STORMTIDE

DEN PATRICK is the author of the acclaimed Erebus Sequence, published in 2014, and was nominated for the British Fantasy Society Award for Best Newcomer in 2015. STORMTIDE is the sequel to WITCHSIGN, and the second of three books in The Ashen Torment series. He lives in London with his wife and their two cats.

You can find Den on Twitter at @Den_Patrick

STORMTIDE

DEN PATRICK

Book Two of The Ashen Torment

HARPER
Voyager

Harper*Voyager*
An imprint of HarperCollins*Publishers* Ltd
1 London Bridge Street
London SE1 9GF

www.harpercollins.co.uk

First published by HarperCollins*Publishers* 2019

This paperback edition 2020
1

A catalogue record for this book is available from the British Library

ISBN 978-0-00-822819-4

Set in Meridien by Palimpsest Book Production Ltd, Falkirk, Stirlingshire

Printed and bound in the UK by CPI Group (UK) Ltd, Croydon CR0 4YY

MIX
Paper from
responsible sources
FSC™ C007454

For Matt

NORDSCALE ISLANDS
VLADIBOGDAN
SPØKELSEA
CINDERFELL
STEINWICK
NORDVLAST
NOVAYA ZEMLYA
SOMMERENDE OCEAN
VEND PROVINCE
NOVGORUSKE PROVINCE
SOLMINDRE EMPIRE
THE SCORCHED REPUBLICS
DRAKEFJORD
SEREIN
VANSK
VANNERÅND
VIROLANTI PROVINCE
SLAVON PROVINCE
ARKIV ISLAND
KHLYSTBURG
MIDTENJORD STEPPE
VIRAG
SVINGETTEVEI
URZAHN MOUNTAINS
THE ASHEN GULF
PROVINCE OF IZHORIA
PROVINCE OF KARELINA
DOS SHANIS
FAR NADRA
DOS UYKHUR
AHSHINI
DOS FESH
DOS KARA
SHANSURA
MUNA
FARZAN
YAMAL PROVINCE
SHANISROND
DOS KHOR
NADIRA
DRAGON TEAR ISLAND
SHIMMER SEA
THE CONTINENT OF VINTERKVELD

CHAPTER ONE

Steiner

It was just before dawn; a prelude to the sun lay across the horizon like shimmering gold. The few clouds that scudded across the sky were a spectral white, travelling over a sea of deep and majestic blue. Steiner stood at the prow of the *Watcher's Wait* in awe, adoring every second of the early morning. Cinderfell, his home of eighteen years, had always existed under a pall of permanent grey cloud. The winters promised grey snow and the spring gritty rain. There were few places more bleak in all of Nordvlast, few places more grim in the whole of Vinterkveld. But not so today. They were many leagues from Cinderfell and the dark red frigate sailed ever further south. Steiner basked under the blue skies, savouring the briny tang of the sea with every league travelled.

'How far south are we?' said a woman's voice behind him. 'Hoy there.'

'Hoy there yourself,' replied Kristofine. He'd left her sleeping below decks so he could enact his new morning ritual of greeting the sun. Kristofine drew close and her arms encircled his waist. She pressed her nose against his neck and made a small, contented noise. Steiner slipped an arm around her waist in return and gave thanks to Frøya that he was free.

'How did you sleep?' he asked. She made a face.

'You're all elbows and knees and you move around in your sleep. If I didn't know better I'd say you're still trying to escape from the island.'

'No double beds on a ship like this.'

'But very thin walls,' she replied, wrinkling her nose. 'Where are we today?'

'We're down by Svingettevei, I think,' he replied. 'Romola said we'd have to put in at Virag for supplies.' He kissed the top of her head and looked out to sea once more. The gilt on the horizon took shape and became a sliver then a soft curve of brilliant gold. The sky took on all the colours of the forge, fading to indigo and darker still where the night persisted on the opposite horizon.

'I'm surprised the food lasted this long,' said Kristofine.

Steiner ran a hand across his scalp. His hair, singed and burned away to nothing during his incarceration on Vladibogdan, had started to grow back. There was hard stubble on his jaw and the many scars across his face and arms were less livid against his pale skin.

'I'll be glad to get my feet on dry land after three weeks aboard,' he said. 'And I doubt I'm the only one.'

'It's so quiet,' said Kristofine after a pause. Steiner nodded and smiled. The ship's timbers creaked or groaned occasionally, and the waves met the hull with a hushed susurrus. Even the gulls, normally so raucous and loud, flew silently as if in reverence for the coming day.

'That's why I've started to come up here each morning,' said Steiner. 'To give thanks for my life and everything in it.' He squeezed Kristofine tighter and her smile broadened.

'You? Giving thanks to the goddesses?'

'Don't tell Kjellrunn or I'll never hear the last of it.'

Romola appeared on deck and approached the prow.

'Strange to see young lovers aboard my ship,' said the

captain. 'Usually it's stolen cargo and dried-out jetsam, right.'

The sometime-pirate, sometime-storyweaver wore her usual attire of a deerskin jerkin with matching knee-length boots. Her wrists were encircled by all manner of copper hoops, bright with verdigris, bangles of shining jet and polished ivory. Steiner wondered if all pirate captains were so flamboyant.

'How are you this morning?' asked Kristofine.

'Concerned would be the word for it.' Romola eyed the horizon.

'Is Virag so terrible?' asked Steiner.

'No telling what we'll find there,' said the captain. Romola didn't look at either of them, peering out to sea as if she might discern some clue of what awaited them once they went ashore.

'We just need food,' said Steiner. 'We don't have to stop for long.'

'Clearly you've never restocked a ship's stores,' replied Romola, raising an eyebrow.

'I overheard some of the novices talking last night,' said Kristofine. Around two dozen novices had come with them from the academies of Vladibogdan, all students of the arcane. The Empire permitted children with witchsign to live only on the understanding that they would one day become Vigilants for its Holy Synod. The escaped children would be hunted to the very ends of Vinterkveld.

'Some of the older children are talking about leaving,' said Romola. 'They want to find their way back to their families.' The captain shook her head. 'I can't imagine that will work out well, but they won't be told otherwise.'

'But that's not what's bothering you,' said Steiner.

'When those children are caught the Empire will squeeze answers out of them, one way or another. And those answers will point back to me and my crew.' Romola sighed. 'But I can hardly keep them prisoner on my ship, can I?'

'Tell me about Virag,' said Steiner, keen to change the subject. He had no solution for Romola's problem and felt an uncomfortable pang of responsibility hearing her mention her crew and the novices.

'Virag is the capital city of Svingettevei. They've always maintained a more *flexible* relationship with the Empire than the other Scorched Republics. Officially there isn't a garrison there but . . .'

'There won't be any troops,' said Steiner. 'Imperial troops only visit the Scorched Republics during an Invigilation.'

Romola rolled her eyes and nudged Kristofine. 'A few months on Vladibogdan and he's an expert on the Empire.'

Steiner had the good grace to cough and feel embarrassed. 'Sorry.' The Scorched Republics clung to their sovereignty by the tiniest of margins, acquiescing to as few of the Empire's demands as they dared.

'Why don't some of you go ashore before everyone else?' said Kristofine. 'That way you can scout ahead and see what's waiting for us.'

'She talks a lot of sense,' said Romola. 'You should make an honest woman of her, Steiner.'

Steiner smiled and felt the heat of a blush at his cheeks. He squeezed Kristofine's waist with one wiry arm. 'All in good time. There's a few things I need to do first.'

'Care to tell me what you're planning?' said Romola. 'I'm not keen on surprises.'

'I've had three weeks aboard this ship to think about my next move. I still can't believe I'm free to be honest—'

'The plan?' pressed Romola.

'Right. The plan. Well, I guess I'll pick a fight with the Empire when I can and hide when I have to. Little by little word will get around, and maybe others will decide to pick a fight too.'

'And you need to tell people about Vladibogdan,' said

Kristofine with a shy look. 'About how the Empire is taking children and pressing them into service.'

Steiner nodded. 'Of course, but my talents lie in fighting, not talking, so the raids will take precedence. Word will spread from there.' Steiner was hoping for some words of encouragement from the pirate but his plan was met with silence, the only sound the lapping of sea against boat.

'Is that it?' said Romola finally, an incredulous look on her face. 'You're going to pick a series of fights and hope you don't get outnumbered or unlucky? And *that* will inspire your uprising?'

'Others will join me, I'm sure of it.' Though he could hear the uncertainty in his own words. 'And I'll find Felgenhauer. Father and I will stand a better chance with Felgenhauer by our side.'

'Right,' said Romola with a slow nod and a concerned look in her eye.

Steiner spent an hour whittling driftwood and chatting to Kristofine on deck. They had rarely left each other's side since he'd escaped Vladibogdan. They talked about everything, heads bowed close together in conversation, their voices low. They shared the details of their time apart and Steiner placed kisses on her cheek or neck when no one was looking. He found himself lost to long seconds of gazing, learning the shape of her, every gesture and expression.

'It will be good to eat something other than ship's rations,' she said, leaning against the gunwale looking towards the coastline where Virag waited for them.

'Can't say I care too much for any more fish stew or ship's biscuit,' replied Steiner.

She smiled. 'Perhaps we could find a room at an inn and have a little privacy of a night-time . . .' The ship was more crowded than anyone liked to admit. It was hard to find a moment's peace amid snoring, chatting, arguing, or defecating.

'Privacy?' Steiner raised an eyebrow and nodded as a slow smile crossed his face. 'That sounds very fine. Think I'm long overdue for some privacy.'

The call went up from the crow's nest that land had been sighted and the ship came alive with people from below decks. Steiner watched them all arrive from the prow of the blood-red frigate. A gang of novices arrived on deck first, seven in number and no older than thirteen summers. Their faces were bright with excitement, and a babble of questions and specu-lation filled the air. The last few weeks had put some meat on the children's bones but they still resembled windswept scarecrows. Steiner wondered if their families missed them, or if their loved ones were ashamed to have had the stain of witchsign sully their history.

'What's troubling you?' asked Kristofine, noting the frown on his brow.

'Just wondering what welcome those children will get when they return home. If any.'

'It's not just the parents that are a worry, either.' Kristofine turned her eyes back to the water. 'The whole town takes against you.'

Marek emerged from his cabin and made his way across the deck to catch his son in a rough embrace. Steiner returned it with fierce smile.

'We've been on this ship for three weeks now,' said the blacksmith. He took a step back and took in the sight of his son once more. 'And every morning I can't quite believe we got you back.'

Steiner looked at his father's scarred hands, so much like his own, with burns and blemishes stark against the pale skin.

'There's a lot that's hard to believe about the last few months,' agreed Steiner. 'Best not to question it. Just be grateful.'

Marek laughed and raised his eyebrows at Kristofine. 'Seems my son is growing up to be a warrior philosopher.'

'Philosophy is fine,' said Kristofine. 'It's the warrior part that bothers me. I'd rather he didn't rush off and get himself killed. I have need of him.'

'I think he'll be yours for a good while yet,' said Marek. 'But for now it's for the best you stay with Kjellrunn once we take to the road.'

Kristofine narrowed her eyes but said nothing and Marek failed to notice her silent disagreement as Kimi Enkhtuya arrived on deck. Marozvolk followed close behind. She still wore her Vigilant's garb, but had eschewed the snarling wolf-faced mask. The two women of Yamal were distinguished by their dark skin and tightly plaited hair – so different to most of the pale-skinned crew and the many novices. Kimi eyed Steiner across the throng of bodies and nodded, but no expression crossed her face. She did not approach and Steiner felt the distance between them keenly. Kimi held hands with little Maxim, leading the boy to a place at the railing where they might watch Svingettevei slide into view. He was olive-skinned and might have passed for Spriggani at first glance, but a profusion of dark curls hinted at a Shanisrond heritage. Steiner felt a pang of something. Jealousy perhaps? Maxim and Steiner had kept an eye out for one another on Vladibogdan but now the boy had fallen in with the Yamali princess. Steiner couldn't say he blamed him. There was a soft buzz of excitement from prow to stern as everyone waited to catch their first glimpse of Virag.

'How are things between you and her highness?' asked Marek quietly, shooting a concerned look at Kimi.

'I think she's avoiding me.' Steiner turned away and looked across the sea. 'She took a big risk in giving me the Ashen Torment. It must be a hard decision to live with.' Steiner released a long sigh.

'Hard to imagine such an artefact could exist,' said Marek. 'Hard to believe in a simple carving with all that power to bind the spirits of the dead.'

'And command them,' added Steiner, his voice a whisper. Kristofine squeezed his hand.

'You did the right thing when you destroyed it.' Kristofine had been full of questions about Vladibogdan, of course. Telling her about the Ashen Torment had been difficult. He'd woken in the middle of the night more than once in the last three weeks, haunted by the remnants of a dream. It was always the same. He had not escaped the battle in Academy Square but had died instead, becoming a cinderwraith bound to the island, bound to toil in service to the Empire for all eternity as the Vigilants watched over him from behind their masks. Steiner blinked away the nightmare and turned his eyes towards Kimi.

'I promised her I'd find a way to stop the Empire harming the Yamali people, but I'm just one man and that promise is a far heavier weight than I ever thought.'

'We'll figure something out,' replied Kristofine.

'That we will,' agreed Marek. 'I'm all done with a life lived quietly. It's time to take the fight to the Empire.'

The ship edged ever closer to the white and jagged cliffs of Svingettevei. Every league they sailed brought wider smiles and greater laughter.

'Here he is,' announced a gravelly voice from behind them. 'The dragon rider of Nordvlast, if you can believe such a thing!' Tief clapped Steiner on the shoulder and nodded to Kristofine and Marek. Tief was a Spriggani in his forties, his dark hair touched with grey. He wore patched trousers with a threadbare smock. A thick strap of leather crossed his body from shoulder to hip, festooned with tools and knives.

'The dragon riding was a one-time thing,' replied Steiner with a laugh. 'And I'm glad to keep it that way.'

Sundra and Taiga joined them on deck moments after Tief's arrival. The women spent a few moments greeting Marek and Kristofine warmly, which is to say Taiga was warm while Sundra merely greeted them. No one could accuse the high priestess of Frejna of being overly friendly. Sundra was attired in her usual black, the colours of her priesthood, while Taiga wore her customary green. Tief set about fixing his pipe for a smoke and Steiner felt a pleasant rush of relief that his friends had escaped their fate on Vladibogdan.

'Do the bones still whisper my name?' Steiner asked the high priestess, a small smile on his lips. Sundra looked at him from the corner of her eye and pursed her lips.

'I have not communed with my goddess of late,' she said. 'And you would do well not to mock my methods of divination.'

'I didn't mean to mock,' replied Steiner. 'But if the goddess or her high priestess have any advice in the coming weeks . . .' He let the request go unspoken, afraid he might reveal just how daunting he found the endeavour.

'You're a good boy, Steiner.' Sundra's usual severe demeanour softened and she patted him on the shoulder. 'Not a Spriggani boy but no one is perfect.' Steiner chuckled and ran a calloused palm over the long stubble on his jaw.

'I've not been a child for a while now.'

'You all look like children from where I stand,' replied Sundra. There was a quietness to her words that almost hid the pang of sadness. Steiner was suddenly aware of the high priestess's papery skin. The usual olive hue, so common to the Spriggani people, carried a hint of grey that had nothing to do with the forges of Vladibogdan. Her hair was run through with strands of dull silver, while her eyes, usually so quick and piercing, were heavy-lidded with a great weariness. Steiner offered her his arm.

'The sooner we get you back on land the better.'

'You'll get no complaints from me,' said Sundra, linking her arm with his. 'Though I'd prefer Shanisrond to Svingettevei. Or Yamal for that matter.'

'I'll speak to the captain,' replied Steiner. He cast his eye across the deck, over pirates and novices, pale-skinned and dark. It was hard to imagine where such a disparate gathering might settle in peace, if such a thing could be found.

CHAPTER TWO

Kimi

Seen from afar, Virag was a sprawling port city that discoloured the Svingettevei coastline like grey lichen. Plumes of smoke dissipated above the buildings creating a fug over the winding streets. The pall of grey reminded Kimi of Vladibogdan.

'I never thought I'd set foot on the mainland again,' said Kimi. She was almost shaking with nerves. Tears of relief shimmered at the corners of her eyes despite the fierce wave of happiness she felt.

'How long were you on the island?' asked Marozvolk.

'Five years,' replied Kimi. 'Five years as a political prisoner. Five years as a token of loyalty to the Emperor.'

'You must have arrived just after I finished my training,' said Marozvolk. Kimi could feel her trepidation. There had been no jailers on the island: the number of soldiers and Vigilants present was more than sufficient for the task. 'I served on Arkiv for a time but found myself back on Vladibogdan four years later.'

'Why didn't you come to me sooner?' said Kimi with a note of frustration in her voice. 'I spent five years without hearing my mother tongue. Five years without even meeting another Yamali.' A pained expression crossed Marozvolk's face but Kimi received no answer. 'Five years in the forges,' continued Kimi, 'with only the Spriggani and the souls of the dead for company.'

'I'm sorry.' Marozvolk avoided her eyes. 'It wasn't as if I could simply visit you and take off my mask. I had duties. I was lost when I first reached the island, unsure of myself, unsure who I could trust. The academy fill your head with strange ideas. They instil a sense that we couldn't possibly survive without the Empire.'

'So you could be loyal to Felgenhauer but you couldn't make yourself known to me?'

'Vigilants watch each other with constant suspicion,' said Marozvolk. 'Especially the young ones, and especially the Vigilants close to Felgenhauer.' The ship drew closer to Virag and sailors made ready to drop anchor.

'Well, it seems you've figured out who you're loyal to now,' said Kimi over her shoulder as she walked away. 'And who you are.'

Marozvolk watched her go. 'You don't sound very convinced, your highness.'

The view had not improved as the *Watcher's Wait* made port. Kimi waited to disembark with Maxim, drumming her fingers against the side of the ship with impatience.

'All these beautiful chalk cliffs and the city looks like this,' muttered Marozvolk. The pirates tied off the *Watcher's Wait* at the long pier they'd been assigned to and Kimi clenched her fists with impatience. 'I'll never understand why people would willingly live in a city.'

'I've never been in a city before,' said Maxim, staring wide-eyed at Virag. Kimi could feel his excitement. She dropped to one knee and took his hand in hers. For a second she thought of her younger brother, though Tsen would be fully grown now, ready to take on the responsibilities of a—

'Kimi, why are you holding my hand?' asked Maxim, frowning slightly.

'Sorry, I was miles away.' Kimi smiled, aware even as she knelt beside the boy just how large she was. 'You reminded me of my brother for a moment there.'

'Can we go ashore now?' he asked, eyes straying to the city and all the wonders and terrors therein.

'I'll need you to stay on the ship.'

'But I wanted to see—' Kimi held up one finger to silence the boy's protests the way her mother had gently quietened Tsen when they were little. He was so like Tsen at the same age. Their mother had still been alive then.

'It's safer on the ship,' explained Kimi, her tone calm and even. 'We don't know how unfriendly the locals are, or if there are Imperial soldiers here.'

'But I can be useful!' pleaded Maxim.

'And more useful besides if you're not dead,' countered Kimi. 'I don't want to argue about this, Maxim.'

The boy's shoulders sagged with defeat. 'I'll go up to the crow's nest and watch you from there,' he said solemnly.

'Good. Keep an eye out for anyone unusual and stay up there if any fighting starts.' Maxim nodded earnestly, then scampered off to start his long climb to the crow's nest.

'That's your idea of safety?' said Marozvolk, staring up the main mast to the crow's nest above.

'He'll be out from underfoot,' replied Kimi, 'and so far away from trouble it might pass him over.' She paused and waved to a tall woman with long, dark red hair who served with the crew and went by the name of Rylska.

'Can you keep an eye on that boy up there?'

Rylska beamed a broad smile and saluted enthusiastically. 'Of course! I don't know much about children, but then I didn't know much about sailing when the captain took me on, so why not?' She began climbing, whistling cheerfully as she went. Kimi watched the red-haired pirate ascend to the crow's nest.

'That didn't exactly inspire confidence, did it?' Marozvolk chuckled and then looked at the city. 'Will our reception really be that bad?' she asked.

'Two unescorted, dark-skinned women on the west coast of Vinterkveld.' Kimi cocked her head to one side. 'I don't know what to think.' She looked over Marozvolk's cream robes. 'But I do know we should get you some new clothes. Clothes that don't hint at your former occupation.'

The boarding ramp had barely made contact with the stone pier when Kimi set foot on it. A few steps and she was swiftly on dry land. For the first time in weeks she felt as if she could breathe again, away from the novices, away from Steiner.

'Shouldn't we wait for the others?' said Marozvolk, hesitating as she reached the cobbled pier, but Kimi was already moving, keen to be among the bustle of Virag's winding streets.

'Romola said we should split up and scout ahead,' shouted Kimi over her shoulder. 'So that's what I'm doing.' Maxim and Rylska waved from the crow's nest while Steiner stood at the prow, watching her leave.

It took Marozvolk a few minutes to weave through the crowds at the docks and catch up with the princess. Kimi held her sleeve up to her nose and mouth as they pressed deeper in to the city.

'It smells worse than the Izhorian swamps in summer,' she muttered darkly in her mother tongue.

'And what do they smell of?' replied Marozvolk.

'Death, mainly. Anyone travelling from Yamal to Midtenjord rarely survives that journey.'

'I'm from the south coast,' replied Marozvolk. 'Or . . . I was before I was taken. There was never much call to go anywhere near Izhoria.'

'Just as well,' said Kimi with a grim smile. 'The swamps don't really smell of death, but they do smell of sulphur and I don't know what's worse.' The two women turned a corner and found themselves on a wide thoroughfare full of carts and horses. Dung, mud, and rotting food spattered the cobbled street.

'What kept you?' said Kimi as she stepped around something foul.

'What do you mean?' replied Marozvolk.

'You took a while to catch up after I disembarked. Did Steiner ask you to have a word with me?' Marozvolk shook her head, then caught the stern glint in Kimi's eyes and sighed.

'He did speak with me. He's concerned about you. He doesn't blame you for being angry with him—'

'I should think not,' snapped Kimi.

Marozvolk cleared her throat. 'What happened between you two?' Kimi stopped walking, then pulled out the sliver of stone that hung from a chain about her neck.

'This is all that's left of the Ashen Torment. One of the mightiest artefacts in all of Vinterkveld and this' – the jagged rock was no larger than Marozvolk's little finger – 'is all that's left of it.'

'Felgenhauer told me about its existence. And what it does,' replied Marozvolk. 'What happened? How did it . . . ?'

'I lent it to him so he could command the cinderwraiths to rise up against those loyal to the Empire.' Kimi's eyes became hard, her mouth a narrow line. 'When he was done he destroyed it with that damn sledgehammer he's so fond of waving about.'

'No ordinary weapon could unmake an artefact of such power,' said Marozvolk with a frown. 'The Ashen Torment was crafted by Bittervinge himself.'

'The sledgehammer is most decidedly not ordinary, that much is clear.' They resumed walking at a much slower pace.

'But the destruction of the Ashen Torment is a good thing,' said Marozvolk slowly. 'Those souls could pass on to the afterlife once they had been released.'

'True enough, but when the Emperor hears that I let his most powerful artefact be destroyed he'll send soldiers south to Yamal and wipe out every last one of us as punishment.' Kimi felt tears prickle at the corners of her eyes and told herself it was the city's smoke that made them smart. 'I'd forgotten how *fragrant* western cities are.' She coughed behind her sleeve.

'Why didn't you stop him from destroying it?' asked Marozvolk, her voice low, a note of caution in her words.

'I've been asking myself the same question ever since we left the island,' Kimi growled with frustration. 'He wanted to make sure no one else rose up as a cinderwraith. It's hard to say no to something like that.'

'And what will you do now?'

'I need to return to Yamal and speak to my father. We need to gather the tribes and prepare for war. I owe the sly bastard that much.'

Marozvolk remained silent and looked uneasy.

'What is it?' asked Kimi.

'Nothing. I just . . .' Marozvolk, stripped of her snarling wolf-faced mask, was an open book. Her expressive face told of a deep worry that consumed her. 'I'm not sure I can go back to Yamal, Your Highness. I want to. I want to help you, protect you if I must, but . . . my parents disowned me when I failed the Invigilation.' Marozvolk shook her head and looked away.

'What would your parents do if they saw you?' asked Kimi gently, slowing her stride. 'What *could* they do? They should be grateful you're alive at all.'

'Part of me would give anything to see my family again,' said Marozvolk, eyes downcast. 'But they disowned me in a heartbeat. I can't go back to that.'

Kimi eyed the other woman for moment. They'd shared a cramped cabin for three weeks but carefully avoided any difficult conversations. Until now. All their efforts at interaction had been directed at caring for Maxim. Without the distraction of the boy, Kimi was painfully reminded that Marozvolk had been one of her former jailers, but it seemed even jailers had problems of their own.

The women continued into the city in silence. The buildings stood three storeys tall, so different to the nomadic tents of Yamal. Virag's rooftops were adorned in grey slate as opposed to the thatch more common in the northern reaches of Vinterkveld.

'Everything is grey and damp here,' said Kimi. 'It's a wonder anyone gets out of bed.'

'Hard to disagree with that,' replied Marozvolk. The further they ventured away from the docks the more people watched them pass. Eyes filled with suspicion followed their passing, or was it merely curiosity?

'I imagine most sailors from Shanisrond or Yamal stay near the docks,' said Marozvolk.

'We're not sailors,' replied Kimi. She looked at the shingles hanging outside each of the shops. Each bore an illustration of the profession practised inside. They appeared to be on a street of scribes, judging by the depictions of quills, scrolls and even the odd book. 'We just need to find a . . .' Kimi turned into an alley and pressed on before coming to an abrupt stop. Marozvolk walked into the back of her, apologising in hushed tones until she spotted what Kimi had seen moments before. Three dockers waited at the end of the crooked cobbled alley. All were heavy-set men with deep frowns and mouths set in flat lines. The largest of them clutched a cudgel in a scarred fist.

'It's a shame Romola didn't have a few weapons to spare for us to come ashore with,' said Marozvolk under her breath.

She clenched her fists and a silvery glimmer of arcane power moved across her skin. Her fists began to turn the colour of granite.

'You can't use the arcane here,' said Kimi just as quietly, grasping her arm quickly. 'It will attract too much attention. Come on.' She took Marozvolk by the hand and led her through a door.

The tailor was a gentleman who had not seen fit to die despite his great age. The elderly man's spotted pate and rounded shoulders stood in stark contrast to his sharp eyes and firm jaw, and Kimi doubted she had ever met anyone so old. Even Sundra and Mistress Kamalov demonstrated a blush of youth compared to the tailor. Weak light filtered into the shop through the uneven windows at the front. It smelled of dust and sandalwood, stewed tea and quiet desperation. A fire snapped and popped in the hearth, lending the shop a reprieve from the dismal chill outside.

'I do not make clothes for women,' said the tailor slowly, first in his own tongue, then in Solska when it was clear he had not been understood.

'I don't want clothes for *women*,' replied Kimi with a lift of her chin. 'I want britches, a shirt, a good coat and some boots that just happen to fit my friend.'

'And how do you propose to pay for all of this?' replied the tailor, pursing his lips. He had a sour look about him, but Kimi imagined she'd be sour too if she'd lived a long life in Virag. She unfastened her thick leather belt and laid it across the counter, then slipped a few coins out of a false lining on the reverse side. Each was solid gold and bore the profile of the Emperor.

'Given you speak their language, I assume you'll take their coin?'

'Solmindre crowns are very welcome here.' The tailor

attempted a smile but the expression might have easily been constipation.

'Half now, half on completion,' said Kimi.

'As you wish,' replied the tailor, smooth as silk. 'Will there be anything else?'

'Make the three shirts and as fast as you can. I don't know how long we're going to be in town.' She cast an eye over his bony hands. 'You have assistants to help you, I hope?'

The tailor rolled his eyes, then held up one forbidding finger and shook his head. It took Kimi a moment to realise the gesture was not for her but the three thugs waiting in the alley outside. They looked even more brutish through the uneven glass.

'Friends of yours?' asked Kimi.

The tailor took up a measuring tape and bade Marozvolk stand on a low stool. 'They are not even friends to each other,' said the tailor. 'And they are only friendly to me when they come to collect their due.'

Kimi eyed the thugs in the alley. They stared back with dead-eyed indifference. 'Is there somewhere close by that I can buy a weapon?' asked Kimi in an idle tone. She held up four fingers in an obscene gesture at the thugs outside.

'There is always somewhere to buy a weapon in Virag,' muttered the tailor. 'Which is entirely the problem.'

The tailor ignored the women in his shop once the measurements had been taken. A young girl was sent to round up seamstresses to begin the work. Kimi and Marozvolk left the shop and headed back to the main thoroughfare. They had barely walked a hundred feet when they spotted an Imperial Envoy, dressed in the customary blue robes of his office, with a soldier's black cloak across his broad shoulders. His hair and beard were close-cropped, and he could not have looked more different to the men of the Scorched Republics, who wore their beards long and their hair longer still.

'Frøya save us,' hissed Marozvolk as Kimi pulled her behind a stationary wagon. The Envoy was escorted by four soldiers, looming over the crowd in black enamelled armour. Each helm bore the red star of the Solmindre Empire proudly on the brow. The soldiers were led by a sergeant carrying a two-handed maul, while his subordinates carried maces and shields.

'What are they doing here?' breathed Marozvolk, barely daring to peek around the corner of the wagon.

'I think we're about to find out,' replied Kimi as the Envoy mounted the steps of an impressive but dilapidated building.

'Citizens of fair Svingettevei!'

'I loathe Envoys,' muttered Marozvolk. 'What is this place?' she added, looking up at the building.

'An old temple to Frejna if I had to guess,' said Kimi. 'Look at the crow sculptures over the windows, and the tree motif above the door.'

'I speak to you today on behalf of the Emperor himself,' called the Envoy in a booming voice. 'I bring you warning of a terrible danger growing in the south.' A crowd was starting to form around him. 'As many of you know, the cities of Shanisrond are teeming with pirates!'

'We should go,' said Marozvolk, still remaining out of sight behind the wagon. 'It's not safe.'

'I just want to hear what he's going to say,' replied Kimi.

'Envoys are failed Vigilants that are too useful to kill,' hissed Marozvolk. 'If he has the sight then I could be in a lot of danger.'

'These thieves have harassed Imperial shipping for many months,' continued the Envoy. 'And now we suspect they will come north.'

'What do you mean, "sight"?' Kimi frowned.

'It's how Vigilants detect witchsign. They can see the arcane about you. Some say they can smell it but it's usually called the sight.'

'You head back to the ship,' said Kimi. 'I just want to hear him out.'

'Their agents may even be among you as I speak,' added the Envoy. 'And you will know them by their dark skins.' At this, several of the people turned to glare at Marozvolk and Kimi.

'I'm not leaving without you,' said Marozvolk through gritted teeth. 'Can we go now?'

Kimi stared at the crowd with a frosty look, then turned on her heel and slipped away into the next street.

'I think it's best I listen to you a bit more in future,' said Kimi when they were safely away.

'I'm not just trying to protect myself,' replied Marozvolk, her words clipped with frustration. 'I'm looking out for you too, Your Highness.'

CHAPTER THREE

Kjellrunn

Kjellrunn had stayed in her cabin all morning. She had no wish to be among the press and clamour of bodies as they vied for position on deck, no wish to squeeze past pirates and novices for the chance to sight land. Kjellrunn had never left Nordvlast before, never gone more than a dozen leagues from Cinderfell in any direction, and now the *Watcher's Wait* approached Svingettevei with all its wonders and dangers but she felt nothing.

She had endured three weeks of nightmares, endlessly seeing her Uncle Verner killed by the Okhrana, and feeling her powers swell again with murderous fury. Over and over she dreamed of smashed corpses and the desolation she visited on the Imperial agents sent to hunt down Mistress Kamalov.

'Kjellrunn. Do not tell me you are still in bed?'

Kjellrunn groaned and squeezed her eyes shut at the sound of Mistress Kamalov's voice. She turned over in her bunk as the door creaked open and the renegade Vigilant pushed into the room. The old woman shook Kjellrunn firmly by the shoulder.

'Up! There is much to do. We have made port at last.'

Kjellrunn pulled the blankets higher, as if they might fend off the day's problems.

'Come. I know you are dressed.' Mistress Kamalov spoke Nordspråk with a harsh Solmindre accent that left no one in any doubt where she hailed from. 'It's time for you to get off this ship. We will have meat and wine and conversation with someone other than pirates and children.'

Kjellrunn rose from the bed without a word. It wasn't wise to disobey the old woman once she'd set her mind to something.

'I suppose Steiner has already gone ashore?' Her voice was a sleepy mumble as she pulled a comb through the tangle of her blonde hair.

'Of course,' replied Mistress Kamalov as she fixed her headscarf. 'But Kimi went first. She could barely wait for the boarding ramp to fall.'

'Wouldn't it be wiser to wait until they come back? We don't know what we may run into.'

'Wise? Yes. But ship's biscuit and dried meat are no good for children already half-starved from Vladibogdan. We must eat! And you most of all. Like a bag of bones, you are.'

Kjellrunn's stomach rumbled as if on cue and she smiled with reluctance. 'I'd just rather avoid running into the Okhrana again.'

'This is good. It means you have some sense, but sense is no good if you starve to death on this stinking ship! Come on now, out of this cabin.'

They made their way through the dark confines of the *Watcher's Wait* and up creaking steps to the main deck, where the escaped novices of Vladibogdan waited. The children were pale and slender in the main and numbered around two dozen.

'Never much food on Vladibogdan,' Mistress Kamalov had explained. Steiner had been little more than sinew and scars when he'd returned. The novices' clothes were ragged and threadbare and many had naked feet. The faraway look that so often haunted the children's eyes during the journey had been replaced by the fervour of excitement. The cadre of children fell silent as Mistress Kamalov crossed the deck. That she had escaped the Empire and lived as a renegade Vigilant had imbued the old woman with a legendary status among the children. But none had been told about the day a dozen Okhrana came for Marek and Verner in the woods north of Cinderfell. None knew that Kjellrunn had defended her father and the old woman. Not a single novice would be able to imagine Kjellrunn's fury, manifested in such a display of arcane power that she had almost destroyed the old woodcutter's chalet. Kjellrunn still saw the faces of the men she had killed when she slept, swept up in a storm of her vengeance, dashed against the trees and ground until they were bloody pulp.

'Come,' said Mistress Kamalov with a clap of her hands. 'Cease your wool-gathering. You must keep your wits about you today, yes?'

Kjellrunn flinched and shivered. Even a passing thought of the dead Okhrana was enough to distract her.

'We go to the city,' said Mistress Kamalov to the children. 'Stay close.' Mistress Kamalov had never been given to ceremony or pomp and today was no different. The rag-tag band of two score children followed the elderly woman down the boarding ramp. Kjellrunn ushered the last of them off the ship and encouraged them to keep together. Such a large rabble of children attracted stares and comments from the dock workers as they went. Kjellrunn fell into step beside the old Vigilant and returned the hard stares of the locals, daring them to make trouble for her charges.

'Kjellrunn. You are clenching your fists.' The old woman directed a forced a smile at a nearby port official. 'Try to relax, yes?'

'This isn't just a bad idea,' said Kjellrunn under her breath as the children followed behind. 'It's a terrible idea.'

'These children have been incarcerated for years,' said Mistress Kamalov. 'They have faced each day not knowing if they might live or die. Do you really think there is anything we can do to keep them on that ship?' The old woman frowned. 'Better we keep an eye on them if possible.'

Kjellrunn thought of all the times she had gone to spend the afternoon in woods north of Cinderfell.

'I suppose I slipped away often enough to come and see you in the forest.'

'Yes, for training. But these young souls want to spend their coin on stew and bread, clothes and boots, and Frejna knows what else.'

'I don't know how they're going to pay for all this,' said Kjellrunn, glancing over her shoulder at the ragged children in their threadbare clothes.

'They looted the corpses of their captors.' Mistress Kamalov grinned wickedly.

'Corpses?'

'There were a lot of soldiers on the island, a lot of loyal novices and Vigilants. These children have fought and killed for their freedom.'

Kjellrunn looked back over her shoulder at the novices with renewed interest. Some of the children were her own age but the majority were much younger.

'Hah. You thought you are the only one who has killed, yes?'

Kjellrunn shivered as she tried not to think about the dead Okhrana. 'I still think it's a bad idea to head into Virag . . .' Kjellrunn trailed off as they reached a wide thoroughfare, far more imposing than the crude roads and humble tracks of Cinderfell and Nordvlast. Carts and wagons filled the view and the various ethnicities of Vinterkveld hurried in all directions, bearing heavy loads.

'Are you unwell, Kjellrunn?' said Mistress Kamalov. Kjellrunn had stopped walking to take in the vista while the novices clustered around them, all whispering, bickering and laughing.

'I . . .' Kjellrunn blinked and looked around. 'We're really not in Nordvlast any more, are we? Cinderfell, I mean. We're not home any more. We can't go back.'

'Darling girl,' said the old Vigilant in a rare moment of tenderness. 'We spend three weeks cooped up on a stinking ship, and only now you begin to understand.' The old woman squeezed her close. 'It's to be expected, I suppose. Do not worry. We will make a new home, yes?'

'Where?'

'I do not know.' Mistress Kamalov looked away. 'But I do know two children have already slipped away.' The old woman pointed down the street and frowned. 'Come now. Quickly.'

Mistress Kamalov had many talents but moving quickly was not among them. The old woman hobbled as best as she could. Kjellrunn supported her and they followed the two novices a few hundred feet down the road. The other children whispered and pointed.

'Go find your friends,' snapped Mistress Kamalov at two of the older children. 'Find them and bring them back here.' She held up a finger in warning. 'And no trouble!' The children sprinted down the street, pleased to be given such a task by their hero. Kjellrunn glared at the other novices, daring them to wander off from Mistress Kamalov's protection. Sounds of yelling up ahead forced Mistress Kamalov to walk faster.

The crowds scurried away, parting to reveal an Imperial soldier who had grasped one of the older children by her neck. The raven-haired girl struggled and spat. She cursed as if she'd been born to it, filling the air with profanity in three different languages.

'It *would* be Trine,' said Mistress Kamalov, sounding exasperated.
'Who's Trine?' asked Kjellrunn.

'Only the most unruly novice I've ever crossed paths with.'
The renegade Vigilant glowered as three other novices argued
with the soldier. An Envoy across the street stared and pointed,
his mouth hanging open in shock. His gaze alighted on Mistress
Kamalov, Kjellrunn, and the other children.

'I sense witchsign on a scale I have never . . .' He said no
more as the girl called Trine jerked free of the soldier's grasp.
Kjellrunn could only watch as events unravelled, powerless
to stop them.

The soldier lost his patience, and backhanded Trine with a
heavy gauntlet. A trio of boys ran to protect their friend but
the soldier stepped forward and punched one of the boys in
the face. The boy was all of twelve summers old and weighed
no more than a bushel of potatoes. He crumpled to the ground
and his head smacked against the cobbles, silencing everyone.
The boy's friend, a sandy-haired youth from Nordvlast called
Eivinde, knelt down beside him.

'He's bleeding!' shouted Eivinde, plaintive and desperate.
'He's not moving.'

The soldier hesitated, feeling all eyes in the street fall upon
him. Trine shook her head and wiped her bloody nose on
her sleeve.

'You fucking pigs.' There was a fury in her eyes that
Kjellrunn knew all too well. It had been the same fury she'd
felt when Verner had died.

'Capture or kill them all,' bellowed the Envoy. 'I don't care
which.'

The soldier hefted his mace and Kjellrunn ran toward
Eivinde, hands outstretched in desperation. Trine opened her
mouth and her neck glowed blood red. She breathed out,
exhaling a torrent of flickering orange and yellow. The soldier's
head was engulfed in arcane fire.

'We'll kill you first,' screamed Trine, turning to the Envoy. The soldier stumbled backwards, clawing at the searing metal of his helmet, desperately trying to remove it. Kjellrunn felt the acid burn of sickness in the back of her mouth. Her hands were shaking.

'Not again.'

Chaos broke across the street like a wave. The people of Virag fled as the soldiers advanced on the novices. Far from being afraid, the children unleashed their talents. An unnatural gale pushed one soldier back, tearing fitfully at his cloak. A choir of five Vozdukha novices laughed as they summoned the dire wind, sending the soldier tumbling backwards down the street until he lost his footing and crashed into a wagon.

Another soldier leapt aside to avoid a ball of fire and landed on the cobbled street in a clatter of armour. He lurched to his feet only to discover his cloak was alight. Three Academy Plamya novices held their ground with looks of terrible concentration etched on their faces, hurling more fireballs at their attackers.

'Kjellrunn!' barked Mistress Kamalov. 'Don't just stand there!' But Kjellrunn's legs were locked, every muscle tense, she could barely breathe. 'So much death,' she whispered.

A gang of four novices from Academy Zemlya ran forward, calling on their arcane affinity with the earth. Their skin darkened to granite grey as they closed on the sergeant, still bearing his two-handed maul. Kjellrunn could only stare as the novices punched with fists of stone. The sound of rock slamming against armour joined the cacophony in the street. The sergeant stepped back and swung hard with the maul. The strike caught the largest of the novices square in the chest and sent him sprawling. Two other novices fixed themselves to the sergeant's legs, trying to wrench his armour off with brute strength. The third novice scaled his back, pulling herself up with fistfuls of his cloak. She clamped her hands around the sergeant's helm, one hand covering the eye slit.

And still Kjellrunn did nothing. Everything was happening too quickly. Indecision held her fast as if she'd been run through with a spear. She stood in the centre of the street and witnessed a struggle everywhere she looked. All the novices had joined the fight in any way they could. Mistress Kamalov remained behind her, though she had been accosted by a soldier who tried to snatch hold of her arm. The old woman stepped out of reach, muttering something dreadful. The soldier faltered, then swung with his mace, but Mistress Kamalov stepped neatly past the weapon, slipping behind the man. Her knife flashed in the sunlight and disappeared beneath the soldier's helm, the tip sinking deep into his throat.

The Envoy was shouting at the top of his lungs in Solska. He drew a short sword from a jewelled sheath and swiped at the nearest novice. The boy stepped towards the man and parried the blow from a stony forearm, the metal sparking as it glanced from his granite skin. The Envoy raised a leg and stamped on the novice's chest, sending the boy sprawling backwards, then grabbed a young girl by the shoulder. He held his short sword to her throat, thinking to save his wretched skin by threatening hers, but no one was watching, no one but Kjellrunn.

The sergeant cast off the stone-skinned Zemlya novices one by one. A wild strike from the maul caught the girl clinging to his back square between the eyes. In her stone form the first blow merely caused her to flinch, but the second blow sent her to the ground where she lay unmoving. The two boys grasping the sergeant's legs didn't last much longer. The maul was reinforced with metal and the novices' concentration faltered under a series of punishing blows. One boy retreated while the other wailed in shock as his stony arm shattered apart.

More soldiers emerged from the side streets and from behind, arriving in groups of four until sixteen of the number loomed over the novices, in black armour, maces grasped in armoured fists.

'You will stand down,' screamed the Envoy, still holding his short sword to the young girl's throat. The sergeant continued his onslaught, swinging wildly with his maul at the novices, who fled and ducked and dodged back to Mistress Kamalov at the centre of the street. Kjellrunn counted at least four children strewn across the cobbles.

'Kjellrunn,' whispered the old woman as rain began to fall. 'We are surrounded.'

CHAPTER FOUR

Silverdust

The wind howled around the jagged black peaks of Vladibogdan, ushering in a grey shimmer of rain from the Sommerende Ocean. Silverdust gazed at the sky from a tower in Academy Vozdukha as the waves crashed against the cliffs far below with a hushed roar. Rare were the times a wind blew in from the north east. Such winds had a way of invading the very island itself. Up through the darkened cove the winds would race, ascending a hundred blackened steps, keening through the gatehouse which lay quiet and empty, and into Academy Square

The square had been cleared of rubble since the uprising and the shattered pieces of the dragon statue had been committed to the sea. The many bodies of the fallen had been taken below to the forges, where Silverdust himself had immolated them with arcane fire. No one had assigned him the role of the cremator, yet it was important to him that each body meet a decent end. Silverdust had taken a quiet relief in this. No one would rise as a cinderwraith since Steiner destroyed the Ashen Torment and the vast statue at the centre of the island. No longer would dead souls toil in eternal service to the Empire. Silverdust was now the last of his kind. His fate would not be passed on to another generation.

The dark pall that had lain heavy over the island for years had dissipated, drawn this way and that by winds from all cardinal points. Silverdust had enjoyed three weeks of peace until the north-eastern wind gusted in. Three weeks of peace until now.

A knock on the door roused the Exarch from his reveries. He reached out with his mind and found Father Orlov waiting in the corridor outside.

Come. Silverdust sent the word with telepathy; he had lost the ability for speech long ago. The door creaked open and Father Orlov edged into the room. He was a heavyset Vigilant, broad in shoulder and thick of arm.

'Exarch,' said Father Orlov with a half bow. His mask was a handsome face with nine stars embossed down the right-hand side, one star for each province of the Empire.

Father Orlov. Silverdust inclined his head, though in truth he had no respect for the Vigilant. *We have not had a chance to speak since the uprising.*

'You have kept yourself very busy, Exarch.' Father Orlov edged further into the room and Silverdust could sense the man's wariness. 'Appearing only at night to take the corpses from the courtyard. You have given the children much to talk about.' Father Orlov paused a moment. 'And much to fear.'

Cremation. A rotting body causes pestilence and we can ill afford a plague taking hold on the island. Not after everything that has happened.

'Your wisdom is a guiding light in these dark times,' replied Father Orlov. Silverdust ignored the sarcasm. 'Will you walk with me, Exarch? I think it would do everyone good to see the highest-ranking Vigilant in the academy taking an interest in the living.'

I will walk with you, Father Orlov, though rank is rarely a comfort in the wake of disaster.

'And truly this has been a disaster,' said Father Orlov as he exited the room. 'And someone will have to answer for it.'

Silverdust wondered if there were a note of warning in Orlov's words, or if the man had tipped his hand.

There is always a price to paid.

Father Orlov glanced over his shoulder to check Silverdust was following him down the dark stone corridor. The children called him Cryptfrost behind his back, on account of his chilly temperament, and for the power he wielded over water and wind. Orlov would be keen to blame Silverdust for Steiner's destruction of the Ashen Torment and his subsequent escape.

The Exarch and Father Orlov emerged in Academy Square and looked over the battered flagstones. Novices swept the square of grit and sand as best they could despite the wind.

'I barely recognise the place now,' said Father Orlov, unable to disguise how forlorn he was at the disarray before him. The Vigilant clenched his fists and Silverdust could sense a fierce eddy of disgust, shame and anger for what had happened during Steiner's uprising.

It is much changed.

Blood stained the flagstones of Academy Square, each mark a reminder of someone who had risen up against the Empire or died to defend it.

'It was quite the scene,' said Father Orlov, after taking a moment to compose himself. 'The Spriggani priestess killed a great many of our men, turning them to stone with her gaze.'

I had heard as much.

'Your absence during the fighting was noted.'

I stayed close to Academy Vozdukha, protecting loyalist students.

This was lie, but one almost impossible to disprove. Academy Vozdukha was home to the school of wind, and though it had been a long time since Silverdust had taught, he had reason to be there.

'I also heard you . . . negotiated with them. At the end.'

Father Orlov stopped walking and cradled a gloved fist inside the palm of his other hand. 'With the Vartiainen boy and the Spriggani.'

Silverdust turned to the Vigilant, his curving mirror mask reflecting the nine stars of Father Orlov's proud visage. The Exarch loomed over his subordinate.

Careful, Orlov, you are perilously close to accusing me of treason.

'And yet you were seen in the company of the dragon rider—'

I was merely trying to broker a temporary peace. The Vartiainen boy did not want to rule the island. He wanted to escape and to take his friends with him.

This much at least was true. Steiner had never wanted dominion over Vladibogdan. Destroying the Ashen Torment had been testament to that.

My intent was to put an end to any further killing. It is by my actions that we have any loyal novices left alive at all.

Silverdust could feel Father Orlov's gaze upon him, sense the Vigilant's own telepathy brushing against his mind for some clue to the Exarch's dishonesty.

You will not find what you seek with the arcane. Silverdust touched two fingers to his temple. *My aged mind is as bewildering and impenetrable as any forest.*

Orlov bowed. 'Forgive me, Exarch, but you can understand my caution. We have suffered the worst setback in the history of Vladibogdan. I need to know who I can trust.'

I can understand your caution, Father. Silverdust walked to the centre of Academy Square and for a moment the battle raged all around him, phantoms conjured by memory. Arcane fire flared brightly, guttering as renegade students summoned winds to fight it. Soldiers fell choking as cinderwraiths robbed them of their dying breaths.

Tell me how things stand on the island now the dust has settled.

'Loyalty has largely been determined by academy,' said

Father Orlov. 'The novices of Plamya are the most loyal, with Zemlya close behind.' It stood to reason. The students of Plamya, the fire school, were wild and capricious, but loyal to the Empire nonetheless. Zemlya, the earth school, had always been headed up by hardline Vigilants. Their fanaticism had been duly passed on to their charges.

'No one trusts the few novices of Vozdukha and Voda that remained.' Vozdukha, the school of air, had ever had a reputation for difficult or eccentric students, while Voda, the school of water, was barely seen as an academy at all. Its students had never amounted to anything.

And yet those students did remain. Does that give indication of their loyalty? I will be most displeased if there is any more death on this island. Do I make myself clear, Father Orlov?

'So I gather you're taking command then?' said the Vigilant, taking no pains to hide the sneer in his tone. 'At last.'

This is why you summoned me from the tower, is it not?

Father Orlov said nothing.

I am the highest-ranking Vigilant on the island.

'Perhaps you can drag yourself away from the cremations to start acting like it,' replied Father Orlov, before turning smartly and marching towards Academy Plamya.

Silverdust would have sighed had he still had lungs to breathe with. The north-eastern wind howled more loudly in Father Orlov's absence and Silverdust turned towards the gatehouse and approached the top of the stone stairs. White-tipped waves smashed against the dark stone of the cove far below. For a fleeting second Silverdust saw the ghostly outline of a ship. A second later and the vision had gone. A vision of the future, Silverdust decided. Guests would soon arrive on Vladibogdan.

Silverdust delegated as much as possible to the few Vigilants who had survived the uprising in the days that followed. He appointed Father Orlov as his deputy for no other reason than to keep a close eye on the man. Taking over Felgenhauer's old office didn't sit well with Silverdust, but necessity demanded his discomfort. The Matriarch-Commissar had never been given to decoration but had kept a fine selection of books, which Silverdust distracted himself with, despite having read them all a long time ago. A knock sounded on the door and Silverdust set aside the book he was reading with a flicker of irritation.

Enter.

The door creaked open and a half-starved waif of around ten years stared at the Exarch with wide eyes.

Fear not, I will do you no harm. There is a message, I assume.

The boy nodded, then blinked and shook his head.

'No, not really. A ship has arrived and all the other Vigilants have gone down to the cove to greet it. I . . .' The boy swallowed. 'I thought you should know.'

I imagine Father Orlov is keen to make a good first impression and give his side of the story.

The boy nodded. 'C-can I do anything for you, Exarch-Commissar?'

Silverdust wanted to laugh at hearing such a title.

Fetch me tea from the kitchen and instruct the cooks to make a fine stew – one fit for an Envoy. Go now and do not delay.

The boy pushed his fringe out of his eyes and raced out of Felgenhauer's office as fast as he could. His office – not Felgenhauer's office, Silverdust lamented, not any more. The boy departed with such haste he failed to close the door behind him, giving Silverdust a clear view to the antechamber beyond and the doorway that led to the stairwell. He spread his hands on the wide featureless table, waiting to meet the person he would have to spin a web of lies to.

The Envoy, when she arrived, appeared in the antechamber sheathed in blue silk with a stole made from a winter fox,

the fur white and stark. Her smile was bitter and she sauntered into the room with a swagger that was almost theatrical.

'Silverdust. There you are! Well, I thought *I'd* suffered a
setback or two, but it seems Vladibogdan has endured nothing
less than a catastrophe.'

Silverdust rose from his chair and bowed deeply. Now wasn't
the time for petty acts of ignored etiquette.

*Envoy de Vries. We are honoured by your presence. How fares the
Empire?*

De Vries approached the office door, a circular portal, and
made herself a work of art, leaning casually on the door frame.

'The Empire is strong as ever, dearest Silverdust, but her
forces.' Envoy de Vries pursed her lips and tutted. 'Shirinov
and Khigir both dead, I hear. And a half dozen other members
of the Holy Synod. And your precious Felgenhauer . . .' The
Envoy sighed and looked away as if she had become distracted,
though Silverdust knew full well she was waiting for his
reaction. He gave her none and the silence stretched between
them until the Envoy turned to face him once more.

How may I serve, Envoy de Vries?

'So inscrutable, Silverdust. So mysterious.' The Envoy slunk
into the room and sat down, putting her feet up on the desk.
'What is it you actually do on this island, Exarch?'

I serve at the Emperor's pleasure. Silverdust did not sit. He
could sense Father Orlov waiting on the staircase, out of sight,
yet close enough to eavesdrop. Silverdust could practically
feel the man straining to hear, though the conversation would
be one-sided due to his reliance on telepathy.

'You don't teach' – the Envoy counted off on her fingers
– 'you don't run the stores, you don't organise the soldiers.
You don't perform any role or task as far as I can see.'

I am old. Felgenhauer, in her mercy, let me retire here. Not true,
of course. Silverdust had carefully delegated more and more of
his teaching duties until none remained.

'I see,' said the Envoy. 'Well, Felgenhauer, in her mercy, gave me the slip while I was escorting her back to our beloved Emperor.'

How very unfortunate, Envoy de Vries.

'Indeed.' She forced a smile that could curdle milk. 'The Emperor is very keen to hear what manner of events were taking place here on Vladibogdan leading to the uprising.'

He has always been the most curious soul. He was also impatient and bloodthirsty and petty, but Silverdust declined to mention this.

'It seems the Emperor should have heeded Shirinov's repeated requests, official and otherwise, for an audience.'

You would need to speak to Shirinov regarding his grievances. He never shared his concerns with me.

The Envoy stood and slammed her palm on the desk, but Silverdust did not flinch.

'Shirinov is dead! And here you are, a supposed-retired Exarch, running Vladibogdan. What the Hel happened here? Who is Steiner Vartiainen, and why were you seen speaking with him after the uprising here?' She leaned over the desk, struggling to keep her composure.

I stand behind this desk for no other reason than Father Orlov asked me to. Felgenhauer had some attachment to the boy, a boy without witchsign no less. He was brought here by mistake. Silverdust leaned over the desk, looming taller than the Envoy. *Brought here by Shirinov's mistake. The boy was sent to work in the forges and somehow entered into an agreement with the cinderwraiths. They massacred the soldiers and then the Vartiainen boy took wing on a dragon. He returned with a ship and took off with two dozen novices and most of our food. The ship sank in bad weather no more than two miles after they set out.*

Envoy de Vries straightened up, adjusted her stole and smoothed back her hair. She stared at Silverdust for long moments then smiled, before giggling. Before long she had slipped into the chair, laughing uncontrollably. She all but shouted when her laughter stopped.

'He left the island on a fucking dragon!'

Silverdust said nothing. The silence was interrupted as the waif entered the room and set the tray of food and tea down on the desk.

'Well, I can't fault your hospitality, Silverdust,' said the Envoy as she lifted the lid of a small ceramic pot to reveal the stew inside. 'Even if your storytelling leaves much to be desired.'

What happens now? He barely needed to ask. Silverdust could sense the Envoy's thoughts and knew full well what she would say next.

'We leave in the morning. You are to give a full account of the uprising here to the Emperor himself at Khlystburg. I failed him once by letting Felgenhauer slip through my grasp. You' – she pointed at Silverdust with her fork – 'will appear at the Imperial Court even if I have to chain you and drag you before the Emperor on a leash.'

There will be no leashes, Envoy. I will present myself to the Emperor willingly.

Envoy de Vries shook her head and began to eat. Silverdust said nothing more, lost to his thoughts, imagining how he might kill the Emperor before his courtiers.

CHAPTER FIVE

Steiner

'I'm looking for a man called Tikhoveter,' said Marek to the barkeeper. They had left the *Watcher's Wait* shortly after Kimi, and Marek had led them from tavern to tavern since. Steiner was pleasantly muddled by the ale and stole kisses from Kristofine whenever his father wasn't looking. They were sitting in the snug in a dimly lit tavern called the Silvered Palm while Steiner's father spoke to the man at the bar.

'Don't you think it strange . . . Hoy! Stop that,' said Kristofine. She moved away from where Steiner had been nuzzling her neck. 'Strange? What's strange?'

'Don't you think it's strange that your father wanted to come ashore for something decent to eat and yet all he does is drink with the locals and chat with them about an old friend of his?'

Steiner shrugged. 'What's strange is that we don't just leave him to it and book that room. Get ourselves some of that privacy you were speaking about back on the ship . . .'

Kristofine half-smiled, half-pouted, then shook her head. 'I need you to think with your head, not your britches. What's your father up to?'

'I'm not one to sit around guessing. Why don't we just ask him? Here he comes.'

Marek's expression was serious as he took a seat in the snug. He stared into the bottom of his mug for a moment, then flicked his gaze up to Steiner.

'What?'

'Are you going to tell us who this Tikhoveter is then? You've been talking about him with just about everyone else here. Why not us?'

Marek snorted a laugh. 'You've always been one to speak your mind, but those three mugs of ale have really loosened your tongue.'

'He has a point, Marek,' said Kristofine, her tone placating. 'He's curious. *I'm* curious. Who is it you're looking for?'

'I knew a man once. Not a Vigilant, but a man who could hear whispers on the wind and send words of his own. A messenger of sorts.'

'Whispers on the wind,' said Steiner with a frown. 'That's a trick of the wind school. You're talking about someone from Academy Vozdukha.'

'That's who I'm looking for, but it's been years since I was here and I've no way of knowing if he's still alive or which side he's on.'

'Sides?' Kristofine rolled her eyes. 'What sides?'

'There's the Empire,' said Marek. 'And then there's everyone else.'

Steiner stood up from the table. 'I want to meet this old friend of yours. I'm going to need all the information I can get if I'm going to keep my promise to Kimi.'

'I don't understand how you're supposed to protect the Yamali people when we're on the other side of the continent,' said Kristofine.

'I'm hoping that if I create a big enough distraction in the west the Emperor will be too busy to send troops to

the east.' Steiner threw back the last of his ale. 'What do
we do now?'

'I managed to get an old address.' Marek eased out of his
chair and didn't look hopeful. 'We'll have to hope Tikhoveter
still lives there.'

It was just starting to rain as they stepped outside the tavern
and a deep chill settled over Virag, numbing Steiner's fingers.
Kristofine huddled close to him and he flashed her a smile
and squeezed her waist.

'So you're a lusty drunk then?' she said with a smile of
her own.

'Better that than maudlin or violent, I suppose.' Steiner
chuckled. Marek walked ahead, keeping a keen eye out for
Imperial soldiers.

'Can I ask you something?' said Kristofine. Something was
clearly on her mind from the way she chewed at her lip.
'About the island, I mean?'

'Of course.'

'When you destroyed the Ashen Torment it set the
cinderwraiths free.'

'That's right. They were no longer bound to the island, free
to pass on to the afterlife.'

'So why didn't Silverdust go with them?' Steiner thought
on that for a moment as they walked the streets of Virag,
following Marek in the rain.

'He said he was going to stay on at Vladibogdan.' Steiner
thought of the strange Vigilant and his mirror mask. 'He was
going to stay there and lie for me, buy me time before the
Empire found out what happened on the island.'

'Will it work?'

'Who knows?' said Steiner, his mouth twisting unhappily.
'The Empire has powers I can't begin to guess at. Will the lies

of one Vigilant make a difference? I hope so. Strange old thing that he is.'

'You miss him?' she asked, as the rain continued to fall.

'I can't say I really knew him, but I owe that old ghost a lot. I can't say I'm happy that we left him on Vladibogdan now that I think about it.'

Marek pressed on through streets that grew more narrow and winding with each mile. The rain and the cold were sobering and Steiner grew tired and irritated in equal measure.

'Slow down, old man,' he growled, but Marek didn't hear him.

'Are we avoiding the main roads so we don't get caught?' asked Kristofine when they reached an abandoned alley thick with shadows and refuse.

'Not exactly,' said Marek, stopping outside a narrow townhouse with a battered front door. He beat the wood with a scarred fist and looked over his shoulder. 'Keep an eye out for soldiers. The Empire might be watching this place.'

No answer came from inside the townhouse. No sound of muffled surprise, no holler or shout that they should wait a moment.

'Not a promising start,' said Steiner, taking shelter at the side of the street.

'Come on, you old bastard,' said Marek.

'We should go,' said Kristofine, her eyes darting to the end of the street. Steiner saw her then for the tavern-keeper's daughter that she was. He felt a pang of guilt for dragging her into the chaos of his life. Marek opened his mouth to speak as the door creaked open. A woman peeked through the narrow gap between door and frame. She had a serious look on her deeply lined face that changed to a scowl as she realised there were three of them.

'Well? Are you just going to stand there?'

'I'm here for Tikhoveter,' said Marek so quietly the rain near drowned out the words. The diminutive woman looked from Steiner to Kristofine. Her scowl deepened and she opened the door. 'You'd best come in.'

The townhouse was a place of dark wood panelling and darker shadows. The candles remained unlit and the fireplaces held no cheer. The only light emanated from the lantern the woman held. Now they were inside Steiner could see her properly. Barely five feet tall, she had the olive skin and the dark eyes of the Spriggani.

'Don't say anything,' said Marek, catching the look in his son's eye.

'This way,' said the woman, crooking a finger at them. The stairs creaked under their weight and every footfall seemed a crime against the silence of the house. The woman opened double doors onto an empty room and gestured they should wait inside.

'What happens now?' whispered Steiner after the Spriggani woman had disappeared.

'Now we wait,' replied Marek, peeling off his wet cloak. 'And hope he speaks with us.'

'And what if this friend of yours still works for the Empire?' said Kristofine with a frown. She shook the rain out of her cloak and her eyes darted around the room.

'He was never a man that followed orders easily,' said Marek and crossed to the window where he could watch over the street below. 'Mistress Kamalov isn't the first person to turn her back on the Empire. Or even the second,' he added, as if remembering his own former allegiance. Steiner peeled off his own cloak before settling in to make a fire.

Tikhoveter, when he finally appeared perhaps half an hour later, did not look like the Imperial soldiers they were avoiding, nor did he look like an Envoy. Tikhoveter did not look like anyone the Empire would employ for anything. He was stooped with the passage of years, at least fifty of them if Steiner had to guess. Wild corkscrews of white hair fell about his shoulders and he was wiry-thin. His beard was trimmed but in all other aspects Tikhoveter was a shambles. His britches were patched and stained, his shirt and jacket no different, and the smell of drink was overpowering. Tikhoveter belched loudly, leaned wearily against the door frame, belched again and blinked a few times.

'Hoy there,' said Marek. 'Did we wake you?'

'On a day like this there's little to do except nap and read old books.' Steiner struggled to place the accent. The wiry man drifted past them and presented his backside to the fireplace. He smiled a moment and whispered, 'There is nothing more wonderful in all of creation than having a warm arse in damp weather.'

'Are you Tikhoveter?' asked Steiner. Marek made a growling sound and Steiner fell silent.

'No Tikhoveter here,' said the man. 'He died about ten years ago.' His words sloshed against each other, and there was a tipsy sing-song quality to the way he spoke. 'We still get Imperial sorts wandering in here from time to time. Looking for shelter mostly, or somewhere to hide for a night or two.'

'That's a real shame,' said Marek. He remained at the side of the room watching the street outside through the window. 'But we're not Imperial sorts. At least these two aren't.' He nodded to Kristofine and Steiner, then returned his gaze to the street outside. 'And I haven't been for over twenty years.'

Their host turned his back on Marek and held out his hands to warm them. 'Is that so?'

Steiner frowned, confused at the two men who seemed to be speaking yet ignoring each other.

'I met Tikhoveter once,' said Marek, not breaking his vigil at the window. 'He was a sickly little runt with a hacking cough. The Empire had posted him to Arkiv Island. They had him working in the library but the dust was no good for his lungs.'

The man by the fireplace stiffened and turned his head just a fraction to glance over his shoulder. 'Never met him.' Steiner noted the drunken pretence slipping away.

'And the strange thing about him,' continued Marek, as if he hadn't heard the man, 'was that he had long hair that fell all about him like corkscrews. Never touched a drop of booze on account of his health, but always had an eye for women. Especially Spriggani women.'

The rain continued to drift down in the street and Steiner couldn't help but smirk. Tikhoveter gave a long sigh and his shoulders slumped forward. He was very quiet for a moment.

'Fuck my boots,' he mumbled in defeat. 'So who the Hel are you then?'

'I'm the soldier who had you reassigned from Arkiv Island,' replied Marek with a slow smile. Tikhoveter stood up straighter and frowned a moment.

'Marek Vartiainen?'

Marek turned to the man at last and nodded once.

'Have you come to kill me?' asked Tikhoveter, a wary expression crossing his face like a dark cloud.

'Do you think we'd just calmly knock on the door if the Emperor wanted you dead?' said Marek.

'I'm not so charming as to warrant a social call after all these years,' said Tikhoveter. 'What do you want?'

'Are you still playing both sides?' asked Marek.

'Not so much these days. I get word to a few old friends who prefer to avoid the Holy Synod. The Empire leaves me alone by and large.'

'Something big happened at Vladibogdan recently,' said Marek. 'We need to learn just how much the Empire knows.'

'Information doesn't come cheap,' said Tikhoveter, running

a hand across his beard. 'And information about the Empire is more expensive still.'

Steiner reached into his pocket and fished out a guilder. 'What do you know about Matriarch-Commissar Felgenhauer?'

'Hel's teeth, Steiner,' muttered Marek.

Tikhoveter eyed the guilder and pursed his lips. 'So the boy has money?'

'He's no mere boy,' said Marek, anger flashing in his eyes as the fire roared in the hearth. 'And he's done more to fight the Empire in a few months than you or I have in two decades.'

Tikhoveter held up his hands. 'I meant no offence.'

'Yes you did,' replied Steiner, hefting his sledgehammer. 'But I'm more interested in Felgenhauer than trading slights.'

'Last I heard,' Tikhoveter cleared his throat, 'is that she was summoned to the Emperor himself by an Envoy. They almost made it back to the Imperial Court at Khlystburg when she went renegade.'

'Renegade?' Steiner stood open-mouthed for a second. 'And then what?' Tikhoveter shrugged and looked away. Steiner tossed him the guilder and the wiry old man snatched it from the air.

'Just rumours,' said Tikhoveter. 'Some are saying she's started a mercenary company operating around Slavon Province. That's all I know about her.'

Marek held up another two guilders. 'We need to know what the Empire is talking about, and we need to know it quickly.'

'Come back tomorrow,' said the old spy. 'This kind of work can't be rushed. I'll reach out to a few contacts and see what I can discover.'

'Can we stay here?' asked Kristofine. Tikhoveter started laughing, a cruel sort of sound that gave way to a painful cough.

'You don't have to be so rude,' she replied.

'Safer for everyone is we stay at a tavern,' said Marek. Steiner led them down the stairs.

'I'll have word by tomorrow,' said Tikhoveter from the top of the staircase. He did not see them out. The rain had slackened during their brief stay at Tikhoveter's house but the temperature was dipping.

'I don't understand,' said Kristofine. 'It takes weeks for a man on horseback to carry messages from one town to another. How does he expect to have answers for us by tomorrow?'

'It's what makes the Vigilants of Vozdukha so necessary,' said Marek. 'They can set whispers on the wind and send them over hundreds of miles, faster than any man on horseback could ever dream of riding.'

'Like Mistress Kamalov?' asked Kristofine.

Marek nodded. 'It's why a Troika of Vigilants usually has one graduate from the Vozdukha Academy in its ranks.'

'So they can stay in touch with the Empire, wherever they are,' said Steiner.

'And some folk with witchsign,' explained Marek, 'those who are too sick or troublesome, are pressed into service as envoys or spies.'

'Folk like Tikhoveter,' said Steiner, glancing over his shoulder. 'Can we trust him?'

Marek shrugged. 'Who knows. But he's our best bet right now, so we have to take that chance.'

Steiner looked back at the townhouse and tried to feel some hope, but uncertainty carried a dread all of its own.

CHAPTER SIX

Kimi

The noise could be heard a few streets away. Kimi and Marozvolk exited the blacksmith's where they'd purchased swords.

'Smoke,' said Kimi, nodding to the pale blue sky. Dark clouds had crowded in over the city and it was just starting to rain. She set off against the flow of people who hurried past them, hurrying away from trouble. Violence had come to Svingettevei and Kimi knew in her bones it was no mere sailor's brawl. Panic was written across the face of every person who fled down the street or cowered in a doorway.

'It could just be a house fire,' said Marozvolk. They exchanged a glance that confirmed neither of them really believed such a thing. A brisk walk became a jog and then, on some unspoken agreement, they both ran towards the sound. Kimi shouldered her way through the crowd, staring down any that blocked her way. She kept one hand on the hilt of her sword to make her intent clear. There was a wail of pain from ahead of them, cries of dismay, people calling out to each other. Most of the voices were children.

'It has to be the novices,' muttered Marozvolk.

'What in the Hel is . . .' Kimi got no further. Marozvolk

rounded a corner and almost ran into three soldiers, lurking at the edge of the street in their black cloaks and heavy armour. No doubt the soldiers were as shocked as Kimi, trying to make sense of the unfolding chaos in Virag's streets. A wagon was bright with fierce flames and a handful of children lay strewn on the cobbles, unmoving, bleeding or both. Mistress Kamalov and Kjellrunn stood in the centre of the street, shielding the children as best they could. The renegade Vigilant looked both severe and forbidding, while Kjellrunn was ashen with fear, her eyes wide with shock.

'This is bad,' muttered Marozvolk.

Kimi searched for Steiner, cursing under her breath when it was clear he was nowhere to seen. 'Where is that damn fool?'

'Stand down and cease all use of the arcane this instant!' bellowed a man's voice. Kimi noted the speaker; he stood on the opposite side of the street, holding a short sword to a young novice's throat. It was the Imperial Envoy they had seen earlier. Kimi gritted her teeth in frustration. She should have gone back to the ship to warn people.

'He won't do it,' muttered Marozvolk, nodding to the Envoy.

'How can you be so sure?' whispered Kimi.

'The children are more useful to them alive. Always have been.'

A burly sergeant with a two-handed maul kicked one of the children on the ground, who cried out and curled up into a ball. Somehow the many soldiers – Kimi guessed over a dozen – hadn't noticed the Yamili women emerge from a side street. Nor had they seen the vast cloud of birds that stared balefully from the rooftops, nor the knot of Spriggani who appeared beside the burning cart. Mistress Kamalov, Sundra and Kimi shared a nod and all the terrors of Hel descended on Virag that day.

Mistress Kamalov reached into the sky, urging a commotion of gulls, cormorants, and gannets to dive from above, summoning them with the arcane. Her lips moved silently and she frowned in concentration. The various birds buffeted the soldiers. Individually they had no hope of harming the armoured men, but their confusion was all Kimi needed. Kimi caught the first soldier square across the back of the neck with her sword. There was a bright gout of blood as the blade cut deep, all but decapitating him. Seconds later he was an armoured corpse littering the cobbles.

Marozvolk grabbed the nearest soldier from behind, one hand clamping over the man's faceplate, blocking the eye slit. The soldier jerked backwards but Marozvolk pulled with all of her strength and the helm came free. Confused and off balance, the soldier had barely turned to see his attacker before Marozvolk slashed him across the throat in a bright torrent of crimson.

'Worth every penny,' said Marozvolk, hefting the new blade.

Kjellrunn used the cover of screeching birds to circle around the soldiers and reach the Envoy. A fallen mace leapt up from the cobbles and her eyes widened in surprise. She hadn't meant to use the arcane, but the weapon had come to her as if summoned. The Envoy stared in disbelief, hands shaking, face pale, as Kimi and Marozvolk carried out their grim trade of death, besting the soldiers.

'Surrender your weapons at once!' the Envoy shouted as Mistress Kamalov's birds swooped and slashed at him with their claws. Kjellrunn closed on the Envoy with a snarl on her face. She pulled back the mace, every muscle tense for the strike to come.

'You will surrender!' shouted the Envoy in desperation.

Sundra glowered at the scene, her eyes a dark and terrible grey. A soldier raised his mace to strike her brother, Tief, as he fought another attacker. Sundra muttered an invocation to her goddess and streaks of grey covered the soldier's armour. The man inside the armour stiffened and became still, until with a final gasp the soldier was petrified. Tief shoved the newly formed statue, grunting a curse. The soldier fell backwards and shattered apart on the cobbles with a terrible crash. Tief snatched up the soldier's mace and, wielding a long knife in his other hand, snuck up to a soldier attacking the children. The long knife took the soldier in the back of the leg. The soldier fell to his knees and turned just as Tief caved in his helm with three savage blows.

Marozvolk and Kimi bludgeoned and slashed a bloody path through the soldiers, but were soon split up. Marozvolk fought to defend the many novices, while Kimi surged forward to kill the Envoy. The children, initially cowed after the loss of their friends, saw their allies fighting for them and began to rally. Trine, the dark-haired, fire-breathing novice, hurled a javelin of arcane flame, which punched through a soldier's armour and into his chest. Another of the men was lifted into the air by a trio of Zemlya novices, only to crash to the ground seconds later. He screamed as his legs broke.

Kimi was a dozen feet from Kjellrunn when she reached the Envoy but no matter what she did, she couldn't find a way past the soldiers. Kimi deflected and dodged their strikes and replied with thrusts of her own, but she drew no closer.

The Envoy still clutched at the young girl, his short sword at her throat, his hand visibly shaking. He backed away from the fight but there was no escaping Kjellrunn. Her first strike came down on his sword arm, smashing the elbow. The sword fell from the Envoy's numb fingers and clattered on the cobbles. The second strike almost connected with the Envoy's head, but was nothing more than a glancing blow to his temple. The young novice slipped free of his grasp and fled.

'Who are you people?' mumbled the Envoy as he staggered backwards, holding his head with both his hands.

Kjellrunn didn't answer him, but hefted the mace, making her intentions clear. The Envoy's expression hardened before spreading his feet wide and gasping down a breath. There was a tell-tale orange glow at the Envoy's throat that Kimi had seen before.

'Kjellrunn! Get down!' Kimi was locked in combat with another soldier a dozen feet away and had no way of reaching her. The Envoy breathed a gout of fire that engulfed Kjellrunn's head and torso.

'Kjellrunn!' screamed Kimi. She slashed the knee of the soldier she was fighting with her blade and sprinted towards Steiner's sister. The Envoy stared ahead in disbelief. The young woman he had immolated had not dropped to the ground in agony. Kjellrunn had barely flinched. Her blackened skin showed traces of stone beneath the scorch marks. She threw down the mace from granite hands and seized the Envoy by the throat before punching him with a series of wet smacking sounds.

'Kjellrunn! Stop. You're killing him.' Kimi stared from the Envoy to the barely recognisable girl. 'I didn't know you could change your skin.'

'Neither did I,' said Kjellrunn. She released the bloodied Envoy and stared at one hand, a look of sickened worry on her stony face. Her granite skin shimmered a moment before returning to its normal colour. Marozvolk emerged from the violence to stand beside them.

'Kjellrunn,' said the former Vigilant in quiet awe. 'It takes years to learn how to do that.'

But Kjellrunn paid no attention. She gestured at a cobble by her foot, which she wrenched out of the road by arcane force. Then cobble shot over Kimi's shoulder, barely missing her ear.

'You nearly took my head off!' Kimi shouted before turning to follow Kjellrunn's furious gaze. The cobble had dented the sergeant's chest plate and knocked him back a step, but he was still within arm's reach. Kimi raised her sword but staggered backwards as the soldier slammed her in the face with the butt of the maul. Kimi fell into Kjellrunn and they both sprawled across the Envoy in a heap of limbs.

'Get *off* of me!' complained the Envoy, through a bloody and ruined mouth. Kimi stamped on the man's face as she regained her feet. Marozvolk parried the sergeant's next strike, stepping aside and looking for an opening. His armour was scored and dented, but the man showed no sign of giving in.

'The Envoy has fallen!' shouted the sergeant, then stepped in closer and swung his maul in a wide arc. Kimi sidestepped the blow and swiped at the sergeant's knees but the armoured man was surprisingly nimble. Her sword missed its mark and the sergeant replied with a strike at Kimi's head. The princess folded at the waist to avoid the maul and Marozvolk charged into the man, catching him in the midriff and knocking him down. There was a frenzied scrabble as Marozvolk grasped the sergeant's maul at each end and pressed down on the man's throat. He pushed and punched and clawed at Marozvolk but her skin shimmered and turned to stone, weathering his frenzied and desperate attacks. Long seconds passed before the sergeant stopped moving. His arms went slack, his legs stopped kicking, and a dreadful silence descended on the street.

Kimi offered Marozvolk a hand, helping the former Vigilant to her feet.

'I thought he was going to kill you, your highness,' said Marozvolk, breathing hard, suddenly formal.

'I thought the same thing. Thanks for saving me.'

All around were bodies of soldiers. Tief was finishing off the ones who still drew breath, while Sundra attended to the dead and wounded novices.

'So much for going ahead and scouting to make sure things

are safe,' said Kimi as Romola rounded a corner and looked at the scene of carnage.

'What have you done?' said the pirate captain quietly.

The rest of the day was spent disposing of the dead soldiers in the bay. Marozvolk hauled another corpse from the back of the wagon. The novices watched from their position on the ship. They stared down with pale faces, too shocked to speak. They were six less in number now, just seventeen souls. Mistress Kamalov had retired to her cabin, refusing to speak to anyone.

Tief helped Romola and her crew loot the soldier's bodies, setting aside the coin and stripping the armour. 'How long before the Empire notices they're missing?' he asked quietly.

'I count eighteen bodies,' said Kimi.

'There's usually ten men to a section,' said Marozvolk, 'and three sections to a troop.'

Tief swore under his breath and Romola pressed a hand to her forehead. 'So there's another twelve soldiers out there?' said Tief.

'We don't know that,' said Marozvolk. 'They might have been under full strength. The other section might be in the next town.'

'We keep three crew on watch at all times,' Romola said to her crew. 'As soon as we sight Imperial soldiers I'm casting off, and I don't care who's still ashore.' She flashed an angry look at Kimi. '*Where* is Steiner?'

Kimi shrugged. 'I haven't seen him. I was scouting ahead. That was what we agreed.' She eyed the captain with a sour look. 'Who let Mistress Kamalov off the ship with all of those children?'

'I was overseeing the resupply,' countered Romola, squaring up to the princess. 'I can't be everywhere at once.'

'You didn't notice two score of children and an old woman

sneaking off your ship?' said Kimi, taking a step closer. 'Are you blind?'

'This isn't helping,' said Marozvolk quietly. 'We dispose of the bodies, we get the supplies, we cast off. You two can blame each other all day long once we're at sea.'

CHAPTER SEVEN

Kjellrunn

Kjellrunn sat on a coil of rope at the back of the ship, hunched and folded in on herself, one hand resting against her brow. Time and again she had tried to clear her mind of the street battle, tried not to remember the dull echo of weapons on armour or the shrill calls of the dying. Every noise from the docks sounded threatening to her. Every raucous voice belonged to a Solmindre soldier. She snuck a look over the side of the ship, holding her breath until she was sure they were safe.

The corner of the stern and the coil of rope were a poor substitute for her cabin, but she had no wish to be close to Mistress Kamalov. Kjellrunn didn't know what was worse, the way the old woman cursed under her breath or the moments she gave in to silent weeping for the dead children. Kjellrunn nested down on the rope once more and blinked away the memories of the carnage. Six children beaten and bloody on the streets of Virag. Beaten until they stopped moving and breathing. Beaten for bearing the 'taint' of witchsign and the misfortune to run across an Envoy with the sight.

'Frøya save us,' whispered Kjellrunn as a chill wind whipped across the deck, bringing spots of rain with it. The crew of the *Watcher's Wait* went about their tasks under a pall of surly silence, keen to sail away under the cover of night. The glee of ransacking Vladibogdan had subsided and the men and women shared sidelong glances, muttering bitterness when they spoke at all. They wore their weapons openly and all humour had been cast aside. Romola directed the resupply of the ship's stores and not one of them shirked under her stern gaze. Mistress Kamalov appeared on deck and scowled at the grey sky and the promise of rain as if it were a personal affront. She spoke with Sundra and Tief for a moment.

'They can't wait to be rid of us,' said Tief, indicating the pirates. 'We're bad luck. We're worse than bad luck.'

Kjellrunn couldn't hear Mistress Kamalov's response, but moments later the old Vigilant was hobbling across the quarterdeck and up the steps. She approached the stern of the ship as if she hadn't seen her pupil then leaned against the rail a dozen feet from where Kjellrunn sat.

'It is quite a thing to hide in plain sight,' said Mistress Kamalov, staring out to sea. Kjellrunn shrugged, too tired to argue, but there could be no question that hiding was what she was doing.

'Sometimes it's good to hide,' continued Mistress Kamalov. 'Sometimes hiding is necessary but sometimes hiding costs people their lives.'

Kjellrunn flinched at the last word and felt the heat of anger in her cheeks.

'This isn't about me sitting in the corner of the ship, is it?'

'I always said you were a smart girl.' Mistress Kamalov looked out to the city of Virag and curled her lip. 'This entire city smells like rotting fish heads and wet dung, but I doubt the cities of Shanisrond will be any better.'

Kjellrunn released a breath of relief, glad for the change of subject, glad that the old woman hadn't taken her to task for failing to protect the children. She was more than capable of doing that for herself. Neither woman spoke for a moment and Kjellrunn stood up, keen to reach the quiet of the cabin and avoid anyone else.

'Strange that you take up arms against that Envoy but not fight with the arcane the way I taught you.'

'I can't do it,' said Kjellrunn quietly. 'I couldn't do it. I couldn't . . .'

'What can you not do?' asked Mistress Kamalov, hobbling forward, a frown fixed above her furious eyes.

'I have nightmares,' said Kjellrunn, 'dreams where the souls of all those dead Okhrana drag me back to the woodcutter's chalet in Nordvlast. They take me down to the deep places in the earth. I can taste death, feel the decay of creatures gone to their rest. Those Okhrana want me dead for what I did. I can't use the arcane like that again. I can't destroy a score of people in a heartbeat.'

Mistress Kamalov looked away and rubbed her face. The dark circles beneath her eyes spoke of sleepless nights and Kjellrunn suspected there would be many more to come.

'You killed the Okhrana with the arcane to avenge Verner,' said the old woman quietly. 'And you should have killed those soldiers with the arcane to protect those children. Now they are dead. They are dead because they trusted an old, foolish *kozel* and a student who has suddenly lost her nerve.'

'What?' Kjellrunn stepped closer to the old woman.

'You had no such qualms about sinking an entire ship of Imperial sailors off the shore of Nordvlast.'

'That was to stop the Empire coming to Cinderfell.'

'So.' Mistress Kamalov held up one finger. 'It is permissible to use the arcane when you wish to avenge a loved one, or to protect yourself, but not to protect anyone else.'

Kjellrunn pulled back her hand to slap the old woman across the face when she noticed the raven-haired novice just a dozen feet away. Kjellrunn lowered her hand. The remaining novices had gathered at the stern and were watching the exchange.

'What do you want?' said Kjellrunn. She eyed the girl with an unfriendly glare and the girl returned it with one of her own. For a brief moment Kjellrunn was back in the street, watching the girl breathe fire, killing the soldier who gripped her arm while Kjellrunn did nothing.

'I'm Trine,' said the girl. Kjellrunn took a moment to look at her more carefully. She was around the same age as Kjellrunn with the same pale complexion, made stark by the shock of black hair that tumbled down her back. Kjellrunn stood a little straighter but no good came of it. They were roughly the same height, the same scrawny build. They might have been twins if not for their hair. 'I came to tell you' – the girl looked at Mistress Kamalov – 'that we're staying on the ship. All of us. We'll come with you to Shanisrond.' For a fleeting second the girl looked apologetic. 'And we promise not run off and get into trouble.' The young girl looked over her shoulder with a hard expression, as if warning the other children.

'How old are you, Trine?' asked Kjellrunn.

'Sixteen.' Trine jutted her chin and stared at Kjellrunn with a note of challenge. 'And I'm *not* scared of using my powers.' Kjellrunn felt the rebuke as clearly as if she'd been struck.

'Then perhaps you should be Mistress Kamalov's new student.' Kjellrunn pushed her way through the centre of the novices and kept walking until she was at the prow. She didn't look back.

The crowds at the end of the pier shifted uneasily but Kjellrunn couldn't see any soldiers among them from her place on the ship. A small contingent of guild masters lingered for a time, locked in discussion despite the inclement weather.

Only three guild masters remained as the evening drew on, along with four of the city watch. A cruel wind whipped at their tabards and coats and Kjellrunn shivered. 'Where are you, Steiner?' she whispered, knowing all too well that her brother was spoiling for a fight with the Empire. She'd rather not lose him so soon after getting him back from Vladibogdan.

'Frøya's teeth, Steiner. Don't leave me on this rotting ship.'

The guards on the pier intercepted two people before letting them approach the ship. Kjellrunn didn't recognise them at first in their new clothes, but it was unmistakably Kimi and Marozvolk that stalked down the pier and not Marek and Steiner. Kimi looked cold and furious, much as she'd done for the whole voyage, while Marozvolk spared a backwards glance towards the city. Kjellrunn watched the former Vigilant bend closer to the Yamali princess and exchange words before both of them broke into a run. Marozvolk had seen something.

'Not again,' said Kjellrunn. Her mouth went dry.

The crowds at the docks broke apart and a single scream pierced the confused mumbles of the city folk. More soldiers in black enamelled armour and black cloaks approached. Kjellrunn counted a dozen at least, possibly twenty.

'Cast off now!' bellowed Romola.

Kjellrunn's stomach turned to ice. Kimi and Marozvolk hit the boarding ramp even as two sailors attempted to drag it on board. The soldiers were moving down the pier as fast as their heavy armour would allow.

'Archers!' Romola's voice again. She had drawn her sabre and pointed towards the pier. Kjellrunn ran, heading for Romola at midships. Sailors were heaving and grunting as they drew up the anchor and Kjellrunn struggled to slip past them.

'Wait!' she called out. 'Wait, gods damn it! My brother is still ashore.'

The pirates' arrows raced through the air, embedding in the thick wood of the soldier's hastily raised shields. Other arrows clattered off the stone pier and ricocheted into barrels and crates near the guild masters. The soldiers had dropped to one knee behind their shields, their advance slowed.

'Keep firing!' shouted Romola.

Kjellrunn reached the captain and took her by the arm. 'We have to wait for my family!'

'It's your family or my ship and my crew,' shouted Romola. She shook Kjellrunn off.

'Just a few more minutes!'

'A few more minutes and there won't be a ship to come back to.'

Sundra emerged at Kjellrunn's side and took her hand. 'Come away from the captain, no good will come of it.'

A soldier on the pier had slung his shield across his back and ran towards the ship, sprinting as best he could in the heavy armour.

'Cast off, damn you,' shouted Romola. 'Push off from the pier.'

The soldier leapt on, mounting a pile of crates as arrows fell all around him. He was almost at the gunwales when Romola planted a foot against his head and forced him off the ship. The deck was a flurry of action as sailors went about their tasks.

'Look out!' shouted a pirate beside Kjellrunn. Moments later a handful of grappling hooks streaked over their heads, ropes arcing behind them after. The metal clattered on the wooden deck and the ropes became taut. Someone screamed and Kjellrunn discovered a sailor pinned up against the side of the ship, a grappling hook, thrown from land, embedded in his thigh. Kjellrunn drew the pirate's cutlass as the pinned man clutched at his leg and howled in agony.

'What are you doing?' he gasped. Kjellrunn severed the rope attached to the grappling hook and a soldier on the pier collapsed backwards.

'I have wounded here!' shouted Kjellrunn.

More grappling hooks were thrown, prompting more calls of alarm.

'How did they know to bring grappling hooks?' said Romola. 'They're soldiers, not marines.'

'Whatever they are,' said Kjellrunn, pointing to another contingent of soldiers further up the docks, 'there are a lot more of them.'

'Marines don't wear armour, halfhead,' said the captain. 'Keep firing, you filthy dogs!' she bellowed at the archers.

The hissing sound of fabric unfurling filled Kjellrunn's senses as the main sail dropped from its boom. Kjellrunn caught a glimpse of Mistress Kamalov at the stern of the ship with four novices, all standing with feet spread wide and arms outstretched, fingertips splayed. The sail snapped out and the ship lurched forward. The shouting stopped as all aboard clung to whatever was closest to hand. Kjellrunn dropped to her knees and blinked through the unnatural wind. There was a moment where no one said a word and the only sound was the shrieking arcane gale and an almost unhinged laughter. Kjellrunn turned to see Romola staring up at the main sail with a wide grin.

'May you have witchsign!' shouted the captain above the howling gale. 'Glorious witchsign and a fair wind at your back!'

The *Watcher's Wait* surged away from Virag and the sailors dropped more of the sails. Kjellrunn ran to the stern, ignoring Mistress Kamalov and her charges, who squeezed their eyes closed in concentration. The pier was taken over by black-clad soldiers, who stared after the ship in mute fury. Kjellrunn watched the city as it grew smaller and smaller with distance. Somewhere in that sprawl of people was her brother, her father. Did they even know they had been left behind?

CHAPTER EIGHT

Steiner

The docks were awash with people, some shouting, some crying. Most were staring slack-jawed at the blood-red frigate heading for the open sea. The sails were full with a wind that shouldn't have existed.

'Seems our good fortune didn't last long,' said Marek. Steiner could just make out the gaunt frame of Mistress Kamalov standing at the stern, arms outstretched, summoning a gale to speed them on their way. Four novices stood beside her, following the renegade Vigilant's lead. Was that Kjellrunn staring from the back of the ship? He hoped so.

'The pier is crawling with soldiers,' said Kristofine, clutching Steiner's hand with a wild look in her eyes. The crowd near the pier started to dissipate, keen to be away from the armoured men in black cloaks.

'I can't believe it,' said Steiner as the *Watcher's Wait* departed Virag. 'Romola left without us.'

'She did warn us she'd set sail if soldiers came,' said Marek. He rubbed his stubbled jaw with one calloused hand. 'At least Kjellrunn and the children will be safe.'

'That's good for Kjellrunn,' said Steiner. 'But what about us?'

'We need to get out of the city,' said Marek. 'The Empire

will be asking a lot of questions over the next few days.' He walked away and headed towards a side street. Kristofine and Steiner followed, their gazes lingering on the ship as it receded into the distance.

'Shouldn't we try and book passage on another ship?' asked Kristofine with a worried glance over her shoulder.

'No one will be going anywhere for about a week,' said Marek. 'They'll forbid the captains from leaving port. Every hold and crate will be inspected.'

'You don't know that,' she replied. 'We could still catch up with them at the next port.'

'Actually I do know that.' Marek's voice was low and his words clipped. 'I used to serve with those men. I used to give the orders.'

'Fine,' replied Kristofine, though her tone of voice said otherwise. 'But we're on our own and need to be prepared.'

'If we delay we'll be caught,' said Marek, his expression grim. Steiner could tell his father was struggling to keep his anger in check.

'But we have nothing but the cloaks on our backs,' replied Kristofine from between gritted teeth. 'What's the point of escaping if we starve to death on the road?'

'She has a point,' said Steiner, stepping between them. He pointed out a handful of market stalls further up the street. 'Come on.'

There was a perfunctory attempt at haggling, but Marek was more committed to being on his way than commanding a good price. Moments later they were outfitted with a satchel and two packs filled with food that would keep them going for a few days at least. The stalls were packing up for the night and the rain, which had never really stopped, began anew.

No sooner had they gathered their supplies than two Imperial soldiers appeared and began to question one of the vendors. As one, Steiner, Kristofine and Marek pulled up their hoods to shield them as much from prying eyes as the drizzle that fell in Virag's crooked streets. Steiner hid the sledge-hammer beneath his cloak and prayed they were not searched.

'What else do we need?' he said.

'Something to sleep on,' replied Marek. 'And Kristofine should have a blade.'

'But I don't know how to fight.' The tavern-keeper's daughter from Cinderfell looked at the older Vartiainen, shock and worry writ plain on her face.

'Not yet you don't,' replied Marek. 'But you're going to learn now that you're on the road with us.'

'Is that wise?' Steiner wanted to say more but couldn't find the words.

'Do you have a better idea?' Marek's impatience was clear as he paced down the street, away from the soldiers. Steiner leaned in close to his father.

'I just don't want her getting hurt is all,' he whispered.

'That makes two of us,' replied Marek.

'Three of us,' added Kristofine, with a curl of her lip. 'And I can hear you. What do I say if the soldiers ask us our business?'

'We'll tell them we're mercenaries,' replied Marek. 'There's never a lack of violence in Vinterkveld.'

'Fine,' said Kristofine, though this time Steiner had the sense she had made up her mind about something. 'Where do I get one of these swords, then?'

It took around an hour to get what they needed. The rain fell harder with every coin they spent and a deep chill settled over Virag as the sun slunk towards the horizon from its hiding place behind the clouds. Steiner clenched his numb fingers into equally numb fists and Kristofine huddled close to him.

'If we leave now we'll never know if Tikhoveter discovered anything,' said Steiner, slowing his pace.

'We can't be sure Tikhoveter didn't sell us out to the local garrison,' said Marek, clearly wanting to be on his way.

'But he may be my best chance of finding out where Felgenhauer is.' Marek shook his head and cursed softly. 'We don't have the luxury of time for that sort of thing.'

'Luxury? She's family! Family isn't a luxury. I've already lost Kjellrunn to gods know what port in Shanisrond. I may never see her again.'

'I've more a mind to search for Kjell than Felgenhauer,' said Marek, his expression hard. 'Come on. Now isn't the time for this.'

'Your father has a point,' said Kristofine. 'Let's leave.'

'If this uprising is going to stand a chance I'm going to need someone with the arcane on my side. I'm going to need Felgenhauer.'

'Steiner.' Marek's tone was pleading now. 'She's likely dead, and us along with her if we go back to Tikhoveter.'

'I'm going to speak with the spy,' said Steiner. 'We paid him and he owes us.' He set off down the cobbled street as the drizzle continued to fall.

'Gods damn it,' muttered Marek, but he followed his son all the same.

'Is there any chance we'll agree on anything today?' said Kristofine to Marek as they followed Steiner through the winding streets.

'I don't have much hope,' said the blacksmith.

Smoke rose up over the city and obscured the few stars that peeked through the dreary clouds. Every chimney on every street gently exhaled more soot into the darkening sky.

'Cities are wretched places,' said Kristofine. 'I feel like I'll never be clean again.'

Steiner was too tired to form any sort of reply, could think of nothing else except Tikhoveter and what the spy might know about Felgenhauer. He hadn't realised how much he'd missed the Matriarch-Commissar until the old spy had mentioned her name, but now her whereabouts consumed his thoughts.

A shout of alarm from the next street was their first clue something was wrong. They pressed on through the winding streets, keeping a bleary eye out for Imperial soldiers.

'There shouldn't be this much smoke,' said Marek, struggling not to cough.

'Surely it can't be much further.' Kristofine said no more as Tikhoveter's townhouse came into view. Tongues of fire spoke destruction from every window. The stones of the beautiful old house were blackened and Steiner guessed the wooden beams had surrendered during the fire. The roof had collapsed, no doubt killing anyone inside that hadn't already burned to death. Dozens of neighbours stood in the street clutching buckets. They did their best to ferry water from the nearest well, but the blaze had done its fearsome work.

'We need to go,' said Marek quietly. 'The Empire will be watching this place to see who comes calling.'

'You don't know it was the Empire that did this,' said Kristofine, but she became silent as she caught Marek's stern gaze. The old blacksmith disappeared into a side alley. Marek didn't speak as he strode away, hands balled into fists. Kristofine held Steiner's arm tightly.

'Do you think Tikhoveter escaped?'

Steiner shrugged. 'The Empire are thorough. When they take an interest in someone . . .' He grimaced. 'They usually end up dead.'

'Will we end up like that?' said Kristofine. 'Burned in our sleep?'

'They'll be looking for me too,' replied Steiner. 'You're only caught up in this because of me. If things get bad you start running and don't stop. Understand?'

Kristofine looked at him from under her hood, neither nodding in agreement nor refusing his request. He wished she was on the ship with the others.

Marek led them to a canal at the edge of the city where an inn hunched low under a rickety roof. The low din of merchants could be heard from within, no doubt arguing about the day's events and the losses they had suffered.

'What are we doing here?' asked Kristofine hopefully.

'Change of heart,' said Marek. 'You two are dead on your feet, and I'm not much better. Smithing is one thing but dashing around takes its toll. We stay here tonight and set off in the morning with a proper meal in our bellies. It may be the last time we eat well for some time.'

'That's the first bit of good news I've heard all day,' replied Steiner, shouldering the door open and stepping out of the rain.

'Seems we all agree on something after all,' said Kristofine as Marek held the door open for her.

The night at the inn was far from restful. There was a low rumble of conversation from the bar until closing time and occasional shouts from the city outside their window. Steiner took first watch, waiting outside their chamber door, watching for the Imperial soldiers he feared would surely come. Kristofine took a turn and Steiner was deeply asleep by the time Marek took a shift.

'Is this how it's going to be now?' asked Kristofine the next morning as they packed their things. 'Always looking over our shoulder for trouble?' There was a stillness to her that Steiner hadn't seen before, as if the gravity of their situation had settled on her shoulders overnight.

Marek nodded. 'It's been that way for us for some time now. Welcome to the family.' He smiled but Kristofine didn't laugh at the joke and Steiner felt a pang of guilt. He took her hand in his as Marek stepped out of the room.

'I'm sorry,' he whispered to her.

'It's not your fault,' Kristofine replied, but her gaze was fixed on the floor. 'When I left Cinderfell I simply wanted to be away from my father. I didn't really know what I was getting myself into.'

'It is my fault,' replied Steiner. 'If we hadn't spent the night together, the night before I was taken to Vladibogdan, then people in Cinderfell wouldn't have suspected you of witchsign.'

'Even if that hadn't happened I'd still have had to flee Cinderfell. It's not every day a man arrives on the back of a dragon and burns an Imperial ship to ashes.' Finally she looked up and forced a brave sort of smile.

'One day we're going to find a place we can live without worrying about the Empire,' said Steiner.

'One day.' Though the way Kristofine said it made Steiner wonder if that day would ever come.

They enjoyed a repast of warm porridge, hot tea, and dash of honey that made everything seem better. The canal was filled with boats that bumped up against one another. The air was filled with the sound of fraying tempers and stifled curses.

'What's happening?' asked Kristofine.

'People are trying to get their cargo out of town by canal now the port has closed,' said Marek. 'A lot of people, all with the same idea.'

Steiner took an anxious breath. An idea was starting to form. A woman passed them in the street and glanced at Steiner. There was a frozen moment as she recognised the three of them before she turned away. It was the Spriggani woman from Tikhoveter's house. Steiner sprang forward and caught her by the arm.

'Wait! What happened?'

'What do you think happened!' hissed the woman, one hand straying to her hood, making sure it stayed up. Now Steiner was closer he could see she had a pack on her back, just as they did. She too wore a cloak for the road and sturdy boots. 'They killed Tikhoveter and waited nearby for you. I set fire to the house to warn you off.'

'You set fire to your own house?' said Kristofine.

'I only stayed because he wanted me to. I've begged him to leave for Shanisrond for years but he couldn't give up his old life.' Her mouth creased with grief and tears shone at the corners of her eyes. 'I think he liked the danger, but I didn't need a hero. I just wanted a husband. Now I have neither.

'I'm so sorry,' said Marek. 'Did he tell you anything before the soldiers came?' The Spriggani woman blinked away her tears.

'He was excited. Said he couldn't believe it. The Emperor has learned of what happened on Vladibogdan and flew into a rage so terrible his own court feared to attend for three days.'

'Did he mention any names?' asked Steiner. 'Anything about dragons?'

'Dragons?' The woman scowled as if he were simple. 'How dare you speak to me of children's stories now.' She took Steiner by the hand, her grip hard and icy cold. 'The greatest monster to stalk Vinterkveld is no dragon. The Emperor is by far the most dangerous creature to have ever lived.' The woman looked away, her shoulders slumped as the energy drained out her, and then she walked away without farewell or a backwards glance.

'We should follow her,' said Kristofine. 'If she's headed to Shanisrond—'

'No,' said Steiner. 'I made a promise to Kimi. I said I'd find a way to lead an uprising against the Empire. People are going to find out about Vladibogdan soon enough, they're going to find out about the novices, and we need to tell people why these things are happening.'

'Steiner, this is madness.' Marek looked away. 'We'll be caught in no time at all and everything you've fought for will be for nothing.'

'And if we don't? Then what?' Steiner struggled not to raise his voice. 'How many more people like Tikhoveter will be killed? How many Yamali people, how many Spriggani will continue to suffer?' Kristofine and Marek said nothing. 'I'm going to catch a barge down river and start telling people what happened on Vladibogdan,' said Steiner. 'If you want to sail for Shanisrond' – he shrugged – 'I can't stop you, but I'm headed for Slavon Province.'

Kristofine took his hand and kissed his scarred knuckles. 'You can't go on your own, I won't let you.'

'Just my bad fortune to have a son as stubborn as I am.' Marek shook his head and gave a weary smile. 'We do it your way. We tell people what's happened, and we fight when we can.'

'And we find Felgenhauer,' said Steiner. 'Now let's find a barge and leave this place.'

CHAPTER NINE

Silverdust

The Envoy was true to her word and the novices worked through the night to unload the supplies though the chill was deep and bitter. Silverdust had no need to pack for he had long given up the mundane pleasure of possessions. He took a spare uniform and packed a handful of curios so that he might pass as human.

No one spoke as he headed across Academy Square. The gaunt novices, wrapped up against the cold, shared wary looks at Silverdust's passing. The remaining Vigilants of the Synod assembled to watch Silverdust depart. None had words of farewell for the Exarch. He nodded to them and turned his back. It would be many hours until the sun rose at this time of year, yet Silverdust's aura of arcane light emanated brightly around his feet. He turned to take in the brutal splendour of the four academies. It pained him to know he would not return here. Vladibogdan had been his prison these long decades but it had also been his home. The Envoy slunk from the shadows, the white fox stole that hung from her shoulders ghostlike in the darkness. She joined him at the centre of the square and followed his gaze to take in the buildings.

What will happen to these children?

'Such sentimentality.' Envoy de Vries grinned. 'Come, pay no mind to them. The Emperor needs new Vigilants now more than ever. I am sure they will be treasured.'

Silverdust began the many steps down to Temnet Cove where the Imperial galleon waited in the darkness. The silver light followed him and threw weak shadows all around.

'I've long been aware that individuals of certain power manifest the arcane in strange and forbidding ways,' said the Envoy from behind him. 'For Khigir it was tongues of flame that danced at his feet.' She paused. 'They never did find his body.'

Most unfortunate. Though in truth Silverdust had hated Khigir. He'd been glad to hear Steiner had put an end to the hateful man.

'I trust you can suppress this nimbus of heat that surrounds you?'

I am sure I can accommodate you, Envoy de Vries.

'I don't like you, Silverdust,' said de Vries dispassionately. 'I don't like the way you never speak.'

I was injured. My face. It is difficult to form words and so I use the arcane. He didn't really care if she believed the lie; she had no way of proving him false short of wrenching off his mask. They were halfway down the countless steps to Temnet Cove, the stone worn smooth by the passage of time. How many novices had scaled these steps only to die during their training?

'I don't like the fact that you retired,' continued the Envoy, her voice quiet but no less dangerous for that. Silverdust reminded himself de Vries needed him alive.

'And I can never tell if you're mocking me or not.'

I would never mock you. You are the Emperor's representative.

'I don't like your mask, and how it reflects my face back at me.' Silverdust reached the bottom of the steps and made a mental note, adding Envoy de Vries to the list of people he wanted to kill.

I will think on what you have said and make efforts to appease you.

The Envoy stopped and stared up at him. Silverdust could feel her frustration as she tried to get the measure of him. She released an irritated sigh and headed towards the boarding ramp. The ship was lit by lanterns, the masts gilded in soft light. A dark shape awaited them on the main deck.

'Father Orlov,' said Envoy de Vries with a smile. 'Have you been waiting long?' The Vigilant gave a shrug as if it were no matter. Silverdust approached the man with the sense that something was amiss.

I trust the island will be safe in your hands, Father Orlov.

'In my hands? Ah, you are mistaken, Exarch. I am not staying on Vladibogdan.' Silverdust looked at Envoy de Vries, who smirked at him with her hands on her hips. 'I too am journeying to Khlystburg,' continued Father Orlov. 'So that the Emperor may benefit from both of our accounts of what happened here.'

Silverdust nodded. His hopes to assassinate the Emperor wavered with this new complication. No matter. It was a long way to Khlystburg and a plan would present itself in good time.

It did not take the galleon long to reach Cinderfell with Father Orlov and Silverdust lending their talents. Both of them had studied at Academy Vozdukha and could summon arcane winds with a gesture. The white sailcloth billowed out from the mast and snapped taut as more and more wind was conjured into being. The day favoured them with a lazy drizzle and pale grey skies. Silverdust was grateful that the Envoy stayed below decks. Her endless affectation of boredom made him want to burn things.

Soon the ship had crossed the Spøkelsea. Cinderfell was just as drab and dreary as Silverdust remembered. The cottages and hovels were squat, built from drab grey stone with thatched roofs, scattered over a steep incline that looked out to sea. Envoy de Vries emerged from her cabin and stood at the prow. The town was silent as a tomb.

'Where is everybody?' she whispered.

'Perhaps Shirinov put them all to the sword when he came here,' said Father Orlov. 'He was always keen in that regard.'

Orlov, Silverdust and de Vries took a small boat to the stone pier, escorted by two soldiers who rowed without a word.

'Why was Shirinov so desperate to come here?' asked the Envoy.

I do not know. Silverdust wondered if the Envoy believed anything he said. He couldn't blame her for distrusting him.

'The Vartiainen boy had a sister,' said Father Orlov, happy to oblige the Envoy with facts. 'It was concluded that she should have been brought to the island instead of her brother. This was Shirinov's and Khigir's mistake.'

Khigir never had the sight. He could not have detected witchsign even if his life depended on it.

'This sister,' said de Vries, striding down the pier. 'Her name?'

I did not learn it. Another lie in service to Steiner, another attempt to keep someone safe.

'It doesn't make any sense,' said Father Orlov. 'Shirinov took a ship to Cinderfell with around twenty soldiers. Surely they can't all have disappeared.' Silverdust left the pier and crossed the beach, noting large pieces of blackened driftwood tumbling to and fro at the water's edge. The Envoy joined him and looked around.

'Damn you, Steiner Vartiainen.'

Something troubles you, Envoy?

'Your talent for understatement is masterful, Silverdust. Where is the ship? Where are the soldiers?'

Silverdust pointed to the several pieces of burned driftwood.

Your missing ship has been ravaged by fire. It sank close by, or perhaps it washed ashore and the locals broke the hull down out of fear of reprisal.

Silverdust studied the beach. Three weeks had passed since Shirinov's ill-fated journey. The rain and tide had long since washed away any tracks that might tell a useful story.

'Emperor save us,' said Father Orlov from further up the beach. Silverdust and the Envoy made their way to where the Vigilant was pulling something free of the shingle.

'It seems you have found Ordinary Shirinov,' said the Envoy. Father Orlov shook the sand from a silver mask with a gently smiling expression. A smear of blood had dried at the corner of one eye.

'B-but where is the body?'

Silverdust extended one arm and pointed out to sea.

'Shatterspine,' said de Vries, invoking the name the novices had used for the man. 'The old bastard really is dead after all.'

Or gone renegade.

The envoy laughed bitterly. 'Shirinov would sooner sprout wings and fly than turn against the Empire.' She stalked off towards the town without a backwards glance. Father Orlov cradled the mask in his trembling hands.

Are you unwell, Father Orlov?

'No.' Orlov straightened up and gripped the mask more tightly. 'I'd never known a Vigilant be killed before the uprising. Now this Vartiainen peasant appears and even the most venerable of our number fall. It is . . . It is unseemly.'

Did you think us invincible, Father? Immortal?

Father Orlov shook his head, and though Silverdust could not see his expression he knew the man felt disgust. Disgust for Shirinov's fate and disgust at Silverdust's insolent question.

Father Orlov tossed the mask onto the stony beach and followed the Envoy. Silverdust watched him go and waited, feeling the wind whip all around him. It must have been a fight to inspire the storyweavers, he decided. A lone peasant boy riding a dragon, taking on a seasoned Vigilant and twenty soldiers. This was the stuff of legend. Something the people of Vinterkveld would grow drunk on. Silverdust stooped to retrieve the mask and drifted into town, though he was certain all the inhabitants had fled. To stay would be madness. To stay would invite difficult questions and a swift death.

They found rooms in an abandoned inn and the soldiers took roles as cooks, servants, and waiters. Envoy de Vries insisted on a hot bath and Father Orlov turned in early. He had said little since uncovering Shirinov's mask. Silverdust waited in his room, sending his focus out beyond the wooden walls to ponder at the soldiers in their company. His attention brushed against the minds of men drawn from many provinces across the Empire. Most of the soldiers were useful fools that cared nothing beyond getting paid and fed, but one approached, younger than the rest, who he sensed was different. Silverdust opened the door before the young soldier could knock. He held a tray with a bowl of borscht, a plate of dark bread, and a stout mug of ale.

Come in.

The soldier hesitated at the door, then entered the room with a wary expression on his face. Silverdust knew full well what the rank and file thought of him. The way he seemed to glide rather than walk unnerved people. That he never spoke aloud but dropped the words directly into a person's mind earned him greater mistrust. And there was the question of his loyalty.

What is your name?

'Streig,' said the young soldier as he set the tray of food down. He was barely older than Steiner, with a downy fuzz masquerading as a beard, and hair shorn down to stubble across his scalp.

I have already eaten, Streig. So I invite you to stay and enjoy this food.

'I . . . I can't do that,' said the soldier.

You and I both know that the Emperor has so many soldiers he cannot afford to feed them properly.

'That's no secret,' replied Streig. 'The peasants in the Scorched Republics eat better than we do.'

And you are hungry, are you not?

Streig's stomach chose that very moment to growl.

I wish to take the air outside. Being cooped up in these sombre dwellings does not suit me.

Streig had the good sense to remain quiet and watched Silverdust leave. The streets outside the inn were shrouded in the deep darkness of winter night but Silverdust had his own illumination. He drifted along the lonely winding lanes of the town. Something else was in Cinderfell, some other presence that he could not put a name to. The buildings became fewer as he drifted onward, following the steep incline up through the town. The Exarch paused, staring up at the star-flecked heavens, before turning north and advancing into the woods. The leaves and grasses at his feet grew black as he passed by, scorched by the aura of argent light. This was novel; for decades he had only walked the corridors of Vladibogdan and now he travelled in the shadow of moonlit trees, beckoned by an unknown feeling, almost a sound to his arcane senses.

Something wailed in the darkness, something pained and anguished. The trees crowded around Silverdust with dark and threatening branches, then all at once opened out to a clearing. The ruins of a chalet stood on the far side and scores of broken branches littered the ground. Silverdust paused at the edge of the clearing.

You can step into the light, Envoy de Vries.

'And here I was thinking I'd been so good,' she said, stepping out from behind an old oak tree a dozen feet behind him. 'I do so hate the cold.' She shivered in the night's chill and stared up into the Exarch's blank mask. 'And what brings you out so late at night, Silverdust? What have you seen?'

Silverdust cast his gaze over the clearing where writhing ghostly forms stood weeping and moaning. There had to be a dozen of them, broken in body and mind, cradling old swords and crooning to themselves like tired children.

Can you not see them?

'What?' The Envoy drew her knife from the golden belt that hung from her hips.

The ghosts of the Okhrana haunt this place. They linger over shallow graves and cry out for absolution. I hear them.

'This is nonsense,' replied de Vries. 'No Vigilant has ever had such gifts.'

They speak of a peasant girl with terrible power. She summoned the stones from the earth and smashed everyone alive to a pulp.

'More of your cryptic foolishness. Don't you think I know you're hiding something, Silverdust?'

I am not hiding the ghosts of the Okhrana from you, I give you my word on that.

The Envoy looked over her shoulder and for a second Silverdust wondered at how easy it would be to kill her in the darkness of the forest. It was no good, he decided. He needed her to gain audience with the Emperor. Only after the Emperor was dead could he rid himself of the Envoy once and for all.

They haunt this clearing and yet remain hidden from you.

'There is much that remains hidden from me.' There was a sour curl on her lips. 'Not least the events of Vladibogdan.'

The ghosts say one name, over and over.

'Vartiainen,' said the Envoy. Silverdust nodded. She stepped closer and dropped her voice to a deathly hush. 'I don't believe you can see these ghosts. You've told me nothing I did not already know.'

You knew a dozen Okhrana had been sent to Cinderfell, Envoy?

Her silence confirmed she had not.

We could return in the morning and dig them up if you need proof.

Envoy de Vries looked around the clearing as if it might come alive with stalking nightmares at any moment.

'Perhaps you can see ghosts. I don't care. I'm going back to the inn. You will keep me informed if you learn anything else.'

Silverdust said nothing and watched the woman leave. He wandered the clearing for long moments, drifting between the phantoms who cried or wailed in the night. As a man he might have fled from such a vision, but as a cinderwraith he had no fear of death. Never before had he seen such apparitions, but much had changed since Steiner had taken his hammer to the Ashen Torment.

Finally he came to a grave with a marker. The soul that had belonged to these bones had moved on to whatever rest awaited. Silverdust crouched down and leaned closer to the wooden marker. A name had been carved into the wood.

Verner.

Silverdust stood slowly and nursed a pang of jealousy. How he longed for the peaceful slumber of death's cold embrace. How he yearned to pass on from this existence. Silverdust glided from the clearing back towards the town. There would be no peace, not while the Emperor still drew breath.

CHAPTER TEN

Steiner

It took two weeks to make their way along the Rusalka River. Steiner had never travelled anywhere by barge before, nor had he ever been so absolutely bored. The persistent damp leeched any good mood out of the three travellers. The owner of the barge was a stooped man called Rezkh who might have been any age from fifty to seventy years old. Long, iron-grey hair emerged from under a battered grubby hat and he rarely said much on account of missing most of his teeth. When he did communicate, in a series of grunts, mumbles and gestures, the conversation was directed at Marek.

'There's not even a view to look at,' said Kristofine, gesturing to the ever-present mist surrounding them. The river was the colour of unquenched steel and the riverbanks were thick with reeds the height of a man on both sides. Trees would emerge from the mist like ghostly sentinels as the barge slunk along the river. In the distance crows called out to one another in strident tones muffled by distance.

Kristofine spent the time learning swordplay from Marek, though there was scarcely enough space for the lessons. Rezkh the boatman would let Marek teach for an hour or so before complaining bitterly about 'the gods-damned racket of swords crashing against each other'.

It was after one of these training sessions that Kjellrunn and Marek joined Steiner at the prow and stared ahead into the gently swirling mist. They settled down under their cloaks and pressed their hands into their armpits to keep warm.

'Just our bad fortune to be travelling in winter,' said Marek.

'Better this far south than up in Nordvlast,' said Kristofine, still catching her breath from the lesson.

'Why is it called the Rusalka River?' asked Steiner, trailing a hand over the side of the barge and into the water. 'Why not just the Virag River?' Marek cleared his throat and looked around to check that the bargemaster wasn't eavesdropping on them.

'Before the Empire came into being it was more common to meet things on the road that weren't human. And sometimes they lingered near the canals too.'

'Things that weren't human?' said Kristofine.

'The old stories tell of water nymphs who served the land,' explained Marek. 'It was seen as good fortune to have one close to home. The fields and forests were more fertile when a nymph was happy, so they said.'

'And when they weren't happy . . . ?' asked Kristofine.

'The Emperor's hatred wasn't merely confined to dragons. He hates all arcane beings. The Empire placed a bounty on the heads of the nymphs and for a time the men of Virag earned coin by murder.' Steiner pulled his hand back under his cloak, his water-chilled fingers clenched into a fist. Kristofine huddled closer to him.

'But the Emperor hadn't counted on the true power of the nymphs. They didn't pass on to Frejna's realm and die like the Emperor had hoped. The nymphs came back but now they called themselves rusalka. Where once they had brought life, now they brought only death.'

'What happened to them?' asked Kristofine.

'The rusalka wrought a terrible vengeance on the living for their treachery. Trade by barge stopped completely in Vannerånd, Svingettevei and Drakefjord. The Empire sent Vigilants to kill the Rusalka and many were slain on both sides. Some say the Rusalka were wiped out, but I think some still exist near lakes, where it's quiet and people are few.'

The barge bumped against something and Steiner flinched. He looked around with one hand on the haft of his sledge-hammer, then breathed a sigh of relief. Rezkh had found a small pier to tie up to for the night.

'Maybe it's time we went ahead on foot?' said Steiner. 'I think I'd like to spend some time among the living. This endless mist is getting to me.'

Marek smiled and clapped a hand on his son's shoulder. 'We're close to the final stop anyway.'

'How do they get you?' asked Kristofine. 'The Rusalka, I mean. How do they, you know, kill you?'

'A rusalka appears as a beautiful woman bathing in the river. When a man gets close by she calls to him, and the man can't help but draw close to her.'

Kristofine rolled her eyes.

'And when the men are close enough the rusalka's hair comes alive and wraps about the man's neck, dragging him under the water and drowning him.'

'We should *really* go the rest of the way on foot,' said Steiner.

'Seems to me the people of Vannerånd, Drakefjord and Svingettevei could have maintained their barge trade if they'd had any brains,' said Kristofine, gathering her bag.

'How's that?' asked Marek.

'If the rusalka lured only men to their deaths, they should have employed women to run the barges.'

Marek laughed long and deep and Steiner found himself

caught up in the sound, laughing along with him. It was the first time any of them had laughed since Tikhoveter had been killed.

The riverside inn was a welcome sight after two weeks aboard the narrow barge. A small village spread out from beside the canal though most of the buildings were little more than shadowy outlines in the mist. Once they had settled in, Steiner took a bath and joined Marek and Kristofine downstairs in the bar.

'We've wasted two whole weeks on the barge,' he said. 'I need to start telling my story now.'

'Steady now, Steiner,' warned Marek in a hiss. 'We only just escaped Virag. We need to be cautious. The Empire has ears everywhere.'

'Even here, in a riverside inn lost in the mist?'

Marek shrugged. 'I'm just saying we should be careful is all.'

Steiner cast his gaze around the bar and searched the faces of the local men and women. Wasn't it the business of spies to blend in and look like everyone else? He approached the bar and nodded to a handful of heavyset men in muddy smocks and forced a smile.

'Hail, friends.'

'Friends?' said tallest of them. He was a bull-necked man with a heavy brow and black beard shot through with grey. 'Were only friends if you're buying the drinks.' The men around Bull-neck chuckled and looked away.

'I bring news about the Empire. A story really.'

'A story!' Bull-neck grinned. 'What a delight.' Steiner couldn't tell if he was being sarcastic on account of his accent. 'An' you come all the way from . . . ?'

'Nordvlast,' supplied Steiner.

'So you come all the way from Nordvlast to interrupt our

conversation with a story about the hated Empire. The Empire that took my niece three summers ago.' The man's expression darkened. 'Go back to Nordvlast, halfhead.'

'There have been two uprisings against the—'

'Go back to Nordvlast,' repeated the bull-necked man. 'There'll be no uprising in Svingettevei. We prefer to keep our heads attached to our shoulders. Go.'

Steiner headed back to his table where Kristofine waited with an anxious look. Steiner slumped down in the seat beside her and stared into his mug of ale.

'I need to get better at that,' he said quietly.

'People are strange creatures,' said Kristofine. 'Territorial. You can't just walk into their place and tell them a thing. It makes them feel stupid, ignorant. You need to make them curious. I used to see this done a lot in my father's tavern. A person would come in and hint that they had just arrived from somewhere or perhaps knew something everyone else didn't. Just a hint really, to make people curious, make them ask a question or two.'

'Making people curious,' repeated Steiner. He looked at his father over the top of his mug. 'And what do you think?'

'I think I'm an old soldier who doesn't know much about storytelling. But I think Kristofine has a point,' said Marek. 'Let's try it her way next time.'

Marek insisted that he needed a room of his own on account of not having a moment's peace in the last month. 'We have a little coin to spare,' he said. 'One night's luxury won't kill anyone.'

And so Steiner found himself alone with Kristofine that night when the bar finally stopped serving and the lanterns downstairs were extinguished one by one. They headed up the creaking wooden steps hand in hand and spent a minute fussing at the candles before Steiner sat on the bed and gave a deep sigh.

'What's got you frowning so, dragon rider?' said Kristofine, running her fingers across his scalp and down his neck. She pressed closer to him and he rested his head against the soft curve of her stomach. Her fingers continued to trace the muscles in his neck and shoulders.

'Dragon rider?' He huffed a bitter laugh. 'They called me the Unbroken back on the ship. At Nordvlast I wielded the Ashen Torment and fought Shirinov in single combat. Out here I can't even make a handful of men listen to what I have to say.'

'It will come in time. You'll work out the trick of it. We'll work it out together.'

'Everything will fail if I can't make people pay attention.'

'I'm paying attention to you,' she whispered. 'And we have our own room for the first time since you were taken by the Empire.'

'When you put it like that . . .' Steiner gave her slow smile and stood up to kiss her.

'Much better,' said Kristofine as he began to unbutton her skirt.

They were late joining Marek for what passed for breakfast the following morning, and even the paucity of the fare couldn't dim Steiner's spirits.

'Took us a while to pack,' said Steiner, setting down his bag and sledgehammer, which he hid under his cloak. Marek raised an eyebrow. Kristofine blushed and Steiner took a seat. They ate their food in the bar and tried to ignore the stale smell of ale and the sweat of men long in their beds. Kristofine smiled a lot but said little, and Marek approached the innkeeper and his wife at the counter.

'Folks are talking of trouble up north,' said the innkeeper after the usual round of pleasantries. The innkeeper looked towards the door and then conspiratorially over his shoulder, even though the bar was empty save for Marek, Kristofine and Steiner. 'Never heard anything like it, I tell you.' The innkeeper was a thin man in his fifties, with a ratty ponytail of greying brown hair and a patchy beard. He'd introduced himself as Gerd or Ged – Steiner wasn't quite sure on account of the man's accent.

'We've been on the road for a few weeks now and not heard a thing,' replied Marek loud enough to attract Steiner's attention.

'Word is that the Empire have a fortress on a secret island.' Gerd leaned across the bar and dropped his voice. 'An' they've been taking the children there this whole time.'

'You know,' whispered his wife. 'The children with witchsign.' She was a short bulb of woman called Lena, as generously proportioned as her husband was lean. She'd been pretty once, but decades spent ushering drunk fools out of her establishment had given her a hard look. 'An' to think, this whole time we supposed they were taking them to be slaughtered in Khlystburg.' She raised her eyebrows.

'That's quite a tale,' said Marek. 'How did you come by such news?'

'A trader came into the village late last night,' said Lena. 'He told us some Nordvlast man escaped the island.'

'Said he was seven feet tall an' covered in scars,' explained Gerd. 'Said he wielded a sledgehammer that could fire lightning bolts.'

Steiner half-laughed, half-snorted, as he attempted another spoonful of thin porridge, drawing affronted looks from his hosts.

'Sorry.' He coughed. 'Excellent breakfast, by the way.' Steiner shared a look with Kristofine and they both held their breath to keep from laughing.

'Ignore my son,' said Marek with a frown. 'He's a touch simple. I shouldn't let him drink ale of an evening, but it helps him sleep.'

'Never seen no enchanted sledgehammer,' said Lena in a frosty tone of voice. 'An' our trader friend said the man flew on the back of a dragon and killed a dozen men an' a Vigilant.' She rolled her eyes. 'But he was drunk as a lord and I'm not so foolish as to believe everything I'm told.'

'She's not foolish!' crowed her husband, his eyes wide and earnest in his thin face.

'And what will happen now?' said Kristofine, rising from the table to join the conversation at the bar.

'Same as always happens when someone crosses the Empire,' replied Lena with a scowl. 'They'll find this man an' kill him, fancy sledgehammer or not.'

'Probably send those wicked Vigilants after him,' moaned Gerd.

'How much of what your friend told you do *you* believe?' asked Kristofine. Gerd blinked at her and Steiner supposed he wasn't asked for his opinion on a great many things.

'Can't say I know.' He looked to his wife. 'I suppose there could be one or two dragons hiding out from after the war. An' I suppose it might be possible to ride one.' He sighed. 'But a sledgehammer seems like a stupid weapon for a man to carry. Never seen anyone fight with a sledgehammer before.'

'And the lightning,' said Marek. 'That seems like pure invention.'

'Aye, invention,' said Gerd, nodding.

Steiner chose that moment to stand up and pull his cloak around his shoulders, then picked up his bag and hefted his sledgehammer. Gerd and Lena stared at him and he could almost feel their eyes counting the many scars on his face, scalp and the backs of his hands. He approached the counter. 'Sorry I'm not seven feet tall,' he said to Gerd and Lena, before turning to Marek and Kristofine. 'Come on, we need to get going.'

They were a dozen feet from the inn when Gerd called out

to them from the doorway. 'Don't be leaving so quick now.' Steiner looked over his shoulder. 'Is any of it true?' said Gerd and Lena joined him in the doorway.

Steiner nodded. 'The island. The children. They train them to be Vigilants.'

'And the lightning?' said Gerd, and Steiner could see the tiny spark of hope in his eyes.

Steiner shook his head. 'I'm afraid not, no lightning.'

'You're not him,' scowled Lena. 'Come on now!' And she ushered her husband inside.

Marek, Kristofine and Steiner walked for some time, leaving the misty village until at last Steiner spoke.

'Think he'll tell anyone?'

'Without a doubt,' said Marek with a slow smile.

CHAPTER ELEVEN

Kjellrunn

'They caught us by surprise, right.' Romola was sitting against the edge of the table in her cabin with a hard look on her face, her head cocked to one side. She'd patiently listened to Kjellrunn's complaint, waiting for the stream of anger and frustration to abate. 'I'm not happy about it either. I've known your father for a long time and I like Steiner. I like him a lot.'

It had taken Kjellrunn a restless night to get up the necessary courage. Her frustration and dismay had grown with every hour that passed, and with every league they sailed further south.

'We have to go back. They won't stand a chance.'

'We *have* to, do we?' Romola shook her head and moved around the table to pour a drink. 'Let me tell you how it works.' She poured two tots of rum and downed the first before she'd finished pouring the second. 'The Empire has graduates or cast-offs from the Vozdukha Academy in most towns, especially the ports. They're not Vigilants but ones with a gift for sending whispers on the wind, right? Messages can be sent for leagues with the arcane, far faster than men on horseback or birds with scraps of parchment tied to their legs. Word of your street fight may have spread across the

Empire by now. The Emperor himself will be spitting blood when he finds out.'

'The Emperor is hundreds of miles away!'

'But his soldiers are close. Closer than we think sometimes. They'll be looking for us, just as Imperial ships will be looking for us.'

'Then we'll fight!' replied Kjellrunn.

Romola raised an incredulous eyebrow. 'Like you fought in Virag?'

Kjellrunn felt the anger drain out of her.

'I'm a smuggler, not an admiral,' replied Romola. 'And the *Watcher's Wait* is a fast frigate. She can't take on those big Imperial galleons. She just doesn't have it in her.'

For a moment the woman and girl eyed each other over the captain's table. The ship creaked as it voyaged further south.

'What will happen to them?' said Kjellrunn quietly. 'Do you even care?'

'I care about plenty of things. My crew, my ship, my skin. And I care about rum, of course.' Romola knocked back the second tot. 'Marek and Steiner are more than capable of slipping out of a city unnoticed. Maybe you forgot, but Steiner the Unbroken escaped from Vladibogdan. I don't think Virag will give him any problems.'

'You don't understand,' said Kjellrunn, hating the pleading note in her voice. 'I may never see them again.'

'But you'll be alive to miss them. And so will I. The *Watcher's Wait* is not returning to Virag, Kjellrunn. You can get off at the next port if you don't like it, but we are not going back.'

The door to the captain's cabin slammed open and a tall woman with red hair entered, one of the crew. Kjellrunn scowled but the pirate simply grinned.

'Hello!' She turned to Romola. 'Here's the inventory you asked for.'

Romola took the parchment from the tall pirate and it was

clear the conversation was over. Kjellrunn sighed in defeat. She slunk out of the cabin, not bothering to close the door behind her.

She was halfway across the deck of the ship when her fingers strayed to the hammer brooch her father had given her.

'None of this would be happening if you'd just stayed pinned to my cloak.'

The brooch had no answer, which only put her in an even worse mood.

Kjellrunn spent the afternoon sitting in the prow of the ship running over her conversation with Romola and cursing herself for not persuading the captain to turn around. She'd wrapped herself in her cloak so that it came up under her nose and only the top of her face could be seen. The gunwales shielded her from the worst of the wind, but the weather was cold enough that she half considered going below decks. It was almost nightfall when Mistress Kamalov appeared on deck. Trine, the fire-breathing novice, hovered nearby, shooting dark looks at any sailors who came too close to the old woman. The renegade Vigilant hobbled across the deck and Kjellrunn felt another pang of irritation.

'You hurt no one but yourself when you don't eat.'

'I'm not hungry,' replied Kjellrunn, looking up to the rigging in order to avoid the older woman's eyes.

'As you wish. The food is gone now. Too many mouths to feed.'

'I just want to be left alone.'

'It's right that you are upset for your family, but you must see the sense in the captain's decision.'

'I must, must I?'

'It was going to happen anyway, Kjellrunn.' Mistress Kamalov rested a hand on the side of the ship, supporting herself as the waves rocked the slender vessel. 'Your brother would have disembarked sooner or later. He is keen to take the fight to the Empire. His path is not yours—'

'His path is going to get him killed!' Kjellrunn stood up, feeling the familiar heat of her anger stoked to life once more. 'What was the point of escaping Vladibogdan if he's going to run back to the Empire so that they can kill him?'

'He has found his purpose, Kjellrunn. Now you must find yours.'

'Purpose? What purpose? The Empire has taken everything from me. My home, my father, my brother, my uncle.' Her voice broke slightly. 'I never had the chance to meet my mother.' Mistress Kamalov shook her head, pursing her lips in a look of disappointment Kjellrunn knew all too well.

'And you are the only person aboard to have lost something precious to the Empire, I suppose?'

Kjellrunn turned her back on the renegade Vigilant. 'I just want to be left alone.'

'Soon we will reach Shanisrond,' said Mistress Kamalov. 'Where people with witchsign are not hunted. We can live quietly with the novices.'

'And I'll spend the rest of my life wondering what happened to my family, wondering if they're still alive. What's the point? I want to get my family back and I'm going to leave this stupid ship and find them.'

Mistress Kamalov bowed her head and made her way back across the deck. Trine did not follow, but eyed Kjellrunn with a curious, unfriendly stare.

'Hoy there,' said Kjellrunn, more out of habit than any desire to speak to the girl.

'Are you always such a whining bitch?' replied Trine.

Kjellrunn stepped forward. 'They're my family. I wouldn't expect you to understand. I imagine the Vigilants stripped all the decency out of you on the island.'

'Mistress Kamalov said you were her best student, but you just seem like a snivelling child to me.'

'You have some some cheek. Those six children might still be alive if you hadn't snuck off in Virag.' Trine's eyes widened in surprise at Kjellrunn's rebuke. 'Perhaps you'll consider other people in future, now that you have blood on your hands.'

Trine shrank back a step, shaken by Kjellrunn's words, then remembered herself and followed after Mistress Kamalov. Kjellrunn watched her go, anger beating loudly with her pulse. She slumped down in the prow, tired beyond reason with tears of loneliness brimming at the corner of her eyes. Maybe she was a snivelling child, she decided. A snivelling child who wanted nothing more than her family returned to her safely.

The scent of pipe smoke and the sound of soft voices woke her. Sundra and Tief had sat down next to her and were chatting.

'What time is it?'

'Too late to be sleeping on deck when you have a perfectly reasonable cabin,' said Tief with a crooked smile. He toked on the pipe and breathed out a few smoke rings. 'What foolishness is this?'

'I had an argument with Mistress Kamalov. Two actually.'

'You and your brother have a fine gift for stubbornness,' said Sundra. She stared up at the night sky and clucked her tongue. 'I do miss that boy.'

Kjellrunn felt the beginnings of tears at the mention of Steiner. 'As do I. And that seems to be a problem for some people.'

'I've got something for you.' Tief reached under his jacket and pulled out a small sack. 'Steiner would kill me if I let his little sister starve, so eat up.'

Kjellrunn reached into the sack and pulled out an apple. 'Thanks. Is this bread too?'

Tief nodded. 'I'll give you nip of rum too if you don't tell Mistress Kamalov.'

Kjellrunn ate for a time and they listened to the shushing sound of the waves against the prow. Stars shone overhead and the ship rumbled and groaned as the timbers moved. The sails billowed from the masts and Kjellrunn felt calm in the presence of the two Spriggani.

'What will you do?' asked Sundra.

'What do you mean?'

'What will you do in the weeks ahead? We won't always be on this ship.' Kjellrunn couldn't quite believe what was happening. Here was a high priestess of Frejna, representative of a proscribed religion, asking about her future. Here was a woman four times her age if not more, speaking to her as if she were an adult with a plan.

'I don't know. My family . . . It seems we're destined to be pulled apart. I'll never be able to find them on my own.' It was tough to admit to such a thing, but the words needed saying.

'It is difficult to be away from the ones we love,' said Sundra, though Kjellrunn realised the words were intended for Tief rather than her.

'I'm going on to Yamal with Kimi and Marozvolk,' explained Tief. 'We're going to present ourselves to the Yamali king and explain what happened, try and rally the tribes for the forthcoming war.'

'You don't know they will go to war,' snapped Sundra.

'Hopefully Steiner will raise such a ruckus the Emperor will be too busy to send an army to Yamal.' Tief toked on his pipe a moment. 'But if he does send an army . . .'

'And Taiga has decided she has to go with him,' said Sundra to Kjellrunn with a note of disgust in her voice. 'Everyone rushing off to get themselves killed. Did we escape the island for nothing!' The old priestess rolled her eyes in a rare display of pique and Kjellrunn almost laughed, though she shared the sentiment entirely.

'And Taiga is coming,' agreed Tief. He blew out the smoke and cleared his throat. 'The thing is—'

'The thing is,' said Sundra, her voice brittle with irritation, 'is that I am too damned old to go wandering around this continent. I will leave the ship and stay with Mistress Kamalov and the children. I should very much like it if you were to become my apprentice.' Kjellrunn nearly choked on her apple. She stared at the older woman in disbelief.

'Apprentice?'

'I am getting old and our religion has all but died out. I need someone to carry these traditions and beliefs on to the next generation.'

'But I barely know anything about the goddesses,' said Kjellrunn.

'As it is in all the provinces of the Solmindre Empire and the Scorched Republics. There was a temple in Virag, you know? Dedicated to my goddess. They boarded up the windows and the doors were locked.'

'All knowledge of the old ways is prohibited in Nordvlast,' added Kjellrunn.

'But this did not stop you, did it, Kjellrunn?' Sundra narrowed her eyes with a smile of admiration on her thin lips.

'Well, no,' Kjellrunn admitted. 'I always loved the old stories.'

Sundra clucked her tongue and shook her head. 'They are not just old stories!'

'Pah! You've upset her already.' Tief gave an earthy chuckle. 'You'll make a fine initiate.'

'And what of my family?'

'I'll be out there,' said Tief, jerking a thumb towards land. 'There can't be too many people rushing towards Khlystburg in the hopes of killing the Emperor. I have hope that I'll cross paths with your brother before too long. I'll be sure to bring him back to you.'

Kjellrunn smiled.

'That's it, girl. You keep smiling. There's too much pain in the world and every smile is a rebellion against it.'

Sundra made a dismissive snort. 'So says the grumpiest man I know.'

'Nothing to say I can't be a grump and hypocrite at the same time,' replied Tief proudly.

'An initiate of Frejna,' said Kjellrunn, testing the words out. Sundra nodded. 'And we'll live in Shanisrond and wait there until my family comes back?'

'We will.' The high priestess got to her feet, though it took her some time and a helping hand from Tief. Sundra was quickly swallowed by the darkness as she retired for the night. Kjellrunn stood to watch her go.

'Thank you for that,' said Tief when his sister had gone. 'I'll be glad to know someone will be keeping an eye on her.'

'You looked after my brother on the island, didn't you?'

He grinned. 'I did, although Frøya knows he was a pain in the arse more often than not.'

'I'm beginning to think everyone is a pain in the arse,' said Kjellrunn as her thoughts turned to Mistress Kamalov and the ever-present Trine.

'Maybe you're right,' said Tief. 'But some of them are worth fighting for.'

CHAPTER TWELVE

Kimi

The *Watcher's Wait* had not lingered in the week since they had left Virag. Mistress Kamalov and a few of the children took it in turns to summon favourable winds. Kimi sat on a barrel on the mid-deck and watched the novices learn from the older woman, manipulating the air to serve their interests. The sails billowed out above her, the white cloth taut.

'It troubles you?' said Maxim.

'How do you mean?' replied Kimi. The boy was so quiet she often didn't notice he was there at all.

'The arcane. Does it trouble you?'

'I suppose it does. I don't trust it. Bittervinge made the Ashen Torment with his powers.'

'The father of dragons.' Maxim paused to bite his lip, then looked at Kimi from the corner of his eye.

'For decades the dragons came and went as they chose, eating whatever and whoever they liked.'

'I'm glad I wasn't alive back then,' said Maxim.

'But are things any better?' asked Kimi. 'The Empire makes people disappear just as surely as those dragons did. The Emperor is no better than Bittervinge.'

'I'd never thought of it like that,' replied the boy. He looked out to sea with a serious expression on his dark face.

'And now something is troubling you,' she replied. 'What is it?'

'Why did you ask Silverdust to release the dragons from Vladibogdan after we left?'

'Can you imagine being chained up beneath the island?' She frowned. 'And starving to death in the darkness?' Kimi shook her head. 'I couldn't have that on my conscience. Better they go free and find their way in the world. I'd rather they had a fighting chance than no chance at all.'

'It certainly seems like they've found a fight,' replied Maxim. Kimi stood up and looked port and starboard. The coast greeted her on one side as a distant blur of tan and white, while the dark blue ocean stretched away to the horizon on the other.

'What are you talking about? What fight?'

The boy didn't answer but swayed with the motion of the ship. For a moment Kimi thought the boy might pass out. She took him gently by the shoulders and saw his eyes had rolled back.

'Kamalov!' Kimi held the boy tightly to her chest and cast a desperate look over her shoulder. 'I need you, Kamalov!' The old woman hurried as best she could from the stern of the ship, aided by Kjellrunn, who glanced at Kimi with undisguised rancour. The Nordvlast girl hadn't forgiven anyone for abandoning her family in Virag. Kimi couldn't say she blamed her. She'd be no different under the same circumstances.

'What is going on?' said Mistress Kamalov sternly. 'Is the boy sick?'

'I don't know.' Kimi held him at arm's length again, but his eyes showed only their whites. Somehow he remained standing, which unsettled her deeply.

'They will come for us too,' he muttered in a faraway voice.

'He is having a vision,' said Mistress Kamalov. 'What did he say before this happened?'

'We were talking about dragons,' replied Kimi, 'and then he became very quiet.'

'I did not know he had come into his powers,' said Mistress Kamalov as she pressed a hand against Maxim's forehead. 'I would have kept a closer eye on him.'

'All hands on deck!' shouted a woman's voice from the crow's nest. 'All hands, damn you, Imperial ship sighted.' Romola sauntered onto the deck from her cabin, her hair tousled. She squinted at everyone with bleary eyes. The captain shouted up to the crow's nest.

'This had better be good, Rylska, I was in the middle of a particularly good nap.'

'You'd better see it for yourself, captain,' the woman in the crow's nest shouted back. 'You'll never believe me.' Everyone on deck rushed to the prow, leaving Mistress Kamalov to take Maxim below. Romola shielded her eyes with the flat of her hand and stared out to sea.

'If she's been at the vodka again I'll cut her wages for a month,' said the captain as she approached the prow. Kimi followed her and the crew made space for them.

'It looks like three large gulls are flying around that ship,' said a pirate, peering into the distance. They were a good three miles away. 'But why is the ship on fire?'

'Because they aren't gulls,' said Kimi with a dreadful certainty. 'They aren't birds at all.'

'And we're heading straight for them,' said Romola. Her face shot back to the crow's nest. 'Rylska! Get down from there.' The captain looked towards the stern where three novices were dutifully summoning more winds for the sails.

'Stop that right now!' shouted Romola, but the novices couldn't hear her over the sound of the arcane gales that sped the ship ever onward. Kimi broke into a flat run, her feet pounding the deck. She waved her arms at the novices imploring them to stop. The novices ceased their conjuring, but only after Kimi had scaled the steps to the poop deck.

'I don't take orders from you,' said a young, dark-haired girl.

'No,' said Romola, coming up behind Kimi, 'you take orders from me. Now get your scrawny arse below decks.'

Trine and her coterie of air witches slunk off, flipping the sign of the four powers at Kimi as they went.

'I'm never having children,' muttered Kimi.

'That makes two of us,' replied Romola.

'I think one of the dragons has seen us, captain,' shouted Rylska from the crow's nest.

'What do I do?' said Kimi. Marozvolk had joined her and the feeling of rising panic was difficult to resist.

'Not much you can do,' replied Marozvolk.

'Rylska, get down from there!' shouted Romola. A dark, winged shape was growing steadily larger on the horizon, perhaps just two miles away. The Imperial ship behind it was marked by a column of dark grey smoke that coiled up into the skies. Kimi wanted to run, but where would she go?

'Everyone who isn't crew get below deck!' shouted Romola from the ship's wheel. 'Fetch up the crossbows and bring plenty of bolts.'

'We won't stand a chance,' whispered Marozvolk.

'Stay here and keep an eye on Romola,' replied Kimi.

'Where are you going?'

'I've got an idea, but I'm going to need some help.' Kimi scrambled down the steps and headed below deck just as the dragon flew overhead, a vast shadow above them.

'It's really fucking big!' shouted Rylska from the crow's nest.

'Tell us something we don't know,' growled Kimi as she searched for Sundra. The priestess emerged from her cabin just as Kimi reached the door.

'Is it true?' asked Sundra.

'Yes, and I need your help.'

The prow of the ship was on fire by the time Kimi escorted Sundra from below decks. A handful of pirates attended the flames with buckets of water and a great deal of harsh language. The dragon swept in towards the ship from the starboard side, great wings unfurled. The scales were all the colours of a forest in autumn: a profusion of brilliant reds and warm oranges, deepest browns and hints of green. The creature's underside was a pale eggshell blue. It had transformed itself from the ragged and spent creature kept underneath the island. The creature flew low, just a dozen feet above the ocean, then pulled up just as Romola steered hard to port. The dragon clipped the top of the mast, and the crow's nest disintegrated in a heartbeat.

'Rylska!' shouted Romola, clutching the ship's wheel in fury. Of the tall red-haired woman there was no sign. The pirates aimed at the dragon with their crossbows, keen to avenge their crew mate.

'Aim for the face,' shouted one of the pirates.

'Wait!' shouted Kimi, turning to Sundra who stood alongside her at the burning prow. 'Can you contact it? Like you did with Steiner?'

'That was a very different set of circumstances,' replied the high priestess, with an alarmed look on her slender face. In the distance the dragon wheeled around, turning to face the Watcher's Wait once more.

'Can you try?' said Kimi. 'This might be our only chance.'

'I don't see we have much choice,' said Sundra, her eyes fixed on the dragon as it sped towards the ship once more. 'But it's not like sending a message. You have to think in images.'

'Images,' breathed Kimi. The dragon was almost upon the ship. 'Send it an image of me with a bucket of meat. Send it an image of me feeding them each day.' She'd been on the island for five years, and every day she'd done what she could to keep the creatures alive.

'I hope this works, Kimi.' Sundra reached out with one hand and closed her eyes. The ship rocked as Romola changed course to try and avoid the dragon and Kimi wrapped an arm about the priestess's shoulders to steady her. Waves crested the edge of the ship and broke across the deck in a fine spray.

'We can't outrun it,' shouted Romola. 'And we can't outmanoeuvre it.' The dragon slowed and turned side on to the ship, matching them in speed.

'Hold your fire!' shouted Kimi to the crew. 'Don't shoot it!'

'Have you lost your mind?' Romola shouted back from the stern. 'This is our best chance.'

'What's happening?' Kimi whispered to Sundra. The priestess looked more pale than usual and a fine sheen of perspiration covered her brow. 'It . . . It seems to be sending back images of you. Images and sounds. You used to sing to them?'

For a brief second Kimi was transported back to the deepest parts of Vladibogdan, feeding the dragons, willing them to survive, crooning folk songs to them in the hope that anything would help. One prisoner reaching out to another.

'I'm not sure how much longer I can keep this up,' whispered Sundra, sounding tired and hoarse.

The crew had extinguished the fire at the front of the ship and Kimi headed to the blackened prow, her heart racing. The dragon surged ahead with beats of its huge wings, much wider than their main sail. The creature circled around in front of the red frigate then hung on the air, waiting for them.

'Stow the sails!' shouted Kimi, and to her surprise the sailors raced up the rigging to do just that.

'It's me,' she shouted, feeling about as foolish and terrified as she ever had. 'It's me. From the island!' The dragon was still two hundred feet away. Sundra appeared at her shoulder.

The ship slowed and the dragon remained ahead of them, hovering above the ocean with steady beats of its vast wings. The sailors stared with open fear on their faces and no one spoke.

'I know you!' shouted Kimi. 'I fed you. I'm sorry you were kept in the darkness for so long.'

The dragon snorted a plume of smoke and altered its position, hovering lower, so it was closer still to the burned prow. The creature made a terrible sound, as if it were clearing its throat, then snorted another plume of smoke into the air.

'You remember me.' Gods, she hoped it remembered her. 'We were both prisoners under the island.'

The dragon extended its sinuous neck and Kimi reached out until she could press her hand against the still-warm snout.

'It knows you,' whispered Sundra in awe. 'It recognises you.'

Kimi balanced on the prow and pointed with her free hand at the Imperial ship. 'Those people are your enemy. The people on this ship are with me. We are friends.'

The dragon flapped down hard with its wings and ascended a dozen feet, releasing a terrible sound – something between a growl and a roaring fire. Kimi stumbled back, certain she was about to be bitten in two.

'Dragons don't really understand the idea of friendship,' said Sundra with a worried look on her face.

'What do they understand?'

'This one seems to understand your words,' replied Sundra.

'Yes, but how do they think?'

Sundra shook her head. 'These dragons are infants, primal and angry. Appeal to their anger.'

'We hunt the Emperor!' shouted Kimi. The dragon beat its wings and flew away, circling the ship before heading off in the direction they had just sailed from. The dragon dived out of sight, disappearing underwater. Everyone aboard stared at

Kimi with undisguised awe and no one spoke. Sundra sat down and cradled her head in one hand, exhausted and speechless.

'I have never seen anything like this before,' said Marozvolk. 'I didn't even know it was possible.'

'It's coming back!' shouted Romola. Kimi ran from the prow of the ship and the crew made way for her. She arrived at the ship's wheel just as the dragon appeared at the stern and dumped the bedraggled form of Rylska on the deck at Romola's feet.

'Frejna save us,' whispered Romola. The dragon took off, heading towards its kin. Rylska looked up at Romola and Kimi and opened her mouth to speak but no words emerged. She waved her hands around, trying to explain that she'd just been saved from drowning by the same dragon who'd knocked her clean out of the crow's nest.

'Get this woman a very large vodka,' said Romola. 'Wait a moment.' She sighed. 'Get everyone a very large vodka.' The captain shook her head and stared at Kimi for a long moment. 'You're full of surprises, aren't you, your highness?'

Kimi stared after the dragon. 'It remembered me.'

It was another week before the *Watcher's Wait* made port in Dos Khor. The sun shone high in the sky and the ever-present damp of the north no longer troubled them. They had mercifully avoided any more encounters with dragons and Kimi spent her time thinking long on the majestic creatures.

'Never in my whole life will I voyage again from Vladibogdan to Shanisrond in such remarkable time,' said Romola from the docks of the desert port. They had all come ashore in small ships and the novices huddled around Mistress Kamalov obediently. The events of Virag lay heavy in everyone's mind. Kjellrunn lingered behind the old woman, glowering at Romola with tight-lipped disgust.

'I'll miss you,' Romola said to the novices. 'If only for the fair wind in my sails, right.' Trine was standing with them, scowling in much the same way she always did. 'You I will not miss,' admitted Romola.

Trine tossed her hair and sidled closer to Madam Kamalov. 'And I won't miss your horrible boat, or your stinking pirates.'

'It's a *ship*,' said Romola. 'And you're lucky I didn't make you swim.' The captain walked away to attend to the supplies.

'You are headed to Yamal?' said Mistress Kamalov, turning to the princess, though it barely needed saying. Kimi nodded. Maxim pressed himself against her and threw his arms around her waist.

'I have to warn my father that I'm no longer a political prisoner and we can no longer expect a truce with the Empire. Marozvolk will come with me.'

'And the boy?' said Mistress Kamalov.

'His name is Maxim,' said Kimi, looking down and frowning. 'And that's what you'll call him. He's not just a boy.'

'I see,' said Mistress Kamalov. 'So he is to come with us?'

'No,' said Maxim. 'I don't want to go with them.'

'It's too dangerous where I'm going,' said Kimi. She knelt down and stroked his cheek, rubbing the tears away with her thumb. 'I have matters to attend to. When I'm done I'll come back for you.'

'No you won't,' said Maxim, his arms falling to his sides.

'Steiner came back, didn't he?' said Kimi, dropping to one knee.

'And where is he now?' replied Maxim. 'Everyone leaves.'

Sundra appeared out of the crowd of pirates and passengers on the docks, escorted by Tief and Taiga. The high priestess laid a hand on Maxim's shoulder.

'I'm staying in Dos Khor too,' she said, her words heavy with sadness. 'My sister and my brother are going with Kimi, so I will be all alone. And I will need a friend.'

Kimi stood and realised this might be the last time she ever saw Sundra. 'Thank you. For everything you did for me on the island, and . . .' A deep pang of sadness robbed her of speech.

'Hush now, child,' said Sundra. 'I will see you again, in this life or the next. I will think of you often and send my prayers.'

'I will come back,' said Kimi, though she had no idea how. 'For all of you,' she added, looking at Maxim, though in truth she didn't expect to survive the coming months. Maxim gave her one last hug, then took Sundra by the hand and walked away from the docks. Kimi, Tief and Taiga watched the young boy and old woman leave the docks hand in hand until they were lost from view.

'So you're coming with me?' said Kimi to Tief and Taiga. 'I have to admit to being a little surprised.'

'Pah! We're with you until the end,' said Tief. 'You can bet your boots on it.' He tested the edge of his knife with his thumb then looked up and grinned.

'Marozvolk is coming too. She's my bodyguard.'

Tief curled his lip and a frown chased the good mood off his face. 'Why do you want to get yourself mixed up with a Vigilant? We just got rid of one.' He gestured to the departing form of Mistress Kamalov.

'She's a *former* Vigilant, and more than that she's from Yamal. She wants to go home.'

'Fair enough,' said Tief, though there was nothing fair about the look on his face or the tone he used.

'We'd best get aboard the ship,' said Taiga.

'Romola has a habit of leaving people behind,' said Tief.

'No one is getting left behind,' said Kimi.

CHAPTER THIRTEEN

Silverdust

The soldiers had begun marching inland, much to Silverdust's disappointment. *Are we not taking ship to Khlystburg?* he asked as he emerged from the inn.

'The dragons were set free during the uprising,' said Father Orlov in a mournful tone. 'Two Imperial ships have been lost to attacks from them in the last week.'

'And there are rumours of four merchant vessels that suffered the same fate,' added Envoy de Vries.

Silverdust knew all of this. Whispers had been set on the wind and he had listened for them in the long hours of the night. It was a cruel consequence that his act of kindness in releasing the beasts now hampered his journey across Vinterkveld.

'Strange that the dragons didn't escape until after Steiner had left,' said Father Orlov, his implication painfully clear.

I simply brokered a peace with the Vartiainen boy so the remaining novices would not be slain. I did not free dragons.

'So you have said.' Envoy de Vries started off down the street, following the column of soldiers.

'This is all your fault.' Father Orlov hefted his pack on his shoulders and set off after the Envoy. Soon they reached the outskirts of Cinderfell and the road was no more than a leaf-strewn muddy track. The trees on either side reached out to one another, their boughs meeting overhead. The sky would have been obscured had there been leaves on the branches, but spring was still two months off. Instead it felt as if they trudged through the ribcage of an unending serpent with chaotic black bones.

Was it really necessary to come this way? Silverdust sent the question to both Orlov and de Vries.

'It's the fastest route between Cinderfell and Steinwick,' said the Envoy. 'Don't you like the view, Exarch?' She gestured grandly to the stark trunks and leafless trees. The ferns had withered and turned brown during the winter and only the thorny gorse had kept its colour.

'I like the forest,' said Father Orlov. 'It is good to be among living things after so long on Vladibogdan.'

This forest is half-dead, along with everything in it. This is a poor time of year to travel.

Envoy de Vries slowed her pace until she walked beside Silverdust. Father Orlov walked on ahead and the Envoy stared around the forest with a growing frown.

'Have you experienced anything else since that night in Cinderfell?' she said quietly. 'Do you think this is a new school of the arcane?' After a pause, the woman added in awed tones, 'Could it be taught?'

I am experiencing something at this very moment.

The Envoy's pace slowed and she cast an anxious glance over her shoulder. One hand drifted to the hilt of her knife, for all the good it would do her against the dead.

'What do you see?'

Dead bandits come to the edge of the track to watch our passing.

'Bandits?' De Vries smiled and shook her head. 'I hope they were killed by Imperial soldiers.'

Silverdust looked at the phantoms in the forest. Some came

right up to the track itself, close enough to touch the soldiers who walked past unaware they were being watched. To Silverdust's senses the ghosts resembled white and blue flames, springing up from the earth. The pale blue lights resembled men and women, no older than forty if Silverdust had to guess, all whip-thin and ragged. A few opened their mouths to cry pitifully, but no sound emerged from the mouths of the dead.

They starved to death. Silverdust could feel his patience for the Envoy waning. *Nordvlast is not an Imperial province. There are no soldiers here to kill the lawless.*

'It won't be long until we claim this cheerless corner of Vinterkveld for the Empire,' said de Vries, sounding bored. 'Surely you know this, Exarch?'

Nordvlast can barely afford to build decent roads much less afford to keep and feed barracks full of soldiers. The Envoy waved off his words and rolled her eyes.

'This could change everything in the Empire,' said de Vries, with a breathless intensity that put Silverdust on edge. 'This gift of yours could give us the edge in the war with the south.'

This will change nothing. The Emperor has long known secrets denied to the Synod. Do you think the man who dominates an entire continent would be content with mastering air, water, earth and fire?

'No one has ever developed skill in all four areas of the arcane,' said de Vries with curl of her lip. 'Not even the Emperor.'

He was some forty summers old when the war against the dragons reached its climax. By now his years number more than a century. Imagine what one could learn given two lifetimes.

The Envoy said nothing. For once she was less sure of herself and her expression was troubled.

'You seem to know a great deal about the Emperor for someone who has spent decades on Vladibogdan.'

It was not always so.

They travelled in silence for some time, the wind gusted in

the trees and the Envoy shivered as much from fear as cold if Silverdust guessed the truth of it. The phantoms continued their vigil from the side of the track, appearing in groups of twos and threes every few miles. Some appeared to be weeping, other stared with a dreadful intensity.

'When did you first notice this power?' asked de Vries.

The first time was in Cinderfell.

'How?' De Vries shook her head, and her usual assured guise slipped to show something of the frustration and confusion she felt. 'How did this come to pass?'

I was close at hand when the Vartiainen boy destroyed the Ashen Torment. The artefact contained vast power, particularly power over the dead.

'And you think it has something to do with your new sight?'

It would make a certain sense, but the arcane does not always follow a straight path.

'Nothing like this has ever happened to a Vigilant before,' said de Vries in a thoughtful tone.

I am not as most Vigilants.

The soldiers settled into a routine each day and the deep darkness of the long Nordvlast nights required they stop to make camp. Silverdust remained apart from the main group, never straying far from the Envoy. He stared into the woodlands with the aura of heat and light playing around his feet, a sombre beacon in the gloom.

'Keeping to yourself again.' It was the young soldier, Streig. Silverdust was not surprised; he had felt the boy's curiosity, noticed him approach with senses other than eyes. 'The other soldiers say you can see the dead.'

Is that so?

'Alexandr overheard the Envoy speaking with Father Orlov. She said you were dangerous.'

All Vigilants are dangerous.

'True enough, but she seems particularly worked up about you.'

The Envoy is conflicted. On the one hand she suspects me of treason, and yet I have a power she can only dream of. She cannot decide to deliver me to the Emperor as a unique prize or a deadly prisoner.

'So it's true then?' Streig looked at Silverdust from the corner of his eye.

That I have committed treason or that I can see the dead?

Silverdust regarded the endless darkness of the night-time forest. A pair of blue-white lights shimmered in the distance, two phantoms lingering perhaps half a mile away.

'I don't imagine you'd admit to betraying the Empire.' Streig stared into the forest and Silverdust could feel the young man's fear grow steadily stronger.

There is nothing to be afraid of. The dead are content simply to watch, it seems. Unlike the Empire's leaders, who live only to kill.

'Are you going to eat that?' said Streig, carefully ignoring Silverdust's dissent. He pointed at the bowl of thin broth that sat forgotten beside Silverdust's pack.

I am not. But you may.

The soldier took the bowl and spooned the greasy broth to his lips, pausing to cast a glance at the camp fire where the other soldiers sat and drank and played dice.

You have kept this irregularity between us, I trust?

'The fact you never eat?' Streig nodded slowly. 'Double portions for me.'

Exactly. It is to your benefit. Silverdust watched the young soldier finish the broth, felt the swirl of thoughts in the man's head. He was neither tall nor short, but heavy in the chest and arm in the way of Imperial soldiers. The young soldier viewed the world through wide, honest eyes and Silverdust sensed a question gnawing at him. *And you are not bothered by this?* The Exarch gestured towards the bowl. Streig shrugged.

'There's plenty of things I don't understand and plenty of things about Vigilants I don't know. I've always been told not to ask. This is another one of those things.' Streig glanced at the Exarch a moment. 'Though maybe this is particular to you.'

You are astute.

'Well, it works out rather well for me, so I suppose I'll stay with not asking. And I'm not going to ask why you never seem to sleep either.'

You are an attentive soldier, Streig. You could go far in the Imperial Army.

Streig shrugged and looked away, then snorted a weary and incredulous laugh. 'As long as I don't ask any questions. The Envoy has been very clear about that, stuck up . . .' Streig stopped himself and eyed Silverdust warily.

I have no great love of the Envoy, your indiscretions will not reach her ears.

'Just our bad fortune that we have to escort Father Orlov across the continent,' added Streig, quietly. 'He was in charge of troop inspections on Vladibogdan. The pointless nonsense he had us do, just to show us who was in charge.'

He is a man who grasps after power to the exclusion of all else.

'You sure have a way with words.' Streig looked back to the camp to make sure he hadn't been missed.

If you should overhear anything else between Father Orlov and Envoy de Vries . . .

'You'd be amazed what important people say in front of lowly soldiers.' Streig looked back towards the camp fire. 'I'll take your bowl back for washing. Do you need anything else?' He let the question hang between them for a moment. 'No, I don't suppose you do.'

Silverdust watched the young soldier go and felt a glimmer of amusement. It was good to have an ally again.

*   *   *

It was another week before they reached Steinwick, and Silverdust was grateful when they emerged from the seemingly endless tunnel beneath the bleak boughs of the Nordvlast forest. Steinwick served the nearby villages and hamlets, acting as a focal point for trade. The merchants had fared well, and a succession of headsmen had raised walls around the town. Smoke drifted lazily from numerous chimneys and lantern lights glimmered from the watch towers.

Why are there Imperial soldiers at the gate?

Envoy de Vries stared down the track and squinted into the distance.

'Surely you must know, Exarch?' She smiled smugly. 'A garrison was left here. Two Vigilants were killed in their sleep months ago while lodging at an inn. Another went missing though her body was never found. The novices called her Sharpbreath.'

Khigir's sister.

'The soldiers are a friendly reminder to the townsfolk. The innkeeper and his family were not much help during our investigation, which was unfortunate. More unfortunate for them as it turned out.'

Silverdust fought the urge to set the woman on fire and stopped walking.

Why would the innkeeper and his family know anything about the killer?

The Envoy stopped beside him and looked back towards the forest, before ignoring his question and continuing her train of thought. 'We have to assume the assassin came from out of town. Perhaps Cinderfell.'

Steinwick is part of Nordvlast. We have no right to station soldiers here. The terms of the treaty we made with the Scorched Republics specifically forbid the Empire's interference.

'You've been on the island too long, Exarch.' The Envoy smiled without humour. 'We are the Solmindre Empire.

We do as we please and if the Scorched Republics feel slighted . . .' The Envoy pouted and shrugged. 'Well, they may just end up like the innkeeper and his family.'

That remains to be seen. The people of the Scorched Republics will not be so easily subjugated, I think.

'Careful, Exarch. You sound perilously close to sedition.'

What does it matter? The innkeeper and his family knew nothing of the assassinations, and yet they perished at our hands all the same.

'Innocence isn't protection from punishment, Silverdust.' The Envoy stroked the curving mask with a single fingertip. 'An example had to made here. And the Emperor does so like to make examples.' She grinned girlishly. 'You may want to ponder on that. We'll be at Khlystburg before too long.'

CHAPTER FOURTEEN

Steiner

'I thought we were seeking out small towns and villages,' said Kristofine. 'So we can spread the word of rebellion and incite uprisings.'

'We are,' said Steiner, 'and we will.' He pulled his hood up against the faint drizzle that appeared to fall almost continuously. 'But for now I'd simply be happy to be out of the rain.'

They had been trudging across the dreary landscape of Svingettevei for two weeks, walking along the edge of the Great Western Forest in the hopes they would avoid being spotted. They dined on hare and, when the goddesses smiled upon them, boar, but food was scarce in the main. The trees watched silently, evergreen branches sheltering them from the worst of the north wind.

'We've barely seen a soul since we left the barge,' said Kristofine, a note of impatience in her voice.

'I know. We'll in the Empire soon and things will change.'

'Is this because of what happened at the canal-side inn?' she asked. 'You might find a friendlier audience next time.' Steiner winced as he remembered his failure to make any impression on the men in the bar.

'I'll try again, I'll make people hear me. They will listen,

I'm sure of it.' But with every word he felt more uncertain. 'Besides, people are talking about what happened. The innkeeper will talk about Vladibogdan and the dragon. Word of the taken children is spreading.'

'But shouldn't you be the one telling it?' said Kristofine. 'It's your story after all.'

'When we get to the next town,' replied Steiner, frowning. 'I promise.'

A cold wind whipped at the tree tops and pulled at their cloaks. The forest they had walked beside for so long finally parted ways with them. Marek waited for them on a knoll a half mile ahead. The land here was unclaimed, miles of grassland between the forests and lakes.

'Because if you are worried about talking to people,' continued Kristofine, 'I could try for you.'

Steiner shook his head. 'No.' He felt a flash of irritation with her. 'I said I'd do it.'

'I just want to help,' said Kristofine quietly. Her words were clipped, hinting at her frustration.

'I know,' he replied. 'But I made a promise to Kimi. It should be me that fulfils it. It should be me that tells the tale.'

Marek gestured that they hurry and the conversation was abandoned, but the irritation Steiner felt hung at his neck like a millstone. They walked in silence and if his father noticed the tension between them he didn't mention it.

'This is the border where the Karelina and Virolanti Provinces meet Svingettevei,' said Marek. 'And those' – he gestured to a clutch of small black dots wandering along an ill-defined track – 'are Imperial soldiers patrolling the border.'

'And that' – Kristofine pointed to a huddle of dour buildings a few miles away – 'looks like an opportunity to get dry and eat something other than hare or boar.' Steiner eyed the tiny settlement and pursed his lips, knowing he'd have to try and speak to the locals.

'I can only see about five,' he said, squinting through the rain at the Imperial soldiers. 'If we surprise them somehow we might be able to . . .' He caught Marek's stern look and said no more.

'I don't like those odds,' replied Marek. 'We go into town and we see if we can find a few people interested in our tale. Maybe they've already had word here.' He held up one finger. 'We keep our heads down.'

Steiner sighed. He'd rather fight with bad odds than try winning people over in a bar.

'Come on,' said Kristofine with a glimmer of renewed hope in her eyes. 'Let's find a good inn with a large fireplace.'

The hamlet was barely more than a few roads that had the good fortune to run into each other. A muddy square formed the centre and a number of houses in dark timber had been thrown up. The houses had been covered in now-flaking plaster, while the thatched roofs were verdant with moss and stained with guano.

'Welcome to the Solmindre Empire and all of its riches,' said Marek.

'Cinderfell doesn't look so bad now that I've seen this place,' said Steiner.

'So is this Karelina Province or Virolanti?' asked Kristofine.

'Well, actually,' said a local man who slouched in a nearby doorway, 'this isn't one place or another. We're right on the border.'

'Does it have a name?' said Steiner. The man had a patronising tone that made Steiner clutch his sledgehammer a little tighter.

'You don't know where you are?' The man stepped out into what passed for the main street. He was a little younger than Marek, balding and narrow-shouldered. His cloak was a tired grey colour that matched his face. 'Fancy not knowing where you are.'

'If we knew we wouldn't be asking,' said Kristofine.

'It's not wise to start travelling and not know where you're heading,' replied the man with a sneer.

'We're heading east,' said Steiner. 'Come on. I'll not waste my breath speaking with halfheads.'

'Too bad the inn is full,' said the man with a broad smile. 'Full of Imperial soldiers. Soldiers looking for someone, I'd say. Looking for people coming from the west.'

Marek pulled back his hood and glowered at the man. 'This is Trystbyre.'

'Ah, one of you has a clue then.'

'We're headed to the far side of the lake in Virolanti to see my sister,' said Marek. 'She's had a fever for many weeks now. My son and his wife have never travelled before and don't know the land like you do.'

'Ah, well, no one knows the land like I do.' The local man preened. 'I've been here for longer than . . .' But Marek had already walked away.

'Why did you tell him all those lies?' asked Kristofine.

'Now he feels like he has something on us,' replied Marek. 'A little story about who we are. We're not mysterious strangers any more, and that makes us unremarkable. People don't gossip about unremarkable things.'

'I wanted to smack him in the mouth,' said Steiner.

'I know,' replied Marek. 'And that's exactly the kind of thing that will get us noticed.' He frowned. 'What's got into you? You don't normally let fools rile you so easily.'

Steiner shrugged and tried not to think of performing speeches about sedition to rooms full of people who didn't care to listen to him, or worse yet didn't believe him.

'Just cold is all,' he lied. 'Cold and hungry.'

'Well, you're going to have to stay cold and hungry for a good while yet,' said Marek. 'We can't stop today, not with the soldiers here.'

*　　*　　*

The weather, like Steiner's mood, did not improve during the next few days. Only when they reached the tall pines of the Karelina Forest did Steiner relax. 'I don't care for walking out in the open like that,' he admitted that evening as they settled down and made a fire. 'Too easy for people on horseback to see you from afar and come riding over.'

'You mean Okhrana,' said Kristofine. Steiner nodded. The sun had long begun to set and the shadows reached across every part of the dreary land.

'Okhrana aren't so bad,' said a voice from deeper in the forest.

Marek, Steiner and Kristofine looked at one another for a stuttering heartbeat, then lurched to their feet and brandished their weapons.

'They have teeth,' said another voice from nearby.

'Aye, and some spirit too.' A shadow within the forest emerged and stepped into the meagre light of the camp fire. He was a tall man, taller than Marek, but wiry and thin. His sandy beard was long and unkempt and a dirty bandage covered one eye.

'Hoy there,' said Steiner.

'So you're on the run from the Okhrana?' said the one-eyed man. He nodded as if considering this. 'Exciting, eh, Nils?'

'Very exciting,' said another man, stepping from the treeline. He was younger, darker, and more heavyset than his friend. 'I've been in trouble with the Empire myself, but never the Okhrana. Sounds serious.'

More men stepped into the light, emerging from the forest with sodden cloaks and ragged boots and trousers. All were armed.

'Steiner,' whispered Kristofine. 'We're surrounded.' He nodded and gripped the sledgehammer tighter; there had to be about a dozen brigands.

'It seems you have the numbers,' said Marek. 'So now what?'

'Now?' The one-eyed man stepped forward. 'Now we invite you to dinner of course!'

'Do we have a choice?' asked Steiner.

'No,' replied Nils. 'Not really.' Steiner and Kristofine gathered up their things as Marek stamped out the fire.

'What will we do?' said Steiner under his breath.

'Not much we can do,' replied Marek quietly. 'If we're lucky we'll get out of this with our lives, but we won't have much coin to show for it.'

'Come,' said the man called Nils. 'No need for the long faces.'

The brigands hadn't confiscated their weapons, but remained twenty feet away, forming a loose circle around their captives.

'So what brings you to my beautiful county?' asked Nils brightly.

'We're heading east—' said Steiner.

'I wasn't asking you.' Nils' expression became stony in a heartbeat. He nodded to Kristofine. 'You. What brings you here?'

'Ah, you wouldn't believe me if I told you.' Kristofine sighed and an irritated look crossed her face.

'I think this one likes to game, Einar,' said Nils, smiling again.

'Aye.' The brigands' leader scratched at his bandage and nodded. 'Speak up, little girl, we'll hear you out no matter how outlandish the tale.'

'What if I told you we had come all the way from Nordvlast, from the farthest town north you might ever care to visit.'

'Then I would imagine you wish you hadn't left,' replied Nils. The brigands laughed.

'We had to leave, had no choice in the matter,' said Kristofine. 'The whole town learned of Vladibogdan, and the Empire would kill every single one just for knowing such a thing.'

The brigands muttered to each other until their leader, Einar, spoke up. 'Never heard of Vladibogdan.'

'It's an island,' said Kristofine, looking around and seeing she had gained their attention. 'A secret place where they take children with witchsign. Steiner here escaped in order to try and save us.'

'Hah! Secret islands and forbidden powers,' said Nils. 'This tale gets better and better. Go on, little girl.' They trudged further into the forest, only stopping for the brigands to light lanterns.

'The Empire took my husband by accident, thinking he had witchsign. In their haste they overlooked his sister, who has considerable power.'

Steiner mouthed the word 'husband?' to Kristofine in the darkness and she shrugged.

'And where is this sister now?' asked Nils, hoping to find a hole in the story.

'Questions later!' said Kristofine with a sly smile. 'For months Steiner was held captive on the island and he learned that a Vigilant was coming to claim his sister and set the town afire. The Vigilant was called Shirinov, and had a mask of smiling silver.'

'Shirinov, you say?' said Einar. He'd come a little closer now as they continued their march into the forest.

'Steiner's father, Marek, who you see before you now, saw fit to gift his son with a mighty sledgehammer, and this was how Steiner fought Vigilant Shirinov on the freezing beach as a mighty storm rumbled and shook the skies.'

'A scene worthy of the sagas!' said Nils. 'And this Shirinov, was he a worthy opponent?'

'Vigilants are far more than they seem,' said Kristofine. 'But I doubt you'd believe that part of the story, and besides, it's one of the Empire's greatest secrets.'

'Ha!' Nils grinned. 'She's good. I'll give her that. I'm but a fish on the hook of this tale.'

Kristofine returned the brigand's grin. 'The children who are taken each year are trained. They're trained to become Vigilants, though they keep their powers hidden.'

The brigands took a moment to absorb this piece of information, and a few muttered or grumbled hard words to each other in the gloom of the night-time forest.

'So it was that Steiner had to endure all the powers of the arcane that the Vigilant could conjure, even turning his skin to stone to survive their fight.'

'But the sledgehammer . . .' said Einar.

'But the sledgehammer was Shirinov's undoing,' agreed Kristofine. 'For stony skin might protect against knives and swords, but a hammer is quite another thing.'

They reached a clearing littered with pots and pans and a sunken fire pit with a spit. A half-collapsed cottage had been taken over, the roof replaced with canvas for want of something better.

'And this is why the Okhrana want you?' said Einar.

'Partly,' agreed Kristofine. 'And also because my husband helped the stolen children escape and set the dragons free.'

'What dragons?' asked Nils. His mocking tone had given way to genuine curiosity.

'Why don't we light a fire,' said Kristofine, 'and I'll tell you the whole tale, including the parts I missed out. Though my husband tells the story best. After all, it's his story.' She squeezed Steiner's hand and smiled at him. Steiner forced a smile and felt sick to his boots.

Steiner woke to a dreadful pain behind his eyes and his mouth was dry. He could barely move but desperately needed to make water.

'Frøya keep me close. What happened?' he grunted. Kristofine pushed her cold nose under his ear and chuckled.

'You're hungover is all.'

'What? How?'

'Turns out at least two of our new friends have lost children to Invigilation. I don't know when it happened, but there came a point where they realised I wasn't making the story up.'

'And we're not dead?' asked Steiner, though he felt somewhat otherwise. He pressed his fingers against his eyelids.

'I'm not,' said Kristofine. 'But you might be. You wouldn't be the first person from Nordvlast to die of vodka poisoning.'

Steiner opened his eyes and realised they'd been given a corner of the tumbledown cottage to sleep in. Slowly, he dragged himself to his feet and stepped outside, grunting like an old man and wanting to throw up. Kristofine linked her arm in his and smiled at him. The brigands were lounging around the fire pit. Some had fallen asleep where they sat the previous night, and some continued to sleep. A dim light made its way into the clearing and for once no rain fell from the skies.

'You actually persuaded a gang of brigands not to kill us by telling them a story.' Steiner shook his head in disbelief.

'Not any story. Your story.' She looked at him fondly, with more than a little pride. 'Our story.'

'That she did!' shouted Nils cheerfully. Steiner flinched and mumbled a curse. 'Feeling delicate today, are we, dragon rider?' The brigand clapped a hand on Steiner's shoulder. 'Who knew dragons still lived, eh?'

Steiner stared at Kristofine for a moment. 'You really told them everything, didn't you?'

'We told them everything,' she replied.

Marek and Einar sat by the fire pit. Einar would prod a large pot of porridge every so often, but his attention was fixed on Marek for the most part. The men's heads were bowed in conversation.

'Father?' said Steiner, wary of interrupting the two men.

'Good news,' said Marek with a smile. 'Einar and his men have agreed to escort us through the forest, right up to the mountain pass that will take us to Slavon Province.'

'An escort?' Steiner gestured at the brigands preparing to travel. 'How did this happen?'

'It happened because Kristofine made it happen,' said Marek with a smile. 'She could charm crows from a battlefield.'

Steiner opened his mouth to speak but Marek had already turned away to discuss the journey ahead with Einar. Kristofine was retelling parts of the story to Nils, leaving Steiner feeling hungover and useless.

CHAPTER FIFTEEN

Kjellrunn

Dos Khor was at least triple the size of Cinderfell and different in every way. The roads were dusty and the buildings were made from pale stone or sun-baked mud, so unlike the thatched hovels Kjellrunn had known. There were no hills or rises nor were there any trees, and grass was a distant memory. The people were dark-skinned and slender and wore robes in varying shades of sand, earth and cream. They looked at the rabble of children and the two elderly women with unflinching gazes.

'They're not shy about who they stare at,' muttered Kjellrunn as they made their way from the shore, walking deeper into the town.

'It's not rude to stare in Shanisrond,' said Maxim. 'You're Steiner's sister, aren't you?' Kjellrunn nodded. 'We looked out for one another on Vladibogdan.' The boy said this with all the gravitas of a veteran four times his age.

'You looked out for Steiner?' Kjellrunn hid her amusement behind her hand, faking a cough. 'How old are you?'

'Eleven,' he replied. Kjellrunn cast a sidelong glance, noticing him properly for the first time. 'Shatterspine . . . I mean, Vigilant Shirinov, he almost killed me the first day we got to the island. Steiner stopped him.'

'I heard you at the docks, talking to Kimi. You miss my brother.'

'We should never have left him behind in Virag,' he said matter-of-factly.

Kjellrunn grinned. 'It's good to meet you, Maxim. I'd like to know you better once we get settled here.'

The boy gave a shy smile and looked over his shoulder. 'I'd best go and check on Sundra. I promised Tief I would.'

'That makes two of us.'

They pressed on through the town as the afternoon heat threatened to stifle their enthusiasm for their new home. Twice Mistress Kamalov attempted to speak to the local people and twice she was waved off.

'This is not what I was hoping for,' said Sundra, though her voice was a hoarse whisper. She was sweating freely and looked particularly pale in the fierce daylight.

'We need to get you into some shade,' said Kjellrunn, looking about the street for somewhere to shelter.

'What is wrong with these fools?' Mistress Kamalov glared at the passersby. 'Anyone would think I had brought soldiers here directly from Khlystburg.'

The novices milled about looking fearful, but stayed close to the high priestess and the renegade Vigilant. It was clear to Kjellrunn that the two women were keeping a polite distance from one another, just as they had done on the ship.

'What's that?' said Maxim, pointing at a strange building in the next street. Four towers rose up from the ground, stained black, unlike the dun-coloured mud homes of Dos Khor. Each was straight along one side, curving at the other to taper at the top.

'It can't be,' whispered Sundra. She headed towards the

towers without waiting for the others. Mistress Kamalov urged
the children to follow.

'It looks bad,' said Trine, wrinkling her nose. 'Is it a prison?'
But no one answered because none knew, save for Sundra.
She drifted towards the building as if she were sleepwalking.
Once they were closer Kjellrunn could see that the towers
rose up perhaps five storeys and were arranged around a
circular building at the centre. A wide semicircular door
opened out onto the street, almost hidden beneath a ragged
awning of faded teal. A slender, dark-skinned man sat on the
steps enjoying the shade.

'Sundra.' Kjellrunn touched the woman gently on the arm.
'What is this place?'

'We Spriggani never built temples to the goddesses. We
never really believed you needed them. Simply being in
nature, in the forests was good enough, but I often heard tell
that things were different in the south.'

'This is a temple?' said Kjellrunn, grimacing. The four towers
were slender and graceful, but the soot-coloured building
looked ominous rather than calming.

'The four towers represent the wings of Frejna's two crows,'
replied Sundra quietly. 'This is a temple to Se and Venter, a
place for spirits to pass over to the afterlife. The bones whispered the name of this town to me, over and over, but never
did I think to find a temple here.'

The man on the temple steps raised his head, revealing
shrunken, sightless eyes.

'Frejna,' he repeated softly. He spoke a stream of words a
moment later, but Kjellrunn understood none of it.

'He said the temple has been abandoned,' translated Maxim.
'Imperial soldiers came here by ship years ago and killed the
priestesses.'

Maxim spoke to him briefly and the man replied.

'No one has been in the temple since the soldiers came.'

Maxim sighed. 'He says everyone is scared that the Empire will come back.'

'What language is that?' asked Kjellrunn.

Maxim shrugged. 'I only know that my mother spoke to me with these words before I was taken. Some of the words sound different the way he says them, but it's close enough.'

Sundra looked at the vast wing-like towers and a glimmer of a smile crossed her face for a moment. She took Maxim's hand and leaned close to the boy. 'Tell the beggar that a new priestess has arrived.'

Maxim did as he was told and the man reeled off a long and winding ribbon of words.

'He says the soldiers will come back if a priestess enters the temple.'

'Tell him we won't let them,' said Mistress Kamalov, her expression dour.

'I'll fucking burn the lot of them,' said Trine.

'Do not use such language,' said Sundra with a hard look. 'Do your ears not work? I quite clearly said this is a holy place.'

'We can't stay here,' said Kjellrunn quietly. 'It's a temple. It's not right.'

'And I suppose you have a palace nearby where we can stay, your highness?' said Trine. The novices behind her sniggered and exchanged knowing glances.

'It's better than sleeping in the street,' said Maxim. 'Come on.'

They followed the high priestess into the silence of the old temple, exchanging the dust of the arid street for the dust of abandonment. They explored for perhaps half an hour before Kjellrunn emerged at the doorway again.

'You may as well join us for lunch,' she said. 'This was your home before it was ours.' The blind man smiled and babbled cheerfully, nodding as they went. 'Maxim?' Kjellrunn hoped the boy might appear to translate. The old man kept up his unfathomable ramble. She guided him into the temple and sat him down on one of the many low benches that faced the simple altar.

She looked down at the old man and sighed. 'I'm going to need to learn this language of yours if I'm to stay here, aren't I?'

'I thought you could have this one,' said Sundra as she opened the door. They were on the first floor of the north-east tower. Kjellrunn entered the dimly lit room with Maxim close behind. 'You'll have the one above,' added Sundra to the boy. 'I will be in the room below. These old legs of mine have had quite enough of stairs over the years.'

Daylight shone through horizontal gaps in the shutters, throwing blades of golden sun over a narrow bed, a table with two chairs, and a dusty rug.

'All of this is for me?' said Kjellrunn. The room had to be twice as large as the kitchen in Cinderfell and contained none of the clutter.

'Not the most homely of places, I grant you,' said Sundra, looking over the room with a disapproving eye.

'It's perfect.' Kjellrunn sat on the bed. 'We only had a loft in Cinderfell, with thin walls to divide different parts. Just straw and blankets, nothing like this.' She looked around the room with a smile on her face.

'Perhaps this room once belonged to an initiate of Frejna just like you,' said Sundra. 'And it is our good fortune to have found such a place.' She rested a hand on Maxim's shoulder. 'Come, let's get you settled in upstairs.'

As much as Kjellrunn liked her new room, it contained nothing to keep her or entertain her, and so she wandered down the tiled steps. The walls and floors inside the temple were the colour of pale white sand, while doors and wooden panelling were a rich if dusty mahogany. Cinderfell had only ever been endless shades of grey by contrast. Small wonder she'd gone to the forest whenever she was able.

'Hey! Get off of me.' The voice was male, young and loud, coming up the stairs from the main hall of the temple. Kjellrunn felt a moment of panic before racing down the steps. She glanced around, her heart beating loud, a cold sweat at her brow. Two men had grabbed one of the novices and were dragging him to the main door. It was Eivind, the boy who'd lost an arm in the fight at Virag. The men wore riding boots and dirty cream robes, with short curving scabbards hanging from their thick leather belts.

'Hoy there!' shouted Kjellrunn with far more bravery than she felt. The men stopped and Eivind wrestled himself free and ran to Kjellrunn. 'What the Hel is going on here?'

The men conversed among themselves and smiled, then turned on Kjellrunn and the novice, clearly intending to drag them out of the temple. Other novices emerged from doorways in the temple. Kjellrunn could sense they were drawing on the arcane in preparation. All of them had been restless and full of fearful energy since the street fight in Virag.

'What are you doing?' said Kjellrunn, drawing herself up and staring down her nose as best as she could. The men paused and one gave a long whistle with his fingers. Three more men appeared through the temple door. One had drawn his sword.

'They're slavers, halfhead,' said Trine, appearing at Kjellrunn's side. 'Isn't it obvious?' The dark-haired girl curled her lip and spat at the feet of the nearest man. His eyes widened in disbelief that quickly turned to anger. The slaver drew his arm back to strike her but Kjellrunn stepped forward, placing herself between the fire-breathing novice and the man

'Wait!' she said, holding up her hands. To her surprise the man lowered his fist. Maxim appeared beside her and spoke in his mother's tongue, low and quiet. The man answered him with a cruel smile and the rest of his crew laughed bitterly.

'Tell him I am an initiate of Frejna,' said Kjellrunn. 'And you are all in my care.'

'Tell him I'm going to burn his face off,' said Trine.

'I'm not going to do that,' said Maxim to Trine over his shoulder. He looked up at the slaver and spoke calmly. The man replied and Maxim's expression changed to one of dismay.

'He said he has no time for old goddesses and will happily shit on the altar once he's sold all of us.'

The man drew his sword and Maxim flinched backwards. In the space of a heartbeat Kjellrunn was back in the woods of Nordvlast, floating above the ground as the corpses of twelve Okhrana spun and swirled about her, caught up in a vortex of her pain and hatred.

Pain.

It flared across her shoulder as the sword bit deep and Kjellrunn fell to the tiled floor, shocked at the bright blood staining her shirt. A bright flare of fire illuminated the dim interior of the temple as Trine exhaled her arcane power. The slaver's leader screamed in agony and ran into the street, hair ablaze and features scorched. Other slavers raced forward to cut Trine down, only to find Sundra stood before them. The priestess pulled the girl behind her and a slaver raised his sword for a killing blow, but Sundra's eyes had changed colour. The man gave a shocked gasp and his skin was riddled with streaks of grey before his pace slowed as he turned to stone altogether.

'Leave my temple this instant!' said Sundra to the remaining slavers. And for once no translation was necessary.

Kjellrunn bit her lip so hard it almost bled as Mistress Kamalov sewed up the cut on her shoulder. The old woman said nothing, but her silence was rebuke enough. Maxim held her hand as the renegade Vigilant went about her grisly work. Sundra waited outside of Mistress Kamalov's room wringing her hands and occasionally shooing away the novices who came to see the gory spectacle.

'Good. I am finished with you,' said Mistress Kamalov. 'Keep it clean and get some rest.' Kjellrunn stood up and dared to look at the wound. 'All that training we did in Nordvlast.' Mistress Kamalov shook her head as she put away the needle and thread. 'Why did I waste my time?'

Kjellrunn left the room with head bowed and rounded shoulders. The novices watched her go, whispering as she passed while Trine waited at the temple door. She leaned against the wall and stared out into the street as if her expression alone would deter further troublemakers. The raven-haired girl called after Kjellrunn as she descended the temple steps.

'You don't have to thank me.'

Kjellrunn paused and looked over her wounded shoulder and felt a pang of irritation.

'Thank you for what?'

'Burning the man who cut you, halfhead. It's clear you're too stupid to defend yourself.'

'I was hoping we could avoid anyone getting hurt. There's nothing stupid about that.'

Trine flipped the sign of the four powers and Kjellrunn continued into town, keen to be away from the temple, though the heat made her feel faint with the effort of walking.

The docks of Dos Khor were a humble affair, more concerned with fishing than commerce. A few rickety wooden piers reached out into the sea like ancient fingers but Kjellrunn headed north, wanting to avoid the fishermen and a language she couldn't speak. The beach was dominated by the sculpture of a hand that rose up out of the sand. The white stone palm faced the Shimmer Sea as if it might command the tides to halt in their endless ebb and flow. Kjellrunn let out a long sigh and let herself cry for a moment; her shoulder throbbed with pain. The water was a breathtaking azure and the sunlight dappled the waves like the promise of gold. Someone cleared their throat behind her and Kjellrunn turned to find Sundra standing a few feet away, looking out to sea.

'This is so different to Cinderfell,' she said. 'It's desolate, but beautiful in its way.'

'Shanisrond and Cinderfell have much in common,' said Sundra, drawing closer. 'Neither are particularly kind or accommodating.'

'I miss the forests of the north, but that's all I miss.' A moment of quiet companionship lingered between them and the gulls called out in the distance as the quiet hush of waves on sand filled their senses.

'Maxim told me you introduced yourself to the slavers as an initiate of Frejna.'

Kjellrunn nodded. 'Was I wrong to do so?'

'No, no. Far from it.' The old woman smiled. 'It makes me proud that someone would introduce themselves so.'

'Shall we sit?' said Kjellrunn, unsure how to behave in her new role.

'If I get down I may not get back up again.' Sundra made a face. 'And I hate sand.'

Kjellrunn stood beside the high priestess and they looked out to sea, feeling small in contrast to the vast white clouds that drifted across the sky in the distance.

'It is good that you tried to defend the children,' said Sundra. 'But words alone are not sufficient in such dangerous times. Why did you not call on your gifts?'

'I've killed before.' Kjellrunn released a shaky breath. 'In Cinderfell. And not just a single person but a dozen of them.'

'It is unfortunate,' said Sundra. 'But it is also necessary. As a servant of Frejna we watch, we wait, and sometimes we act.'

'When I killed . . .' Kjellrunn tried to breathe but every word was a struggle. 'It was so easy. It was too easy. I plucked the people off the ground, along with the rocks and old branches of the woodland, and I spun them, faster and faster until everything and everyone was broken.'

'Mistress Kamalov mentioned you had great power, Kjellrunn. She also told me you killed Okhrana to protect yourself. There is no shame in this.'

'No shame?' Kjellrunn blinked away fresh tears. 'But I feel it every day and every night. I see those men in my dreams. I see myself caught up in an irresistible power. Did Mistress Kamalov tell you I nearly killed her?' Kjellrunn gave a bitter laugh. 'She doesn't know because she was unconscious at the time. I nearly destroyed the cottage she was living in.'

'You were young,' said Sundra softly. 'You *are* young. And you are untested.'

'I think I was tested enough that day. No one should be able to kill so many people so quickly.'

'So this is why you hesitate to use your gifts.'

Kjellrunn nodded and to her surprise the severe Spriggani woman pulled her close and hugged her. 'You are much too young for such burdens. I am sorry, Kjellrunn.'

CHAPTER SIXTEEN

Kimi

'I've waited so long for this,' said Kimi in her mother tongue, though in truth the breathless excitement she felt was almost as bad as the pangs of dread in her stomach. The *Watcher's Wait* approached the west coast of Yamal, the ship rocking gently beneath them as mile by mile they drew closer. The sun blazed high in the pale blue sky, warming their faces. Marozvolk stood next to her at the burned prow and said nothing, one hand gripping the hilt of the sword where it rested in its scabbard.

'I never thought I'd see Yamal again,' said the renegade Vigilant.

'What I said before, back in Virag.' Kimi sighed. 'I'm sorry. I was frustrated, angry. I can't imagine what it was like for you to be indoctrinated into the Holy Synod, or fed all those lies about the Empire.'

'All my life I had wanted to do something to bring honour or glory to my family, my country.' Marozvolk's face creased in anguish. 'But I found myself being drawn further and further into the Empire's embrace.' She looked away a moment, overcome by painful memories.

'What is like?' asked Kimi. 'To be part of the Empire, I mean?'

'It's to live in fear. Fear is the flesh and blood of the Empire at every level.' Marozvolk's gaze had a faraway quality to it, deep in memory and thought. 'Everyone fears the Emperor, of course. Even his own trusted coterie, the Envoys, the generals and the nobles. That fear reaches right down to the lowliest rank of soldier and novice, and is used to stifle even the idea of dissent in the regular folk.'

They stood together in silence as the ship edged closer to the mainland. 'Do you know what you'll say to him?' said Romola, joining them at the prow for the view. She'd sat up long into the night with Kimi. They'd discussed how a princess might reintroduce herself to a father who was complicit in her imprisonment. None of the options looked attractive.

'He was never a particularly even-tempered man,' said Kimi. 'And that didn't improve when my mother died.' Marozvolk frowned into the distance while Romola took a sip from a metal hip flask. The silence, like the humidity, grew stifling.

'You know, I've been coming here for over a decade,' said Romola, 'and I still don't know where the capital city is. That's strange, right?'

'That was a deft way to change the subject,' replied Kimi with a smile. 'The capital city is wherever the Xhan, I mean the king, chooses it to be. We're nomads for the most part, though the ports are permanent settlements.'

'That makes sense.' Romola offered her flask to the two women but both declined. 'I'm going to have a word with my navigator. We have to sail up river a way before we can weigh anchor.' She looked over her shoulder at the crew who had already busied themselves. 'Let me know if you need anything, all right?'

'She has a point,' said Marozvolk after the captain had left. 'Yamal is a big place and the Xhantsulgarat could be anywhere.'

'It'll be near one of the lakes and close to a forest,' said Kimi. 'There's much that's unpredictable about the Xhan, but he loves trees almost as much as he loves fresh water.' She smiled. 'Xhantsulgarat. I haven't heard that word for years.'

Romola guided the *Watcher's Wait* into the mouth of the river Bestnulim, which divided Yamal from the swamps, mists and forests of Izhoria in the north.

'This is as far as we go,' said Romola. 'I'm going to be taking on supplies from this port town here, and seeing if I can pick up some work.'

'The town is called Bestam,' said Kimi. 'And thank you.'

'You don't have to thank me,' said Romola. 'My crew have plenty of Imperial gold in their pockets, right.' The captain gave her a look, as if sizing her up. 'How are *you* for money?'

Kimi frowned.

'You're a Yamali princess, right? You could be running this country one day. Think of this as early tribute.' Romola dropped some coins into Kimi's hand. To her surprise they were Yamal Shüd, the currency of her people. Kimi laughed.

'What?' said Romola. 'Did I do something wrong?'

'I haven't seen one of these in years!' She looked at the coins and laughed, then embraced the captain tightly.

'Marozvolk is waiting for you in the boat with Tief and Taiga.' Romola looked over the edge of the ship. 'Quite the crew you've got yourself. My people will row you ashore. Are you ready?'

Kimi nodded. 'Look for me in a year's time. If I'm not here, then I'm probably dead.'

'Well, that's easy then. Don't get dead, right?' Romola grinned. 'Farewell, Your Highness.'

Kimi clambered down a rope ladder that hung against the side of the ship to the boat that waited below. The only seat left was beside Marozvolk. Kimi wanted to offer her some words of encouragement or consolation, but the renegade Vigilant fixed her gaze on the shoreline.

'Good to be on dry land again,' said Tief, who sat across from Kimi. Taiga forced a smile.

'Let's see what surprises Yamal has for us,' said Kimi.

Kimi wasted no time once they were ashore, gaining an audience with the headsman of Bestam just as the sun dipped below the horizon. The settlement was bathed in soft red light as they waited outside a grand-looking tent. The outside was made of countless goat skins, all neatly sewn together. An old tree branch had been pressed into service as a banner pole and a long rectangle of cream fabric fluttered in the breeze. There was no design on the banner save for two blue chevrons pointing downward.

Kimi looked around, still not quite able to believe she was home. The headsman exited his tent and looked over the four of them with a curious gaze. He was taller than Kimi, with a shaven head and pale scars on his dark skin, his craggy face unreadable. A hoop of gold pierced his eyebrow and a great many copper bangles hung from his wrists.

'Darga Bestam,' said Kimi in her mother tongue. She bowed her head and clasped her right fist in her left hand. The big man smiled.

'We're not so formal this far north, my child. You may call me Chulu-Agakh.'

'With respect, I'm not a child.'

'My youngest daughter is about your age,' said Chulu-Agakh. 'You have twenty summers unless my eyes are fading.'

'Your eyes serve you well.'

'Then you're still a child,' he replied. 'At least to an old man like me.' Kimi found his words warm rather than condescending and felt a moment of deep contentment. Being back among her people, speaking her own tongue, was nothing short of extraordinary. 'Will you come in for some tea?' He paused a moment to look at Tief and Taiga. 'Strange that you have Spriggani with you. I had thought the Empire destroyed all of them.'

'What did he say?' asked Tief, frustrated at being unable to understand the exchange.

'He's invited us in for tea,' said Kimi.

'I don't like it when I can't work out what people are saying,' grumbled Tief.

'You don't often like it when you *can* understand what people are saying,' said Taiga. Marozvolk snorted a laugh despite wanting to keep a straight face in front of the headsman, and Tief shot her a dark look.

The inside of the tent featured a fire pit at the centre and rugs at the edge of the circle. A soldier stood inside the opening, cleaning his nails with a strange knife. One by one they handed over their weapons and Chulu-Agakh was already pouring tea into small porcelain bowls as they took their places.

'Now let me try to guess,' said the Darga of Bestam once they were all seated. 'Could it be you have come to join the tribe by Ereg Bestnulim? Or perhaps you have a dispute with one of my people? Or are you a long-lost relative, come back from abroad?'

'I am the latter, but not a relative of yours,' said Kimi. 'I come asking for information. I am keen to find the Xhantsulgarat.'

'Ah, a lowly Darga is not a worthy enough audience,' replied Chulu-Agakh, raising his eyebrows at Marozvolk. Kimi couldn't be quite sure who he was mocking.

'You are a fine audience and serve fine tea, Darga Bestam.' Kimi inclined her head respectfully. 'But I have business at the Xhantsulgarat.'

'Is there any chance you two can speak in Solska,' said Tief quietly. 'I'm getting pissed off with not understanding what's going on.'

'Your Spriggani friend is unhappy?' asked Chulu-Agakh.

'He is keen to know what we speak of,' replied Kimi in her mother tongue. She turned to Tief. 'A Darga would never learn Solska. It is a low thing and brings dishonour to sully one's mouth with the language of our enemy.'

'You've never had a problem speaking it,' muttered Tief. 'And you're a princess.' Kimi frowned at him and the Darga gave a deep chuckle.

'You are correct,' said Chulu-Agakh in his mother tongue. 'I hate to sully my mouth to speak Solska, but I do understand it.'

'Oh,' said Kimi. Chulu-Agakh sipped his tea and smiled as if this were just another meeting.

'So you are a Yamali princess making your way to the Xhantsulgarat after spending time abroad?'

'I'm sorry. I should have told you who I was when we first met, but I wasn't sure anyone would believe me.' Kimi forced a smile. 'I've been gone for such a long time.'

A moment of realisation passed as Chulu-Agakh's eyes widened with the full import of her words.

'And not just any Yamali princess, but the daughter of the Xhan himself.'

Kimi nodded and felt herself blush as Chulu-Agakh shuffled around until he was on his knees, then pressed his forehead to the ground.

'I didn't think you were so formal this far north,' said Kimi. It was a strange feeling to have someone bow to her after all this time.

'We are not barbarians, Your Highness. And I have never had a princess in my tent before.'

Kimi sighed, glad to be rid of the secrecy. 'What can you tell me of the Xhantsulgarat and my father?'

Chulu-Agakh took an uneasy breath and Kimi knew in her bones she was about to receive bad news. 'You've been away a long time,' he said. 'Much has changed.'

'Letters were sent to me, but I've not had word for months.'

The Darga cleared his throat and Kimi realised she was holding her breath. 'Much has happened with our ruling tribe,' said Chulu-Agakh. 'And it gives me great sadness to have to tell you.'

The Darga of Bestam gifted Kimi with two tents and presented her with food, tea and servants, though Kimi declined the latter.

'And your brother is coming here?' said Tief. They were sitting around the fire after breakfast. Kimi prodded the fire with a stick, raking through the ashes as if some meaning might be hidden there. Marozvolk had wandered into town and Taiga was tidying up the tent.

'It's customary for the new Xhan to travel the country and go to each of the port towns. That way everyone knows where he is and can make tribute to him.'

'And if the Xhan doesn't come calling?' asked Tief.

'Then you know that you are out of favour and that your time as Darga is coming to an end.' Kimi stopped prodding the ashes and snapped the stick in two. 'But Chulu-Agakh has had word the Xhantsulgarat is on its way here. My brother will be here soon.' She snapped the stick into smaller pieces and eyed the flames with a stern expression. Tief shifted around until he was sitting closer to Kimi, then lit his pipe and smoked a while.

'We've been through a fair bit, you and I.' Kimi nodded and forced a smile, though in truth she felt the beginnings of hot tears behind her eyes. 'We've seen some bits and pieces, and we've finally escaped that island, and that counts for something.' Tief sighed. 'But to come all this way only to . . . I'm sorry, Kimi.'

'My father was never any good at giving me what I wanted,' said Kimi. 'And now he's gone and I can't warn him about the trouble in the north. I can't . . .' Her head drooped forward and her shoulders shook with silent sobs. Tief slipped an arm around her shoulders.

'But you and your brother, that has to be a better relationship than the one you had with your father, right?'

Kimi raised her head and dashed away the tears that tracked down her cheeks. 'We only had each other growing up. But I've been away five years and a lot can happen to a person. Chulu-Agakh said he'd heard rumours from more than a few of his close friends at court. They're saying Tsen poisoned my father, but no one can prove it.'

Tief stared at her as the words sank in. 'Should we really be meeting with him? If he's ruthless enough to poison your father then there's no telling what he may do to you.'

'I have no choice. Word of my arrival has already spread. I am expected to be here to meet my brother—'

'So he can kill you?' Tief shook his head with a scowl. 'I think I'd rather steal a boat and take my chances in Izhoria.'

'Let's hope it doesn't come to that.'

Bestam doubled in size over the course of two nights. The Xhantsulgarat had all the characteristics of a thriving bazaar, a circus, and most importantly a royal court. The tents were large and dyed in vibrant colours. All manner of merchants and nobles wandered the temporary town looking for entertainment and opportunity.

'This will surely set the cat among the crows,' said Chulu-Agakh. 'Are you sure you want to go through with this?' Kimi and Marozvolk waited outside the main tent with the Darga.

'I have to see Tsen,' said Kimi quietly. 'I have to know if it's true or not.'

'This is madness,' said Marozvolk. 'If it is true then he's hardly going to let you go free and do as you wish.' The renegade Vigilant stepped closer. 'I won't be able to protect you once we're in there, this is the royal court.'

'And I am a princess of the ruling tribe.' Kimi took a deep breath, steeling herself for what was to come. 'I still have some sway.'

'But you have been gone a long time,' said Chulu-Agakh. 'And things are much changed.'

A soldier came for them, bowing respectfully to Chulu-Agakh, then gestured that they follow. Kimi took another deep breath and entered the royal tent. The interior was a riot of sky blue and purple silks and incense burned from braziers with the strong scent of sandalwood. Bronze charms the size of birds spun and dangled from the ceiling, some chiming faintly, barely audible over the voices of the three dozen courtiers. Grim-faced horse and cattle traders rubbed shoulders with silk-robed watercleansers. The horse and cattle trade had been a male profession for as long as anyone could remember. They were lean and surly men who usually displayed their wealth with bright red robes, yet all were dressed in solemn black out of respect to the grieving Xhan. The watercleansers by contrast were only ever women, touched by the arcane. They acknowledged the dead Xhan with a sash of black worn at the waist, yet retained their blue robes. A handful of high-ranking soldiers and aides were scattered throughout the tent, but Kimi recognised none of them.

Chulu-Agakh sank to his knees and pressed his forehead to the floor before the Xhan. Kimi and Marozvolk did the same, as the crowd whispered to one another. Tsen-Baina Jet stepped forward and helped Chulu-Agakh to his feet then clapped him hard on the shoulder. Kimi barely recognised her brother. Little Tsen was gone, the slim youth with the surly cast in his eye had become something more. Here was a man of heavy muscle, who held his head high, dressed in the finest leathers and a cloak of startling blue.

'My father spoke very highly of you, Chulu-Agakh. He said you were a straight-talking man without pretence.' Tsen eyed Marozvolk for a moment. 'But what's this? Have you brought me gifts in order to win my favour?'

'I am humbled by your father's praise,' said Chulu-Agakh. 'But I think there has been some mistake in communication. The women I bring are not gifts.'

Tsen circled Chulu-Agakh and inspected Marozvolk. 'Is it not strange that you seem to have a woman for a bodyguard, Darga Bestam?'

'One sword is much like another when it finds you, your highness,' replied Chulu-Agakh. 'The person wielding it hardly matters.' That provoked a few chuckles and Kimi saw a flash of annoyance cross Tsen's face. Perhaps the surly boy she remembered had not gone so far after all.

'And this one?' Tsen approached Kimi. 'Does she lay well?' The laughter stopped and all eyes turned to Chulu-Agakh, waiting to see if the Darga might take offence.

'Your highness, has word not reached you that your sister has returned?' Chulu-Agakh struggled to keep the pained expression from his face. 'It is she that stands before you.'

Tsen stared at Kimi and for the briefest moment she saw the bloom of recognition in his eyes. Then he turned his back and took his seat on the throne.

'I have no sister,' he said with disgust. 'She was taken by the Empire a long time ago.'

Kimi felt as if a sinkhole had yawned open beneath her feet and almost staggered at her brother's dismissal. Her life as a sister, a daughter, a princess, had suddenly been crushed.

'And now I have returned,' she said, but struggled to make herself heard above the courtiers who openly gossiped and speculated. Tsen-Baina Jet held up his hand for silence once he was seated and the crowd obeyed.

'My family received word that my sister died while held

captive. It was the letter that told of her passing that broke my father's heart. He did not recover, as you are all aware.'

'I can assure you I am very much alive, little brother,' said Kimi, her voice loud and her anger clear for all to hear.

'You will not address me in such a way,' shouted Tsen, lurching to his feet.

'I am Kimi Enkhtuya of the Jet Tribe, daughter in exile, a political prisoner of the hated Empire.' The courtiers barely hid their shock, to see someone shout back at the Xhan. 'And you are not the boy I left behind five years ago!'

'Take them away,' said Tsen-Baina Jet, with a wave of his hand. 'I will not tolerate such disgusting lies.'

'But your highness,' said Chulu-Agakh. 'I believe she tells the truth. I respectfully—'

'And I believe you should stop speaking, Darga Bestam,' said the Xhan. 'My patience has a limit, and you are not so valuable that you cannot be replaced.'

Kimi looked to Marozvolk in a daze as they were bundled out of the tent by guards.

'He did it,' she whispered in disbelief. 'He killed my father. The rumours are true.'

'And now he's going to kill us,' said Marozvolk. She clenched her jaw in frustration.

'He killed our father,' said Kimi again, her gaze unfocused. 'My little brother . . .'

CHAPTER SEVENTEEN

Silverdust

They did not stay in Steinwick long, much to Silverdust's relief. The soldiers had two days to rest and a cart was purchased for the journey ahead. Silverdust did not leave his room during that time, barely communicating with the soldiers who brought his meals. Streig was noticeably absent and Silverdust poured his meals out of the window. Before long they were leaving the cheerless, smoky town and the garrison of Imperial soldiers who remained there. Envoy de Vries and Father Orlov rode in the cart, along with the supplies.

Silverdust glided along behind the cart. His patience with the Envoy had grown thin and he had no wish to be near Father Orlov. Streig walked alongside the Exarch, while the rest of the soldiers marched ahead of the cart.

I have not seen you recently.

'They kept me busy in Steinwick,' said the soldier. 'It comes from being the youngest in the troop. You get all the shit jobs.'

And am I one of these shit jobs? Streig had taken off his helmet and stowed it on the cart. The expression on his face told Silverdust exactly what he had suspected.

'You're a job no one else wants,' said Streig after pausing a moment to choose his words.

So I am under guard then, on Envoy de Vries' orders?

Streig nodded, his mouth a tight line as if he wanted to say more.

And none of your comrades care to walk beside me keeping watch?

Streig nodded again but said nothing.

So I am indeed the shit job.

'Like there's anything I could do to stop you doing what you wanted.' Streig shook his head and shot a dark look towards Envoy de Vries. 'For all I know you shoot fireballs out of your arse and strangle people with a thought.'

Despite your flippancy you are painfully close to the truth. Except the part about by my nether regions.

Streig laughed with embarrassment and looked away. 'Where the Hel are we, anyway? What is this place?'

They had turned south-east after leaving Steinwick and each long day of travel took them across a barren featureless steppe. The ground was stony and sandy grit swirled around their feet at the wind's insistence. Yellow grasses grew in tufts and small shrubs clung to life through sheer stubbornness. The horizon was always too far away and the sky above them too vast.

This paradise is Novaya Zemlya. The Emperor's so-called 'new land'.

'I've never heard of it,' said Streig. 'We've not seen a single village or town in a week. Not one that had a living soul in it.'

No one comes here because the ground yields no crops. A person needs to eat to raise a house and a family.

'You don't,' said Streig.

I thought we had agreed that my lack of appetite was one of those things you don't ask questions about.

'As you wish,' said Streig, though Silverdust could sense his frustration and the curiosity behind it. The cart had come to a stop a few dozen feet ahead of them. 'You should join us by the fire tonight,' said the young soldier. 'Pretend to sleep if you have to. The soldiers are unsettled by your strange ways and you're attracting attention when it's clear to me you'd rather not.'

You are attentive as always, Streig. I had noticed the very same thing and will do as you say. Besides, I may not need sustenance but conversation is always welcome.

The young soldier gave a small and tightly guarded smile, then sighed with relief. It had been a risk for a lowly soldier to suggest a course of action to a lofty Exarch.

I will not forget this kindness you have done me, Streig.

An uneasy look crossed Streig's face and Silverdust sensed the young soldier's distress.

Why do you keep doing these small, and not so small, kindnesses?

Streig's armour clattered as he shrugged. 'Damned if I know why, but I trust you far more than I trust that Envoy. I don't like her. And I don't like her fancy ways, or the way she talks to us. That's all.'

And the other soldiers?

'They don't care for her either. And not just the Envoy. The older soldiers are tired of the Empire and want a quiet life. The last thing they need is a war with the south.'

Silverdust thought on Streig's words. The men escorting him were unwilling pawns, loyal only by the narrowest of margins. What might it take to undermine that loyalty even further?

Silverdust sat on the ground, though in truth he had no need to sit. The many miles had not tired him, one of the advantages of being dead. The soldiers were sullen and quiet with the Exarch in their midst. They concentrated on their food, only glancing at Silverdust from the corner of their eyes if they dared to glance at all. Father Orlov and the Envoy continued to speak as if nothing had changed. Silverdust watched as a few soldiers sidled up to Streig and asked him what was going on in conspiratorial whispers. Why had the strange and aloof Exarch joined them at the camp fire now, weeks into the journey?

'I don't know,' replied the young soldier. 'You'd have to ask him.'

Food was brought and Silverdust made a show of clutching his stomach.

'Are you not eating tonight, Exarch?' said the Envoy.

I am unwell and my appetite is greatly diminished. I will be fine, it is a passing thing, nothing more.

'And yet you have not joined us on the cart,' said Father Orlov. 'It seems foolish to walk when you are unwell.' He laced his words with concern, but not for one moment did Silverdust believe the man's sincerity. 'You could have told us all about this new power you supposedly have.' Everyone froze around the camp fire. 'This ability to see the dead.' Mumbled conversations between soldiers fell silent and meals were forgotten as all attention turned to Orlov's challenge.

Do I detect a note of disbelief in your tone, Father Orlov? Silverdust projected the words into the minds of everyone present. If this were to be a public duel, then so be it.

'Envoy de Vries asked me not to mention it but it seems to be an open secret among our band of travellers.' None of the soldiers contradicted Father Orlov. Their gazes slipped from the mask with nine stars to Silverdust's expressionless mirror.

Let us speak of open secrets then, Father. Silverdust rose to a standing position. It had been a long time since he had needed to hold the attention of a crowd.

'Please do,' replied Father Orlov.

The light of the fire is a comforting nimbus on this endless steppe. Silverdust turned to look over his shoulder at the darkness beyond. *And yet I see lost souls lingering in the darkness beyond, no more than two dozen feet away. They call to me.*

'Bullshit,' said one of the soldiers. Silverdust caught the Envoy smirking before she covered her mouth with a hand.

The Emperor tired of the Spriggani after the war. He disliked their way of life, hidden in the forests, and he was uncomfortable with their access to the arcane. The Spriggani were rounded up and brought here, to Novaya Zemlya, within a decade of the dragons' defeat.

Silverdust drifted around the outer edge of the circle, half his form illuminated, half lost to darkness.

'And does this ancient history lesson have anything to do with this power you've convinced the Envoy of?' said Father Orlov.

The phantoms I can see beyond the light of our fire are the spirits of dead Spriggani. He felt a deep pang of sympathy for the phantoms, caught between their existence here and what waited beyond. The wind picked up and sent the flames of the camp fire dancing erratically.

'Spriggani?' said Father Orlov. 'Then it's likely they were too lazy to grow crops and died of starvation.' A few of the soldiers chuckled.

Then why do the ghosts I see before me have their throats cut?

Silverdust moved very quickly and clapped a hand down on Father Orlov's shoulder. The Vigilant flinched violently, then sprang to his feet, knife in hand.

Careful now, Father. Envoy de Vries has been entrusted to bring me before the Emperor. It would be unfortunate for her if I died before I reached Khlystburg. Though it would take something altogether more powerful to kill a cinderwraith than a humble knife.

'The Spriggani were vermin,' shouted Father Orlov. He pointed the knife at Silverdust like an accusing finger. 'They were vermin who refused to help the Emperor fight the dragons during the war.'

You speak of open secrets between men who serve the Emperor, but you do not know that long ago the Spriggani also waged a war against the dragons. A quiet war, a war of hit-and-run attacks, of guile – using arcane power the Emperor coveted.

'Careful now, Exarch,' said the Envoy, 'you're painfully close to treason.' Silverdust paused. How badly he wanted to tear down the lies the Empire told and retold, how badly he wanted a glimmer of truth to exist in the hearts of these unwilling and tired soldiers. If even a splinter of doubt troubled them they might ask more questions and find their own answers. Silverdust looked at the faces of the soldiers and felt his anger subside. This was not the time or the place.

The phantoms cannot harm you, though they may wish otherwise. You should all sleep and rest up for the journey ahead. We are still many miles from Khlystburg.

Silverdust drifted away from the fire and pulled a blanket around his shoulders before sitting on the unmoving cart. He kept watch all night, watching the many dead souls mourning for themselves and their cruel fate.

The following day brought a chilly morning of tense silences. At first light, Father Orlov had stalked away from the camp fire to brood and the Envoy had gone after him. They spent long minutes conversing while the soldiers packed up the simple camp and squinted into the distance at the path ahead. Silverdust resumed his place behind the cart, lost to thoughts of dead Spriggani, last night's anger settling about him like a pall. The Envoy barked something at the soldiers as she took her place on the cart and Streig slunk towards Silverdust, a frown set on his face.

You slept well?

'Of course not,' said Streig. 'None of us did. Spent the whole night thinking about the ghosts of murdered Spriggani wanting to strangle us in our sleep.' They travelled in silence for a while until the cart drew ahead of them taking de Vries and Orlov beyond earshot.

'I take back what I said about you not wanting to attract attention,' said the young soldier. 'You seem to like attention as much as the next man, but your performance last night didn't win you any friends.'

The fate of the Spriggani people is a subject that is close to my . . . Silverdust paused. He hadn't had a heart for a very long time, he was as much a phantom as the ones that haunted Novaya Zemlya.

'How do you know so much about them?' asked Streig. 'And how do you know so much about the war?'

Can I trust you to keep my secrets though I angered you last night?

Streig thought on it for a moment. 'Of course,' he replied, though his expression remained sullen.

I myself am a Spriggani, though it has been decades since I lived among them. I lived through the Age of Fire when the war with the dragons could be felt in every province, and it seemed every family had lost someone to the claws or teeth of those terrible creatures.

'As if the Emperor would allow a Spriggani child to rise through the ranks of the Holy Synod.' Streig shook his head. 'I'm beginning to think you're full of shit. Seeing ghosts that no one else can see? Come on, stop gaming with me.'

Things were different during the Age of Fire. The Emperor merely resented the Spriggani mastery over the arcane. He coveted that mastery, hoped it would be what the world needed to save the lives of men. Humans were almost wiped out during the Time of Tears and it was only when the dragons started making war between themselves that people had a chance to regain their strength, their numbers.

'I'd heard that before,' admitted Streig. They travelled the lonely steppe in silence for a time but Silverdust could feel the young soldier's curiosity increase with every heartbeat.

What else do you want to know?

'Is what you said really true? About this place and the Spriggani?' Silverdust nodded and cast his mind back to that time, though it pained him to do so.

My people were always blessed by the power of the goddesses. The Emperor gleaned enough about the arcane from a small number of sympathetic Spriggani to make a difference in his war against the dragons. Once the dragons were defeated he turned his fury on those Spriggani who had denied him aid. A number which chiefly counted the followers of Frøya and Frejna, which is why those religions are now proscribed. Almost every Spriggani in Vinterkveld was brought here by Imperial soldiers, including my family, though I didn't know it at the time. The Emperor told them that as thanks for the help he had received, they would have their own province, but few believed him. When they reached this place they found entire regiments of soldiers with eager knives. Those who did not die on the first day spent the next week digging shallow graves for themselves and their kin. They died in their hundreds and just as the killing ended, more Spriggani were brought from other provinces. No one knows how many were killed. No exact tally exists. Their tale was never told.

'Why didn't the priesthoods of Frøya and Frejna simply share their secrets with the Emperor?' said Streig, trying to make sense of what he was being told. 'They all wanted the same thing, surely? An end to the dragons.'

Because the wisest of the Spriggani, the priestesses of Frøya and Frejna, had looked into the heart of the Emperor and seen only darkness. This is why all right-thinking Spriggani refused to teach him the ways of the goddesses. In time their instinct proved true. The Emperor cut ties with the goddesses. He found a way to draw the power of the arcane from the dragons instead, becoming the very thing he had fought against for all those long years.

'So the Emperor is a liar and hypocrite?' said Streig.

And many more things besides. Khlystburg is the most dangerous place in Vinterkveld, and all because the person who rules there will do anything to hold onto power.

'And you have to give evidence to him.'

I do.

Streig looked at the Exarch and Silverdust could feel his

dread like a sickness. 'Even if you persuade him you're innocent of the things Father Orlov is saying about you . . .' The young soldier rubbed his stubbled chin with a calloused hand, then shook his head.

Even if I persuade the Emperor of my innocence, I may yet still perish. This is the Empire you are serving, Streig. It is an Empire of old lies and new violence.

'We need to think of a way to keep you alive,' said the young soldier. Silverdust would have smiled had he still had a mouth. The soldier's regard for him was a pleasant reprieve from the endless suspicion of the Holy Synod.

I simply desire to look the Emperor in the eye one last time.

Silverdust kept his true intention to himself; he had no need for conspirators just yet.

CHAPTER EIGHTEEN

Steiner

The trek east through the forest gave them a measure of shelter from the elements and prying eyes, but the even the company of brigands and Nils' near-permanent cheerfulness couldn't keep Steiner's fears at bay. He was restless with his need to be in Slavon Province, desperate to discover where Felgenhauer was hiding. He'd convinced himself that it was her power he needed to make the uprising take hold.

'Less cold this morning,' said Einar, falling into step beside Steiner and Kristofine.

'The seasons are on the turn,' she agreed. 'Back in Nordvlast we wouldn't see spring for another month at least.'

'So this Felgenhauer . . .' Einar glanced at Steiner from his one good eye. 'You have any idea how to find her once you're in Slavon Province?'

Steiner released a slow breath, not quite a sigh. Kristofine, sensing his anxiety, took his hand in hers and gave a reassuring squeeze.

'Truthfully, I don't,' said Steiner. 'I'm hoping fortune will smile upon us but I'm more concerned she'll have moved on elsewhere before we arrive. This hike across the country is taking forever.'

'If you know a faster way then by all means, let's hear it.' Marek had joined them and answered in his usual no-nonsense fashion that did little to ease Steiner's fears.

'I'm just saying is all,' snapped Steiner. Father and son shared a hard look, neither caring much for what they saw.

'I understand that she's a powerful Vigilant—' began Kristofine.

'Renegade Vigilant,' interrupted Steiner.

'But *why* are you so keen to track her down?' A brief frown crossed Kristofine's face. 'Can we trust her?'

'Kristofine has a point,' said Marek. 'Felgenhauer always played her cards close to her chest. We don't know what to expect when we reach Slavon Province.'

'She kept me safe on Vladibogdan,' replied Steiner, feeling his irritation building. 'That's why she's wanted by the Emperor, because of me.'

'Renegade or not,' said Marek, 'we don't know for sure we can trust her.'

'She's my aunt.' Steiner had raised his voice a bit and a few of the brigands turned their head on instinct. 'I don't have too much family left since we lost Verner. And now Kjell's in Shanisrond . . .'

None of them had spoken of Kjellrunn since leaving the port. He hoped fiercely that he would find her in a Shanisrond town under the protective gaze of Mistress Kamalov and Sundra when all this was done.

Kristofine released his hand and picked up the pace, storming ahead of them until she fell into step with Nils and a few other brigands.

Steiner stared after her with a puzzled frown. 'What's got into her?'

'Oh, I don't know,' said Marek. 'Maybe it's that she lost her mother just over a year ago. Or maybe it's because she left her father behind in Nordvlast.'

'That's hardly the same,' said Steiner. 'He suspected her of witchsign. He barely spoke to her while I was on the island.'

'She has no one, Steiner,' said Marek, looking about as stern as Steiner had ever seen him. 'No one but you.'

Steiner's anger drained out of him. 'I didn't think of that.'

Einar, who had listened to all of this, leaned close to Steiner and spoke in a soft rumble. 'Would you hear something from an old man? Something that might help?'

Steiner nodded. He could use all the help he could get and wasn't too proud to admit it.

'No one likes to be taken for granted,' said Einar. 'And you've a fine woman there who's following you to the ends of the earth—'

'Slavon Province is hardly—'

'But it feels like it,' said Einar, holding up one finger. 'To her, having lived in Cinderfell her whole life, every step must feel like a step into a different life.'

Steiner felt like a child again, embarrassed for what he didn't know and angry for not learning it sooner. 'What do I do?'

'Let her know that she's appreciated,' replied Einar. 'I don't know many people who turn away from that. We all need kindness just as the crops need sunshine and rain.'

Steiner approached Kristofine when they stopped to eat their meagre lunch. She was sitting with Nils who looked delighted at having such attractive company.

'I'm sorry about before,' said Steiner as he sat down, not quite able to look her in the eye. Kristofine looked at him blankly.

'Is that it? That's the full extent of your apology?'

'Maybe I should go and check on the horses,' said Nils, standing up, keen to be away.

'We don't have any horses,' said Kristofine.

'Just in case,' replied Nils and left the couple alone.

'I'm sorry,' repeated Steiner. 'I didn't think how hard all of this must be for you. The strange thing is, well, you seem to be doing better at this than I am. You seem more, I don't know, confident?'

'I'm not under the same pressure as you,' she replied. 'But I'm right here, Steiner, without family, without home or work. Most days I barely know which way is north. All I have is you. You're my north. And when you behave like a—'

'Whining arsehole.'

'Not my first choice of words,' she replied, but for a moment her stony anger slipped and a smile appeared on her lips. They sat together and ate for a time, chewing slowing, thinking over what had been said and what still might need to be said.

'I feel so out of my depth,' he said at last.

'Maybe you should stop trying to do everything by yourself. I know you're "Steiner the Unbroken" now but you're just one man. Every man I've ever met needed friends. Every woman too for that matter.'

He slipped his fingers into her palm, hoping she wouldn't snatch it away. They entwined their fingers and shared a moment of just looking at each other, seeing each other a little more clearly.

The brigands were not half as dangerous as Steiner had imagined them to be. For every cut-throat and ne'er-do-well among them, there were two men who simply wished to remain hidden from the Empire.

'How did you come to live like this?' said Steiner to Nils later that day as they picked their way through the silent forest, breath steaming on the air.

'The old story.' Nils' usual smile slipped, replaced by a more reflective expression. 'They took my daughter. Said she had the taint of witchsign.' He gave a resigned shrug. 'My wife never recovered from the loss. Three years to the day after the Empire took my daughter . . .' Nils sighed. 'Three years to the day, that's when my wife left me. There was no big argument or fight. We simply became strangers to each other in the months that followed. I don't know where she went. She was my last link to a normal life. I'd already lost my job, and my friends had long since stopped calling.'

'I'm sorry,' said Steiner. 'My sister has witchsign too.'

'Einar's story is much the same,' added Nils. 'The Empire doesn't just steal children, it destroys families, friendships, marriages.' Nils was quiet a moment. 'It's not enough to whisper in dark taverns about rebellion, Steiner. Someone has to kill the Emperor, someone has to break him down.' Nils stared at the sledgehammer. 'Tell me you'll kill him, dragon rider. Tell me you'll smash his black soul with your great hammer.' Steiner thought about his duel on the beach at Cinderfell with Shirinov. It had nearly killed him just to defeat one Vigilant, and he'd had the Ashen Torment at his command.

'I'll try,' replied Steiner. 'I'll try for all of us.'

Nils looked at the boy with the hammer, grimaced, then stalked away to be alone.

The forest thinned out and eventually the brigands were marching across open grasslands again. The mountains rose in the distance, wreathed in mist and capped with snow. The mountain pass, invisible at first, became more apparent beneath them with every mile.

'There's your problem,' said Einar when they had stopped to catch their breath. They were well past the foothills now. The ground was rocky underfoot and the wind spiteful cold. The brigand's leader pointed to a small point of flickering light in the distance.

'What it is?' asked Steiner, squinting to see better.

'A garrison of soldiers. They'll have a few questions for you, I imagine.' Einar gave a humourless smile. 'And like any soldier at a border, they'll want a few coins for the brief pleasure of their company.'

'What?' Steiner frowned.

'A bribe!' said Einar. 'Frøya's teeth, but you're naive.'

'Never had any soldiers to bribe in Nordvlast,' said Marek by way of explanation and Steiner felt less foolish for it.

'True enough,' said Einar. 'Not much of anything in Nordvlast except snow.'

'I can't argue with that,' replied Marek.

'I don't care too much for bribing soldiers,' said Steiner. They didn't have so much coin that Steiner was willing to part with it for soldiers. And they'd no doubt see the sledge-hammer and that would lead to some difficult questions. 'We'll have to find a way to sneak past them.'

'Did you not hear me?' Einar jerked a thumb towards the garrison. 'It's a mountain pass. Only one way through.' Nils said nothing, but stared at the pass as if it were a personal affront.

'I guess we could do things the old-fashioned way,' said Steiner, looking at his sledgehammer meaningfully. 'We'll have the advantage of surprise if we do it right.'

Nils grinned. 'I like the way the dragon rider thinks. We take the fight to the black-hearted bastards.'

'The dragon rider is going to get himself killed,' said Kristofine with a frown.

'I'm not paying Imperial soldiers for the privilege of being searched and arrested because I'm carrying this.' He held up the sledgehammer. 'Besides, it's not like we can sneak past.'

'She has a point though,' said Einar, rubbing at his band-aged eye. 'We're hardly at fighting strength.' He looked over his band of men. All were gaunt with hunger and ragged from a life outdoors.

'The garrison will have food,' said Steiner. 'And it will be a few days before a new patrol comes. You can rest up and get fat at the Empire's expense.'

Nils gave a low chuckle. 'Tell us more.' At least half the brigands crowded in a little closer to hear Steiner out.

'We'll need to attack in a few different places at the same time to cause confusion,' said Steiner.

'And we need to get someone scaling the walls,' added Marek. 'Get someone inside. All this will be for naught if they bar the doors and wait us out.'

'This will be a raid worthy of a great song!' said Nils with a wild glint in his eye.

'It has to be a fight,' said Steiner to Kristofine. 'We can't talk our way through this one.'

Kristofine nodded. 'Fine. We do it your way.' She shook her head. 'Just don't get yourself killed.'

'I like being alive just fine, I promise you,' he replied.

'This plan had best be good, dragon rider,' said Einar and Steiner looked towards the pass and set to thinking.

'I can't make this plan alone,' he said. 'So I'm open to suggestions.'

The Empire took no chances with security and the garrison was no exception. A sturdy stone gatehouse blocked the pass with wooden doors twice the height of a man, studded with black iron. The walls were twenty feet high with battlements lining the top. The Empire had done their best to clear as many trees as they could, but ancient pines crowded the treacherous slopes above the pass.

Marek carried a lantern and walked down the middle of the pass right up to the garrison's gates, singing an old soldier's song in Solska with a rough and deep baritone. The two soldiers standing guard on the battlements took notice and ceased their pacing to watch the stranger approach, leaning over the walls to get a better look.

'I don't like this,' whispered Kristofine beside Steiner. They were hiding behind an outcropping of rock just a hundred feet from the gatehouse.

'No one likes it,' said Nils. The man jigged from foot to foot with impatience, barely bothering to hide. 'Stay back if you're scared. Boil up some water and prepare some bandages. We might have need of them.'

Kristofine scowled but Marek made the sign before she could reply. The old blacksmith raised the lantern above his head and many things happened simultaneously. The brigands hiding at the base of the walls threw up their ropes and nooses, snaring the patrolling soldiers. Marek had guided them with subtle gestures on his approach. Four men threw ropes, but only two made their targets. The soldiers wrapped in rope struggled in shock and Steiner sprinted along the road from his hiding place, sledgehammer tucked into his belt, a length of rope in his hand.

The brigands on the left succeeded in hauling their lassoed soldier, dragging him over the battlements. The soldier had enough time to cry out but was quickly silenced by the fall. The remaining soldier could not call out; the rope had snared his throat. He fought and staggered and writhed as the brigands below tugged and heaved, but against all odds the soldier would not be dragged from the wall. Steiner reached the gatehouse doors and threw his own rope high. The noose fell around a battlement and he climbed up, pulling hard and grunting with the effort.

The snared soldier finally cut through the rope around his neck with a knife, though he was half dead with the effort. Marek, still haloed by the lantern light, gave a low whistle and pointed to the half-strangled soldier. A heartbeat later two arrow shafts appeared, one protruding from the soldier's neck, the other from his shoulder. He stiffened in shock and sank to his knees. Steiner was on him in seconds, finishing the man with his knife, quickly and quietly in the dying evening light.

Nils followed Steiner up the rope. The brigand waited in the shadow of the battlements, crossbow held close to his body. Einar was next, followed by Marek and more and more of the brigands.

Steiner stared down into the courtyard from the shadows of the battlement edge, some three hundred feet long and fifty feet wide. Many of the soldiers were at their evening meal, gathered together in a long hall at the side of the court-yard. It was a low building made from logs, and stables had been built on the opposite side of the courtyard. Steiner eased himself over the side of the gatehouse wall and slipped over the edge, rolling when he hit the ground, feet stinging, knees aching. A curse escaped his lips. He ran towards the stable bent low, waiting for someone to call out, dreading the moment an arrow might suddenly appear, protruding from his chest. Fortune favoured him and he slipped behind the stable, shielded from view, then took a moment to catch his breath and wrestle the hammer from his belt. Smells of straw and dung lay heavy on the air and Steiner ran on towards the wall ahead of him, sparing a glance over his shoulder. The two archers kept watch over the pass, one at each end wall, huddling beside braziers.

Einar and Nils snuck up to the hall unseen. The other brigands were dark shadows sliding across the courtyard and for a moment Steiner was reminded of the cinderwraiths on Vladibogdan.

'Here's your uprising, Kimi,' he whispered through gritted teeth. 'This will surely get the Emperor's attention.'

Steiner raced up the steps at the eastern wall and had almost reached the top when the soldier saw him scaling the stairs. Steiner pressed on, knowing his opponent had the advantage of higher ground even as the soldier raised his mace.

Something whistled past Steiner's shoulder, shockingly close. There was a sound of metal on metal as the soldier's head snapped back. Nils' crossbow had found its mark. Steiner lunged forward, grasping his sledgehammer at either end. He rammed the shaft across the soldier's chest, shoving him backwards until he had slammed the man over the battlements. The soldier reached out to him as he fell and hit the ground with a dull crump. A look back to the courtyard revealed Nils reloading his crossbow. The brigand grinned and saluted, then gestured to the last soldier on the eastern wall, just sixty feet away. To Steiner's surprise the soldier lay down his weapon and removed his helmet. He wasn't much older than Steiner, his eyes wide with fright, sweating in fear.

'No trouble,' said the soldier in heavily accented Nordspråk.

'No trouble,' agreed Steiner in Solska.

The hall was now ablaze and Einar and Nils had blocked the door with a heavy crate. Smoke tumbled from the windows and soldiers tried to escape only to be cut down by the brigands waiting outside. They were brutish scraps, crude fights, fought with daggers and wild panic. Some of the soldiers were on fire as they fought to be free of the hall.

Steiner looked to his father. He was no longer carrying the lantern he had lit just minutes earlier. The hall burned and the howls of dying men subsided as the heat and ash took them one by one. Steiner felt tears prickle at the corners of his eyes. He told himself it was the smoke and not the screams that made it so.

'Come down to the courtyard,' said Steiner to the young soldier. 'Lose the knife.' The young soldier did as he was told, eyes fixed on the burning hall and the many corpses in the courtyard.

'The dragon rider is victorious!' bellowed Nils, holding his arms out to the heavens. Steiner couldn't tear his eyes away from the hall as the fire continued to roar. The roof collapsed inward and the brigands roared in triumph as a shower of fiery cinders rose up into the night sky.

A burning soldier emerged from the hall and made it a dozen feet across the courtyard before collapsing. The stench of burning flesh was overpowering.

'Why did they have to burn them?' asked Kristofine. She appeared from the gloom ashen-faced and glassy-eyed.

'It wasn't part of my plan,' said Steiner quietly. 'But I suppose one death is much like another.'

Kristofine stared at the still-burning corpse of the soldier. 'What have we done here?'

CHAPTER NINETEEN

Kimi

Kimi and Marozvolk were tied and gagged following their visit to the Xhantsulgarat on the orders of the Xhan himself. They spent a miserable afternoon in a damp tent waiting to see just how cruel Tsen-Baina Jet could be. A lone guard stood watch, no more than twenty years old with a soft, downy moustache that only served to emphasise his youth. The guard ignored them when he could and looked about as guilty as person could be when he couldn't.

'You know I am who I say I am, don't you?' said Kimi, testing her bonds for the fiftieth time that afternoon.

The guard shrugged. 'I was barely fifteen when they took the princess away. You could be anyone, an imposter with nothing to lose.' He had a point, she had nothing to lose but her life, and it seemed her own brother might be the one to take it.

'And nothing I can say will convince you?'

'I don't need convincing,' said the youth. 'Anyone with eyes can see you're a princess. It's in the way you walk.'

'So why not free me?'

The guard turned away. 'Your own brother poisoned his father. There's no telling what he'd do to the likes of me if I disobey him.'

'Shit,' snarled Marozvolk. 'We came all the way across Vinterkveld for this?'

The Darga of Bestam came for them after dark, stealing into the tent with a handful of men who wore scarves over their faces.

'You,' said Chulu-Agakh to the guard, 'tell His Highness that this one is a witch and used her powers on you.' He pointed to Marozvolk. The guard looked at him, his expression unconvinced.

'What are you talking about? Used her powers on me?'

'I'm taking the princess and her friend away from here,' said Chulu-Agakh.

The soldier opened his mouth to protest, took a long, guilty look at Kimi, and then decided to leave the tent.

'If anyone asks, you're my prisoners,' said Chulu-Akagh as he pulled Kimi to her feet. 'We don't have much time.'

They walked through Bestam in the deep quiet of the small hours, when all the camp fires were merely embers and the tribespeople dreamed of fat herds and fine weather. Kimi followed the Darga until she could hear water lapping against the riverbank. A flat-bottomed boat waited for them in the light of the crescent moon. Marozvolk followed behind, her expression unreadable, mouth spilt apart by the gag.

'Trust me, this is the safest place for you.' Chulu-Agakh led them onto the boat and sat them down. 'You're due to be killed come the morning, so I had to act quickly.' He untied their wrists and the women removed their gags.

'What?' Kimi could barely believe what she was hearing.

'The Xhan is not taking any chances. A few people said they recognised you. Rumours are already circulating at court.' Chulu-Agakh poled the boat away from the shore.

'I don't understand,' said Kimi. 'The heir to the throne is always the son. I can't challenge his authority. I'm no threat to his rule.'

'Your merely being alive has raised a few questions about your brother's honesty, Your Highness.'

'There was never any letter,' said Marozvolk, curling her lip in disgust. 'The Empire wouldn't send a letter revealing that they'd killed a political prisoner.'

'I spoke with a few of the courtiers who were loyal to your father,' said Chulu-Agakh, looking back to the shore to check they had left unseen. 'None recall seeing such a letter.'

'Tsen was always very adept at telling stories,' said Kimi quietly, looking out over the endless inky darkness of the river. 'But I never thought him capable of such ruthlessness. I'd hoped that family trait had died with my father.' A coldness was spreading through her that had little to do with the chill of night. She pressed a hand to her mouth to stifle her disappointment.

'All I can give you now is your life,' said Chulu-Agakh, 'though it may cost me my own.'

'Where are Tief and Taiga?' said Marozvolk.

'They were supposed to meet us at the boat,' said the Darga. 'But it is possible that your brother arrested them.'

Kimi thought of Taiga's smile. Of Tief's grin. Their group had already been torn apart because of her.

'Take me back,' said Kimi, feeling both conviction and anger awakening inside herself.

'I cannot do that,' said Chulu-Agakh calmly.

'What will happen to them?' pressed Marozvolk.

'I'll do what I can to make sure they don't come to harm, but Tsen is hardly a temperate Xhan.' The boat crept across the inky darkness of the river, heavy breathing the only sound as Chulu-Agakh struggled to fight the current and navigate by the stars.

'Hand it over, old man,' said Kimi.

'Your highness?' The Darga looked confused.

'The pole.' Kimi took it from him. 'I'm more than capable

of crossing this river by myself. It's been a long day and you're tiring.'

Chulu-Agakh chuckled. 'Far be it for me to disobey the orders of a princess.' The Darga took a seat in the boat and soon he was nodding off.

Kimi looked back towards the southern bank of the river, but there was nothing there. No country, no father, no brother, just an implacable darkness that swallowed everything. She sobbed quietly as she poled the boat across the river. Marozvolk and Chulu-Agahk pretended to sleep or not to hear, which was just what she needed.

'We drifted more than I would have liked,' said Chulu-Agakh come the morning. He had awoken earlier and taken another shift poling the boat, much against Kimi's wishes. 'But you can take shelter at the edge of the forest tonight.' He pulled the boat up onto the shore and slung a few bags on the yellow grass where it was dry. 'There's food, water skins, clothes, and a cloak for each of you,' he added as he caught his breath. 'I thought a tent would be too much to carry.'

Kimi reached out and laid a hand gently on his shoulder. 'Thank you.'

'I revered the old Xhan very much,' said the Darga. 'He was a good man, though not much of a father if I am to judge him by your brother's actions.' Kimi felt a flare of indignation, then realised the anger she felt wasn't for Chulu-Agakh alone.

'You're right,' she admitted. 'He was a terrible father. He lost interest in us altogether after our mother died. Tsen must have felt truly abandoned after I was taken by the Empire.'

'That's a poor reason for wanting you dead,' said Marozvolk, sounding weary.

'He knew I'd call him out for killing our father.'

'It is for the best there is no proof,' said Chulu-Agakh. 'Think no more on this place, your highness. Head north and

take a ship to Shanisrond.' He looked back across the river.
'I must return. May the goddesses keep you, Kimi Enkhtuya.'

They watched the old Darga guide the boat back across the
river for a time and Kimi struggled to believe how things had
gone so wrong, so quickly.

'I should have strangled your brother when we were in the
tent,' said Marozvolk. Kimi couldn't miss the bitterness in
the woman's voice.

'And I'd be the princess who had her brother killed
in order to seize the throne. I'd be no better than Tsen.' She
shook her head. 'We head north.'

'You said only fools try to cross Izhoria.' Marozvolk didn't
look afraid, just angry. Kimi envied her; all she could feel was
bleak desolation.

'We can die over there in Yamal,' said Kimi, looking across
the river, 'with Taiga and Tief, or we can die here.'

'I'd rather not give your brother the satisfaction,' said
Marozvolk. They turned away from the river and began
marching north towards the forest. The forge of Vladibogdan
had made Kimi hard, but she had not walked so many miles
in years. Her body ached in response to the distance they
covered but her mind remained numb. In the space of a
single day she had lost everything. They travelled together
in silence all morning and it was only when the pair reached
the edge of the forest that Marozvolk spoke.

'You look terrible. We should eat something hot.'

'I'm fine. I just need to catch my breath is all.' Kimi removed
her pack and let it fall to her feet.

'I'll get wood for a fire,' said Marozvolk. 'Stay here, you're
dead on your feet.' Kimi nodded and sat down without a word.

Marozvolk slipped out of the forest a while later with
enough wood for a small fire. 'It seems we've gained some
friends,' she said, nodding towards the horizon. Two figures
could just be seen in the distance coming from the south.

'I can't see at this distance.' Kimi shook her head. 'Who are they?'

'Your brother wants you dead,' said Marozvolk. 'Perhaps these are your assassins.'

'We'll eat later,' said Kimi, grabbing her pack and heading into the forest, keen to avoid the approaching strangers. Marozvolk caught up with her and they hurried past the trunks of dead trees that were like slumbering giants on the forest floor.

'I'm beginning to wish we'd signed on with Romola,' muttered Marozvolk. Kimi ignored her, heading onward with a hard expression and firm stride.

'Kimi!'

'Not now, Marozvolk. I'm not in the mood to talk and—'

'Don't move!'

Kimi stopped and stared at Marozvolk. 'There are assassins coming for us and you want to stand around talking?' Kimi followed Marozvolk's gaze. Something was moving in the gloom of the forest a few paces ahead, something low that walked on four legs. There was an awkward motion to the creature's gait and it stepped forward slowly into the dappled light.

'It's just a wolf,' said Kimi, squinting ahead. 'They rarely attack people. Besides, this one looks old and starved. It looks half dead.'

Marozvolk drew her sword and the wolf began growling. 'It's not just half dead,' she whispered. The creature stepped further into the light. Parts of the fur had rotted away and rancid muscles and sinews showed where the skin had parted. The eyes were missing, the sockets crusted with blood. Black lips pulled back in a snarl from teeth that were brown and yellow and cracked.

Kimi drew her own sword with a shaking hand when another growl sounded behind them. Marozvolk flinched and her skin turned a stony grey on instinct.

'We're surrounded,' said Kimi as a third wolf slunk from the trees to her left. The second wolf leapt at Marozvolk. Kimi turned just in time to see Marozvolk's sword slip through the creature's chest even as her friend crashed to the ground underneath the pouncing wolf. Kimi dodged backwards, watching another of the rotting creatures pass in front of her as a third wolf pounced on her back. Only the hood of her cloak stopped the creature's shattered teeth from ripping into her neck. The weight of the animal forced her to her knees and she gripped her blade with both hands, stabbing wildly over her shoulder. Marozvolk was writhing underneath her attacker, her blade stuck fast in the creature's ribcage. The wolf savaged her throat but her stony skin refused to yield. Kimi tried to stand but the wolf on her back bit down again; the cloak's hood continued to stick in its jaws. The last creature had turned and prepared to lunge and Kimi struck out as best she could. The bright metal caught the creature across the face, shearing one ear from its rotting head. The wolf shook itself and growled more loudly.

Marozvolk had released her sword and settled for punching her attacker in the snout with granite fists. She held the creature by its throat and pummeled the wolf's face, knocking out teeth with the force of her blows. Kimi envied the woman her impervious skin and feared she wouldn't last much longer, outnumbered as she was.

The wolf with the missing ear lunged again and Kimi fell on her side to avoid being bitten. The creature on her back withdrew a moment and struggled to its feet just as another wolf stepped out of the darkness to join them. The newcomer was larger than the rest by a handspan, the fur more mangy, the scent of death strong. It bore the same gouged eyes as its kin and stared with hollow sockets at the two women fighting for their lives.

'Frøya save us,' said Marozvolk as she stood up. The wolf's

teeth marks were white scratches on the dark stone of her throat. The undead wolf lay at her feet, its skull mashed to rotten pulp by her granite fists. 'Watch out!' said Marozvolk, ripping her sword out of the creature's corpse to the sound of snapping ribs.

The largest of the wolves dashed forward and Kimi grasped the hilt of her sword with both hands, swiping upwards and catching the creature in the shoulder. But the wolf's momentum carried it forward, crashing into Kimi, knocking her down. Another of the wolves had clamped onto Marozvolk's arm and was snarling furiously, even as another was circling.

A flash of light and Tief and Taiga rushed to their sides, wielding flaming torches, grim expressions on their faces. The undead wolves snarled but came no closer and even the largest of them backed off into deeper shadows. Kimi was speechless to see them again.

'They're called Grave Wolves,' panted Tief. The smaller wolves were circling a dozen feet away, growling low. 'Or Sombre Wolves if you're feeling poetic.'

'We thought you'd been captured!' said Marozvolk, breathless with shock.

'Can't say I care for it,' said Tief. 'Not again. Gave them the slip.'

'What happens now?' said Kimi as she struggled to her feet. Despite everything she flashed her friends a smile. The largest of the Grave Wolves followed, its hollow eye sockets seemingly fixed on the flames. Black lips pulled back in a dire snarl.

'We back out of the forest slowly,' said Taiga. 'Stay near the fire and do not run, no matter how bad things get.' Kimi and Marozvolk did as they were told and the largest of the Grave Wolves let out an unearthly howl.

'There's one behind us,' whispered Taiga. She turned to face the new threat, thrusting the flaming torch towards its face. The largest of them continued to follow, one rotting paw following the other. Others followed, more Grave Wolves joining their number from the depths of the forest. Kimi counted five and her sword arm shook in terror.

'Steady now,' said Tief, sensing her panic. 'Hold up your sword and show them you aren't going down easy. You can bet your boots they can taste fear, so don't give them any.' Marozvolk broke ranks and surged past Taiga towards the edge of the forest. She impaled the wolf behind them through the head, the tip of her sword sinking deep just below the creature's eye socket. She punched down with her free hand, once, twice, three times until the creature's skull came apart. The other wolves growled and the leader howled once more.

'We're almost there,' said Taiga. 'The edge of the forest is close by. Almost there.'

The trees around them thinned as they stepped into the midday light – and out of the forest. The largest Grave Wolf snarled at his pack and slunk back into the woods. A few, more persistent wolves followed for a time, but all turned away as Taiga and Marozvolk stumbled out from beneath the trees, back onto the grasslands of Izhoria.

'Why didn't you wait for us earlier!' breathed Tief, rounding on the Yamali women. 'I ran to you – I was trying to warn you.'

'Earlier?' replied Kimi. 'What do you mean?'

'We were coming to meet you. Chulu-Agakh's brother brought us across the river in his boat but we couldn't find you.'

'We didn't know you were coming,' said Marozvolk, understanding dawning on her face. 'We did see you, but we couldn't see who you were.'

'So you took off into a forest full of Grave Wolves?'

'Go easy on them, Tief,' said Taiga, collapsing on the ground. 'It's been a long couple of days for everyone. Go easy.'

'Why on earth did you go into the forest?' he said, stamping out the flaming torch.

'My brother is telling everyone that I'm an impostor,' shouted Kimi, returning his anger in kind. 'We thought you were his men, we thought you were assassins.' Tief and Taiga looked at one another. The shock of battle and Tief's anger ebbed away until finally Taiga spoke.

'Your own brother?'

'He pretended not to recognise me,' said Kimi with tears in her eyes. 'But I could see he knew me. And the moment he turned his back I knew, I just knew, that my life as a Yamali princess was over.'

'What do we do now?' said Tief.

'We go to Shanisrond and meet up with Mistress Kamalov and Kjellrunn,' said Marozvolk.

'No,' said Kimi. 'I'm heading north. I can't depend on Steiner to create this uprising alone. I'm going to Khlystburg to kill the Emperor before he can hurt my people.'

'You're a little late for that,' said Marozvolk. 'Your brother seems to be doing a fine job.'

'Tsen won't wipe out our entire people with armies from the north. The Emperor wouldn't think twice about it.'

'I'm not going back to Khlystburg,' said Marozvolk. Her anger wavered and fear shone brightly in her eyes.

'Then I won't ask you,' said Kimi. 'But I have to do this thing, though I've no idea how I'll do it.'

'We'll think of something,' said Tief.

'Anywhere he goes I go,' added Taiga.

Marozvolk looked at each of them and shook her head. 'We'll all die long before we cross this infernal country,' she muttered before setting off at a march, putting distance between herself and the others.

CHAPTER TWENTY

Kjellrunn

The high priestess had insisted that Kjellrunn and Maxim join her on the temple steps the dawn after the slavers' attack. In the early morning, Sundra had read a short passage from a tiny, battered black book concerned chiefly with the tenets of Frejna.

'Just as Frøya prepares and nurtures us for life, so Frejna prepares and nurtures us for death. Just as Frøya gives us spring, summer, and new life, so Frejna ushers in autumn, winter, and an end to days.'

Maxim fidgeted on the step and Kjellrunn slipped an arm around his shoulders.

'Is it always so . . .' Kjellrunn struggled to find the words.

'Yes?' said Sundra with a patient expression, not quite a smile.

'Is it always so full of death?' she said. Maxim sighed as if relieved she'd asked the very question he'd not been able to form.

'These are catechisms,' explained Sundra, seating herself on the temple steps. 'The priestess calls out the first part of the sentence, and the congregation replies with the latter part.' Sundra poured tea from a kettle that was as black and battered as the tiny book she had read from. 'But it has been a long time since people gathered in such numbers to revere Frejna.' Kjellrunn caught the note of sadness in the old woman's words. 'The Spriggani, specifically those who revere Frejna, live each day knowing they will die, and use it as a focus—'

'That sounds depressing,' mumbled Maxim, staring into his tea bowl with a forlorn look.

'The Spriggani use it as a focus, to consider what consequences may occur, to be grateful for the present moment, to not linger in the past regretting events that cannot be changed.'

'I'd have to agree with Maxim,' said Kjellrunn. 'It does sound bleak.'

'It is merely a different way of thinking,' said Sundra, laying one hand on top of Kjellrunn's own. 'It is this difference that makes the Emperor nervous. He, more than anyone else in history, takes great pains not to think about death unless it is someone else's.'

They chatted quietly for a time of small things, before seeking out breakfast while Sundra delegated tasks around the temple. This became the routine in the two weeks that followed. Kjellrunn had loathed the early mornings at first, but now she was glad when Maxim knocked softly on her door and enjoyed the simple pleasure of greeting Sundra each daybreak. Maxim often sat beside her on the steps, so closely that it was churlish not to put an arm around his shoulders. There was a deep peace on the temple steps before the other novices woke and Mistress Kamalov started shouting orders.

'It is better to die on your feet than to die on your knees,' said Sundra, reading an aphorism from the black book. It was early morning, long before the midday heat of Shanisrond stifled the sprawling town of Dos Khor.

'I'm not sure dying on your feet is so great either,' said

Maxim. 'I'd rather keep out of harm's way altogether.' The boy said this so earnestly that Kjellrunn laughed and Sundra allowed herself a smile. The high priestess smiled a little more every day now that they were ashore and colour had returned to her cheeks.

'And what happens when harm comes looking for you?' asked Sundra. Maxim shrugged and sipped his tea.

'Mistress Kamalov came to speak to me yesterday,' he said. Kjellrunn had the feeling this wasn't so much a change of subject as a continuation of a theme.

'And what did she have to say for herself?' replied Sundra, holding her tea bowl in front of her face with both hands. She looked over the bowl's rim with a guarded expression. The two women had rarely come into contact with each other over the last two weeks, other than when it seemed absolutely necessary. Kjellrunn had noted the subtle game they played, making excuses to be elsewhere where the other appeared, or busying themselves with a task so as not to have to give the other attention.

Mistress Kamalov had taken up the role of organising the children with a vast rota of cooking, sweeping, laundry, and now paying jobs in the town itself.

'Some of the older children have found work in the town. They're bringing money back for food and so on.' Maxim looked from Sundra to Kjellrunn, sensing something occurring beyond the possibility of his employment. 'And she asked me when I might also work.'

'Did she now.' Sundra drank her tea and sighed. 'You'd think with sixteen novices at her beck and call she could spare me one pair of hands.'

'I told her I was only eleven and I promised Tief that I would look after you.' Maxim looked to Sundra, clearly hoping for confirmation this had been the right thing to say.

'Vigilants,' sighed Sundra, after a pause, and clucked her

tongue. 'That said, she raises a fair point. You can't play nursemaid to me day in, day out.'

'I'm not a nurse,' grumbled Maxim.

'What do you have in mind?' asked Kjellrunn. It had been nice to settle into their new home over the last two weeks, but she feared the day Sundra would insist on teaching her to use the arcane.

'I have a job to keep both of you busy.' Sundra set her tea bowl down. 'Two jobs in fact. You may not be an initiate of Frejna, Maxim, but I will need your help all the same.' She gestured and Maxim stood and collected the high priestess's bowl.

'I don't really like Vigilants,' he said. 'I'd much rather work for you.'

'A temple of Frejna should be a place people can come to bid farewell to the dead,' said Sundra. 'It can be a place of grieving and a place of healing for those left behind. Now that we have settled here, we will need to think about the more practical considerations: burial rites and ways of preparing the dead.'

'People will bring dead bodies here?' said Maxim, pulling a face.

Sundra nodded.

'You want us to go out into town and tell the people we're here for them,' said Kjellrunn.

'I do,' replied Sundra. 'It's time for the people of Dos Khor to know that the old ways are still alive.'

Kjellrunn looked at the largely abandoned buildings around the temple. Any number of people lived in the other districts of Dos Khor, people who looked at Kjellrunn strangely as she passed them in the street – much like her days in Cinderfell.

'Something troubles you?' said Sundra, responding to the unconscious grimace that had formed on the girl's face.

'I don't like people,' said Kjellrunn, surprised she'd said the words aloud. 'Not really. I don't think I ever have.'

'It's understandable. Growing up in Nordvlast with witch-sign can have been no easy thing. This task I have set you will be part of your learning. Part of your healing. People can be fragile, angry, relieved or even happy when they lose a loved one, and we must be ready to meet them all, no matter their mood.'

'I'm ready,' said Maxim.

'Not just yet you aren't,' replied Sundra with a slow smile. 'Wash up the tea things first. Then you can take the word of Frejna to the masses.'

Kjellrunn looked upon Dos Khor with anxiety fluttering in her stomach.

'But I can't speak the language,' she said, once Maxim had gone inside.

'Then you have even more to learn.' Sundra frowned. 'And there is another matter that needs attention.'

Dos Khor became more alive the further one travelled from the temple of Frejna. The houses had bright awnings or shutters painted in vibrant blue. Wide doorways led to courtyards with tiled mosaic floors, while lush green ferns and succulents grew in the shade. Kjellrunn felt the weight of an enquiring gaze and looked up to a balcony, where an old man chewed on a dark root and squinted at them.

'What about him?' said Kjellrunn. 'He might like to hear about the old ways.' Maxim called up to the balcony in the flowing language of his mother tongue. The man replied with a frown, his voice strident. Maxim replied in turn before the old man threw up his hands and disappeared into his home.

'That didn't look promising,' said Kjellrunn.

'He said the temple is in a bad part of town. Lots of slavers there.'

'Shame he couldn't have told us two weeks ago,' said Kjellrunn, running her fingertips over the scar on her shoulder.

The wound had healed quickly, but served as a painful reminder of their unwelcome arrival.

'And he said people don't go to temple any more since the Empire came. He wouldn't say any more than that.'

They walked further into Dos Khor in silence, feeling the heaviness of the old man's words. The morning was spent strolling the streets, learning the locations of shops that might be helpful. Maxim taught her the odd word of his mother tongue as best he could and eventually they came to a place where Kjellrunn could fulfil her second task.

'Why do you need a fabric shop?' asked Maxim as they entered the cool darkness. The main interior was separated from the street and the ever-present dust was held at bay by a small vestibule and a white gauze curtain. Once inside the shop they were surrounded by rolls of fine cotton, canvas, linen and even silk, displayed on wide tables beside exquisite shears with turquoise enamelled handles.

'Sundra said I couldn't be an initiate without having the correct attire,' explained Kjellrunn. The owner of the shop was a wizened, dark-skinned woman with bright green eyes. She wore a gold necklace and earrings and a multitude of other jewellery made from glossy black beads. The owner frowned as Kjellrunn ran her fingers over the fabric, but her expression softened once Maxim explained the nature of their errand. Maxim smiled as the owner slipped out through a door behind the counter.

'She's very impressed you're an initiate of Frejna,' he whispered. The owner returned a short time later with a roll of black fabric. She set about cutting off a length of the black cotton, talking all the while to Maxim as she did so. Soon Kjellrunn and he were heading back to the temple.

'So are you going to tell me what that was all about?' said Kjellrunn. She'd had her fill of not understanding a word of anything.

'She said she heard a rumour about people moving in at the temple and that a thug had received a nasty surprise.'

'That's a good description of Trine,' said Kjellrunn.

'Do you mean she's a thug or a nasty surprise?'

'A little of both, I think,' replied Kjellrun with a small smile.

'Why do you think Trine dislikes you so much?'

Kjellrunn shrugged. 'I'm not sure she likes anyone.' Maxim gave her a worried look but Kjellrunn ignored it. 'Tell me more about the shop keeper.'

'Well, she hopes to come to the temple soon. She wants to pay her respects to her ancestors.' Maxim fell silent and gave Kjellrunn a wary look.

'And what else?'

'Uh, she hopes you sort your hair out if you become the local priestess.'

'She said what?'

'It just needs a comb is all,' said Maxim, wincing. They walked in silence and the sun climbed to its apex, the heat hammering the street until it was almost too hot to think. People retired indoors and Kjellrunn wiped the sweat from her brow, her skin hot to the touch. She patted her yellow matted head.

'So we live in a bad part of town, surrounded by thugs, the Empire killed the last priestess and I have bad hair.' Kjellrunn sighed. 'It's not exactly the quiet life I was hoping for.'

'A quiet life?' Maxim rolled his eyes. 'I'm not sure such a thing exists.' He reached out and took Kjellrunn's hand in his smaller one. 'Don't worry though. I'll look after you.'

'I know you will.' Kjellrunn smiled. 'I know.'

Sundra's morning gathering was not the only routine Kjellrunn had adopted in their first two weeks in Dos Khor. The blind beggar, who had earned himself a place at their table each night, took himself away from the temple after the evening meal.

'Keep an eye on him, will you,' said Sundra on the second night, and so Kjellrunn had followed. The old man walked through the deserted part of Dos Khor and headed east, bent and stooped and blind as he was. He bore a white staff just a fraction taller than himself, tapping the sides of buildings and doorways as he went. Kjellrunn wondered how many times he had made this lonely pilgrimage. Every night it was the same journey; the beggar left the temple with the same destination in mind. The great white stone sculpture of the flat hand rose from the beach, a calm yet forbidding gesture. The sand was not so easy to navigate for the blind man, and many were the nights where Kjellrunn had gently taken him by the elbow and guided him to the tall stone.

'Here you are,' she'd said, fully aware he'd not be able to understand her. The blind man rested his stick against the sculpture and pointed to his free hand. The shape he made with his hand was identical to the sculpture.

'Kolas,' he said, then pointed to the sculpture. 'Kolas.'

'Hand!' said Kjellrunn.

'Kolas.' The old man smiled. 'Hand.'

Kjellrunn took his hand in hers and tapped his finger on her chest. 'Kjellrunn.' He nodded and became very still. 'Do you have a name?' The man didn't answer but turned his head as if staring out to sea. 'Frøya save me, why didn't I bring Maxim?' The old man seemed to sense her frustration and pointed to himself.

'Kolas,' he said.

'That doesn't make any sense,' muttered Kjellrunn. 'You can't be called "hand".' The old man walked towards the water and sat down. Kjellrunn joined him and he held a finger to his lips then tapped his ear twice.

'You want me to listen?'

'Lis-sen,' he replied.

Kjellrunn did as she was told, hearing every roll and ripple of water as it met the beach. The old man had a blissful look of contentment on his lined face, his breathing deep and even. He turned to her again and gestured to his eyes with two fingers.

'*Haerthi*,' he whispered. Kjellrunn closed her eyes and now the sound of the waves was her everything. Only the soft beat of her heart provided distraction from the gentle song of the Shimmer Sea. Kjellrunn left a little of her worries on the shore with every hushed and sibilant incoming wave. Her clashes with Trine, her frustrations with the language, her avoidance of Mistress Kamalov, all receded with each wave. In the end all she had left was her deep and abiding sadness for her father, Steiner, and Kristofine.

'Where are you?' she whispered and the sea whispered back in a hundred hushed voices, but not one answered her query. She remained on the beach with her eyes closed for a good time longer until a chill wind sent a shiver up her spine. A feeling of dread followed but this sensation was different, not something she carried inside, but something else; something vast and old and unknowable was out there – and the awareness of it filled her with fear.

Kjellrunn lurched to her feet and looked around but the blind man had abandoned her. The sun had dipped low behind the town and the enchanting azure of the sea had darkened. The feeling of dread remained, and though Kjellrunn couldn't say how, she knew it was imperative to get off the beach that very moment. Her feet kicked up clouds of sand as she fled, not pausing even when she had reached the houses at the edge of town, only slowing to a walk once the sea was hidden from view. Her heart raced and her ragged breathing sounded all too loud in the abandoned streets.

The blind beggar was sitting in his customary space on the

temple steps when Kjellrunn returned. Maxim was next to him, chatting cheerfully.

'You're back then. I wondered where you'd fetched up to.' Maxim's expression fell. 'What's wrong? Why are you so pale?'

'I followed him to the beach.' Kjellrunn gestured to the beggar. 'Just like I always do, but it was different tonight. There was something out there. Something in the sea.'

The old man gestured to his chest. '*Haerthi*.'

'What does he mean?' said Kjellrunn.

'I think' – Maxim frowned – 'you need to close your heart.'

'That doesn't make any sense,' replied Kjellrunn. 'He's not made much sense all night. Said his name was Hand.'

'He's making plenty of sense now,' said Maxim. 'He's said more to me tonight than since we first arrived.'

'Such as what?' said Kjellrunn, still deeply unsettled.

'He just told me he used to be a sculptor,' said Maxim. 'The best in the whole town apparently.' The boy stood up on the temple steps, almost eye to eye with Kjellrunn despite his stature. 'What was in the sea, Kjellrunn?'

'Nothing.' She shook her head. 'I just lost track of time is all, and frightened myself.' Maxim frowned and the look he gave her made it clear he hadn't believed her.

'We'd best get him inside,' the boy said. 'It's nearly curfew and Mistress Kamalov is in a foul mood.'

Kjellrunn nodded and helped the old man to an alcove in the temple where he slept on a bundle of old blankets. She hurried to her room as soon as she could, glad to put the day behind her. Her thoughts lingered at the Shimmer Sea's edge until she finally surrendered to sleep in the small hours of the morning.

CHAPTER TWENTY-ONE

Silverdust

'What's that?' said Streig, squinting into the distance. They had taken up their usual place some half a mile behind the cart that carried Envoy de Vries and Father Orlov. The soldiers ambled along, thoroughly sick of the long journey and spiteful temperatures. 'There's something on the horizon,' added Streig, shielding his eyes with the flat of his hand, and continued looking to the south. The winter sun was low in the cloudless sky and a keen wind blew at their backs.

That is the most northern of the Urzahn Mountains. They stretch from Novaya Zemlya and divide Virolanti Province from the Slavon Province, then continue through the Province of Karelina and into Shanisrond. If the world has a spine then it is the Urzahn Mountains.

'Virolanti,' said Streig, almost whispering the word with reverence.

Your home, I presume.

The soldier nodded. 'Though I've not seen it for over a year now.'

Nor will you see it any time soon. We are crossing over the border into the Vend Province. And then I expect we will take a ship to Khlystburg so the Emperor can hear my account. Who knows where you will be sent after that.

'This is a border?' said Streig, looking around. The ground underfoot was greener, the grasses thicker, shrubs more common, but no great barrier divided Novaya Zemlya from Vend. No watchtowers haunted the barren expanse. No river or mountain separated one province from the other.

Borders are imaginary lines drawn by men who would rather divide than unite.

'You need borders,' said Streig with a frown. 'It would be chaos without them. No one would know who they had to pay their taxes to, or if they were being invaded or not.'

All of that may be true, but they only exist on paper, no different to fiction.

'And what fiction will you tell when we reach Khlystburg?' There was a dangerous edge to the young soldier's words that Silverdust didn't care for, but he was in a dangerous mood himself. The mood had lingered since his confrontation with Father Orlov at the camp fire.

I doubt the story really matters. The Envoy will say that I was the highest-ranking Vigilant on the island, and that I should have been in control. The Envoy will then follow up by asking where I was during the fighting, and how an Exarch of my experience could let a lowly peasant kill all the soldiers and half of the Holy Synod on the island.

'She has you cornered there.' Streig paused. Silverdust could sense the young soldier's reluctance to ask the next question, knowing the answer may not be to his taste. 'Why didn't you fight?'

I missed the fighting because I was quietly murdering Vigilants in their rooms.

Streig looked stricken, his pace slowed and for a time he said nothing. 'Why?'

Because I hate them. Because it is barbaric to take children from their families, no matter if they have witchsign. It is barbaric to let those families think those children are dead. It is barbaric to persecute

the Spriggani because of a decades-old enmity. Just as the war with
Shanisrond will be barbaric when the Emperor leads his soldiers
south. Soldiers like you.

'Why are you telling me this?' said Streig. 'If I am asked
to speak before the Emperor I will be honour-bound to tell
the truth.'

Because you are no different to the children on Vladibogdan, Streig.
You have been taken from your family and you have not seen them
this last year. I wager you will not see them again.

'I wasn't taken,' said Streig with gritted teeth. 'I took the
Emperor's crown and signed up of my own free will.'

And if you had not? What other future awaited you in Virolanti
Province?

Streig shook his head and swore in a dialect that Silverdust
was unfamiliar with.

'There are no jobs in Virolanti Province. No jobs besides
farming.'

So your choices were few. The children with witchsign had fewer
choices than you and ultimately their fate is the same. Lifelong service
to an uncaring Emperor.

Streig avoided the Exarch for the following week. Silverdust
was escorted by a soldier who refused to give his name. Not
once in seven days did the man remove his helm in Silverdust's
presence. He had not spoken a word for the first two days.
Silverdust was acutely aware the soldier always had his mace
to hand and wondered just how much Streig had told his
comrades.

The barren steppe of Novaya Zemlya had given way to lush
plains, which transitioned to the myriad streams and swamps
of Vend Province. Finally they reached a town where the
swamp organised itself into a winding river. The town itself
perched above the water on a series of wooden posts,
connected by walkways. Smoke dribbled from the chimneys

of the town, reaching into the sky with feeble grey tendrils. Reeds and long grasses grew in abundance and the threat of water was everywhere: to a mortal man, a soaking might bring a chill, but immersion in water was always fatal to a cinderwraith. Silverdust balled his fists in frustration and kept a wary eye on everyone who came close.

What is this place? Silverdust asked the nameless soldier as they drew closer to the town.

'The area is Kulyagesh. The town is also called Kulyagesh. And the river, well, it seems the locals do not have so many names to give.'

The area outside of the town was dotted with spruce, maple and silvery birch trees, though no birds sat in their branches. Wagons crawled in the distance, navigating the narrow strips of land that counted for roads in these parts. Silverdust watched as their own cart passed by a handful of scrawny children who waited at the roadside. The children reached out with dirty hands, gaunt stares on their narrow faces. Father Orlov slapped a hand that strayed too close while the Envoy looked away, pretending not to have seen them. Now that Silverdust was closer to the town he could see people crouching by the trees. They clutched fishing rods by the nearest stretch of water.

So many fishermen.

'Hard to grow crops in a place like this,' said the soldier. 'Harder still to tax a man on the fish he catches if he eats them the same day.'

Silverdust and his nameless escort closed the distance to where the ragged children lingered. The Exarch paused, noting feet wrapped in rags, slender frames, and cheekbones that were too sharp for such young faces. He reached into a pouch and brought forth a selection of coins. The Exarch hadn't needed money in years, insulated from poverty by his position. One by one he pressed a coin into the palm of each child then set off without a word.

'You should have said if you have coin to spare,' said the nameless soldier. He tried to sound as if he were merely gaming, but Silverdust could feel the man's frustration, his jealousy.

You want my coin?

'All soldiers want coin. Everyone knows that.'

Those children will not try to kill me the moment the Envoy orders them to do so. You on the other hand are quite a different matter.

Another miserable town, another equally miserable inn. Silverdust almost wished he'd tried his luck at sea. A knock sounded at the door and Silverdust sensed a familiar presence on the other side.

Come in.

'You should lock your door,' said Streig as he entered with breakfast.

I am under Envoy de Vries' protection. Without me there is no one to punish for the fate of Vladibogdan. I am quite safe.

'And if the Envoy revokes her protection?'

I am well versed in the arcane. Very well versed.

Streig set the bowl down on the simple table and sat down on the bed. The room had little to recommend it. The rug was threadbare and the bedsheets were unclean. Silverdust remained standing as he often did. Sitting lost its meaning when the body no longer tired.

'Why did you tell me those things?' The young soldier sounded weary more than angry. 'It's because I'm young, isn't it? Do you think me foolish? Impressionable?'

Neither. But you have Spriggani blood in you, do you not?

Streig snorted a bitter laugh and shook his head. 'Is there anything you don't know? Anything you can't see from behind that mirror mask of yours?'

So I am correct?

'On my mother's side, my grandmother. How did you know?'

I am a Vigilant. We see what others would keep hidden.

'And what if someone else discovers this? Another Vigilant, perhaps? The other soldiers are already asking questions about you. About me.' He shook his head then pressed a hand to his brow. 'About us.'

Most Vigilants are not as perceptive as I am. I have been doing this a long time. Your secret is safe.

'And if you're wrong? What if I'm found out?'

Then we will face them together. I realise how conflicted you feel, but you have looked out for me on this journey south. You have often taken up the task no one else wanted. You have listened to me when you would rather not have. Now eat. Keep your strength up for the times ahead.

Silverdust gestured to the meagre offering of thin porridge. Streig looked at the bowl and shook his head.

'I've no appetite. Maybe I'm becoming like you.'

I very much doubt that. I am the last of my kind.

Envoy de Vries appeared in the doorway and glanced from soldier to Exarch and back again, then sighed irritably. 'Form up outside as soon as you're ready. And don't dawdle. There is a barge waiting to take us down stream but the owner won't wait.'

Streig and Silverdust followed her out of the inn without a word. The Exarch felt a wave of relief as they took their places on a wide, sturdy barge. He stood at the blunt prow like a figurehead while the soldiers spread out across the rear half of the barge and muttered how grateful they were not to be walking. The Envoy and Father Orlov paced the deck and conferred with each other in whispers.

'I don't like this,' said Streig, looking over his shoulder to de Vries and Orlov. 'I feel like you're walking into a trap.'

Of course I am. But half the danger of a trap is not knowing it is there.

'So the Imperial Court is only half-dangerous?' Streig laughed bitterly.

The Imperial Court is always dangerous, but then, we live in dangerous times.

The days idled by without much to differentiate them and Streig kept his distance from the Exarch except to bring him food, which invariably found itself cast into the river when no one was looking. Silverdust was long-acquainted with his own company, but the barge began to feel like a prison and the close proximity of so much water left him uneasy. They had almost reached the coast when Envoy de Vries approached.

'Father Orlov told me that Steiner came back to Vladibogdan on a ship, a red frigate belonging to a Captain Romola.'

Silverdust nodded, sensing the first of his lies to the Envoy was about to be undone, but it had been important to give Steiner a head start, some breathing room to escape and begin to fan the flames of rebellion. He sat up at night on the barge listening to the whispers of the wind and heard Steiner's name. It had only been a matter of time until the Envoy and Father Orlov heard the same arcane messages.

'You also said the ship sank in bad weather, just two miles from Vladibogdan.' Envoy de Vries should have been gloating to catch him in a lie, but her whimsical smile had abandoned her, and a tightness around the eyes told of her anxiety.

That is correct. A powerful storm in the Spøkelsea. That's when I lost sight of them.

'Both myself and Father Orlov have heard whispers on the wind. The ship was seen in Virag where a street battle took place.'

Is it inconceivable that more than one merchant ship be painted such a colour?

'The local people say a score of young people used the arcane to defeat Imperial soldiers.' The Envoy stood before the Exarch and Father Orlov was just a dozen feet away. Silverdust noticed she clasped her hands together to stop them shaking. 'This is a disaster. Even now rumours are spreading. People are speaking openly of Vladibogdan. Ancient secrets! People are talking about the arcane. How can you be so calm, damn you!' she shouted. The soldiers lurched to their feet on instinct.

Silverdust gazed at the port they were headed towards and hoped Steiner had survived. He brushed his arcane senses lightly against the Envoy's mind, but her feelings were luminous, her heart racing.

You seem very agitated, Envoy. Understandably so. You have nothing to fear. I will not attack you. I will come to Khlystburg as I have always said.

'You'd best get your story straight,' said the Envoy, stepping closer, her voice hushed yet furious. 'It won't matter if you can see the dead or perform miracles. If the Emperor suspects you of treason he'll kill you himself.'

I have seen first-hand how the Emperor dispenses his justice. Silverdust stepped closer to the Envoy, towering over her. *It is a type of sport for him. A blood sport. You have seen it too? How he takes lives with the Ashen Blade?*

The Envoy shrank back. 'You've lost your mind.'

I can assure that is not the case, but I do not fear the end.

'You want to die.' The Envoy's face paled, and her brow furrowed in confusion. 'You welcome it.'

When you are as old as I, death is only natural. Silverdust turned away from her and took his place at the prow of the barge, willing the last of their journey to pass more quickly.

CHAPTER TWENTY-TWO

Steiner

The brigands sat up late into the night, each dealing with the aftermath of the fight in his own way. Some roared their defiance at the stars and spoke of vengeance on the Empire, while others retreated to the shadows. Steiner imagined they were trying to justify the slaughter to themselves. Steiner huddled with the rest of the men near the granary. They'd lit a brazier and stolen chairs from the guardrooms. Nils chanced upon a barrel of mead that added fuel to his already ebullient mood.

'Was it like this on Vladibogdan, dragon rider?' he almost shouted as he sloshed mead into a cup for Steiner and then for Einar. There was a wildness in Nils' eyes that put Steiner on edge, and his wide grin looked unhinged rather than joyous.

'The uprising began and I had to take the fight to Cinderfell.' Steiner took a drink of mead and let out a long sigh. 'I didn't have time to celebrate.' Steiner eyed the long hall where so many soldiers had burned to death. The timbers were glowing a dark red now the fire had dwindled. The scent of charred flesh lay heavy on the air and his conscience.

'What troubles you?' asked Einar. The brigands' leader had

stolen an Imperial cloak and pulled the hood up against the night.

'Childish thoughts is all,' said Steiner, taking another drink.

'There's not a single man here who doesn't carry the child he once was within him.' Einar looked around at his crew. 'Though few would admit it. So. What troubles you?'

'I honestly thought we'd fight them, you know, one on one. A fair fight.' Steiner smiled bitterly. 'I thought we'd overcome them with bravery and skill and . . . I don't know.'

For a time they stared at the glowing embers of the burned hall and drank quietly. Nils worked his way around the courtyard, pouring mead and laughing. 'Bravery and skill rarely last long against men in full armour,' said Einar. 'And the bravery and skill of half-starved brigands lasts no time at all. It wasn't a fair fight, but fights never are.'

'I thought there'd be honour or glory or something to make me feel better about it but . . .'

'You're a good man, Steiner.' Einar laid a hand gently on his shoulder. 'But I'm not sure you have the luxury of acting honourably, not against the Empire.'

The brigands shared out the loot from the granary but Steiner drank more than he ate. The world grew pleasantly blurry.

'What will happen to the soldier I captured?' he asked, a little louder than he intended, fearful he wouldn't like the answer. The brigands fell silent and Nils favoured Steiner with a long hard look then grinned with arms outstretched to both sides.

'He's going to join us!' Nils took an unsteady step forward. 'The Empire's kid soldier,' he slurred, 'becoming a brigand like us.'

Steiner was too tired to reply. A slow smile crossed his face and it took a drunken moment before he realised it was relief he was feeling. There'd been enough killing for one day.

Kristofine approached out of the gloom with a torch and tugged on his sleeve with a wariness in her eyes.

'Come on, there's a guardroom with a bed above the gatehouse. I'm not sleeping outside tonight.' Steiner followed, mute with exhaustion.

'Go to your lady love, dragon rider!' shouted Nils. 'And know the goddesses go with you.' Steiner waved back without looking and paid no attention to the filthy laughter of the brigands

'I'm sorry about before,' said Kristofine, as she led him into the gatehouse and up the narrow stairs. The shadows jumped fitfully in the torchlight and the smell of damp lingered in the darkness. 'I just didn't want to see you hurt is all.' But they both knew she meant *killed*, that she was unable to even say the word.

The room was perhaps ten strides wide with a low ceiling, and featured a fireplace, a narrow bed, and a desk, though the chair was missing. Kristofine set the torch in a sconce and sat against the edge of desk, crossing her arms over her stomach. 'This is what war looks like, I suppose.'

'This is what killing looks like,' he replied. The sweetness of the mead had done little to cover the bitterness of his regret.

'Burning the hall with all those men inside . . .' The torchlight revealed the tracks of her tears, like silver scars on her cheeks. Her gaze was directed at the floor, eyes dazed and unseeing.

'I wasn't expecting that,' said Steiner. 'Not sure I know what I was expecting. A mass surrender perhaps? Was I naive to even think such a thing?'

Kristofine forced a tired smile. 'Perhaps we both were.'

Steiner knelt beside the fireplace and began stacking wood. It was a comfort to perform such a familiar task after living outdoors for so long. He lit the wood with the torch and tried not to think about the screams of burning men.

'Will you hold me?' she asked when the fire was ablaze. He drew close, circled his arms around her waist and rested his forehead on her shoulder.

'I'm sorry.' He breathed the words faintly.

'For what?'

'For being a killer. A murderer, I suppose.'

'It's not murder when they're hunting you,' she replied. 'And there'll be more death to come. A lot more.'

'You're right,' he replied. 'Nils is already talking about travelling back to Trystbyre and killing the soldiers there. I should feel good about it. I should feel good about delivering the uprising I promised to Kimi, but . . .' He slipped free of her arms and stared into the fire.

'I thought this is what you wanted?' said Kristofine, her eyes narrowed in confusion.

'Talking about a thing is hardly the same as doing it. I suppose I'm shocked is all. Killing doesn't get any easier.'

'This is how we bring down the Empire,' answered Kristofine firmly. 'This is how we stop them taking children from their families.' Steiner envied her conviction; it sounded so easy when she spoke of uprisings in a dimly lit gatehouse chamber.

'I'm a blacksmith from Cinderfell. What do I know about uprisings or killing?'

'I'd say you know plenty after Vladibogdan, and a fair bit more after killing Shirinov in Cinderfell.'

'This feels wrong!' There was a snarl to his voice. 'Burning men alive while they're at their dinner is hardly a thing to be proud of.'

'Right or wrong, this is the start of your uprising, Steiner!' She matched his anger with some of her own and the room felt small for it.

'My uprising.' He shook his head slowly. 'I'd say it was your uprising more than mine. If you hadn't told the brigands the story in the forest we'd be dead by now.'

'Get some sleep,' she said with something like disgust or disappointment in her voice. 'Perhaps you'll feel better in the morning, or at least see some sense.' She went to the narrow cot in the room and slumped down, leaving him with the fire and the scent of dried blood.

Steiner would not miss the howling winds of the Urzahn Mountains, nor the constant chill in his fingers. A vast throng of pine trees awaited them as they reached the foothills.

'I'll be glad to be under the cover of trees again,' said Steiner. Kristofine glanced at him but said nothing. It had been like this since the night in the gatehouse.

'Do you miss your friends?' asked Marek. The brigands had remained at the garrison, or headed back to Trystbyre to hunt Imperial soldiers. Steiner shrugged and looked away to the horizon.

'I'd say they were more Kristofine's friends than mine,' said Steiner.

'What's got into you?' pressed Marek.

'I'd say they were friends to all of us,' said Kristofine in a low voice.

'Between her persuasiveness and your fame you make a good pair,' said Marek.

'Try telling him that,' said Kristofine. 'As if having a band of brigands praising him for being the dragon rider, or Hammersmith, or whatever damn foolish folk hero name he fancies this week.'

'I wondered if something was brewing between the pair of you,' said Marek as he looked from Kristofine to his son with a grim expression. Steiner took a moment to frame his answer, caught off balance by Kristofine's anger.

'I wanted to be the one to persuade people is all. I wanted to tell my story.'

'All that matters is that the tale is told,' said Marek. 'Who cares if she's better at the storytelling than you?'

'I care. It's my story.' Steiner could hear how petulant he sounded and hated it. 'And I'd rather people didn't know that we burned two dozen soldiers to death while they ate.'

'I doubt Kimi will care who does what or how it gets done,' replied Kristofine with a sneer, 'just as long as the thing gets done. Then you can crawl back to her. Isn't that what you want?' She took off down the hill, outpacing them until she was a good half mile ahead.

Marek stared at Steiner until his son blurted out, 'What?'

'I'm trying to work out when you filled your head with sawdust is all. Was it in Trystbyre or Virag?'

Steiner opened his mouth to speak and then thought better of it.

It was another ten days before they reached the coast and the walled port town that promised beds, beer and a hot bath. Winter was not yet done with this corner of the world and spring had not gained purchase in Slavon Province. An icy north wind shrieked by night and the days alternated between drizzle, sleet, and on the coldest days, flurries of snow.

'We need to get into this town,' said Marek. 'We won't last much longer in these temperatures.' Any food they'd stolen from the garrison in the mountains was many days gone and the rewards of hunting were few.

The town walls were an unlovely grey that matched the colour of the sea. Travellers waited in a queue outside the gates as the soldiers questioned them. A light dusting of snow fell from the overcast skies, almost dreamlike. Steiner, Marek and Kristofine joined the end of the line and shivered fitfully. The daylight was leeched out of the sky by the oncoming night and a surly mob of darker clouds.

'Well, well,' said the soldier when they finally reached the gate. There was no one else around save the three soldiers who now barred their way.

'Another three starving peasants wanting to come in from the cold.' The soldier spat at the ground by Steiner's boots. 'No shortage of those around here.'

Steiner clenched the shaft of the sledgehammer tighter, and hoped it would remain hidden under his cloak.

'Just passing through, friend,' said Marek in Solska.

'And why should I let you in?' said the soldier. The glow from the brazier cast him in a ruddy light. He'd taken the unusual step of removing his helmet; something Imperial soldiers rarely did. He was missing an eye tooth and his face was deeply lined with age or drink, or perhaps both.

'My family were chased away from our home in the Karelina forest,' said Kristofine in Solska. 'We are carrying everything we own.'

'Chased by who?' asked the soldier.

'Wild men of the forest,' she replied. 'Thieves and killers.

'Very well,' replied the soldier, but he sounded far from happy about it. 'And what will you do here?'

'Look for work of course,' said Marek in Solska. 'I was a smith before I was a farmer.'

The soldier conversed with his comrades a moment. 'Why didn't you simply go to Trystbyre rather than coming all this way?'

'You haven't heard?' said Kristofine in a hushed voice. 'Trystbyre isn't safe, a man with a sledgehammer slew the soldiers there.'

Marek held up two coins. 'Perhaps this will help?' The soldier gestured they should enter the town and spat again, barely missing Steiner's boots. The coins were snatched from Marek's hand. Moments later they were inside the port town, traversing the muddy roads and trying to ignore the sour reek of Frøya knew what.

'We should have just killed them,' said Steiner under his breath.

'I thought you had tired of killing?' replied Kristofine with a hard look.

'Why did you tell them that story about Trystbyre?' said Steiner, irritation itching like a rash.

'Misdirection,' said Marek. 'They won't look for you here if they think you're at Trystbyre. Seems your girl has a head for subterfuge.'

'I'm not his girl,' replied Kristofine. 'I'm a woman.'

'Subterfuge it is then,' replied Steiner. 'But we shouldn't have bribed them. We're not so rich that we can throw coin at soldiers all the time.'

'Marek and I stole those coins from the dead soldiers at the garrison,' said Kristofine. 'While you were drinking with your friends.'

Steiner was stung by the barb but determined not to let her have the last word. 'So when did you learn to speak Solska?'

Kristofine shook her head and hurried down the street before disappearing through the door to an inn.

'Frøya's teeth,' said Marek. 'The words you're looking for are "thank you". Those soldiers would have happily cut our throats just to pass the time.' Steiner scowled but said nothing.

'We've plenty of people to fight, son,' added Marek. 'We don't need to be fighting among ourselves.'

The inn was a much-needed reminder of civilisation after too many weeks claiming shelter from dark forests. The smells of straw, stale beer, unwashed bodies and woodsmoke all vied for attention, and above everything the smell of roasting meat. Steiner wasted no time and ordered meals, beer, and rooms in stilted Solska, glad to have something to do. 'How much?' he asked.

The innkeeper replied and Steiner began to slowly count the coins from the palm of his hand. The innkeeper, who was a stout man with a squint, gave a rough, unpleasant laugh.

'We don't take lousy Svingettevei money here. This is Slavon! This is the Empire.' Kristofine stepped forward, paid the man from her stash of coins and forced a smile at Steiner.

'Like I said, the soldiers at the garrison had a few coins.' She offered a small smile though a sadness remained in her eyes. Marek gave a long, filthy chuckle. 'Did you leave anything for the brigands?'

'I hope not,' said Kristofine with a smirk. 'They got an entire mountain pass out of it, after all.'

'Thank you,' said Steiner, though in truth he was more ashamed than grateful. It seemed he couldn't even pay for a room any more.

Steiner's mood improved drastically as their wet cloaks were hung up to dry. They were given a table near the fireplace on account of yet another small bribe. Steaming bowls were set before them with all manner of cabbage, beef, mushrooms and spices floating in soup. A plate of dark bread was placed at the centre of the table and the innkeeper grinned, his eyes lingering on Kristofine's money pouch as he left.

No one looked up from their food and the soup and the bread were quickly gone. Steiner turned his attention to the beer and was resolved to buy another as soon as he was done. They were all lean from the road; Marek looked fit to drop. Somehow Kristofine remained beautiful despite the journey, and Steiner spent a moment wondering at what had changed between them.

'What do we do now?' said Marek when he was halfway through his pint.

'We could tell these drinkers the tale of the rebels who took a mountain pass against all odds,' said Kristofine. 'Or let them know where children with witchsign are taken.'

'I'm more interested in finding Felgenhauer,' said Steiner, keen to avoid approaching another reluctant audience.

'Come on,' she replied. 'We'll tell the story together.' Steiner felt a pang of guilt for treating her so poorly.

'No stories tonight,' said Marek. He had gone very still but his eyes were fixed on the far side of the room. The cheerful din of raised voices diminished and several locals made space at the centre of the room, for good reason it turned out. A Vigilant approached the bar, flanked by two soldiers.

'Frejna's teeth,' muttered Steiner. The Vigilant wore the usual garb of a red leather surcoat over a padded cream long coat. He wore a black cloak like the soldiers that escorted him. The Vigilant's mask was neither wolf, nor bear, nor dog, but something in between, painted a dark grey.

'What is that?' whispered Steiner.

'It's a wolverine,' said Marek with a scowl. 'Vile creatures that consume every last morsel of their prey. They're not given to sharing their spoils.'

An uneasy quiet settled over the room and the innkeeper's usual squint seemed to become a wince of almost physical pain as he drew close to the masked man.

'C-can I help you?'

'All citizens of the Empire may be of service in some way,' said the Vigilant, loud enough that the whole room could hear.

'Three beers?' said the innkeeper.

The Vigilant gave a low chuckle and shook his head. 'I do not drink, but I daresay my comrades will take two pints of whatever you're serving. I require a room and hot food.' The innkeeper nodded. There was an awkward moment when payment would normally be expected and none was proffered.

'And this will be a service to the Empire?' asked the innkeeper. 'My service to the Empire.' One of the soldiers slammed some coins down on the counter top and few of the locals flinched.

'You will show me to my room now,' said the Vigilant. The innkeeper nodded and made to lead his guest to his room. They were halfway to the door when the Vigilant paused and turned to Steiner. His gaze dropped to Steiner's feet.

'What sturdy boots you have.' The Vigilant took a step closer; the snarling wolverine face bore chips and dents in the metalwork. Steiner guessed it must have been painted over a few times. 'And where did you come by such fine craftsmanship?'

'Hand-me-downs,' said Steiner in Solska, but his pronunciation was poor and he had to repeat himself.

'Not local to these parts,' said the Vigilant, not bothering to turn the statement into a question. 'And who handed these boots down to you?'

Steiner's mouth went dry. He knew full well that Vigilants with the sight could see enchantments on weapons and clothes. He'd learned that lesson the first day he'd reached Vladibogdan.

'They were mine,' said Marek. He stood up from his table and eyed the Vigilant without fear or courtesy. The bestial mask of the Vigilant turned to each of them in turn, taking in the old blacksmith, the pretty girl, and the rough youth.

'You may call me Exarch Zima. We will speak again, I think.' The Vigilant turned and gestured to the innkeeper. There was a stunned moment of silence and Marek sank down to his seat.

'What just happened?' asked Kristofine.

'Steiner's boots are enchanted,' said Marek. 'He can't be knocked down while he wears them, can't fall, rarely stumbles. They were his mother's.'

'And the Vigilant was able to see the . . .' She shrugged. 'The witchsign on the boots?'

'Something like that,' said Steiner.

'We'll be watched,' said Marek. 'And our every word will be reported to Exarch Zima.'

Steiner looked around and had his worst fears confirmed. The locals that hadn't turned their backs stared at the newcomers with unalloyed hostility.

'So much for quietly finding Felgenhauer,' said Steiner.

CHAPTER TWENTY-THREE

Taiga

'Frøya save me,' muttered Tief. 'And I thought Vladibogdan was bad.' They had made camp for the night but finding firewood was difficult. An outcrop of rocks provided a reprieve from the endless wet grasses and constant damp of the Izhorian swamps. Taiga hummed gently to herself as she cooked over a small, smoky fire, sprinkling herbs into the simmering water and slicing carrots.

'At least the food is better than what we had on Vladibogdan,' she said. 'Shame we don't have a roof over our heads, but there it is.' The stars hung in the sky far above them and the full moon emerged from the clouds like a vast eye thick with rheum.

'At least the forges were warm.' Tief crossed his arms and rubbed his shoulders, scowling into the darkness.

'I dislike snow the most,' said Taiga softly. 'Pray that it doesn't snow, big brother.'

'Will you ever grow out of calling me that?' he replied in mock-irritation. She took in his dark hair, shot through with white, and the lines on his serious face.

'Making you feel old, am I?' said Taiga with a smirk.

'I can manage that all by myself,' said Tief, scratching at

his greying hair. Marozvolk sat apart from them on a wide flat stone, sharpening her sword and keeping watch. The sound of the whetstone on the blade set Taiga's teeth on edge; it reminded her of Vladibogdan and the forges. She was loath to ask the former Vigilant to stop. Their survival might depend on the sharpness of that sword in time.

'Dinner will be ready soon,' said Taiga, trying to distract herself from the sound of the whetstone.

Marozvolk had said little in the week they had travelled north east. Tief had been quick to state that suited him just fine when she was out of earshot. Taiga by contrast wondered what it must be like for their companion to be so alone in a land so dismal and desolate. Marozvolk's anger at Kimi's decision to venture to Khlystburg lingered over them all like a pall of smoke.

'At least we haven't had any more trouble,' said Tief, casting his eyes west. They had kept the forest at a safe distance since their encounter with the Grave Wolves, though the undead creatures howled late into the night. The sound haunted Taiga's dreams during the few hours when sleep finally came.

'I lived in Yamal for the first fifteen years of my life,' said Kimi, 'and no one ever spoke about Grave Wolves. Not once.'

'Most people in Yamal know better than to go into the Izhorian forest,' replied Tief. 'I'd have thought they'd have taught you that, highness.'

'Most Yamali never cross the river,' said Taiga in an altogether kinder tone of voice. 'We're originally from the Midtenjord Steppe, near the border with the Novgoruske Province, but we always kept one eye open for Grave Wolves.'

Kimi frowned at Tief. 'No one likes a know-it-all, old man.'

'Knowing it all saved you from being killed,' said Tief. He fixed his pipe and toked a while, his face stern in the firelight.

'Besides,' continued Taiga, 'the folk in the south don't really believe in Grave Wolves. The creatures tend to stay further north.'

'So how do you know so much about them?' said Kimi.

'It comes from having a sister who is a priestess of Frejna.'
Tief smiled sadly. Taiga could tell how much he missed Sundra,
and how much being apart from her was costing him. She
felt the bright pang of missing her sister just as keenly.
She took his hand and squeezed it.

'When I first met you I assumed Sundra was your mother,'
said Kimi.

'Our parents fell pregnant young,' said Taiga. 'Then not
again for twelve years.'

'And then I was born,' added Tief. 'And Taiga followed a
decade after. They say trouble comes in threes.' Tief laughed and
rubbed his eye with the back of his hand, though Taiga couldn't
tell if he was wiping away a tear or the great tiredness that
weighed upon him.

'Sundra would hate this,' said Kimi, looking around at the
moonlit swamps. 'No tent and no tea.'

'I think I saw some tea somewhere,' said Taiga, and began
to rummage through the packs.

'You can bet your boots she'd hate it. If she were here she'd
say that Grave Wolves were never meant to be.'

'They are an affront to Frejna,' said Taiga, still searching
the packs. 'Just as they are an affront to all living things.'

'But where did they come from?' pressed Kimi.

'For centuries there were more wolves than people in
Izhoria,' explained Taiga. 'There were a few villages dotted
around, but nothing significant.

'The wolves were normal back then' – Tief blew out a long
plume of smoke – 'before the curse took hold of them.'

'What curse?' said Kimi.

'It may have been during the Age of Wings,' said Taiga. 'But
could just as easily have been during the Age of Tears . . .
Bittervinge the dragon had a disagreement with one of his kin,
a dragon called Veles. Somehow Veles escaped, but not before

Bittervinge had torn the wings from Veles' back. Veles found his way here, to Izhoria, if the story is to be believed.'

'But the Age of Tears was over a hundred years ago,' breathed Kimi.

'That's true,' replied Tief. 'But curses are persistent, and so was Veles. He killed the few people that lived here and made servants of them.'

'You mean he made cinderwraiths?' Kimi's hand strayed to her neck where the last fragment of the Ashen Torment hung from a chain.

'You should get rid of that awful thing,' muttered Tief.

'No,' said Taiga, cutting off her brother. 'Without the Ashen Torment Veles could only reanimate their bodies. The creatures he made are hideous. Veles called them gholes and declared himself ruler of Izhoria, a dismal kingdom of the dead.'

'And Veles claimed the wolves as well?'

'Not exactly. Gholes exist only to kill. When they encountered the wolves . . .' Taiga pulled a gruesome face. 'The crows came of course, to peck out the eyes of the dead wolves, but then something terrible happened.'

'The wolves came back,' said Marozvolk. She had set aside her whetstone, looking tired yet fierce in the firelight.

Taiga nodded. 'Somehow Veles' corruption had seeped into the land,' she said. 'Into the water, the earth. Nothing that dies in Izhoria stays dead, or so they say.'

'But that was over a hundred years ago,' said Kimi. 'Dragons can't live forever.'

'You know better than that, Kimi,' said Tief. 'Dragons, given the right conditions, can do anything they please.'

'I found the tea!' said Taiga cheerfully, but no one had much to say after that.

Marozvolk led the way after a meagre breakfast the following morning. The renegade Vigilant marched at least a hundred strides in front of Tief and Kimi. Taiga followed close behind them, humming softly to herself.

'You think we can trust her?' said Tief, nodding to Marozvolk. 'She's barely said a dozen words all week. How do we know she's not an Imperial spy?'

'Tief! Don't start with that business,' chided Taiga.

'She's not a spy,' said Kimi. 'She could have given us away in Virag, but she wanted to leave more than I did. I've journeyed with her. I trust her.'

'But we barely know her,' said Tief. 'She could be biding her time, keeping an eye on you until . . .'

'Until what?' said Kimi. 'I barely know what day it is, nor what's on the horizon, and my own brother wants me dead. Hardly a threat to the Emperor, am I?' Taiga could hear the bitterness in her friend's voice, and the irritation.

Tief shrugged. 'I just don't trust her is all. Why did she never come to you on the island?'

'None of us wanted to be here,' said Kimi. 'And Marozvolk's loyalty to the Empire was already waning when Steiner arrived.'

'She has lost so much,' said Taiga. 'First her family, then Felgenhauer, then the island itself. So much loss.'

'As if anyone could miss Vladibogdan,' said Tief over his shoulder with a dark look.

'True, but familiarity is often preferable to . . .' Taiga gestured to the misty swamps. The water appeared as dull steel between thickets of tall grasses, and everywhere mud waited for them. Mud that sucked at your boots. Mud that soaked in and dried to a crust. Mud that slowly sucked you down to the deep places in the earth to drown you. 'Loss and uncertainty.'

'I think she's glad to be free of the Empire,' said Kimi. 'But she can't find her place in the world.'

'You two have a lot in common then?' said Tief. They walked in silence for a time.

'Are you sure about heading north?' asked Taiga. 'I want the Emperor dead as much as the next Spriggani, but there'd be no shame in heading back to Shanisrond.'

Kimi shook her head. 'My place is in Khlystburg, where the Emperor is. It's Marozvolk that wants to set out for Shanisrond.' The princess shot a hard look over her shoulder. 'You're free to go with her if you're having doubts.' Taiga felt herself blush and cursed herself for saying such a thing.

'Let's just escape this infernal swamp,' said Tief. 'One problem at a time.'

The mist grew thicker as the sun edged behind grey clouds and did not return. Marozvolk became a dim silhouette in the distance, another phantom in the desolate swamp. Taiga slipped in the wet reeds and stumbled. She took a moment to steady herself and glared at the marshy ground. A pale grey cat stared at her from the long grasses, the first living creature she'd set eyes on since they'd left Yamal.

'What are you doing out here?' she whispered. The cat bounded from its hiding place, then slunk off into the mist behind her. There was a moment when her vision shifted, and there seemed to be two cats, walking side by side, and then they were gone.

'Diplo? Lelse?' When she looked around the others were long gone, the mist obscuring her view in every direction. 'By the goddess, is this a sign?'

'Tief!' Kimi's voice sounded in the mist ahead. 'Where is Taiga?'

'Taiga?' He raised his voice. 'Where are you, Taiga?'

'I'm here. I saw . . .' She looked around, trying to find the source of her brother's voice. 'I know I saw something,' she muttered to herself.

'What's going on back there?' shouted Marozvolk in the distance, her voice sounding strangely flat in the mist.

'We've lost Taiga!' shouted Kimi.

'I'm here!' shouted Taiga. 'I'm over here.'

'Wait there. I'm coming to find you,' shouted Tief. She could hear the sloshing of swamp waters as he made his way back towards her.

'Is she hurt?' shouted Marozvolk. 'Are *you* hurt, highness?'

'I'm fine.'

The mist did strange things to the sound of their voices, and Taiga stared around, seeing indistinct figures in the shifting grey all about her. Some of the dark shadows were ahead of her, but two more moved in the mist behind her. 'I'm here!' she shouted again, fearful her brother had backtracked too far. The three of them arrived together.

'What the Hel happened?' said Tief, frowning.

'I think the goddess sent a sign,' said Taiga with a hopeful smile. 'There were cats here. Grey cats. I think Lelse and Diplo were here.'

'Well, I didn't see any cat,' said Marozvolk.

'There's nothing here,' said Kimi. 'We need to move—'

A darkness moved in the mist to their left and a dread passed over Taiga like a fierce chill. Marozvolk drew her sword as Tief lunged forward to grab Taiga.

'Get behind me!' he whispered. Other shadows moved in the mist, drawing closer.

'They look too tall to be Grave Wolves,' said Kimi, drawing her own sword.

'Or cats,' muttered Tief.

'What's happening to you?' said Taiga, pointing at Kimi. Pale blue light escaped from the collar of her shirt, glowing through the fabric itself.

'It's the Ashen Torment,' said Kimi. 'But it's been destroyed. I don't understand where this light is—'

The nearest of the shadows emerged from the mist. It was a hunched thing shaped like a man, wearing crude faded black cloth. Its face was hidden in a vast hood and the robes reached as far as the knee, ragged and torn, stained with all manner of filth and dried blood. Tief drew his knife and crouched low.

'Get away!' But the ghole stepped closer, slowly as if prowling, just a dozen feet away. Its hands, if it had ever had hands, were crooked into long claws, the fingernails black talons. Marozvolk drew up alongside Tief and a faint aura of silvery light glittered as her skin turned to stone.

'What do we do?' Taiga hissed at Tief. Kimi checked over her shoulder at them, keen to make sure they hadn't been surrounded as they had been by the Grave Wolves. Nothing moved in the mist behind them.

'I said, get back!' shouted Tief and Marozvolk lunged forward, the tip of her sword plunging towards the cowled head. The ghole stepped aside, almost dropping to a crouch as it did so. For an awful moment Taiga thought it might pounce forward like some feral creature, but then a shriek sounded in the distance and the ghole fled, joining the other shadows in the mist and disappearing from sight. Tief released a sigh of relief and his shoulders sagged. 'Frøya keep me close. I never thought I'd actually live to see one of those things.'

'There was a grey cat right here,' Taiga said with a weak smile.

'You *think* you saw a grey cat in the mist,' said Tief then rubbed his forehead and sighed.

'I know what I saw,' said Taiga. 'I think the goddess sent a sign. A sign that she's with us.'

'We stick together from now on,' said Kimi. 'I know you're unhappy with how things are,' she said to Marozvolk. 'But we stick together.'

Marozvolk nodded her agreement. 'It makes sense.' She dispelled her stony skin with a gesture and sheathed her sword.

'And I need you to stay where I can see you,' said Kimi to Taiga.

'Sundra will kill me if anything happens to you,' said Tief.

'Sundra may not get the chance if those things come back,' said Marozvolk. 'Come on. We move.'

Taiga watched Kimi walking besides Marozvolk. The silence between them was as stout as any shield. Taiga and Tief followed behind, but neither had much to say, casting wary glances behind every so often.

'No birdsong, no croaking frogs, no crickets,' said Tief with disgust. 'You can bet your boots everything here is dead.'

'We'll be in Midtenjord soon enough,' replied Taiga, keen to change the subject.

'And then we'll get to Khlystburg,' said Kimi. 'And we'll—'

'Do you have any idea how well protected the Emperor is?' said Marozvolk, frustration flashing in her eyes.

'No. Not yet,' admitted Kimi. 'But I intend to study his movements before I commit to killing him.'

'Study his movements?' Marozvolk failed to keep the incredulity from her voice. 'He's not an animal to be hunted. He hides behind scores of Envoys and Vigilants, not to mention entire companies of soldiers.'

'I never said I thought it would be easy,' replied Kimi.

'And you've never admitted it's impossible either.'

'I know there will be obstacles—'

'You asked me to be your bodyguard back in Virag,' said Marozvolk, her voice rising. 'And I was glad to have something to do. To have purpose once more. Grave Wolves I can fight. Gholes too if I have to. But I can't keep you safe from the entire Empire.'

'Nothing will change if we don't at least try,' said Kimi. Taiga felt a surge of pride for the woman. Her dedication was admirable if nothing else. 'Those children who died in Virag,' she continued. 'All the Spriggani who have died over the decades, the many Yamali imprisoned for speaking out. We have to change that.'

'Do you know how many people have escaped Vladibogdan in the seventy years since the academies opened?' said Marozvolk.

'I know,' said Kimi, sounding tired. 'We're the first, and we should be counting our blessings and live our lives.'

'I can't protect you from this death wish, your highness. And it's driving me to distraction. I want to be loyal, I want to be a proud Yamali warrior, but not like this.' She gestured north to the horizon. 'This is suicide.'

'Then I release you from being my bodyguard,' said Kimi. 'The clothes and the sword and whatever you're carrying are yours but I can't spare you much coin.'

'This task doesn't have to fall to you, Kimi,' said Taiga. 'Even now, Steiner could be—'

'Steiner isn't here!' shouted Kimi. She turned on her heel and loomed over Taiga, her face twisted in anger. 'I want to meet the bastard that imprisoned me for five years! I want to meet the man who took my country, my family, my life. And I will kill him!'

No one spoke in the moments that followed after. 'I'm sorry,' said Taiga, crossing her arms and clutching at herself. 'I said I'd help you'd do this, and I will.'

'I'm heading for Shanisrond.' Marozvolk said the words so softly that Taiga almost missed them. 'And you should too. We could live good, honest quiet lives and—'

'And then the Empire would invade,' said Kimi. 'It will happen, and in our lifetime. The Emperor will not stop until he has the entire continent in his grip.' Marozvolk looked away to hide her disappointment.

'I'm sorry,' said Kimi. The silence between the two women returned more persistently than ever.

The mist began to clear, revealing the still waters of the swamp stretching ahead for many miles. All manner of wild grasses and reeds broke through the damp earth, some taller than Kimi. Marozvolk squinted into the distance and Tief cursed softly. No more than half a mile away were a dozen dim figures, all hunched and cowled.

'May Frejna's eye not find you,' said Marozvolk under her breath.

'And may Frøya keep you close,' added Taiga from behind them. The gathering of gholes spread out, seeming to break apart like a flock of birds. They ran in all directions, some circling wide to flank their sides, others running headlong towards them.

'Anyone have any bright ideas?' said Tief.

'Romola said don't get dead,' replied Kimi as she drew her sword.

'Something more specific, perhaps?' grumbled Tief.

'We hit them hard and we hit them first,' said Marozvolk. 'And we stay together. Taiga?'

'I'm not going anywhere,' replied Taiga, unsheathing her dagger and pulling a sickle from her pack. 'I'm with you to the end.'

The gholes sprinted through the mist, clawed feet sending up brackish spray.

'Tief,' said Kimi. 'I'm having a bright idea.'

CHAPTER TWENTY-FOUR

Kjellrunn

It was evening in the temple and the novices were slowly tidying away the bowls and washing the pots and pans after dinner. They had dined on a thin soup, and the dark bread had been cut into slivers in order for everyone to receive a piece.

'Not a single person in the whole two weeks we've been here,' said Sundra, shaking her head. She sat with one elbow resting on the table, a lightly clenched fist in front of her mouth. Kjellrunn wondered if she feared to say too much, or if the fist told of her frustration. 'Not a single worshipper the whole time we've been here.'

'It is still early days,' said Mistress Kamalov in a soft tone that Kjellrunn found as surprising as it was tender. Mistress Kamalov ran her finger around the rim of her tea bowl and looked pensive. It was rare for the two women to speak directly to one another. They had, by some unspoken agreement, carved out their own fiefdoms in their new home. Mistress Kamalov looked to the day-to-day needs of the place. She was quartermaster of their meagre supplies, head cook, and stern mother to the children. Sundra's domain began and ended at the temple proper, and Kjellrunn and Max answered to her and only her, for the moment at least.

'It will be hard to survive like this without more money coming in,' added Mistress Kamalov after a pause. Maxim, sensing the conversation was heading in a difficult direction, gathered the last of the bowls and took himself off to the kitchen. Kjellrunn remained by Sundra's side, feeling protective of the small woman.

'It would be helpful if everyone who could work did work.' The renegade Vigilant eyed Maxim as he trotted away to the kitchen, then glanced at Kjellrunn.

'I would rather my initiate concentrate on her studies,' replied Sundra, looking down at the rough surface of the wooden table. 'It would not do for the townsfolk to find a religious figure sweeping the steps like a scullion.'

'With respect, it is not the steps of the temple I am concerned for,' said Mistress Kamalov, careful to keep her tone soft. 'The older children have found work in the town. And work means money.'

'I understand,' said Sundra, forcing a polite smile, 'Let me think on this.' She stood up and touched Kjellrunn tenderly on the shoulder. Kjellrunn couldn't help but wonder if the gesture were also proprietary. 'Come, I would speak with you.'

Kjellrunn followed the high priestess out of the crowded room, surprised when Sundra passed through the main circular hall, and out of the wide doorway, into the street.

'You're going into town right now? This evening?'

'The bones whisper your name to me, Kjellrunn,' said Sundra. 'They speak of a troubled mind.'

'Or Maxim did most likely,' she replied under her breath.

The blind beggar had begun his evening pilgrimage to the beach and Kjellrunn's mouth went dry as his white stick tap, tap, tapped along the street. Sundra caught the look and gestured that she follow.

'Come now.'

Kjellrunn had not returned to the pale hand sculpture since the night she'd felt the vast presence in the sea. She'd taken care to avoid the beach altogether, not escorting the beggar to his sightless vigil, hoping her dereliction of duty had escaped Sundra's attention. Evidently it had not.

'Will you teach me how to read the bones?' said Kjellrunn, keen to avoid a difficult conversation.

'Of course,' replied Sundra. 'But first we must unravel a more pressing mystery.'

'What mystery?'

'Why you no longer escort our friend' – Sundra gestured to the beggar, walking a few dozen feet ahead of them – 'to the beach.'

'I didn't think you meant that I escort him every night,' lied Kjellrunn.

'Nor did you think to tell me that you had stopped,' said Sundra with a disapproving stare. The buildings of Dos Khor thinned out and finally they were slip-sliding through the fine sand of the beach. The pale stone hand rose up into an angry red sky, while the sea had begun to shift from azure to cobalt with the promise of darkest green and midnight blue to come.

'You have taken to wearing your black robes with ease,' said Sundra. Kjellrunn took the old woman's arm to help her across the dunes. 'And yet we speak so rarely. You are still my initiate, are you not?'

'Of course I am.'

'Then tell me what causes your brow to furrow like this. It is not right that we keep secrets from each other.'

Kjellrunn sighed with a feeling of deep unease. Hadn't she kept her witchsign secret from Steiner all those years? Hadn't her father concealed truths for an entire decade? Even Verner had tales left untold. Secrets were the way of the Vartiainen family.

'I've only known you a few weeks,' said Kjellrunn. 'This is all very new to me.'

'This much is true. I myself am finding the changes . . .' Sundra stared out to sea, as if the word she searched for might wash in on the tide. 'I am finding the changes difficult. I miss my brother and sister, and I'm sure you must miss you family also.'

Kjellrunn nodded but didn't trust herself to speak without ushering in a wave of tears.

'I can't force you to speak to me.' Sundra stopped and looked up at the pale stone sculpture. 'All I can do is invite you to share something of yourself.' Kjellrunn watched the beggar approach the shoreline and sit down to listen to the sea.

'I scared myself,' said Kjellrunn, the words tumbling out of her. 'I closed my eyes and I lost track of time. When I opened them I was all alone, and I thought that something' – she felt the breathless panic of that moment return – 'something big, something unknown was out there.' She nodded to the vast cobalt reaches and the rushing waves.

'Can you describe it?' said Sundra, and Kjellrunn felt a surge of relief that the priestess believed her.

'I don't know.' Kjellrunn looked around, fearing a repeat of what she dreaded the most. 'It's huge. I don't know how I know that. I didn't see it, but I felt it.'

'What else?' said Sundra softly. 'How does it make you feel?'

'Scared. I'm scared of it. That's why I haven't returned since.' The old priestess drew closer and stared up into Kjellrunn's face, her gaze unwavering. There was a gentle curiosity in that look, rather than the imperious glare more common to Mistress Kamalov.

'You are blessed with the gifts of earth and water, Kjellrunn. Earth is traditionally the domain of Frejna. We come from earth and we will return to earth. This is the way of things. Water is the domain of Frøya. Life cannot exist without water. Plants, people and all living things. You may well be an initiate of Frejna, but you have a foot in both worlds. This makes you intensely special, Kjellrunn.'

'I don't feel very special. I never seem to know what I'm doing. I struggle to make myself understood here.'

Sundra held up a hand for silence. 'All of this comes with youth. I'm not sure it ever goes away.' She looked out to sea, past the white sculpture and the sitting beggar. 'Can you feel it now?'

Kjellrunn closed her eyes and took a deep and calming breath, letting herself be drawn into the sounds of the waves and the Shimmer Sea.

'Nothing. I feel nothing.' Kjellrunn opened her eyes. 'Am I going mad?'

'This is not madness. The bones whisper your name. They speak of a troubled mind and of something approaching Dos Khor, but what it is I cannot tell.' The priestess began to trudge up the beach, back towards the town. Kjellrunn followed, glad to put distance between herself and the sea.

'And this is another problem I could do without,' said Sundra, making an almost imperceptible gesture to the street ahead. Trine had been watching them from the doorway of a deserted house. She ducked back and scurried up an alley between two of the houses.

'Was she spying on us?'

'On us? I do not think so,' said Sundra. 'More likely she was spying on you.'

'I don't understand. I thought she wanted to be Mistress Kamalov's apprentice?'

'Mistress Kamalov misses you, Kjellrunn,' said Sundra. 'I daresay she sees something of herself in you. You were perhaps her only apprentice, and now you have chosen a different path.' Kjellrunn winced to hear what she could not admit to herself. 'If I had to guess I would say Trine knows this and feels second best,' continued Sundra. 'It is no easy thing to feel second best. I myself feel near useless compared to your former master.'

'That's hardly fair,' said Kjellrunn. 'Mistress Kamalov is . . .' but Sundra cut her off with a raised hand and stern look.

'We're more of an orphanage than a temple. And a poor orphanage at that.' The old woman sighed. 'This is not what I had hoped for.'

Mistress Kamalov was waiting for them on the temple steps when they returned from the beach. Trine lurked just inside the temple doors, half in shadow, black hair tumbling over her face but not concealing her sullen look.

'Kjellrunn,' said Sundra softly. 'Stop clenching your fists. Breathe.'

'Sorry. I just don't trust her is all.' Her mind was racing as she tried to imagine what the renegade Vigilant wanted.

'Do not worry yourselves so,' said Mistress Kamalov in a flat tone that did nothing to reassure Kjellrunn. 'It is good news. There are people here asking for you. I asked Maxim to speak with them until you returned.' Sundra forced a grateful smile and the priestess and initiate passed through the temple door. Kjellrunn took a moment to lock eyes with Trine. The girl sneered and stared back.

'Why did you follow us?'

'I was sent to find you,' said Trine. 'But it was clear you were on your way back when I reached you.'

Kjellrunn wasn't sure she believed a word of it and headed into the temple. 'It's too bad we didn't leave her in Virag,' she muttered.

'Concentrate,' said Sundra. 'First impressions count for a lot.'

The local people stood near the altar, a wide table made from white marble, covered in a vast diamond of black velvet that reached the floor. There were three of them, two women and a young man, all dark-skinned and wearing the flowing robes so popular in Dos Khor. The eldest of the women was stooped, with rounded shoulders and a weariness in her heavy-lidded eyes. Her dark curly hair was shot through with accents of iron grey and soft silver. Maxim bowed to Sundra with one hand over his heart. much to Kjellrunn's surprise.

'This woman lost her husband last night. She would like him to receive the blessing of Frejna before he is cremated.'

'Cremated?' whispered Kjellrunn. 'What is that?'

'The body is burned,' replied Sundra quietly. 'It is not unheard of.'

'I was a bit surprised too,' said Maxim. 'So I asked why—'

'Maxim!' Sundra's face hardened.

'What? I was curious is all.' The boy shrugged. 'They explained that it's the custom here. The desert jackals are very persistent and will dig up buried bodies.'

'It is hardly proper to ask a grieving family to explain their burial rites,' said Sundra. The bereaved man stepped forward and said something to Maxim. Kjellrunn couldn't understand the words but the dismissive look on his face told her all she needed to know.

'He asked if we can do this thing or not. He also wants to know why we're standing around whispering like old fisherman's wives.'

Kjellrunn's eyes widened as she waited for Sundra's stern retort, but the priestess merely turned and smiled at the man. She placed her hand over her heart and bowed at the waist.

'Tell him I apologise,' she said. 'And tell him that we will be honoured to send his father's soul to the afterlife with Frejna's blessing.' Maxim did as he was told and the younger woman stepped forward and took the man by the arm, chiding him with a whisper. Kjellrunn guessed they were brother and sister, though they were a few more years apart in age than Steiner and she.

'Tell them we will come for the body shortly.' Sundra bowed again to the older woman. 'We will prepare the temple and perform the funeral tomorrow.'

Maxim translated Sundra's words and guided the family towards the temple door, where Mistress Kamalov waited with a look of disapproval on her ancient features.

'That could have gone better,' said Kjellrunn.

'Come,' said Sundra. 'We have much to do. I need to teach you the funeral rites of Frejna. And we are going to need help.'

The family reached the temple doors and the young woman paused briefly to look over her shoulder at the altar where Kjellrunn and Sundra conversed. Trine was still lurking by the doorway, watching everything with a sneer.

'Are we really going to set this man on fire?' said Kjellrunn. 'Cremate him?'

Sundra nodded. 'That is the way of things here.'

'Well, if Trine is going to be watching our every move' – Kjellrunn smiled wickedly – 'we may as well put her to good use.'

'Surely you don't mean . . .?'

'She studied at Academy Plamya. Who better?'

'Mistress Kamalov may not be so keen,' said Sundra. 'And I'd rather not stir up that particular hornet's nest.'

'Perhaps it's a way for Trine to stop feeling like second best?'

Sundra considered this for a moment. 'Very well. I will ask Trine to cremate the body.'

Kjellrunn raced down the steps outside her bedroom, blinking away the morning's sleep, roused from her bed by the sound of raised voices. The temple was thick with shadows, the tiled floor cool under her feet.

'What is the meaning of this?' bellowed Mistress Kamalov, who was still in her ankle-length nightshirt. The renegade Vigilant stood outside Sundra's room, hair dishevelled, face flushed with fury. Trine waited in the temple, carefully eavesdropping on the argument, though Kjellrunn suspected the other novices could hear every word.

'The arcane is not some conjurer's trick to be pressed into service for mundane tasks!' added Mistress Kamalov.

'It was my idea,' said Kjellrunn, blocking the doorway with her body. Mistress Kamalov took a startled step back and opened her mouth to speak but Kjellrunn cut her off.

'The fire needs to be hot enough to burn the bones, and we don't know how to do that with firewood alone. Trine is always the first to use her talents, so why not this?'

'The arcane takes a toll on the user!' Mistress Kamalov glared at Kjellrunn. 'You know this better than most. Those who draw their power from the dragons suffer a corruption of the body. This is a religious ceremony. Burn the body yourselves.'

'Frøya and Frejna only grant the powers of earth and water,' said Sundra in a calm tone of voice.

'You know this better than most,' said Kjellrunn, throwing Mistress Kamalov's words back in her teeth.

'I'll do it,' said Trine with a defiant jut of her chin. 'It won't take long, it's a parlour trick is all.' The girl slunk off, past the shocked faces of the other novices who had snuck through the temple to witness the argument firsthand. 'This is most irregular,' muttered Mistress Kamalov.

'We're living in Shanisrond,' replied Kjellrunn, 'running an orphanage, delivering funeral rites in a language we don't understand, and hoping the Empire doesn't find us. We're about as far away from regular as we'll ever be.'

'Perhaps you would prefer a life on Vladibogdan?' said
Mistress Kamalov, looking down her nose at her former
apprentice.

'Why would you think that? You obviously didn't.' Kjellrunn
stepped inside the room and slammed the door. Her heart
was beating loudly in her ears.

A ghost of a smile flickered across the high priestess's face.
'What was that expression you used yesterday? "That could
have gone better"?'

'Why does she have to be such a bitch?'

'Now you sound like Trine,' replied Sundra. 'And I would
ask you not to speak in such a way in this temple.' There was
a knock on the door but Sundra held up a finger before
Kjellrunn could answer.

'I will attend to this. You have already come to my aid
once today, even though I am quite able of holding my own.'
The high priestess opened the door to find Maxim standing
outside.

'Mistress Kamalov asked me to pass on a message.'

'This is ridiculous,' muttered Sundra over her shoulder to
Kjellrunn. 'Out with it then, before I die of old age.'

'She thinks it would be wise to clear up the alcove that
Kolas sleeps in. She said it was unseemly for a ragged collection of blankets to be in the temple during the funeral service.'

'She has a point,' conceded Sundra. 'Take Kjellrunn and
move the beggar's belongings, such as they are, to a safe place.
And wash those blankets!'

'Why me?' said Kjellrunn.

'Because I have to punish you for slamming my door in
Mistress Kamalov's face.' Sundra shook her head. 'We have
a funeral to prepare for and I could well do without a
performance like this in my bed chamber.'

'But I was defending you.'

'Kjellrunn, for the love of Frøya, do as you're told, stop

shouting at your elders, and please, help me prepare for the funeral.'

Kjellrunn nodded and slipped out of the room, her cheeks burning red.

'I thought it was pretty funny,' said Maxim. 'I don't like Vigilants. At all.'

Kjellrunn smiled. 'You're not helping, Maxim.'

'Probably not.' The boy smiled, then looked around to check they were alone. 'But wait until you see what I saw in the beggar's alcove.'

CHAPTER TWENTY-FIVE

Silverdust

Silverdust was tired. The endless miles had taken their toll. From Vladibogdan to the shores of Nordvlast and abandoned Cinderfell, through the forest to Steinwick and on to the vast skies of Novaya Zemlya. Across the cheerless steppe and over the border to the swamps and stillness of Vend. It was not a tiredness of body Silverdust felt, for his flesh had long since passed on, but the daily change of scenery and the need to be wary of danger had sapped his energy. They had taken ship from a stinking, dour port in Vend Province and finally, Streig said the words that Silverdust had wanted to hear more than any others.

'We're here. The captain says we should be in port within the hour.'

Silverdust drifted up from the hold, where he had waited in the gloom. It had comforted him to do so, a reminder of the darkness of the forges on Vladibogdan. 'This is the longest journey I've ever taken,' said Streig, joining Silverdust on deck. 'And now I find myself at the heart of the Empire, about to set foot in the capital city.' Silverdust sensed the young soldier's veneration and an undercurrent of excitement.

Your need to romanticise the city is misplaced. The people here care

only for money and their own skins. The Vigilants are more ruthless
than anyone you will meet, loyal only to their own advancement.

'But this is Khlystburg,' protested Streig. 'Even you can
admit that it invokes a measure of awe.' He dropped his
voice to a whisper. 'You may not love the Empire, or the
Emperor that rules it, but the city . . .'

The word 'khlyst' is an old dialect term for whip. That's what the
Holy Synod are, the Emperor's whips, the ones that purge through the
application of pain. Those who speak out are brought here and disap-
pear below ground to be questioned. No one survives such a thing.

'That doesn't make any sense,' said Streig. 'Khlystburg isn't
a prison.'

What does not make sense is that the capital city is many days'
travel from the rest of the Empire. This was a place where the Emperor
could work in secret and do as he wished without interference.
Khlystburg only became the capital once the Emperor had consolidated
his position.

As the ship drew closer they could see the graceful towers.
The buildings were painted in gaudy colours, as if trying to
fend off the sombre clouds that hung over the city. Many of
the towers featured bulbous domes that tapered at the top,
shining weakly in silver or gold. Other buildings were dressed
in red stone, while others stood resplendent in ivory or cream.

'The city of whips,' said Streig. His expression became subdued
and he leaned against the side of the ship. 'We'll be lucky to
leave this place with our lives.' Streig cast a glance over his
shoulder at the other soldiers. Father Orlov and the Envoy
conversed together at the stern. 'What befalls you here will find
a way to my door too, I suspect.'

You will be fine. Just tell them you were following the Envoy's
orders to stand guard over me. Silverdust couldn't truly say he
believed what he'd told the young soldier, but it was all
he could do.

*　　*　　*

The antechamber to the Imperial Court was a dimly lit room that could have easily homed five peasant families. Candles flickered from six wrought-iron stands, each the height of a man and twice as heavy. Two elderly men polished the intricately tiled floor on their hands and knees. The menials looked up from their labour every so often to tut at the Envoy's soldiers.

The Envoy had taken to pacing like a Novgoruske tiger. Father Orlov by contrast barely moved, as still as one of the many memorial statues outside in the Imperial Gardens. After a full hour had passed, the doors creaked open suddenly and Envoy de Vries turned to Silverdust and smiled sweetly.

'Shall we?' She turned before Silverdust could answer, striding into the hall as if it were no more than her local tavern. Her carefree entrance was interrupted by the Semyonovsky Guard, who crossed their spears, blocking further passage. Black cords decorated their armour, crossing their chest before looping at one side and ending in a tassel. The red star on their helm, the symbol of the Solmindre Empire, had been dyed black upon entry to the Emperor's elite bodyguard.

'What is the meaning of this?' said Father Orlov, who remained trapped in the antechamber with the soldiers.

'The only armed persons who may enter this room are high-ranking members of the Holy Synod and courtiers with appointments.' The man stepped closer to Father Orlov. 'Which you would know had you been here before, Ordinary.'

'I am Father Orlov from Vladibogdan and I am escorting Envoy de Vries.'

'That would make sense,' said the Semyonovsky guard. 'She never could follow the rules. Arrogant bitch.' Then the guard grabbed Father Orlov by the scruff of the neck and slung him through the doorway, before turning his gaze back to the soldiers. 'I suggest the rest of you return to barracks.'

The guard paused as he caught sight of Silverdust. 'I suppose you'll be wanting to come in as well.' Silverdust nodded and the Envoy's soldiers drew back to let him pass, muttering as they did so.

'What shall I do?' whispered Streig. Silverdust directed the words to Streig's mind alone, so no one else could know his intent.

There is a viewing gallery. At least there was last time I was here. Bribe the menials, have them show you the way. And put your helm on. If a lowly soldier like you appears before the Emperor with an uncovered head he will likely remove it.

Silverdust glided forward, past the towering double doors and the Semyonovsky Guard, into the cavernous splendour of the Imperial Court. The vast hall was awash with tiles the colour of palest sand and bluest ocean, while the wood-panelled walls were intricately carved, painted white and decorated with gold leaf. Candles were suspended in chandeliers like constellations of stars. Silverdust's mind drifted to the starving children in Kulyagesh and he felt a surge of irritation. The throne was at the opposite end of the chamber, some two hundred feet from the doors.

Envoy de Vries had taken her place in the loose semicircle of courtiers surrounding the throne. She stood very straight, eyes bright and alert, with a contented smile. Father Orlov stood close to her, casting a glance at Silverdust as the Exarch joined the courtiers. Four Semyonovsky guards stood near the throne clutching heavy spears, each one a veteran of the Emperor's armies, exuding a palpable aura of menace, and yet they were not the most dangerous people in the room.

The Emperor was a dark-haired man, with pale eyes and a high forehead. More slender than the soldiers of his court, he had a wiry strength and a stillness that hinted at years of discipline. He wore knee-length riding boots of deepest black, with britches and a jacket in a matching hue. All manner of medals and black braid covered his chest, while a sash of crimson circled his waist, almost concealing the sheathed dagger on his hip.

The Emperor stepped down from the throne with a brow furrowed in annoyance. A young noble knelt before him with his head bowed, hands clasped together yet visibly shaking.

'I swear to you that I did not take the taxes that are rightfully yours, Your Imperial Highness.' The young man's clothes, silks and velvets in a supposedly fashionable motley indicated he was a person of some means. Silverdust guessed he was a Boyar from one of the provinces, or the son of a Boyar – judging by his age.

'Stand up,' said the Emperor. His voice still had the whispery quality to it that Silverdust remembered, yet there was steel in that whisper that compelled and commanded. It had been many years since Silverdust had stood before the Emperor. He'd had a different name back then, a lower rank, worn a different mask. So much had changed in the decades since then.

The young nobleman stood warily. Sweat shone at his temples and stained the fabric of his velvet coat at the armpits.

'I should cut out your tongue,' said the Emperor with a terrible quietness. 'So you can tell no more lies. What will your father think when he learns that you insulted me here, in my own court?'

'I swear to you.' The young man held out his shaking hands in supplication. 'The money was taken from me two nights ago by thieves in the Voronin District. I would never lie to you, Your Imperial Highness.' The Emperor nodded as if considering the young man's words then circled around behind him, his pale eyes fixed on the floor in deep contemplation. His hand drew the dagger and regarded it for moment as if it were a recently received gift. The metal did not reflect even a glimmer of the many candles in the room, and grey ashes flaked from the dull surface like dismal snow. A sneer had quirked the Emperor's thin lips and something in his pale eyes had hardened.

The young nobleman chose this moment to snatch a glance over his shoulder. His eyes widened in alarm as he caught sight of the blade in the Emperor's hand. He cringed but remained rooted to the spot, blind obedience outweighing his instinct for survival.

The Emperor released a long sigh and paused to look at his audience. He nodded to Envoy de Vries and then turned to Silverdust. For a second the Exarch felt an immense pressure on his mind, like the tension in the air heralding a thunderstorm. The feeling passed suddenly and Silverdust remained content the Emperor had not breached his mental defences.

'I was not always the man you see now,' the Emperor said in his whispering voice. He gestured with the dark knife as if it were no more than a crust of bread, and he a peasant farmer slightly the worse for drink. The semicircle of courtiers edged backwards, all eyes fixed on the blade and the ashes that fell from it. The Emperor approached the throne and took a long draught from a golden goblet on a small table. He turned back to his audience of Vigilants, Envoys, and high-ranking soldiers with a wry smile. 'You might even say I was the Holy Synod's first member.' His expression darkened in a heartbeat. '*I invented the fucking synod!*' he shouted with such force that the young nobleman flinched. Piss pooled by Sokolov's boots in the moments that followed. Silverdust heard a collective intake of breath from the courtiers, felt their unease, their dread.

The Emperor huffed a breath and shook his head, as if trying to shake off his fury. When he spoke again his voice had returned to its customary whisper. 'Some Vigilants can know the hearts of men, know their minds. One who is very skilled might even know a man's memories. I too have this power, and I see you, Dimitri Sokolov. I see you deeply.' The Emperor smiled at the young man and held out his arms as if to embrace the nobleman. 'Dimitri! Of course you would never steal your father's taxes!'

Sokolov. Silverdust knew the name, they were one of the Great Families, with a long and storied past that reached back to the Age of Tears. This must be the son of Boyar Sokolov, who ruled Vend Province. Dimitri shook with nerves, confusion written across his pale face. Did the Emperor intend to embrace him?

'After everything your family has done for me across generations! Of course you would not steal those taxes.' The Emperor stepped forward and swept his arms around the young man, then kissed him on the forehead.

'Y-your Imperial Highness, I—' But Dimitri said nothing more. The dull blade entered his back and several of the courtiers winced or looked away. Dimitri Sokolov shuddered in the Emperor's arms, eyes wide and mouth gasping in shock. Crow's feet appeared at the corners of the young man's eyes and his sandy hair became shot through with grey, before turning white. His hands wrinkled and the knuckles became like knots under the skin. Dimitri Sokolov managed a wheezing breath before he died as an old man. The Emperor stood back from the husk before him and the corpse collapsed to the tiled floor. No blood stained the dull blade the Emperor clutched, and grey flecks of ash floated to the floor, alighting in blood and urine.

The Emperor closed his pale eyes and took a deep and rapturous breath. He swayed on his feet, shivering with pleasure, then sighed with contentment. For a moment the Emperor forgot his mental defences and Silverdust had a brief glimmer of the incandescent rage that lay at the heart of the man, and also the heady intoxication. In one thrust the Emperor had siphoned the life from the nobleman and made himself younger.

'He did not steal from me,' said the Emperor in a calm voice to the courtiers around him. He flashed a warm and gentle smile quite at odds with the corpse at his feet. 'He gave most of the money to peasants who would rise up against me. The rest he spent on whores and wine.' The Emperor mounted the steps to the throne and lifted his goblet to the courtiers in a parody of a toast, then drank deeply. The Semyonovsky Guard dragged the elderly corpse from the room as the courtiers spoke among themselves in whispers.

'Your Imperial Highness,' said Envoy de Vries, stepping forward from the semicircle. She performed a deep bow to the Emperor and smiled. 'I bring two Vigilants from far Vladibogdan. I know you have been awaiting them with great anticipation.'

The Emperor's gaze settled on Silverdust and he breathed deeply, but his stare was glassy and unseeing, attention elsewhere.

'Your Highness?' said de Vries, her smile slipping.

'Not today,' said the Emperor, as if the fate of the Empire's sole training academy were of no consequence. 'I think we have all had enough drama, de Vries. I must write to Boyar Sokolov. I will tell him what a worthless dog his son was. I'll ask him how Vend Province will make reparations for this gross insult.'

'It will be as you say, Your Imperial Highness.' Envoy de Vries bowed again and retreated from the Emperor, her face carefully blank of expression, her eyes lowered. Silverdust could feel her fury, her frustration. The Emperor left from a door at the back of the room and the courtiers began to drift away. Silverdust felt the tension ebb as each commander, Vigilant, Boyar and Envoy turned to leave. Streig was waiting when the Exarch reached the antechamber. Silverdust could tell the young soldier was sick to his stomach.

You saw all of that, I take it?

Streig nodded, gesturing they should leave through a side door. Silverdust led them from the palace and Streig removed his helm once they were in the gardens outside. He was pale and covered in sweat, eyes darting nervously from side to side.

'What was that dagger?'

The Ashen Blade. It takes life from one and bestows it on the wielder.

'And he does that to his own people?' There was a wildness in Streig's eyes that Silverdust had not seen before. Perhaps it had been a mistake to suggest that he watch from the gallery.

Keep your voice down. We are still in the palace grounds. The Semyonovsky will execute you in a moment for speaking of such a thing.

'What do we do now?' said Streig as they walked towards the inner gatehouse.

We find quarters. We should rest. Tomorrow is going to be a long day.

'The Boyar's son . . .' Streig shook his head. 'Do you think such an uprising could occur in Vend? They could barely afford knives, let alone swords.'

The boy was innocent. He was indeed robbed in the Voronin District, just as he said he was.

'But the Emperor said he could read minds—'

And that is undoubtedly true, but the Emperor lied about Dimitri's guilt. I too read the young master's mind. I know Dimitri's truth.

'Then why him?' whispered Streig, leaning close. 'Why kill a Boyar's son?'

Because the Emperor lies. He lies for sport and he lies to manipulate. Imagine the wave of fear that will spread across the continent now. Every Boyar will do their utmost to appear absolutely loyal.

They will seek out unrest and put down any rebels in the most public way possible.

'And you?' said Streig, as they passed through the dim tunnel of the gatehouse. 'How will you fare tomorrow, given the Emperor can reach into your mind?'

My mind is not an open book.

'But Envoy de Vries and Father Orlov—'

I simply wish for the Emperor to hold me close, just as he did to Dimitri. That is all I require, nothing more.

'So you mean to die.'

Only if such a death gives me what I need.

CHAPTER TWENTY-SIX

Steiner

Steiner couldn't sleep that night, knowing the Vigilant was so close at hand. Kristofine lay in the crook of his arm lost to the deep silence of sleep, yet Steiner could get no rest. Long hours he remained awake until the boredom was almost as bad as the tiredness. He took a moment to extricate himself from the tangle of limbs, dressed quietly, and slipped downstairs. The sun had yet to rise but someone else was awake despite the hour. She wore her dark hair in two long braids and hummed to herself as she worked, stacking and cleaning various mugs and cups behind the bar.

'Morning,' said Steiner, wincing as he pronounced the word in Solska.

'We can talk in Nordspråk if you prefer,' said the innkeeper. She had a way of smiling on one side of her mouth. Faint crow's feet lined the corners of her eyes and a few strands of her dark hair had turned silver. Steiner reckoned her to be in her early thirties.

'How did you know?' replied Steiner in his own tongue.

'My husband overheard you last night. He doesn't understand much of it, but he knows Nordspråk when he hears it.'

'Where are you from?'

'Vannerånd, but that was a long time ago. Twenty years or more. You know, the locals here still distrust me because I'm not a Solmindre girl.' She rolled her eyes. 'What can I get you?'

'Water, please.' The innkeeper took a moment to pour water from a jug and set it on the bar.

'Come, sit.'

'What is this town?' asked Steiner after he'd slaked his thirst.

'You don't know where you are?'

'We've been travelling a long time, and without a map.'

'You're in Vostochnyye Lisy,' she replied. 'There was a longer version of the name, but that's what it's called now. Something about "the home of the eastern foxes".'

'You get lot of foxes around here?'

'No, but the locals here often have red hair and there are some strange old myths.'

'I can't imagine the Exarch is too keen on old myths about foxes,' replied Steiner.

'No,' admitted the innkeeper. 'I daresay he's quite opposed to them. Still, that's one problem I don't need to worry about. He left about a half hour before you appeared. It seems to be the morning for early risers.'

'I'm Steiner.' He quickly regretted not using a false name, but something about the woman made him feel safe. 'I'm from Nordvlast.'

'And you're wanted by the Empire,' replied the innkeeper, though there was no judgment in her voice and her expression spoke only of compassion or pity.

'Maybe.' Steiner shrugged.

'It was the same for me when I came here.' She set down the mug she was cleaning and came closer, though the bar lay between them. 'I'm Lidija.' She presented her hand palm up and a tongue of fire sparked to life. Steiner's eyes widened;

he hadn't seen anyone manifest the arcane since Virag. Lidija closed her fingers and the flame disappeared.

'You came here to avoid Invigilation,' said Steiner.

'They'd already taken my sister while we were in Vannerånd. My parents couldn't bear to lose another child, so we took new names and moved here. Somehow it worked.'

'And that's why you weren't working last night,' added Steiner.

Lidija nodded. 'A little bird told me the Exarch was coming. I hear things from time to time.'

Steiner smiled. 'You want to share any of them?'

'I heard an army of children used the arcane in the streets of Virag to fight Imperial soldiers.'

'It was hardly an army,' replied Steiner with a puzzled smile. It was strange to him that stories could grow out of all proportion and how fast they could travel.

'And I heard of a man, seven feet tall, who could smite an Imperial soldier with a single blow from his sledgehammer.'

'I'm a few inches short of six foot, but don't let the details get in the way of a good story.' They laughed and a companionable silence settled in around them.

'They will kill you, Steiner,' said Lidija gently.

'I know.'

'And everyone you have ever cared about.'

'That's why we have to rise up,' said Steiner. 'That's why we can no longer hide.' Lidija's eyes were full of sadness, but the sadness was not for herself.

'This is no small thing. The Emperor has reigned for over seven decades. There are doubts he can be killed. They say he is no longer human.'

Steiner's thoughts drifted to Nils.

Tell me you'll kill him, dragon rider. Tell me you'll smash his black soul with your great hammer.

'You say you hear things from time to time?' he asked. Lidija nodded. 'Well, be careful. We approached a man called Tikhoveter in Virag, but the Empire killed him before he could get much information for us.' Lidija became pale. 'I'm sorry,' said Steiner. 'Did you know him?'

She shook her head. 'Only as a name, a voice on the wind, and rarely at that.'

'He told us about a mercenary company here, in Slavon.'

'I know, it was I that discovered them. Just shadows and rumours mainly. They were camped in the forest like brigands for a time, but no one has spoken of them lately.' Steiner swore softly under his breath. 'Friends of yours?'

'One of them.' He placed the wooden mug back on the bar and gave thanks.

'Be careful not to wake your sister,' said Lidija.

Steiner smiled. 'Who told you she was my sister?'

'My husband. He said you seemed like two kids vying for your father's attention. Did he read you wrong?'

Steiner frowned. 'She's not my sister.'

'Forgive me,' replied Lidija. 'I'm sure your father is very proud of you. You've no need to seek his approval.'

Steiner nodded and forced a smile to hide his shame, then left the room to trudge up the stairs to his room. Approval. The word weighed heavily on him.

'And you're sure the Exarch has gone?' said Marek. He'd joined Kristofine and Steiner in their room later that morning. They were all bleary-eyed, legs aching from the many miles covered in the last few weeks.

Steiner nodded. 'The innkeeper's wife told me. We can trust her. She's called Lidija.'

'Making new friends?' said Kristofine. 'Should I be jealous?'

Steiner smiled. 'Well, I am a famous folk hero now. I'm likely to attract attention from time to time.'

Kristofine snorted an exasperated sort of laugh. 'Well, you're in better spirits today.'

'Thank Frejna for small mercies,' said Marek.

'I have an idea,' said Steiner, 'but it's not without risk.'

'Every day is a risk,' said Kristofine with a shrug.

'I promised Kimi to spread word of Vladibogdan in the hopes we could start some sort of uprising, and I'm keen to find Felgenhauer.'

'And you think she's close by?' asked Marek.

Steiner shook his head. 'I don't know, but if we stay here, in Vostochnyye Lisy, and tell our story, maybe Felgenhauer will come find us.'

'And maybe the Empire will find us first,' said Marek.

'I *did* say it would be a risk, but we can achieve two things at once.' Steiner looked at Marek and Kristofine's grim expressions. 'If Frøya smiles on us,' he added.

'She'd need to smile a lot,' said Marek.

'You really want to find this aunt, don't you?' said Kristofine.

'It must have been terrible for you to lose your mother,' said Steiner.

'Of course,' replied Kristofine. 'But what does that have to do with Felgenhauer?'

'I never knew my mother, or at least I can't remember her. Felgenhauer is a link to her, I suppose.'

Marek shook his head. 'You can't be sure we can trust her. Felgenhauer always looked out for herself.'

'No,' replied Steiner, in a quiet yet firm voice. 'I wouldn't have survived Vladibogdan without her.'

Marek frowned. 'That's as maybe but—'

'And she has men and she wields the arcane,' continued Steiner. 'We need her.'

'I can see your heart's set on this,' said Marek. He opened the door and left the room with a grim look on his grizzled face.

'So we'll tell this story then?' said Steiner. 'Tonight?'

Kristofine grabbed his hand and squeezed it. 'I much prefer it when you're excited about a terrible scheme that will get us killed.'

'Prefer it to what?' said Steiner.

'The endless sulking. You've been acting like a whipped dog for weeks.'

'I'm sorry,' said Steiner, looking down. 'Growing up in Cinderfell as the illiterate blacksmith with a pariah sister never did my confidence much good. I guess there'll always be a part of me doubting myself. And this storytelling thing, well, I reckon it just plays into those fears. Makes me feel like I'm illiterate all over again.'

'Illiterate?' Kristofine frowned. 'After all the things you've achieved and the victories you've won, and you're still worrying about letters and numbers.'

Steiner chuckled and held Kristofine's hand a little tighter.

'We'll tell this story of yours tonight,' she continued. 'And we'll tell it together.'

'We can do this,' said Steiner. 'I know we can do this.'

'What is it that he finds so objectionable about Felgenhauer?' asked Kristofine. She lay against him, drowsing in the late afternoon. Rehearsals had been set aside and the windows of the small room had steamed up. Steiner had been able to forget his worries for a time.

'My father? I've no idea. He's not said much about her.' Steiner cast his mind back. 'Perhaps there's more to it than he's letting on.'

A loud knock on the door made them both start and Steiner was already half out of bed when his father's voice called from the other side.

'Dinner will be served in half an hour. I'll see you two down there.'

'See you down there,' Steiner called back.

They made their way to the bar and settled in at the same table as the previous night. Marek nodded to them both but said nothing and Kristofine blushed and looked away. Food was ordered and provided a welcome distraction from the evening's storytelling. Steiner ate as well as he could, but in truth his gut was knotted with nerves.

'You'll be fine,' said Kristofine. Lidija approached the table with three tall wooden mugs of ale and set them down.

'You're sure about this?' said Marek to her.

Lidija nodded. 'What will be will be. Tell your story. I'm tired of hiding.' She looked around the room and sighed. 'And if a rebellion is going to start somewhere, well, it may as well be here.'

Steiner finished his food, knocked back half his ale, and lurched to his feet. His hand strayed to his sledgehammer, hanging from a loop on his belt.

'You'll be great,' said Kristofine, though Marek's expression made it clear he didn't share her optimism. Steiner held his hand out and Kristofine took it with a frown and a smile.

'What are you doing?' asked Marek.

'You told me there's no need to fight among ourselves,' said Steiner. 'Her Solska is better than mine, her storytelling is better than mine, and Kristofine's a damn sight nicer to look at.' He pulled her to her feet and squeezed her close. 'We're telling the story together.'

Marek nodded with a satisfied smile on his face and raised his mug.

'At last, the dragon rider talks some sense.'

'What changed your mind?' said Kristofine as they crossed the bar. 'I thought you wanted to be the one to tell your story.'

Steiner leaned close to her with a smile. 'The innkeeper thought we were brother and sister vying for our father's attention.' He nodded to Marek. 'And that's when I finally realised, I'm not in competition with you, we're in this together. You're good at some things and I'm better at others. I don't have to resent you for that.'

'And it took you Frejna knows how many weeks to work that out?' said Kristofine, shaking her head.

'Sorry. You know better than most that I'm slow to catch on.'

She kissed him right there at the bar and Steiner kissed her back. The kiss lasted longer than either intended and a great call went up as the locals cheered them on. 'That got their attention,' said Kristofine, looking around the inn with a rueful smile.

'Maybe we should start with that every time?' said Steiner with a grin. Kristofine nudged him in the ribs, then stepped forward and held up her hands for silence.

'Gentlefolk of Vostochnyye Lisy,' said Kristofine in Solska. Her voice carried over the hubbub of the crowd and the many people settled down. 'And the *not*-so-gentlefolk of Vostochnyye Lisy.' A great roar went up from the patrons and laughter followed after it. 'I come to you all the way from Nordvlast with a tale to tell. The hearing of it will not be easy, but I stand before you with the man I love and truth in my heart. Who will listen?'

The crowd mumbled their assent, less raucous now, their curiosity outweighing their wariness.

'Who among you have lost children to Invigilation?' asked Kristofine. 'Because that is how our tale began in the tiny town of Cinderfell way up on the north-western coast of Vinterkveld.'

It was not the beginning Steiner had hoped for, but the room became still and no one spoke. One man departed, slamming the door as he left. Steiner stepped forward.

'I always knew my sister was different,' he said in Solska. 'But I loved her all the same. The Vigilants came as they always do and something strange happened.'

Kristofine took over the tale, weaving in the hammer brooch that kept Kjellrunn's witchsign hidden. She described Shirinov and Khigir and the events that followed, how Steiner had been turned away from her father's tavern, and how they had shared the night in the barn. She nodded to Steiner and he stepped forward.

'And here's the thing I learned: the children of Solmindre and the Scorched Republics are not killed by the Empire. They are taken by ship to a remote island. Their powers are pressed into service by the very Empire that would have you shun them.' The room broke out in a series of disbelieving conversations and Steiner worried they had lost the crowd.

'These children,' said Kristofine, holding up her hands for quiet once more, 'your children, abhorred, hated and reviled for their differences, are turned into Vigilants. Vigilants like the one you saw just last night in this very spot.'

'We need to tell them about the cinderwraiths and the dragons too,' said Steiner quietly, but Kristofine shook her head.

'We've given them plenty to think on. Let's not overdo it.'

'And what of the garrison up in the mountain pass?' shouted a man from the back of the room. 'I suppose that was you too.'

'It depends what you heard,' said Steiner, fixing the man with a hard stare.

'I heard a father and son were seen cleaving through soldiers.' The man stepped forward, long red hair and beard worn in plaits, his leather trousers and boots battered by the weather. Steiner held up his sledgehammer for all to see.

'Not much chance of cleaving anything with this.' That earned him a few chuckles. 'But I was there.'

'If that's so then where's your father?' said the plaited man.

Marek stood up from the table beside the fire.

'I was there,' he said. 'I fought those black-armoured devils, shoulder to shoulder with my son. I've never been more proud of him.'

'It's true,' said an older man with silver-white hair. 'I came through the pass just last week on my horse. Not a soul there, just ashes and bones.'

The crowd responded warmly. A few of the men raised their fists and roared words that sounded part war cry and part exultation. Other patrons conferred with their friends, the shock giving way to a thrill of excitement that such a thing could happen.

'I think the story is taking root,' Steiner said to Kristofine, feeling a great swell of relief.

'And some will pass it on to their friends and so on.' She flashed him a smile and slipped an arm around his waist. 'Your legend grows.'

Marek approached with a hint of a tear in the corner of his eye as the room was filled with the sounds of clapping and shouts of defiance and joy.

'You did it,' said Marek, clapping his son on the shoulder. He leaned forward and kissed Kristofine on the forehead.

'We did it together,' said Steiner. 'The three of us. I'd do well to remember that.'

The door at the back of the inn opened and shout of alarm went up. There was a wet sound followed by a thump and Steiner knew in his very bones that someone had been killed.

'Soldiers!' shouted someone. The room became a blur of motion, and through the chaos Steiner watched Exarch Zima enter the room.

CHAPTER TWENTY-SEVEN

Kimi

Twelve of them came as the mist swirled and retreated. Twelve hunched and sinister forms, sprinting and hobbling and scrambling forward.

'That's your bright idea?' said Tief, drawing his blade with a grim expression. 'Light a torch?'

'It worked on the Grave Wolves, didn't it?' said Kimi. She struggled with the flint and tinder as the gholes rushed ever closer.

'Grave Wolves remember enough of their old lives to be afraid of fire,' said Tief. 'I'm not sure these things are afraid of anything.'

'They can be scared of me,' intoned Marozvolk. She sang something under her breath and her skin shimmered with the subtle arcane transformation. Marozvolk drew her sword and said nothing more, staring down the undead creatures with a flinty resolve. The gholes had covered the half mile with unsettling speed.

'We don't have time for this,' said Tief. 'Draw your sword and get ready to fight.'

'Come on,' whispered Kimi. The torch began smoking then burst into flames as the priestess of Frejna blew gently on the

flint and tinder. 'Thank you,' said Kimi. Tief glared at his
sister but the moment was lost as the gholes rushed at them
from all sides. Marozvolk used her left arm as an improvised
shield as one of the gholes raked her with both hands. The
claws shredded her jacket but the skin beneath remained
resolute. Marozvolk replied with a sword thrust to the guts,
then ripped the blade free and smashed the crosspiece into
the creature's face, sending the ghole sprawling in the swamp
with a splash.

Tief did not have the luxury of Marozvolk's stony skin. He
parried his attacker's foul and fetid claws, once, twice, then
staggered backwards under the onslaught. In desperation he
dodged to the side, swinging wildly. The blade bit into the
back of the ghole's skull as it lunged forward. There was a
jarring crunch before the creature fell face-first into the
brackish water.

It was Taiga that Kimi was most concerned about, but her
fears were misplaced. A ghole had circled around their small
group and raced up behind in jerky strides, desperate to
extinguish the lives of all. Taiga turned to the creature and
crossed her blades. In her left hand she bore a sickle, while
in her right she wielded a slender dagger. The ghole hesitated
at the sight of this, then staggered. Taiga intoned a long stream
of strange words, each syllable forcing the undead creature
to its knees. Taiga rushed forward and sliced the ghole across
the throat with the sickle before thrusting the dagger into the
darkness of the hood. The ghole screeched pitifully, holding
up twisted claws to its mangled face. Taiga withdrew the
dagger and slashed with the sickle once more. The ghole
stiffened, then slumped onto its side, its head rolling loose.

Kimi found herself beset by two of the hooded horrors.
Slashing claws were batted aside with a flurry of clumsy
parries. She was painfully aware she might stumble in the
uncertain footing of the swamp. Kimi stepped to one side,

using one creature as an obstacle to the other, even if only for a second. She dropped to one knee and hacked at the leg of the nearest ghole, then thrust upwards with the torch as her attacker fell forward. For a moment the flames were buried in the mouldering fabric of the ghole's robes and Kimi doubted her plan after all. A heartbeat later and the ghole was shaking and screaming. It lurched backwards and limped away, batting at its smoking hood.

Tief parried and ducked the claws of two gholes. He was losing ground, being separated from the group, but Kimi was powerless to prevent it.

'Tief!' she called out, hearing the desperation in her voice.

'Frejna's teeth,' growled Tief as a claw raked across his shoulder, snagging in the fabric of his heavy coat. Taiga stepped in before him, crossing her blades again, the sickle and dagger dark and bloody against the pale sky. Again she made an invocation to Frøya, her expression stern as more strange syllables did their arcane work. The gholes attacking Tief stumbled sideways as if hit by a cart. One clutched its hooded head and splashed face down into the swamp. Tief grabbed the other ghole by its wrist and hacked at the creature's throat until the head came free.

Marozvolk's initial luck had abandoned her. Three gholes crowded in, one grasping her left arm so she could no longer parry the raking claws. Two more harried her with savage attacks, cutting her clothes to jagged ribbons, but when the blacked talons reached her skin they found nothing but stone. The gholes hissed with frustration and piled onto Marozvolk, forcing her to her knees, then pushing her over, onto her back. Her sword fell from her hand as she struggled to stay upright.

'Kimi!' Marozvolk shouted from lips of stone as the gholes grabbed her around the throat. Marozvolk thrashed, kicking one of her attackers so hard it fell sideways into a bed of reeds. The remaining two gholes forced her head under the turbid

waters, hissing and whispering in frenzied excitement. Kimi
lunged towards Marozvolk's attackers as another ghole swiped
at her; the claws snagged in her cloak but failed to draw blood.
Kimi thrust the flaming torch into the cowl of the first ghole,
shouting wordlessly. The creature jerked backwards and Kimi
used the reprieve to kick Marozvolk's other attacker in the
head, sending it sprawling. Marozvolk needed no invitation
to rejoin the fight. She stumbled to her feet with a look of
rage on features carved in stone. The former Vigilant grasped
the ghole that had fallen next to her and bludgeoned it with
her fist, punching with such force, over and over, that the
creature's head was reduced to a stinking pulp.

'You've got to remove the head,' shouted Tief through
the chaos.

'Thanks,' shouted Marozvolk, holding a headless ghole
by the scruff of the neck. She swung the corpse in front of
her, using it as a shield to fend off yet another attacker. 'How
I love it when men tell me how to fight.'

Kimi had turned her back on her own attacker to rescue
Marozvolk from drowning, and the ghole seized the moment
in a heartbeat. The creature took handfuls of the cloak and
pulled the cord tight against her throat. Kimi coughed, struggling to make words as the ghole strangled her. She flailed
blindly with her sword but failed to strike her attacker. The
creature crowded in close behind her, forcing her down. It
took a breathless moment to reverse her grip on the blade
and the edges of her vision grew dark.

'Frøya save me,' she whispered, then thrust the sword under
her arm, feeling the tip of the sword meet the ghole behind
her. Dead flesh gave way as she thrust again and something
splashed out of the wound, foul and stinking. The pressure
at her throat slackened and she gasped, tasting the charnel
stench of the gholes as she did so. Tief appeared with one
hand extended, hauling her to her feet as he parried the

slashing claws of Kimi's attacker. The ghole's arm came down with startling speed and Tief lashed out on instinct alone. There was a moment when the force of the blow jarred all three of them and the ghole's arm sailed off to splash down in the swamp a dozen feet away. The ghole held up the severed limb, staring at it with mute fascination. Kimi couldn't move, too shocked at the speed and ferocity of the combat. The wounded ghole hissed at Kimi and Tief, then sprinted away. The remaining creatures began to rout, following with alarming speed. Five of their unholy kin lay unmoving in the waters. Tief, Marozvolk and Kimi watched the retreat, breathing deeply, almost too weak to stand.

'I thought we were dead,' said Tief. 'When I saw how many they were . . .' He shook his head in disbelief and wiped his blade clean.

'Thank you for saving me,' said Marozvolk quietly to Kimi. 'Stone skin will protect you from most things, but being drowned isn't one of them.' She shook her head. 'And here I was thinking I was *your* bodyguard.'

Kimi smiled. 'I'm just glad we're all in one piece.'

'Not quite all of us,' said Taiga from behind them. As one they turned and Kimi's heart stuttered in her chest. Taiga held one hand to her side where a ghole's claws had ripped through her clothes. Her fingers were dark with blood. 'It was going so well. The goddess was with me and then one of them charged me from the side . . .' Taiga gave them an apologetic smile. 'I didn't notice at first and then . . .' Her eyes rolled back in her head and she slumped forward. Tief caught her as she fell to her knees.

'This won't end well,' said Marozvolk quietly as Tief called his sister's name over and over.

'Don't speak that way,' said Kimi. 'Find us somewhere close to camp, and find it quickly.'

* * *

Within an hour they had found a huddle of rocks and headed towards them in the hopes of shelter. Kimi realised they were not boulders but a collection of long flat stones. Each stood on its end, side by side with its kin, forming a wall of sorts, arranged in a circle just ten feet wide. There was a gap wide enough for a person to slip into the centre.

'What is this place?' said Kimi as she dragged her fingers across the stone. Moss fell away revealing old runes made indistinct by the passage of rain and time.

'The folk who used to live in Izhoria made their homes of wood,' said Tief as he sat beside Taiga. 'They all rotted away decades ago, but their shrines remain.' He pointed to the base of one of the stones, where moss had grown in the groove of an engraved symbol, forming a green spiral. Kimi began to make up a fire and fetched bandages from one of the packs.

'I'm going to need boiling water,' Kimi said, eyeing the paltry collection of sticks that they had for firewood. 'Or as hot as I can get it.'

'The Ashen Torment,' said Marozvolk, 'it's still glowing.' Kimi took the shattered artefact from around her neck, holding it by the chain. The fragment of stone that remained gave off a faint ghostly light.

'They're still close by,' said Kimi. 'Perhaps they'll come for us at night.'

'Perhaps it's that artefact that's luring the gholes to us?' said Tief. 'Maybe they can sense it.'

'You don't know that,' snapped Marozvolk.

'You should get rid of it, Kimi.' Tief eyed the broken artefact. 'The power is gone, Steiner saw to that.'

'I wore this stone for five years,' said Kimi, 'and I commanded all the souls of Vladibogdan to do the Empire's bidding. I'll not throw it in some swamp to be forgotten so easily.'

'It's a cursed thing,' muttered Tief. 'You can bet your boots on it.'

'That's not what you said to Steiner,' replied Kimi. 'You wanted to lead an army of cinderwraiths across Vinterkveld.'

'When it had power!' said Tief. 'When we had a chance to use it against the Empire. Now it's just a reminder of what could have been.'

'Stop!' shouted Marozvolk. She glared at both of them. 'We've all just come through the fight of our lives. Can we set aside the bullshit until Taiga recovers?' Tief nodded but didn't make eye contact with either woman, tending to his sister's wounds. Kimi stalked away from the stone circle, glancing at the Ashen Torment in the palm of her trembling hand.

'He's just scared is all,' said Marozvolk. She stood a way off behind Kimi and they watched the mist swirl about the gloomy swamp. It was hard to tell if the gholes were still prowling, but the Ashen Torment pulsed with pale blue light every so often.

'I didn't expect them to flee like that,' said Kimi.

'It seems even the dead dislike taking casualties.'

'What if they come back in greater numbers?' said Kimi, searching the mist for some clue.

'Then we use more torches. Your idea to use fire as a weapon was a good one.' Marozvolk searched the horizon for the next sign of trouble.

'I'm sorry I dragged you into all of this,' said Kimi after a moment. 'You would have been better off leaving the ship with Sundra at Shanisrond.'

'That may be true,' said Marozvolk, 'but Mistress Kamalov is a pain in the arse and a reminder of my past I could do without. Dying at the hands of marauding gangs of gholes is almost preferable.'

Kimi smiled. 'I didn't think she was that bad.'

'Renegade Vigilants,' replied Marozvolk. 'You can't trust them.'

'I'll bear that in mind.' Kimi wiped off her sword now that she felt calm enough to sheathe it. 'Answer me seriously. Why did you come to Yamal?'

Marozvolk shrugged and her face contorted in grief before she shook her head, getting a tight grip on her emotions once more.

'You were right, about Vladibogdan. All that time you were on the island and I never once revealed myself to you, or made sure you were looked after or protected.'

'You were on a different side back then,' said Kimi. 'Things change, you've changed.'

'I shunned you the same way my family shunned me when I failed the Invigilation. I want you to know I regret it, though I didn't feel there was a choice at the time.' Marozvolk bowed her head and closed her eyes.

'That's what the Empire does best,' said Kimi. 'It takes even the hope of choice away from us. Get some sleep.' She nodded towards the standing stones. 'I think we're in for a long night.'

Marozvolk glanced at the Ashen Torment with a sickened expression. The pale blue light had grown stronger. The gholes remained hidden by the mist but Kimi suspected they were close, waiting to avenge their fallen kin.

CHAPTER TWENTY-EIGHT

Kjellrunn

'This is disgusting,' said Maxim as they pulled yet another threadbare and tatty cloak from the pile. 'The smell . . .' He held up a wrist to his mouth and Kjellrunn wondered if he might gag. The mess of blankets and rags the blind beggar had assembled did not resemble a bed so much as a bird's nest. Mistress Kamalov had requested the beggar's things be moved from the alcove in which he slept ahead of the forthcoming funeral. 'Is he really called Kolas?' asked Maxim when he had recovered.

'I'm not sure,' replied Kjellrunn. 'That's what he told me on the beach that night. I'm not sure he's always lucid. Surely you understand him better than the rest of us.'

'Sometimes he'll tell me little snippets about the town's history,' said Maxim. 'Then he'll fall silent as if he'd never spoken.' The boy held up a half-burned candle and a conch shell, then shook his head with a puzzled smile. 'The stuff that he has in here.'

Kjellrunn glanced over her shoulder. The novices were watching from across the temple; they had clustered around Trine, who sneered at Kjellrunn. 'This stinks,' complained Maxim as he tugged on another mangy blanket and began folding it. They spent a while gathering up the bedding and taking it to the kitchens, before boiling up some water and doing their best to clean the various blankets and rags that formed Kolas's bed.

'What did you find?' asked Maxim.

'A crow's feather and some driftwood.' Kjellrunn remembered with a heavy heart all the times she had retrieved the very same flotsam treasures from the shores of Cinderfell. Steiner would chide her for hoarding glass fragments made smooth by the sea and pale pebbles.

Don't collect such things, he'd say. *People will think them charms and fetishes and call you a witch.* How she'd give anything to be chided by Steiner right now. Even a chiding would be better than the emptiness of missing her family.

'Kjellrunn?' Maxim's voice was soft with a note of concern.

'Sorry. Just thinking on my family is all. I used to dig up things like these all the time in Nordvlast when I was a child.' She forced a smile.

'I'm pretty sure you're still a child.'

'I don't feel like one. I haven't felt like a child since they took Steiner.'

'I still can't believe Romola left them in Virag,' said Maxim, and Kjellrunn wondered if he had read her mind without meaning to.

'I hope they're still alive,' said Kjellrunn, tracing the outline of the hammer brooch and thinking of her father.

'I'm sure we'll hear from them soon enough.' Maxim pushed the last of the blankets into the cauldron over the fire. The fire crackled and the water bubbled as they boiled up the filthy rags.

'You said you saw something,' said Kjellrunn, eager to change the subject. She closed the door to the kitchen, keen to be done with the eavesdroppers and prying eyes.

'It sounds strange, but I dreamed it first.'

'You had another vision?' asked Kjellrunn in a reverent whisper.

'Yes, it was like the time I foresaw the dragons, but I was asleep.'

'What did you see?'

'I saw the blind man holding this. Crooning to it.' Maxim fished a small book out of the waistband of his trousers and offered it to her. It was a slender white tome with two stylised crows on the front. 'I went to him and asked if he owned a book and sure enough he did. He gave it to me. Obviously he can't read it on account of his eyes, so why hold on to it?'

Kjellrunn opened the book and gave a dispirited sigh. 'I can't read any of this. It's all in . . .' She waved her hand, searching for the word. 'What's the language called?'

'Shanish, I think.' Maxim took the book from her and pointed to each word as he read it aloud. '"This book is chief, ah, chiefly concerned with the lesser-known aspect of Frejna. She is well established as the goddess of wisdom and death in these parts. In other countries she is also credited with having dominion over winter and sincerity, though this volume will cover the more wrathful aspect of Frejna."'

Kjellrunn's heart raced with excitement. She had lived off half-remembered tales in Cinderfell, frustrated that the townsfolk were so reluctant to speak of the goddesses. And here was a book full of information, most likely set down by an old priestess of Frejna.

Maxim looked up from the book. 'Should we take this to Sundra? It seems important.'

'No.' Kjellrunn couldn't say why she answered him so, only that she wanted something for herself. 'It'll be our secret.'

'But Sundra only has that book of dreary reflections, and they're all about death. That's the only book she had left after her imprisonment.'

'We'll just keep it for a day or two longer. You can teach me Shanish and we can both learn something about Frejna at the same time.'

'You want to learn Shanish from this book?' Maxim hesitated, a troubled expression on his boyish face. Kjellrunn took the book from him and looked at the elegant lines and clusters of dots.

'I know it's probably not a book best suited to learning but—' The kitchen door opened and Kjellrunn hid the slender volume behind her back as Sundra entered.

'Come,' said the high priestess, gesturing that they follow. 'We have a funeral to organise. We can't spend all day running a laundry.'

Maxim eyed Kjellrunn, sullen at the prospect of keeping her secret.

'We'll tell her tomorrow,' said Kjellrunn quietly. 'I just want to have a look first.'

The funeral was long and Kjellrunn spent the service standing beside the wide altar, holding up a parchment of script that Sundra read from in a sombre voice. The black-clad high priestess would pause every so often and Maxim would translate for the benefit of the fifty or so mourners. At some point in the day Trine had been outfitted with black robes of her own, marking her as one of Frejna's servants. Kjellrunn found her eye straying to the other girl often during the service, as her irritation grew. Trine ignored Kjellrunn completely, a small smile on her face, her long black hair tied back neatly for once.

'I don't understand why she gets her own vestments,' said Kjellrunn after the service when the mourners had departed. 'All she does is burn corpses. I'm the initiate.'

'I don't know either.' Maxim shrugged. 'I'm just glad I don't have to wear them.' They stood on the temple steps as the sun dipped towards the horizon and the heat began to fade from Dos Khor. 'You're not going to give that book to Sundra, are you?'

'Why don't we go down to the beach before the sun sets? You can try and teach me a few more words. Then we'll give it to her later.' Kjellrunn felt a pang of guilt as the boy smiled. They walked through the town and a trio of men watched them pass from the doorway of a tumbledown house. The men called out to them and followed their footsteps with unfriendly stares.

'What are they saying?' asked Kjellrunn.

Maxim bowed his head. 'That we don't belong here and the temple doesn't belong to us.' He paused a moment. 'And some other stuff.'

Kjellrunn frowned. 'Go on.'

Maxim shook his head. 'The usual sort of thing. Witches aren't illegal here, but that doesn't mean everyone likes them.' Kjellrunn took the boy's hand in her own and they kept walking. Kolas was sitting by the shore when they reached the pale sculpture of the flat hand.

'What's he doing?' asked Maxim.

'Listening to the sea just like he always does. Come, sit down and close your eyes.'

'I thought you wanted me to teach you Shanish from the book?'

'I was hoping we could see if you get a sense of what I can feel' – she gestured to the sea – 'out there.'

'My visions don't come that often,' said Maxim with a frown. 'They hardly come at all.'

'It'll just take a moment.'

'And then we give the book to Sundra. Agreed?'

'Of course,' said Kjellrunn, annoyed he was being so stubborn about it. 'Now come and listen to the ocean.'

Maxim did as he was told and Kjellrunn listened to the

waves as they met the sand and pebbles with a thousand hushed whispers.

'Maybe Dos Khor isn't so bad,' said Maxim quietly into the fresh evening air. 'I could grow to like this.' But no sooner had he said the words than a feeling of powerful dread seeped up from the pit of Kjellrunn's stomach. Her eyes snapped open and she hurried to her feet.

'It's happening again.'

'What is that?' said Maxim, frowning in confusion. He rose to his feet slowly, as if waking from a dream, then stared out to sea.

'You can sense it too?'

'It's big . . .' Maxim looked over his shoulder, panicked, breathing quick and fast. 'And old. Ancient.' He raised one hand to the sea and pointed. 'It's somewhere out there.' Kolas stood up and dropped his white staff, then tripped on his robes and fell. Kjellrunn ran to the old man and Maxim followed.

'Help me get him on his feet,' she said, but the blind man scrambled away from her.

'*Haerthi nam khaidra!*' shouted the old man, then again and louder.

'He's saying you have to close your heart,' said Maxim, glancing out to sea. The sun dipped behind the town and a chill breeze whipped up the fine sand along the beach. The clouds in the sky had been few and wispy but now they were bloated and dark.

'Close my heart? What does that mean?'

'I don't know,' said Maxim. He glanced towards the town, clearly wanting to run from the beach as fast as he could. The old man babbled something else, jabbing an accusing finger in Kjellrunn's direction.

'He said you have to be less angry,' said Maxim. 'Think of something that calms you.' But Kjellrunn didn't feel calm.

The terrible foreboding feeling made it difficult to think. The wind blew harder and vortices of sand twisted and spun around their knees. The old man was shouting now.

'He keeps saying you have to be less angry!' translated Maxim in a panicked voice.

Kjellrunn ran, her feet sliding in the sand until she reached the edge of the town. She ran past Trine, who had been watching them from a shadowed doorway, and into the town. She ran all the way back to the temple until she reached the altar and slumped down in front of it. For long moments her tortured breathing was the only sound in the temple until she buried her face in her hands and began to weep.

'What's happening to me?' she whispered. 'What's happening?'

'Kjellrunn.' Mistress Kamalov was kneeling beside her at the altar, shaking her awake.

'What time is it?'

'Close to midnight. What are you doing here? Were you asleep?'

'Something happened at the beach. Maxim and I felt a presence in the Shimmer Sea . . . Frejna's teeth! I left him there. Did he come back?' Mistress Kamalov nodded, then sat down on the nearest low bench.

'He's fine. He was with the old man. Neither of them looked very happy but they're still with us. What happened?'

'The old man kept pointing at me, telling me I have to be less angry.'

Mistress Kamalov grimaced. 'Small chance of that.'

'I'm not angry,' said Kjellrunn.

'Is that so?' Mistress Kamalov smiled. 'You're not angry about having witchsign, which you didn't ask for?'

'Well, I suppose—'

'You're not angry that the Empire used up your mother like firewood, split up your parents, and then took your brother?'

'Yes, of course I am.'

'You're not angry that Romola left your family in Virag and there wasn't a damn thing you could do about it?'

'Of course, but I don't go around shouting about it.'

'And where does the anger go if you do not shout about it?' Kjellrunn shrugged. 'What kind of question is that?'

'One that still needs an answer. Come, Kjellrunn. You are bright. Sometimes, anyway. Where does the anger go?'

'It doesn't go anywhere.' Hot tears sprang from the corners of her eyes. 'It just stays inside me.'

'Breathe, Kjellrunn,' said the old Vigilant. There was a deep sadness in her eyes. 'I know this is hard.'

'The Empire took your brother too.'

'Oh yes, we are much alike, you and I. Gifted, stubborn beyond reason.' Mistress Kamalov smiled. 'And incredibly angry.'

'I'm sorry I slammed that door in your face.'

'I have that effect on people,' admitted Mistress Kamalov with a quiet chuckle. 'But I am grateful for your apology all the same.'

'That day in the woods, when the Okhrana came . . .' Kjellrunn struggled to find the words, wanting desperately to explain why she feared the arcane and how she'd nearly killed Mistress Kamalov in her fury.

'Go on,' said Mistress Kamalov, leaning forward.

'That day in the woods when the Okhrana came, I nearly lost control. I did lose control, and I . . .'

Trine emerged from the gloom, her dark hair loose. She still wore the dark vestments of Frejna's priesthood and irritation spiked through Kjellrunn. 'A few of the children are asking for you,' said Trine to Mistress Kamalov, ignoring

Kjellrunn entirely. 'Bad dreams again. Something in the sea coming to get them.'

'We will speak more in the morning, Kjellrunn.' The renegade Vigilant stood slowly. 'Go to your room now and get some sleep.'

Kjellrunn watched the old woman leave the temple with Trine by her side, and softly cursed the raven-haired girl.

CHAPTER TWENTY-NINE

Silverdust

'Why are we in the Voronin District?' asked Streig, looking about him with barely concealed disgust. He carried his helm under one arm, and a stout bag hung from his shoulder. 'Is this where Dimitri Sokolov stayed?'

The roads were narrow, and winding lanes led in all directions. The warped and rickety buildings cast a shadow over everyone, and the air was thick with the scents of dung and smoke. Traces of marinated fish competed with the stench from a tanner's. Streig wrinkled his nose and glared at the people begging at the side of the street. The beggars had bound their feet in rags and stared at the world from pale faces, clutching at themselves with dirty hands. There was no warmth, there was no cheer. Voronin District was the most wretched place Streig had ever seen.

This is indeed where Dimitri Sokolov stayed.

'It's nothing more than whores and beggars.' Streig looked around, his young face full of accusation. 'And the *smell*. Can't we find lodgings in a better district?'

Do you think these people choose to live this way?

Streig looked from the Exarch gliding beside him to the many ragged and gaunt souls that haunted the streets. They went about their lives with stooped shoulders and downcast eyes, bowed by unseen burdens.

'Why don't they get jobs?' asked Streig, trying to keep his voice low despite his growing irritation. 'Surely there is work to be had in a city this big.' The locals stopped and turned to stare at the Exarch and his escort as they wended their way down the cobbled streets. It was apparent that there were places where the Holy Synod and the Imperial army were rarely seen, even in the capital. Smoke crowded the sky above the chimneys and an evening mist haunted every street corner. It would soon be dark.

You told me there were only farming jobs in Virolanti Province. You had to take up farming or fighting, there was nothing else.

'That's right,' said Streig, scowling as a beggar approached him.

Which means there are no blacksmiths, no shop owners, no vintners or coopers or cartwrights in the whole province?

'That's not what I said,' replied Streig as they turned a corner. A large building loomed ahead of them in the mist.

But it is what you implied. Tell me, was your father a soldier too?

Streig nodded.

And his father before him?

Streig nodded again.

So becoming a soldier was not so much about taking up a job but an inheritance of sorts. It is what your family have always done. The Exarch ceased walking. *It is the only thing they know how to do.*

'We can do more than just fight. We're not simple thugs.'

Streig and Silverdust stood in a small square where market stalls were being packed up for the night.

'Are you looking for lodgings, sirs?' said a girl of about sixteen summers from the doorway of an inn. She had lank blonde hair and a broken nose. There was a hard look about her no matter how much she smiled.

Ask her if she has always worked at the inn. Silverdust had no
wish to startle the girl with a demonstration of the arcane,
but telepathy was all he had. Streig asked the question, feeling
foolish as he did so, stumbling over the words.

'Why yes, I've worked here since I could walk.' The girl
swept her shawl around her a little tighter and held up her
chin proudly. 'My parents own it and their parents before
them.'

Tell her we shall stay there, but we require a moment to converse.
Streig did as Silverdust asked and the girl scurried away,
looking back over her shoulder to see if they were gaming
with her. The Exarch extended a hand and beckoned a woman
who stood beneath the awning of a closed shop. 'What are
you doing?' whispered Streig, blushing furiously. The woman
was older than Streig, though not old enough to be his mother.
She wore her years in the lines of her face and the scar that
peaked from her hairline. She hesitated with a wary look in
her eye.

Ask her what she does for a job.
'Have you lost your mind? It's perfectly obvious what she
does for a job,' Streig hissed, stepping closer to the Exarch.
'One moment we're in the Imperial Court and the next you're
asking me—'

'Can I help you?' The woman had ventured closer, her
curiosity outweighing her circumspection.

Ask her what she does for a job.
Streig made an exasperated growling sound and turned to
the woman.

'The Exarch, in his all-consuming curiosity, wishes to know
what employment you are currently engaged in.'

So formal, Streig. We will make a courtier of you yet.
The woman frowned.

'I would rather not say, if it's all the same,' she replied with
a flash of irritation in her eyes. Silverdust held up a single

coin and the woman took it from his gloved hand, uncertainty writ large across her narrow face. 'What's this for?'

Ask her what her mother did.

'I'm sorry to have troubled you,' said Streig. 'The Exarch is in a strange mood tonight.' The soldier turned on his heel and marched to the inn and waited on the porch, staring at his boots. Silverdust bowed to the woman and drifted across the street.

Tell me, how are the innkeeper's daughter and the prostitute any different to you?

'I am not a whore!' said Streig, teeth gritted in anger.

And yet your place in this world is predestined, just as hers was. Silverdust gestured at the woman who watched them still, clutching the coin in her hand with a look of bemusement. *There are few choices when one lives with poverty as a constant companion.* The Exarch laid a hand on Streig's shoulder. *And all of us are just moments away from living the life of a beggar.* Streig gave a laugh, though it was tired and bitter.

Look past the rags and see the person beneath, Streig. Never lose sight of the person beneath.

'Can we go in now?' Streig jerked his head towards the door. 'Or are you going to sermonise a little longer?'

The Exarch opened the door. *'Come in from the cold, Streig. Warm yourself.'*

Once inside Streig procured rooms and followed Silverdust as he took the stairs upwards until they were outside again, looking over the street below from the flat rooftop.

I used to watch over Academy Square in the small hours. Mainly I would linger on the rooftops of Academy Voda or Vozdukha. I loved Vladibogdan most at night, when it was quiet and the students were at their rest.

Streig looked around and squinted at the forest of chimneys that emerged from the Voronin District. They were surrounded by the slopes and ridges of tiled roofs, by balconies of rotting wood and crumbling plaster.

'You brought us all the way to the Voronin District so you could stand up here?'

I did. Silverdust cast his gaze at the square below. There were fewer people now, though the ghosts of the city drifted the streets freely. The spirits of the dead came and went, endlessly attempting to find that which had evaded them in life.

You have served on Vladibogdan?

'Colder than a witch's tit.'

I will take that as a yes. Silverdust wanted to say more but three shadows flickered at the edge of his vision. The first emerged on a sloping rooftop while another slunk around a corner in the square below. The last of them lingered on a balcony opposite the inn. The last of the three shadows bore a crossbow, though he tried to hide the weapon under his cloak. It was as Silverdust had feared. Envoy de Vries had sent Okhrana to murder him before he could give his testimony to the Imperial Court.

Leave me now, Streig. Go to your rest. And be sure to lock your door and sleep with a weapon close to hand.

'I always do,' said Streig with a slow smile. 'Be sure to get some rest yourself, or whatever it is you do.' The soldier turned away as Silverdust watched more men in black draw close across the rooftops.

The first attack came from behind, perhaps a minute after Streig had gone to his room. The man pulled himself up over the side of the building, rolling onto the flat roof and coming to his feet in one fluid, near-silent motion. The Okhrana stepped forward with his sword raised but Silverdust was already behind him. The Exarch slipped one arm around his neck and smothered the man with his free hand, though it was not a glove that met the Okhrana's mouth and nose but a wispy limb of soot-dark smoke. The Okhrana coughed and breathed in on instinct, but it was ash not air that he inhaled. Silverdust reached out with his senses, feeling the other men's focus, their fear, their excitement. He could feel the exertion of climbing up onto the roof. The Okhrana in his arms struggled, desperate for breath that would not come. Silverdust held him close for long convulsing seconds until the Okhrana had choked to death.

The crossbowman on the balcony opposite took his chance the moment his comrade slipped from Silverdust's embrace. The bolt flashed in the darkness, piercing the Exarch's vestments. The bolt passed clean through Silverdust, though he was not slowed by such mundane weapons. The Exarch summoned a bright spear of roaring flame and cast it across the square where it caught the man full in the chest. The Okhrana pitched forward and fell to the cobbles below, his corpse a pitiful blaze. Silverdust allowed himself a moment of satisfaction. He had no wish to set fire to half the district in order to survive.

A moment of fleeting fear passed through the Okhrana, and Silverdust could feel it harden to anger. The next Okhrana, realising the time for stealth had passed, threw a grappling hook over the edge the building. Silverdust grasped the rope and sent a surge of white-hot arcane fire through his hand. The rope blackened, crisped, and snapped in moments. The Okhrana cried out as he fell three storeys. Silverdust could sense a brief flare of pain as the Okhrana hit the street before the man's consciousness winked out.

Another assassin had pulled himself onto the roof and charged headlong at the Exarch, a short blade held back for the killing blow. The Okhrana lunged forward, thrusting his blade too fast for the eye to follow. The Exarch stepped aside, aided by prescience, and grabbed the man by the collar. Silverdust could feel the man's panic, knowing he had over-committed himself, caught off balance and now at his enemy's mercy. Silverdust threw him from the rooftop to meet his dead comrade and the burned rope below.

And yet more came for him, up over the lip of the roof and surging forward, cruel shadows in the darkness. Silverdust snatched up the grappling hook and parried a blow from one man, blade and hook sparking in the darkness. The Exarch sidestepped and headbutted another Okhrana with his feature-less mask. The second man fell back, nose bloodied, with tears streaming from his eyes.

The Okhrana I knew were terrible and implacable.

Silverdust parried another blow with the grappling hook, then grabbed his attacker by the face and slammed the grap-pling hook into his exposed neck. The man floundered like a fish, grasping at the metal. Blood gushed from his mouth as he cried out wordlessly.

Standards have slipped, it seems.

The surviving Okhrana wiped his bleeding nose on his cuff and swung again. His eyes widened in disbelief as Silverdust slapped the blade aside with a gloved hand. The Exarch seized the man around the throat with a tendril of ashen darkness, lifting the man off his feet.

'What are you?' said the man, before Silverdust set fire to him and threw him from the roof. By now a huddle had formed in the street below, watching with sickened fascination.

'Silverdust?' It was Streig. He stood in his shirt and britches, mace clutched in one hand. 'What in Hel is happening up here?'

Silverdust did not have time to reply. One final Okhrana had made the climb to the rooftop at the back of the inn. He had shielded his mind from the Exarch's arcane senses, effec-tively invisible to Silverdust's scrying. The last Okhrana was just feet away from Streig's unprotected back, short blade raised for the killing strike. The Envoy wanted both of them dead, it seemed.

Silverdust surged forward and Streig, thinking he was under attack from his master, dived to one side. The Exarch met the Okhrana's blade, felt it pierce his garb, then slammed into the man, catching him in both arms. Okhrana and Exarch sailed from the lip of the roof and Streig turned just in time to watch them plummet to the street below.

CHAPTER THIRTY

Steiner

Panic swept through the crowded bar. Steiner couldn't tell how many soldiers were with the Exarch, but he knew in his bones they were outnumbered.

'This way,' shouted Lidija. Steiner watched as the innkeeper ushered Kristofine out of the bar and up the stairs. Marek followed through the press of bodies and a soldier stumbled through the confusion towards him. Steiner jabbed the sledge-hammer at the soldier's armoured head. A space cleared around him as the sledgehammer clanged against the soldier's helm.

The locals stared in horror. Not a living soul here had ever seen a person take up arms against the Empire.

The soldier took a moment to steady himself, then turned as Steiner swung, hard and low. The sound of the soldier's knee breaking was followed by howling. The soldier fell forward, rolling on the ground and clutching his shattered limb. Steiner backed out of the bar as Exarch Zima punched and shouldered his way through the mass of bodies.

Marek and Kristofine had gathered their things by the time Steiner reached the top of the stairs.

'This way,' said Lidija, gesturing to a room at the end of

the hall. 'There is a window that opens out above the stable. You can hop down to the roof and make your way from there.'

A soldier appeared at the bottom of the stairs and Lidija gestured towards the man with a flick of her wrist. A mote of white light drifted from her hand and down the staircase. The blinding mote pierced the soldier's breastplate with a hissing sound. There was a smell of scorched metal before the soldier screamed. Bright light emanated from the gaps between the black armour as the man crumpled.

Marek and Kristofine hurried down the corridor after Lidija as Exarch Zima stepped over the corpse of the incinerated soldier. The Vigilant's eyes were hidden behind the bestial mask, but Steiner could feel the weight of his gaze all the same.

'Come on!' Lidija led them to an empty guest room and opened the window. 'Quickly now,' she called over her shoulder as she pushed open the shutters. Steiner slammed the guest-room door closed as Exarch Zima reached the top of the staircase. A moment later and the door began to rattle on its hinges.

'He must be from the earth school,' muttered Steiner. Marek had already jumped from the window and waited on the flat roof of the stables below. He held out his hands for Kristofine, who jumped without hesitation.

'You next,' said Lidija.

'We're not leaving without you,' replied Steiner. 'You've done so much for us.'

The shaking of the door reached a fever pitch and the hinges and lock surrendered to Zima's power. The frame splintered and the door shot forward, knocking Steiner to the floor. Heavy footfalls could be heard on the staircase as Steiner shrugged off the remains of the door and clambered to his feet. Lidija gritted her teeth and flicked out both hands, sending another two motes drifting down the corridor towards the Exarch. Steiner watched Zima smash a door from its frame with a gesture, then sidestep into the room. The blinding motes drifted past him, on down the corridor.

'Frejna's teeth,' whispered Lidija. She swung her legs over the windowsill and slipped out of sight. One of the motes of arcane light impacted against the wall while the other hit the door to another guest room. Both motes flared in the gloom and the wood became incandescent; bright flames took hold immediately.

'Steiner!' came Kristofine's voice from outside, barely audible above the shouts coming from downstairs. Steiner jumped from the window and felt the roof of the stables give as he landed. Marek's eyes were wide as the roof shook beneath them all. Steiner reached out to Kristofine as the wooden beams creaked.

'Oh shiii—'

The roof gave way, depositing him in the stables below, where a bed of hay bales awaited him. They were not as soft as he'd have liked. His feet and knees hurt yet he was still standing. Kristofine swung down through the hole in the ceiling and landed close to him.

'Are you all right?' she asked, reaching for his face.

'Clipped my head on the way down.' He pressed a palm to his forehead and felt the hot wetness of his own blood. 'Where's my father?'

They neared the doors to the stable and heard shouting outside. A glimpse through the gaps between the timbers confirmed Exarch Zima had brought all the soldiers he could find.

'It's no good,' said Steiner. 'There are too many of them.' He turned around when Kristofine didn't answer. She was already opening two of the stalls and slipping bridle into place on the horses' heads.

'I can't ride!' said Steiner.

'Then you'd best learn because we don't have a choice.'

No sooner had they saddled and mounted the horses than Exarch Zima floated down through the gap in the ceiling, his descent slowed by his mastery of the arcane.

'Truly the Emperor has guided me in this undertaking,' he said calmly. 'I shall be his vessel of destruction.'

The soldiers outside opened the stable doors and Steiner and Kristofine put their heels to the horses' flanks and raced out into the street. Steiner swung the sledgehammer as he passed, connecting with a soldier's head. The man spun and collapsed to his knees. Crossbow bolts flitted past them and smoke billowed into the night sky. Vostochnyye Lisy was cast in a fiery orange and blood-red light as they fled the inn, the horses throwing their heads this way and that in panic.

'Where is Marek?' shouted Steiner, but Kristofine didn't hear him, urging her mount down a side street and racing away. Steiner shook the reins and somehow the horse seemed to know what was required of it. The chestnut mare followed Kristofine and Steiner clung onto the beast's neck. More crossbow bolts followed them, ricocheting from the stone buildings, or burying themselves in the timber.

'Father,' breathed Steiner as the horse spirited him away from danger, but there could be no turning back.

Kristofine led them down every uninviting backstreet that she could find. People opened their shutters to see the commotion as soldiers patrolled the streets, calling out to each other in the gloom. Kristofine brought her horse to a trot and then halted altogether in a narrow, winding alley. Steiner's mount was not so keen to stop. The skittish horse continued until Steiner wrestled with the reins, forcing it to turn back. Kristofine slipped from the back of her horse with ease and held out her hands to Steiner.

'I'm the dragon rider,' he said. 'I think I can get off one—' but anything else he said was lost as he slipped from the horse's back and slammed into some barrels.

'I thought we were working together now?' said Kristofine. 'Isn't that what you said?'

'I also said I can be really, really stupid,' replied Steiner, rubbing his knee. 'Sorry.' Both took a moment to put their cloaks on and Steiner made sure the sledgehammer was hidden.

'Why are we dismounting?' he asked when they'd set their packs on their backs.

'I didn't want you to fall off and break your neck.' They spent a moment of nervous laughter as the adrenaline coursed through them. 'Truthfully, the hooves make too much noise on the cobbles. They'll attract attention. We'll have to leave them here.'

Steiner took a moment to tie the reins to a door handle and hoped someone would find the animal come the morning.

'What now?' asked Kristofine when they'd composed themselves.

'Now we find my father.'

They spent hours slipping through the city like the lost spirits. They haunted every darkened lane and alley and waited in doorways for soldiers to pass, breathless with fear, hearts pounding. Sounds of shouting could be heard from a few streets away.

'That's them,' said Steiner. 'That has to be them.' He launched himself from the shadows to run down the street. Kristofine called after him but he'd left her no choice but to follow. Fire burned in the night, the streets were gilded with fiery orange and sleepers had stumbled from bed, watching the unfolding chaos.

'Is it the inn?' asked Kristofine, panting to catch her breath. 'Have we run back to where we started from?'

Steiner shook his head and gestured that she follow. He snuck down the street, staying close to the buildings, slipping into shadowed doorways whenever he could. Marek and Lidija stood ahead of them a few hundred feet away at a junction. A building behind them was on fire and soldiers blocked every road. Exarch Zima led an honour guard of four soldiers perhaps a hundred feet in front of Steiner.

'Close your shutters!' the Vigilant screamed at the townsfolk, who had staggered to their windows despite the late hour.

'He doesn't want anyone to see him using the arcane,' said Steiner.

'I think he should be more worried about Lidija,' replied Kristofine.

A fireball blinked into existence between Lidija's hands. She stood back to back with Marek, a look of snarling anger on her face. It was difficult to think of her as the kindly innkeeper Steiner had met just yesterday. The fireball raced down the street and wreathed a group of soldiers, knocking them off their feet. There were screams as their cloaks caught fire; those who were not already dead began to scald and sear. The other soldiers did not hesitate, charging forward with weapons raised. Marek stepped forward to meet them though he was greatly outnumbered, a look of grim resignation etched on his lined face. Steiner started down the street, pulling the sledgehammer free, a single word on his lips.

Father.

The first of the soldiers closed with Marek, who feinted low, sidestepped, and slashed at the back of the man's neck. The man screamed and fell, writhing on the cobbles as he bled out. Marek barely had time to parry the next soldier's strike, stumbling backwards but refusing to fall.

Lidija pierced the darkness with a handful of motes that floated towards their targets with ghostly ease. Three of the soldiers roared in futile fury as the arcane lights found them, piercing the heavy armour and incinerating the men from inside out. The smell of burning flesh and hot metal seared the night air. Two remaining two soldiers were wiser or luckier, throwing themselves to one side, watching the motes sail past them and on down the street.

Steiner reached Zima's honour guard and swung hard. The blow took one soldier's leg with a fierce crack, sending him headlong into his comrade. A moment of confusion seized the men as they realised they had been attacked from behind. All weapons were raised to smite the scarred and swearing youth who had stumbled out of the darkness. Kristofine, trailing Steiner by a dozen feet, ran her sword into a soldier's side. She clutched the hilt like a spear and had put all her weight behind it. The soldier looked down at the fatal wound and tried to grasp her wrists, but Kristofine snatched the blade away, a gout of blood following after. The soldier gasped and fell to his knees, hands pressed to the wound.

Steiner blocked one strike, kicked out a soldier's knee, swung, and smashed a shoulder guard free of the wearer. He spat and swore and promised death like a berserker of the old tales. Another soldier came at him and the sledgehammer knocked the man's weapon from his hand. Steiner spun slightly with the force of the swing, just in time to see two soldiers punching Marek with armoured fists. They had seized him by the collar and held him fast. Marek sagged and his sword fell from his hand.

'Take him to the docks now!' bellowed Zima, who had an arm around Lidija's throat, a knife tip pressed against one ear.

Steiner swung again and heard the soldier's neck snap as the sledgehammer caught him across the jaw. The honour guard were no more.

'Stand still or I will kill her!' shouted Exarch Zima, his bestial mask seemingly alive in the flickering light of the inferno that raged behind him. Steiner looked to Kristofine.

All the soldiers were dead but for the two who were dragging Marek's unconscious body away. Steiner stepped closer to Zima until barely twenty feet separated them.

'Lidija,' said Steiner, 'I'm so sorry.'

The innkeeper grinned at him, her teeth lined with blood. 'You started this, Steiner,' she whispered. 'You gave us hope after so long. I need to you to promise you'll see it through.'

'Be quiet!' shouted Zima. He pressed the tip of the knife to her ear and squeezed her throat with his arm.

'I promise,' said Steiner. 'I'll see it through to the bitter end.'

Lidija closed her eyes. For a single heartbeat there were traces of tears at the corners of her eyes and then her entire body became a searing tongue of fire. Zima, who gripped her around the throat, found that Lidija clung to him just as keenly. The sound he made as he burned was inhuman. He convulsed as Lidija's living flame brightened, sinking the blade through her skull. The fire blinked out and Zima collapsed on the ground, ravaged by fire.

Steiner wasted no time, sprinting down the street, desperate to find Marek. Kristofine ran with him but all they found were more soldiers, more fire, more confusion. The sledge-hammer's weight was reassuring and called out for violence. Steiner was all too keen to obey. Instead he found himself wrenched sideways, dragged into an alley by Kristofine. They ran until they were confident no one was following them, then stopped in a small courtyard and regained their breath.

'I have to get him, I have to find him,' said Steiner, staring at the ground in shock. 'He's all I have.'

'No. You have me,' replied Kristofine. 'And if you go to him now we'll all be captured.'

'But he's my father!'

'You heard what Zima said. They're going to take him to the ship at the docks. We can't see this through if we're captured, can we?'

'And you have a ship of your own, do you?' said Steiner, frowning.

'We can try and stow away. We might be able to free Marek before they set off.'

The thought of his father being dragged down the street made him want to howl with rage.

'We can't sneak aboard a ship full of Imperial soldiers.' Steiner had regained his breath and tried to calm down enough to think. 'It's impossible.'

'They used to say escaping Vladibogdan was impossible too, didn't they?' Kristofine gave a small smile and he heard the challenge in her words.

'I don't have much good fortune when it comes to sneaking onto boats,' replied Steiner. 'They tend to leave without me.'

'Not this time.' Kristofine nodded towards the docks. 'This time we'll do it together, for Marek's sake.'

CHAPTER THIRTY-ONE

Kimi

'It's your watch,' said Marozvolk quietly in the dark. There was barely enough room for a campfire and three people inside the circle of stones, but it was dry and Kimi drew a feeling of calm from the place: Marozvolk handed the Ashen Torment back to Kimi. It still glowed a faint blue, but no more than the starlight far above them.

'They're still out there,' said Kimi, more in irritation than enquiry.

'They were created to kill all living things,' replied Marozvolk as she lay down and pulled a blanket around herself. 'I doubt they'll just give up and go home. If they have a home.'

Tief grumbled and shuffled around in his sleep while Taiga was still and silent beside him. Kimi knelt down and pressed her fingers to the woman's brow, feeling the heat from her clammy skin.

'Dammit, Frøya,' whispered Kimi. 'She's one of yours. She kept the faith.' Kimi looked to the heavens. 'If you let this woman die I will kill you myself.' She passed through the gap in the stones. The vast damp darkness of Izhoria waited on all sides and only the torchlight provided any reprieve.

'Did I just hear you threaten to kill a goddess?' said Tief

from behind her. Kimi looked over her shoulder. The man looked as if he'd been to Hel and back.

'I thought you were asleep.' Kimi cleared her throat, suddenly embarrassed. 'Not one of the best prayers I've made.'

'So you do pray then?'

'I used to. A lot. Especially after my mother died.' Kimi sighed. 'But then my father gave me up to the Empire.' The torch flame flickered and writhed, throwing shadows across her face. 'And I prayed and begged that somehow Frøya would find a way to get me off Vladibogdan. All those prayers went unanswered. So I stopped praying and I stopped paying my respects and got on with the business of staying alive.'

Tief lit his pipe and stared into the night for a moment. 'Maybe Frøya did answer your prayers.'

'Really?' Kimi gave an incredulous smile.

'Maybe Frøya sent Steiner to help us escape the island.'

'I'm afraid I don't share your gift for religious interpretation,' said Kimi with a tired smile. 'Besides, Steiner was five years late. I wouldn't let my followers suffer like that if I was a goddess.'

'That's good to know,' said Tief. 'Maybe I'll start worshipping you.' Kimi almost laughed and for a moment they stood in the peaceful quiet of the night, warm under their heavy cloaks.

'Do you think we're going to make it?' said Tief, toking on his pipe. 'Across Izhoria, I mean. Will we get through?'

'How is she?' said Kimi, nodding to Taiga, keen to change the subject.

'I'm not sure. Out of the three of us it was Taiga that always had the gift for healing. Sundra, well, Sundra is Sundra, and I've always been the practical one.'

'You mean fighting?'

'I mean fighting, fetching, carrying. You name it, these old bones have done it.' Tief paused and struggled to hold back his tears. 'Why in Frøya's name did I never learn medicine? All those years and I left it to Taiga, depended on Taiga. I used to think it was women's work. Now she's depending on me and there's not one damn thing I can do.' Kimi put an arm around the man and held him close. 'I was supposed to be looking out for her. That's what brothers do, isn't it?'

'Not all of them,' said Kimi, thinking of Tsen before her thoughts turned to Steiner and the lengths he'd gone to in order to protect Kjellrunn. 'All we can do is look out for each other,' she said.

Morning came to Izhoria and glorious sunlight scoured the mist off the swamps. The waters, so full of silt and mud and gods knew what else, were bright and clear. The many mangy reeds and yellowing grasses looked healthier somehow. Of the black-cowled gholes there was no sign. It was as if the unholy creatures had vanished with the mist.

'She's worse,' said Tief. He was kneeling beside his sister, fists balled, brow heavy. 'Can you hear that? She's wheezing. I don't know if the damp's got into her or if it's an infection. It could be poison. Frejna's teeth! I don't know anything.'

Taiga was shockingly pale. She had barely moved at all in the night and Kimi wondered how much time the woman had left.

'We stay here,' said Kimi, forcing her feelings down, struggling to think. 'Marozvolk will forage for anything useful, food, wood, anything at all. I'll keep watch.'

'I'm not just going to sit here and watch my sister die,' said Tief, brandishing a small green book. 'There are herbs mentioned in here. I'm going to search for them. If it is an infection then . . .'

'Do it,' said Kimi, knowing he needed to keep himself occupied.

'I'm going north,' said Marozvolk, eying Tief with a stern look. 'I thought I saw some rabbits that way yesterday.'

'Fine,' replied Tief without looking at the former Vigilant. 'It's drier to the south. That's where I'll look for the herbs.'

Kimi watched them go and shook her head. Taiga's wheezing became louder for a moment and the woman grimaced in her sleep. Kimi knelt down next to her and released a long, weary sigh.

'Don't leave us, Taiga. You might just break your brother's heart. Frejna's teeth, you might just break mine.' She pushed her fingers into Taiga's limp hand; the difference between them could not have been more stark. Kimi's hands were large and strong, dark-skinned with calluses. Taiga's hands were slight, with slender fingers for nimble endeavours.

'Many's the time you sat up with me through the night on Vladibogdan when I was sick. That whole time, all five years, and I never knew you to complain about a thing.'

Kimi's gaze wandered around the inside of the circle, noting more of the engravings at the base of each stone, all furred with dark green moss. They did not belong to any alphabet that she knew and they piqued her curiosity with their strangeness. Kimi fetched up her knife and carved the moss from each one, then cleaned out the grooves in the stone with the corner of her cloak. She muttered various threats and promises to Frøya as she did so, pleading and begging for Taiga's life. Only once all the engravings had been cleaned did she realise how much time had passed. Her stomach growled and the sun had begun the slow descent towards the horizon once more. Kimi left the circle and stared into the distance, north and south. Tief and Marozvolk were nowhere in sight and the clinging mist had returned. Kimi shivered. Where were they? Where were her friends?

*   *   *

It was almost dark when Marozvolk returned with three dead rabbits hanging from her fist.

'How is Taiga?'

'Still wheezing. Still asleep.' Kimi stared at the lonely swamp, scanning from horizon to horizon. 'Did you see Tief on your way back?'

Marozvolk shook her head. 'I knew in my bones he wouldn't come with me this morning. He'd rather fight the ghole single-handed than spend time with me.'

'Things change,' said Kimi, 'and people end up on different sides, but feelings . . . they take longer to change, I think.'

'He loathes me,' said Marozvolk. She took a knife to the first of the rabbits and some of the blood splashed on a standing stone. Kimi wondered if it were sacrilegious somehow. Tief would know such a thing, but Tief had yet to return.

'He loathes me,' repeated Marozvolk, her face tight with frustration.

'He loathes an Empire that exterminated and enslaved his people.' Kimi looked at Taiga's pale and fragile form. 'And you were a Vigilant, the most absolute symbol of the Empire. He's going to need some time.'

Kimi stepped out of the gap between the stones and looked around, unable to bear the idea that Tief lay dead or dying in the endless Izhorian swamps. The mist had returned like a sinister tide and the sun's pale disc descended inexorably. The two women cooked in silence, casting anxious glances at Taiga as they ate.

'Full moon,' said Marozvolk when the meal was done. She drew her sword and sharpened it. The sound made Kimi clench her jaw but in time she sharpened her own blade as a distraction from waiting for Tief to return.

'They're back then,' said Marozvolk. Kimi looked towards the Ashen Torment, where she'd hung it on one of the shorter standing stones near the opening. Once again it was glowing, a faint blue that grew steadily stronger the longer she watched it.

'Frøya save me,' breathed Kimi, touching the shattered remnant of the Ashen Torment with her fingertips. 'Frøya save all of us.' She fetched up her sword and the last torch they had. 'Do you think . . .' Kimi paused. It was too awful to think about but she needed to know. 'Is it possible we'll rise from death after they kill us? Will we become like them?'

'Tief would know,' said Marozvolk. She spun the blade in her hand and rolled her shoulders. 'We'd best prepare ourselves.'

Outcast princess and former Vigilant took their places at the entrance of the stone circle. The mist swirled as if alive, glowing with the radiance of the full moon. Marozvolk whispered under her breath and Kimi watched as the silvery glow of the arcane emanated. Her dark skin had shifted to a stony grey when the glow subsided.

'This is like something from dreaming,' said Kimi.

'Or from nightmare,' said Marozvolk as the first of the gholes came lunging out of the mist. Its face was hidden beneath the cowl, arms flung open, blackened claws spread wide. Kimi lunged forward and then sideways, swinging as hard as she could. The blade met resistance and the ghole stumbled, then looked down at the stump of its arm.

'They're hard to kill,' shouted Kimi. 'But their arms come off just fine.'

Her attacker fled into the mist, only for two more gholes to take its place. The first ducked under her wild swing but found its own strike blocked by the flaming torch Kimi carried in her left hand. She forced the flames into the face of her attacker. The robes and cowl began to smoke and the unholy creature gave a wordless shriek before sprinting away, batting at the smouldering fabric. Kimi, sensing the other ghole was behind her, sprang forward to avoid being wounded but lost her footing in the swamp. She stumbled to her knees with a cry. Marozvolk took her place, cutting down with an overhead swing that bit deep into the pursuing ghole's head. She followed up with another strike, a brutal hack that severed the ghole's arm at the elbow. Kimi surged to her feet and grabbed Marozvolk by the shoulder.

'Back to the stones,' she gasped. The fighting had drawn them away from Taiga's sleeping form. They turned their backs on the moonlit mist, hurrying back to the dwindling camp fire. Five more gholes emerged from the mist with long loping strides, clawed feet splashing in the chilly waters.

'You won't take me!' bellowed Marozvolk, hacking at the nearest ghole. The blade bit deep between neck and shoulder and the ghole responded by clamping a taloned hand down on Marozvolk's sword arm. Another ghole grabbed her and pulled her down into the waters.

Kimi found herself beset by two of the creatures before she could rush to Marozvolk's aid. The first ghole slammed against the flaming torch, knocking it from Kimi's grasp. The second ghole swiped at Kimi and she parried, and then her vision exploded into white light. The world pitched sideways and all sound became flat and muted. Her eyes fluttered open and she was lying in the water, staring up at her attacker with a terrible pain at the base of her skull. The ghole clutched a blunt rock in its hand but made no move to finish her. More of the creatures had dragged Marozvolk down into the water.

'You won't take me!' shouted Marozvolk. Kimi tried to stand but her legs may as well have been a hundred miles away. Her eyes closed and the taste of water and iron filled her mouth.

Tief, where are you? was the last thing that passed through Kimi's mind.

CHAPTER THIRTY-TWO

Kjellrunn

'I'm sorry about yesterday,' said Kjellrunn. Maxim said nothing, his gaze fixed on the dark temple interior. It was early morning and they were sitting on the temple steps as was customary. Sundra had yet to join them and Kjellrunn had ventured an apology to salve the silence. 'Maxim?'

The boy shrugged, refusing to meet her eyes, clearly desperate for Sundra to appear with her battered book and its morbid readings.

'Maxim. I'm sorry. I shouldn't have run from the beach.' Kjellrunn's shame almost stifled the words but she forced out her apology all the same. 'I shouldn't have left you.'

'It's just as well you did.' The boy looked down at his dusty feet. 'Whatever was out there, in the Shimmer Sea, it left as soon as you did.' He took a moment to rub sleep from his eyes. 'You should keep away from the shore in future.'

'Maxim, I'm sorry. I panicked—'

'You weren't the only one. I thought Kolas was going to shit himself.' Kjellrunn began to laugh but Maxim stared up her with a stillness she found unnerving. 'I'm eleven years old, Kjellrunn. I shouldn't be the one looking after old men from Frejna knows what.' His mouth twisted with anguish.

'You should have been there.' Kjellrunn flinched as the boy made a statement feel like an accusation.

Sundra emerged in the doorway as Maxim stormed past her and into the temple.

'She has a book for you,' he shouted over his shoulder. Sundra raised her eyebrows and looked down her nose at Kjellrunn.

'You fall asleep at the altar, you've clearly upset Maxim, and now it seems you have something for me.' Sundra set herself down on a step and poured a bowl of tea. Kjellrunn stared at the old woman, not knowing what to say. 'I was hoping we would find some peace inside these temple walls.' Sundra sipped her tea and gazed across the street in contemplation. 'But every week seems to bring a new problem, almost every morning. I don't have the patience for it at my age.'

'I was trying to apologise to him for yesterday. I ran away from the beach—'

'I know what you did,' said Sundra in a quiet yet hard voice that silenced Kjellrunn. 'Spare me the dissembling and get to the point, won't you? Maxim said you have something for me.'

Kjellrunn reached into the waistband of her britches and produced the white book. She held it out to the priestess.

'Kolas gave this to Maxim. I was curious. I wanted to know . . .' Sundra took the book and spent a moment leafing through the pages. Her eyes widened in surprise before she composed herself.

'And you're giving it to me now.' The high priestess had paled and she was trembling with anger as she pursed her lips.

'All I had growing up were folk tales, and half-remembered ones at that. This was the first time I'd seen anything written down—'

'You can't read this in this language,' said Sundra. 'So why keep it? Do you even realise what you have here?'

'Something about a wrathful aspect . . .' Kjellrunn felt she might wither and die under Sundra's disapproving gaze.

'I suppose you were going to let Maxim translate this for you.' Every one of Sundra's words was weighted with disappointment. Kjellrunn was crushed.

'I just wanted to know.'

'I think it would be best if you set aside your duties as initiate,' said Sundra. She sipped her tea.

'I made a mistake,' whispered Kjellrunn.

'I can't trust you. And something like this' – Sundra gestured to the white tome, the crows stark and black on the cover – 'is not to be trifled with by mere children.'

'I am not a mere child!' snarled Kjellrunn. Sundra glared at her before standing up. The old woman slipped the book into her sleeve, frowning all the while. 'I'm not! I'm not a child!'

'And yet you keep acting like one.' Kjellrunn flinched as the high priestess shouted. The silence that followed was almost painful. Sundra shook her head and clucked her tongue. 'Get out of my sight.'

Kjellrunn hid in her room while the novices ate their morning meal, too shocked by Sundra's stern dismissal to eat or think. The few items she owned were gathered in a sheet and she tied the corners together with haste. The staircase outside her room was empty and she descended on silent feet, hurrying through the temple and out of the door. The noisy task of cleaning the bowls and washing the many utensils would prove ample distraction. She would not be missed.

The searing Shanisrond sun had climbed into the sky. Soon she would be away from the stifling heat of Dos Khor, away from the Shimmer Sea. She paused at a junction, not knowing where to go next, glancing back at the temple with regret. Maxim emerged through the temple door and slunk down the steps as Kjellrunn hurried into a narrow street. She had no wish to say goodbye. Hadn't she caused enough trouble? She was almost running in her haste to be free when a voice called out to her.

'Going somewhere, priestess?' One of the slavers slunk from the doorway of an abandoned building and pulled a dagger from its sheath. A crossbow hung from his shoulder on a thick leather strap and the stench of old sweat, leather and strong spirits hung the air.

'We're awfully pleased to see you, aren't we, Daras?' Another man emerged from a building on the opposite side of the street. He clutched a green glass bottle and yawned before fixing Kjellrunn with a sour look.

'That we are, Harein. We could use some religion, I reckon.'

'I'm just running an errand for the high priestess,' said Kjellrunn. 'It would be unwise to interrupt temple business.' Her confidence stalled as she spun the lie and her steps faltered as three more men blocked the street ahead. All carried crossbows and an air of malevolence.

'Maybe this high priestess of yours could perform a funeral for my friend.' The slaver called Harein cleaned his nails with the dagger and sunlight glinted from the blade. 'Do you remember? She turned him to stone with a look.' The man smiled, revealing the pale scar that ran from the corner of his mouth and the missing tooth within. 'And Djendra. He had his face burned off. It worked out well for me. I'm the leader now, but I think it's time we got even.'

More slavers slunk from the buildings nearby until there were at least ten of them, moving slowly, unhurried and smirking. Most of the men carried crossbows and Kjellrunn recalled the clearing by the woodcutter's chalet in Cinderfell. She remembered the Okhrana coming for Mistress Kamalov and the moment Verner died. But mostly she remembered how dangerously out of control she had felt as the arcane coursed out of her.

'No, please,' she said. 'I don't want to hurt you.'

Harein chuckled and he spoke to his gang in a low rumble. Kjellrunn couldn't understand the language he spoke and stared around as the slavers answered with cruel laughter. Kjellrunn turned this way and that, but there was nowhere to go. The slavers closed in, one or two within arm's reach, circling her like sick dogs in the dusty street. Kjellrunn didn't see the strike coming. A heavyset man backhanded her and she crumpled to the floor without a sound. The bed sheet came untied and her possessions spilled out in the dust. Blood stained the back of her hand as she wiped her numb mouth. She tried to speak but nothing came out; she could only gasp with shock.

'So. You're a runaway?' said Harein, smiling his gap-tooth grin. He squatted down and plucked the single crow feather from her belongings. 'Too bad no one's going to miss you, priestess.'

The bed sheet billowed as an unnatural wind swirled around them, raising sand and grit. Kjellrunn closed her eyes and the slavers did the same, cursing in Shanish, stumbling as the wind gusted about them. Kjellrunn ran to the side of the street, almost blind with grit, her pulse pounding loud in her ears. She hunkered down in a doorway and squinted through the angry dust to make out four figures, arms raised towards the sky. The wind intensified and the slavers shielded their eyes with their hands. Suddenly the wind dropped, revealing Mistress Kamalov. She stood in the centre of the street with an expression like thunder. Three novices stood close behind, including Maxim, much to Kjellrunn's surprise.

'Why is it you men are too stupid to learn this lesson,' said Mistress Kamalov. 'Did we not make ourselves clear?'

The slaver's leader reached for the crossbow and curled his scarred lip. 'We learned just fine,' he replied. Kjellrunn sprang to her feet and ran. Harein sighted down the weapon at Mistress Kamalov.

'No!' screamed Kjellrunn. She sprang towards him, terrified he might hurt her former teacher. Harein turned on instinct and Kjellrunn felt a jolt but her momentum carried her forward, knocking him over. The wind went out of her and all she could feel was a bright pain.

'Scrawny bitch!' Harein pulled himself to his knees and drew his knife. Kjellrunn scrambled backwards with a terrible pain in her side. He reached forward, grabbing her by the throat and pulling back his knife hand for the killing thrust. A blur of black shot past the slaver, and another, leaving bright red slashes across the man's eyes. Harein dropped the knife and doubled over at the waist, holding his hands to his face. He shouted in confusion and was answered by more birds, darting from the sky to rake the slaver's scalp, shredding his ears and hands. Kjellrunn dragged herself away from Harein as he wailed and stumbled about, panicking blindly. A huge flock of birds attacked the slavers in concert and the men called out in agony. The air was filled with wings, a vast turmoil of avian bodies. Mistress Kamalov strode through the chaos and plucked the man's knife from the ground, then stabbed him in the throat even as a crow was gouging his eyes.

'This is your last lesson.'

Kjellrunn tried to stand but her legs buckled as pain flared through her body. Her black robes had been torn and she touched the ripped fabric above her hip with a trembling hand. He fingers came away wet and red.

'I'm bleeding,' she whispered. 'Frøya save me, I'm bleeding.'

Those slavers that could stand ran for their lives and Kjellrunn's gaze fell on the corpse of their leader.

'This is like Cinderfell all over again.'

'You survived the Okhrana,' said Mistress Kamalov as she pulled her upright. 'You will survive these thugs.'

The vast flock of birds dissipated over the city, flying back

to a hundred nests and perches, leaving the street empty save
for the novices.

'I'm bleeding,' repeated Kjellrunn, feeling delirious and
faint.

'Yes. You are shot,' said Mistress Kamalov in her no-nonsense
manner. Through her pain and shock, Kjellrunn realised she
had missed the old woman. 'Now start walking or you will
bleed to death in the street.' They started back to the temple.
'One small argument with Sundra and you are running away.'

'She told me to get out her sight,' mumbled Kjellrunn. Her
words sounded far away, as if they came from someone else.

'She did not say anything about getting yourself killed,' said
Mistress Kamalov. 'Or leaving.' The other novices ran forward
to support Kjellrunn. 'Why didn't you use your powers to
protect yourself as I taught you?'

'I didn't want to kill anyone again.'

'None of us do, child,' said Mistress Kamalov in a tender
whisper. 'None of us do.' They were last words Kjellrunn
heard before she passed out.

Pain. Kjellrunn's eyes snapped open just as Mistress Kamalov
pulled the crossbow bolt out of her side. Blood pooled and
Sundra pressed a bandage to the site of the wound. Kjellrunn
groaned before she had the sense to look away and the room
spun slightly as her vision swam. Maxim was kneeling at the
doorway and the other novices had crowded in behind him
to watch the gory spectacle.

'How that bolt did not go through you at such close range
is a miracle.' Mistress Kamalov held up the offending bolt,
slick with blood, then threw it in a bucket. 'Foolish girl. You
could have turned your skin to stone. I have seen you do
this before!'

'Not now,' whispered Sundra. 'She's lost a lot of blood. You
can scold her later.'

'I didn't want to lose control,' whispered Kjellrunn. 'I didn't want to hurt you.'

'What are you talking about?' said Mistress Kamalov. 'You would not have hurt me.'

'Before. In Cinderfell. When the Okhrana came.' Kjellrunn's vision darkened and she knew she was close to passing out. Or death. 'Before. I nearly killed you. I lost control of the arcane and the cottage collapsed. You were unconscious. I nearly killed you.'

'That's enough,' said Sundra, standing in front of Mistress Kamalov. 'She needs to rest.'

The room turned black.

Kjellrunn drifted in and out of consciousness. Faces blurred and the room darkened, but there was always someone beside her, holding her hand. The pain was a constant companion and the iron tang of blood filled her senses.

'What time is it?' she mumbled, her eyes still closed.

'It is night. Now sleep, dear child. Sleep.' Mistress Kamalov's voice, soft and soothing in the darkness. Kjellrunn blinked a few times and found herself staring at Maxim, sitting beside the renegade Vigilant with an earnest look. Sundra sat in the corner of the room, dozing on a rickety stool.

'All this time you have been too scared to use your powers because of what happened in Cinderfell,' said the renegade Vigilant with a sad smile. 'Why did you not tell me?'

'I was . . .' Kjellrunn struggled to find the word. 'I was ashamed. I tried to tell you the night you found me asleep at the altar.' She felt the hot sting of tears as she said the words, but also a relief to have finally said them.

'You have saved my life on two occasions now,' said Mistress Kamalov, squeezing her hand.

'And I almost killed you,' added Kjellrunn, feeling as miserable as she could remember.

'But here I am.' Mistress Kamalov bent forward and kissed

Kjellrunn on the forehead. 'I have missed you, Kjellrunn. I miss teaching you and I miss your company. We will speak of this again in the morning, but know that you have nothing to feel ashamed of. Nothing.'

The old woman rose from the bedside and left the room. Kjellrunn watched her go with a feeling of deep calm. Trine waited in the doorway with a murderous look on her narrow face. She glared at Kjellrunn before Mistress Kamalov put an arm around the dark-haired girl's shoulders and ushered her away. Kjellrunn continued to stare at the doorway where a grey cat stared with a serious expression.

'Kjellrunn?' said Maxim. 'Are you . . .?'

'Still alive?' replied Kjellrunn. 'Yes.'

'What are you staring at?'

'There's a grey cat in the doorway. I didn't know the temple had a cat.' Maxim rose from his stool and approached the doorway, then stepped into the corridor beyond and looked around. He looked back at Kjellrunn over his shoulder with an expression of concern.

'There's no cat here, Kjellrunn.'

'Of course there is,' she replied, starting to fall asleep again.

CHAPTER THIRTY-THREE

Silverdust

The vast chamber of the Imperial Court was heavy with silence. The first rays of sun had yet to venture through the windows and halos of light broke the gloom; trios of candles in tall candelabras stood watch over the scene. The court was empty save for the four old women who polished the floor, hunting down scuffs, stains and imperfections. Streig and Silverdust watched all of this from the gallery, high up on the side of the chamber. The shock of the previous night's attack had passed but many questions needed answers.

'All this time?' said Streig in a hushed voice. The Exarch nodded.

All of this time and for many years before. It is why I do not sleep and why I do not eat.

'The last cinderwraith in all of Vinterkveld.'

Quite possibly.

'Why didn't you pass on why Steiner set the others free?'

In part, because I wanted to buy Steiner some time with lies and misdirection. As time went on I realised that there was something left undone. A wrong I should have righted long ago.

'Why tell all of this to me now?' Streig rubbed his face and blinked away the tiredness.

We have come all this way together, Streig. It feels wrong to keep this last truth from you. Besides, you saw me fall off the roof of the inn. Only a Vigilant of Academy Zemlya could prevent their demise from such a fall.

'You could have lied,' said Streig. 'I'm a soldier, what do I know?'

You are not just a soldier, Streig. You are my friend, perhaps my only friend, and honesty is good currency between friends.

'Friends.' Streig said the word as if trying on a new garment for size. 'Not too much opportunity for friendship in the Empire.'

It is how the Emperor likes it. People fighting among themselves rarely unite to topple their leader.

Streig thought on this, seeing the sense of it. He turned his eyes to the women scrubbing the floor and spoke quietly. 'I was shocked when I learned the Empire lies to everyone about the arcane. Any soldier that serves alongside a Vigilant is told and sworn to secrecy on pain of death.' Streig shook his head. 'All this fear and hatred about witchsign, and here you are setting people on fire in the capital city. There will be consequences.'

There are always consequences. But they were Okhrana and I was unarmed. They would have killed you too.

'No witnesses.' Streig massaged his forehead and sighed. There hadn't been much chance to sleep since the assassins had come for them.

This has always been the Emperor's way. Kill the truth, kill those who know the truth, destroy anything that supports a different view, then tell people what they want to hear to hold on to power.

'And today you'll kill him and make it all stop.' It hardly needed saying. Silverdust had made his intent clear. 'You're all I have now,' said Streig after a pause. 'The other soldiers don't speak to me. I have no section, no troop, only you. And after today . . .'

I must kill him, Streig. It is the only way. His grip on the Empire is absolute.

'But do you have to die with him?'

I will need to gain a private audience; only there might he relax his defences. If fortune smiles upon me I may be able to catch him off guard. Even if I survive killing the Emperor there will be scores of loyal Vigilants in the palace. Escape will be far from certain.

The doors at the back of the court boomed open and Semyonovsky guards stalked in. A pause in their stride indicated they were not used to such early visitors. One of their number marched across the polished tiles and made a perfunctory bow to the Exarch, a nod at best. Silverdust let it pass.

'You must come down from there,' said the Semyonovsky guard to Silverdust. 'And you must leave at once,' he said to Streig. 'Soldiers are not permitted here.'

Silverdust held up a hand. *He is not a soldier, but my aide. His mace waits by the doors outside. Go now and trouble us no more.* The Exarch waved the man away as if he were a serving wench. The guard looked from Silverdust to Streig, then turned on his heel and marched away.

If only the rest of the day passes so smoothly.

'What should I do?' asked Streig.

Go back to the inn. I have left a significant sum of money for you. From there I want you to return home to Virolanti Province. Learn to be a farmer. Take a new name and live a new life.

'A farmer?' Silverdust could sense Streig's shock. 'I wouldn't know where to start.'

Which is why the money will help.

'I want to stay. I want to help you set things right . . .' Silverdust held up one hand to silence Streig's protests.

Farmers make things grow. You should make something of your life that does not depend on death and secrets.

'Like the Empire.'

Like me, thought Silverdust, but he kept these words to

himself. *Yes. Like the Empire. Get away from here. Should I fail they will seek you out. They will have questions. Questions, whips, and knives.*

It was another hour before the courtiers filed into the vast court in dribs and drabs. In twos and threes they came, high-ranking generals and Vigilants of various standing. A few nobles joined their number, splendid in their finery. Silverdust could sense their reluctance, given the recent fate of Dimitri Sokolov. 'What now?' said Streig.

It is time. Go back to the inn. Take the money. Silverdust stood up and placed one hand on the young soldier's shoulder. Neither said anything, knowing that this might be the last time they ever spoke. *Thank you for being my friend, Streig.*

Silverdust exited the gallery and descended the steps to the court. He drifted across the polished tiles and stood directly before the throne, head bowed as if in contemplation. Latecomers joined the huddle of three dozen courtiers, but Father Orlov and Envoy de Vries were the last to enter. The Envoy, who made it her life's work to appear poised and beguiling, had the beginnings of dark rings beneath her eyes. She walked slowly with one arm crossed over her stomach, her other hand pressed against her mouth. She approached Silverdust with a look of dread.

Good morning, Envoy de Vries. I gather by now you have heard the fate of the Okhrana sent to kill me.

Envoy de Vries said nothing. Silverdust probed at her mind and found only shocked turmoil. Her thoughts spun and twisted, too fast to concentrate on or make sense of.

Father Orlov. You are well, I trust? Orlov's expression remained hidden behind his mask, but Silverdust could sense the man's stomach tightening with a dread born of disbelief. Silverdust projected his words into the minds of everyone present.

Thank you for the gift of Okhrana last night. Unfortunately they were not up to the task you set them. How unfortunate. For them and for you.

The courtiers broke out in a frenzy of barely whispered outrage. Envoy de Vries grimaced through a smile of pure fear.

'I have no idea what you are suggesting, Exarch. Only the Emperor and few trusted lieutenants have the authority to dispatch the Okhrana for an assassination.'

Silverdust stepped closer to the woman so they were within arm's reach of each other.

I did not say they had been sent to assassinate me, Envoy.

'Half of Khlystburg is talking about it. My people brought me news a few hours ago.' The Emperor entered the court before Silverdust could reply and all assembled dropped to one knee and bowed their heads. He wore his customary black and his pale eyes slid across the many courtiers with a cold indifference. An unfurled scroll dangled from one hand, while the other traced the sheath containing the Ashen Blade. Four Semyonovsky guards escorted him, taking up places either side of the throne.

'You may stand,' he said in his quiet voice. The courtiers rose and a feeling of dread crept along the necks and spines of everyone like a frost in spring. 'Exarch.' The Emperor looked down at the scroll and returned his gaze to Silverdust. 'I have reports that you slew a handful of Okhrana in the Voronin District last night, even going so far as to use the arcane in public.'

Your reports are almost correct, your Imperial highness. The Okhrana were seven in number.

'Seven.' The Emperor sat on the throne and took a moment to roll the scroll up, his pale eyes fixed on Silverdust, his expression serious. The court waited, barely daring to breathe. 'Perhaps you could illuminate us why you took it upon yourself to kill my servants in such a way?'

My best guess is that the Okhrana had been sent by Envoy de Vries to kill me before I could testify before you today, your Imperial highness.

'Your best guess?' repeated the Emperor, nodding thoughtfully. 'Who else might want you dead, Exarch?'

Perhaps you sent them, Your Imperial Highness, to punish me for Vladibogdan.

Silverdust knew the latter wasn't true, but he also knew the Emperor was attracted to boldness and intrigue. If he could win the Emperor over he might be granted an audience in private.

'This is quite the accusation, Exarch.' The Emperor gave a chilly smile and drew the Ashen Blade from its sheath. 'As it is well known at court that Envoy de Vries is a favourite of mine.'

A shame, Your Imperial Highness. She is no favourite of mine.

The courtiers standing near Silverdust wore such looks of sickly anguish it was almost comical. The Emperor looked at Envoy de Vries, then regarded the tip of the Ashen Blade. Flakes of pale grey ash fluttered to the floor.

'Your Imperial Highness . . .' she began to say but the Emperor gave her a look of such reproach she fell silent immediately.

'We killed fifty people in the Voronin District this morning,' said the Emperor. There was no expression in his voice, save perhaps boredom. His eyes drifted to the tip of the enchanted dagger. 'In order to suppress last night's . . . altercation.'

Silverdust felt a pang of remorse. He had known there would be consequences for such a public display, but he had not considered the consequences would not be his and his alone.

'Not that it matters, of course.' The Emperor stood up and descended the steps from the throne. 'Rumours of people using the arcane are spreading across the whole continent and I can't very well kill *everyone*.' He took a moment to stare at the Ashen Blade then once more looked up sharply and fixed his pale gaze on the Envoy. 'Is this true, de Vries? Did you use my Okhrana without correct authority?'

'Your Imperial Highness. I grew frustrated. I know this man to be an enemy of the Empire. He consorted with the ringleader of the uprising on Vladibogdan and—'

'You decided to send *my* Okhrana to kill him in the middle of the night?' The Emperor's calm expression had changed to something darker, hinting at the anger deep below the surface. For a moment Silverdust wondered if he might use the Ashen Blade on de Vries to make an example of her.

'And you have proof I assume?' said the Emperor. 'Of this consorting.'

'Your Imperial Highness.' Father Orlov stepped forward and bowed deeply. 'I was on Vladibogdan during the fall—'

It has hardly fallen. Unless the island has sunk beneath the Sommerende Ocean since we left.

Silverdust's riposte drew a smirk from the Emperor before he nodded to Orlov to continue.

'Go on, Ordinary.'

'I am Father Orlov, Your Imperial Highness.' The courtiers were absolutely silent, keen to hear the words that would damn the upstart Exarch. 'Silverdust was absent during the fighting; he did not come to the defence of the island. And furthermore, I saw him with my own eyes, conversing with Steiner Vartiainen himself days later.'

The courtiers whispered to one another at the mention of Steiner's name. The boy's fame preceded him. Silverdust could feel some satisfaction from that at least. He had bought Steiner time, just as he said he would.

'Is this true, Exarch?' said the Emperor, keeping his tone level.

I did speak with the Vartiainen boy, but only to secure the safety of the remaining novices on Vladibogdan. Many were slain during the fighting, and many fled afterwards.

The Emperor stared at the Exarch and moved closer. Silverdust felt the immense pressure of the Emperor's regard as the man tried to read his mind. A look of irritation crossed the Emperor's face for a fleeting moment. Silverdust's mind remained impregnable.

'And you were in charge when all of this took place?' said the Emperor, his gaze flickering between Father Orlov and Silverdust.

No, Your Imperial Highness. That responsibility fell to Ordinary Shirinov, who was carrying out Envoy de Vries' wishes after Matriarch-Commissar Felgenhauer left us.

'Another link of treachery, Your Imperial Highness,' said the Envoy. 'The Exarch is a known conspirator with the renegade Felgenhauer.'

'What stopped you from slaying Steiner Vartiainen?' said the Emperor. 'I'm curious how you can kill seven Okhrana when they come for you in the middle of the night, but one peasant boy can cow you into obedience.'

He carries a weapon of immense power, Your Imperial Highness, and wears boots of steadfastness. His allies are numerous and powerful, channelling the powers of the old gods. It felt good to build Steiner's myth here in the Imperial Court. Let them fear him. Let them know the end was coming.

'You didn't even try to kill him?' said the Emperor with an icy calm.

I thought negotiation would be best. And let us not forget, he carries the blood of the Vartiainen family in his veins.

'The Vartiainen family,' breathed the Emperor. 'It seems I'll never be free of them.' The Emperor walked away, regarding his courtiers with tight smiles and small nods, though they shrank back from him with barely concealed terror. The Ashen Blade dangled from his hand. Silverdust saw his chances of gaining a private audience dwindle as the Emperor approached an old, high-ranking soldier.

'Dragons have been sighted all along the west coast of the continent, Your Imperial Highness,' said the elderly general. 'Ships attacked, goods lost, and there is panic in the port cities along the western coast.'

'All of our secrets are undone, it seems,' replied the Emperor.

'There's no telling how many people have seen them by now, Your Imperial Highness,' continued the general.

'Send troops to the borders of the Scorched Republics and await further orders,' said the Emperor. 'We may not be able to control the story, but we can at least control the land.'

Silverdust clenched his fists in frustration. Talk of dragons was an unwelcome distraction.

'Your Imperial Highness,' said Envoy de Vries. 'Obviously the dragons are important, but something terrible happened on Vladibogdan. We have lost over half our students, the Ashen Torment has been destroyed, and Felgenhauer taunts us from her hiding place in the forests of the Slavon Province. Someone must pay for this treachery!' A handful of courtiers broke out in applause, no doubt supporters of de Vries.

'This Ordinary Shirinov,' said the Emperor after a long pause. 'Where is he now?'

'Dead at the hand of Steiner Vartiainen,' replied the Envoy. 'Killed on the beach at Cinderfell. The Exarch was the highest-ranking member of the Holy Synod on the island.'

'Silverdust,' said the Emperor, with a faint smile. 'So the novices still hand out nicknames to their mentors.'

They do.

'What's your real name, Exarch?'

I have not gone by another name in many years, Your Imper—

'Tell me your name!' roared the Emperor.

My family name is Pyli. My parents called me Serebryanyy, on account of the halo of light that I was born with.

'Serebryanyy Pyli.' The Emperor's eyes widened in surprise. For a fleeting second his mental defences faltered and Silverdust was dizzied by the strong feelings of shock that emanated from the Emperor. And there was fear.

'Serebryanyy Pyli?' The Emperor's mouth curved into a sneer. 'Do you come here to mock me in my own court?'

Envoy de Vries looked puzzled.

I meant no offence.

'Serebryanyy Pyli are the Solska words for silver dust.'

My family were Spriggani nomads who lived in Shanisrond. They took the name Pyli as a point of pride before they settled in the Province of Karelina.

'Serebryanyy Pyli.' The Emperor sounded out the words as if they were a particularly repulsive curse.

'I am unfamiliar with the name, your Imperial highness,' said Envoy de Vries, keen to insinuate herself into the conversation. The Emperor gave her a bitter smile, then mounted the steps to the throne slowly, as if a great weariness had overtaken him. He retook his seat and fixed his gaze on Silverdust.

'I knew a Serebryanyy Pyli once, before the Empire was born. So many decades ago now. You are not him. Serebryanyy Pyli is dead.'

And yet you yourself endure down the ages, your Imperial Highness. Such a thing might be rare but not impossible.

The Emperor dispensed with the need for spoken words and sent a question using the arcane. *So you have the other Ashen Blade?* Silverdust did not reply. He had long heard of the Emperor's life-draining dagger, but no one had ever mentioned the weapon being part of a pair.

The doors at the back of the court boomed open and a bedraggled messenger hurried in.

'Exarch Zima has found the rebel Vartiainen in Vostochnyye Lisy! Even now he tracks him through the streets.' The court broke out in a rumble of shocked gossip. The Emperor gestured for the messenger to come closer. The business of Vladibogdan was forgotten with word of Steiner's actions.

'This is not over,' said Envoy de Vries from between gritted teeth. She watched as the Emperor pressed his messenger for more information.

It would seem not. But it would appear to be over for today at least.

'You will not survive this,' said Father Orlov.

I had never imagined I would. Silverdust left them, sweeping from the room even as the Emperor convened a huddle of generals, Envoys and Vigilants.

CHAPTER THIRTY-FOUR

Steiner

'I feel like we've spent the whole night running back and forth across this awful town,' said Steiner. He clenched his numb fingers into fists, hoping some feeling would return. They stood in the shadow of a cart stacked high with bales of straw.

'That's because we *have* spent the whole night running back and forth across this awful town,' said Kristofine, her breath steaming on the bitter morning air. She was pale beneath her hood, the beginnings of dark circles forming beneath her eyes.

'Let's hope we can smuggle ourselves aboard this ship and be done with this place,' said Steiner. The docks were loud and busy with carts and horses delivering or picking up cargo or fish. A stream of surly sailors and fishermen wended their way to and from the sea. The mood was sour and many shot wary gazes at the horizon, where plumes of smoke hung over the town like dire banners.

'Vostochnyye Lisy isn't going to forget about us in a hurry,' said Kristofine, looking ruefully at the red sky.

'Seems like everywhere we go a building burns down,' said Steiner.

A trio of labourers was unloading crates from a wagon on

a long stone pier. The Imperial ship waited at the far end, guarded by half a dozen soldiers.

'Look,' said Kristofine, pointing down the street. Soldiers emerged from a nearby tavern, dragging Marek after them. He was awake, with fresh bruises on his face and rope binding his hands.

'Do you think he told them anything?' said Kristofine.

'I couldn't say,' replied Steiner. 'How about we deliver some straw to those fine men on the pier?' He patted the cart beside them.

'That's your plan? To steal this cart?'

Steiner approached the front of the cart. A wizened old man sat on the driver's seat, squinting at the soldiers escorting Marek. The old man supped at a pipe and fixed Steiner with an unfriendly glare.

'Bad times all around,' growled the old man, nodding towards Marek. 'They say an inn and two houses burned down last night. Seems ten people died and some outsiders were spreading lies about the Emperor. Bad times.'

'Lies?' said Steiner. 'I know a few things about lies. A Vigilant visited that inn with a score of soldiers. They didn't seem too keen on asking questions. They let their maces do the talking. As for the fire' – Steiner shrugged, remembering Lidija launching motes of fiery arcane light at Exarch Zima – 'that was the owner. She set fire to the place by accident in the chaos. She's dead now. Killed by the Vigilant.'

The old man leaned forward and squinted at Steiner. 'You seem to know an awful lot about it, young 'un.'

'I was there,' said Steiner. 'And that man is my father.' He nodded towards Marek, who was slipping further away with every moment. 'Now do you want to drive your cart over there so I can get a little closer, or are you going to make trouble for us?' The old man drew on his pipe for a moment and looked at Steiner from the corner of his eye.

'You'll get no trouble here, young 'un,' said the old man. 'The Empire never did nothing for me but raise my taxes.' He flicked the reins and clucked his tongue. 'Be sure to keep up.'

The cart approached the pier and the driver guided his horses onto the narrow stretch of grey stone. The Imperial ship loomed at the end of the pier, masts reaching high into the sky as a chill northerly wind whipped and snagged at the cloaks.

'Hoy there,' an angry voice called out. 'What in the name of . . . !'

'I was told to deliver my straw to that ship,' growled the old man. 'So why don't you move your damned crates out of my way.'

Steiner smiled at Kristofine and snuck towards the crates. They ducked down behind them when they got close and Steiner dared a glance around the side. Marek was just twenty feet away; the cart had pulled onto the pier directly behind the soldiers.

'We have to do something,' he whispered in desperation. Kristofine shook her head and pointed to the ship. Waiting at the top of the boarding ramp was Exarch Zima. His robes were blackened and one sleeve was missing entirely. The arm was bound up in bandages but Zima was no less fierce, his bestial mask all the more imposing for the scorch marks discolouring the surface.

'How in Frejna's name did he survive that?' said Steiner.

'Vigilants aren't like other folks,' said Kristofine. 'You of all people should know that.'

'We won't be able to sneak past him,' said Steiner, 'we have to get Father now.'

'Then what?' said Kristofine. 'I want him back more than anything, but we're surrounded and there's nowhere to go.'

'I'm going to start a fight,' said Steiner. 'Grab Father as

soon as things turn interesting.' He stood up and approached the cart before Kristofine could reply.

'Leave him alone, you worthless dog,' shouted Steiner to the nearest labourer. He was already swinging before the man had turned around. Steiner's fist caught the labourer under jaw and the man collapsed over the front of the cart, becoming tangled in the reins. A great shout went up from the other labourers and the soldiers looked around. Steiner drew out the sledgehammer and held it aloft.

'Looking for me, arseholes?'

The labourers fled at the sight of the scorched, scarred, sledgehammer-wielding lunatic who had appeared from nowhere. All but one of the soldiers started towards the cart and Kristofine snuck forward from her place of hiding by the crates. She had drawn her sword and Steiner prayed she wouldn't need to use it. He climbed the bales of straw and made the sign of the four powers at the soldiers.

'Come on, halfheads! I killed Shirinov, I can easily kill any of you. In my sleep most likely.' He wasn't sure he got the words right, but he shouted in Solska all the same.

The soldier guarding Marek spotted Kristofine and stepped forward to stop her, but Marek kicked at the back of the soldier's knee, bound up and bruised as he was. The soldier stumbled forward and Kristofine barged into him, knocking him off the pier. The weight of his armour took him to the bottom of the bay in seconds. Steiner had just enough time to see Kristofine start to cut Marek's bonds when the first soldier climbed the bales. Steiner swung and struck the helmet where the red star of the Solmindre Empire rested at the brow. The man fell backwards and crashed to the stone pier below.

'Come on, halfheads. There's plenty of this for everyone.'

Everywhere Steiner looked there were soldiers. Soldiers streaming down the boarding ramp of the ship, soldiers rushing across the docks from the town, soldiers trying to mount the cart and its cargo of straw. He swung again and knocked another soldier from the side of the cart.

Kristofine and Marek fled to the side of the pier where a handful of small vessels had been tied up. Kristofine clambered down to the rowing boats, nearly falling as the choppy waters made them bounce and bob. Marek made to follow her but stopped as if shoved back onto the pier.

'Oh, no.' Steiner looked along the pier to see Exarch Zima. The Vigilant had forgone the usual dictates of the Empire and used the arcane for all to see, though it was subtle. The Exarch gripped Marek with raw concentration, just as Shirinov had done to Maxim. To anyone watching it would seem as if Marek were hesitating.

More soldiers swamped the cart. They had tired of being beaten back and settled for rocking the cart side to side. Steiner swore and grabbed onto the bales but the motion became more intense, more pronounced, as more soldiers joined the effort. With a mighty heave one side of the cart was lifted clear of the ground and the cart plunged into the bay, taking Steiner with it. The shock of the cold water left him breathless and he kicked and struggled under the weight of his sodden cloak and pack. He struggled on, kicking out for shore, half-floating, half-swimming in the chilly water. Soldiers shouted to one another along the pier and pointed.

'Come on, lad,' said a voice from above.

'What?' Steiner turned to see two fishermen looking over the side of their row boat. One had a hand outstretched.

'The game is up. You've had your fun with the Empire. You can drown here or take my hand.'

Steiner didn't see he had a choice. It took long moments to haul him into the boat.

''Fraid we're going to have to turn you in,' said the fisherman. He was a wiry man with a broken nose and spoke

from one side of his mouth. 'The soldiers have seen us fetch
you up. There'll be no peace for us or our families if we
don't.'

'I understand.' Steiner nodded and shivered, then looked
towards the pier for some sign of Kristofine. Marek was being
dragged to the ship and Exarch Zima followed just a few feet
behind.

'Awful shame,' said the fisherman. 'The dragon rider
himself washes up in my boat and I have to be the one to
turn him in.'

'It's not your fault. Bad times all around.' Steiner sighed.
'And the dragon rider is a damn fool who tried to rescue his
father without a plan.'

'The Empire doesn't seem to care too much for other
people's plans, even if they do have them,' said the fisherman.

'Is there anything we can do for you?' said the other
fisherman. He was a stout sort with a broad face, perhaps the
same age as Steiner.

'You tell everyone that Lidija the innkeeper gave her life
fighting the Empire. Her sister was taken when she was young,
and Lidija had to hide her whole life. You tell people that
witchsign isn't a taint, it's a rare gift with a high price. You
tell people Lidija is a hero. That's what you can do for me.'

It took a long time to reach the docks and Steiner suspected
the fisherman had deliberately kept the soldiers waiting. A
sergeant pressed forward and imposed himself among the
armoured bodies. Steiner glanced back over his shoulder and
watched the Imperial ship unfurl her sails and begin to drift
away from Vostochnyye Lisy.

'You Steiner?' said the sergeant. Steiner nodded and
shivered, feeling like a drowned cat.

'Going to need you to hand over that sledgehammer. Slowly
now. We've had enough excitement for one day.'

Steiner did as he was told and let a soldier bind his wrists.

'I can't decide if you're mad or drunk,' said the sergeant.

'Just foolish,' whispered Steiner as he watched the ship sail further away, taking his father to Khlystburg no doubt.

'We'd best get you inside,' said the sergeant. 'You won't be able to answer many questions if you die of cold.'

Steiner spent the night at a dockside inn under guard. He was roused from sleep early the next morning and marched down to the docks, then guided to a galley and led to the centre of the ship. The sergeant tied him to the mast.

'Just so I can keep an eye on you,' said the sergeant. 'If you can escape Vladibogdan then anything's possible.'

'I had help on Vladibogdan,' admitted Steiner.

'You may want to keep that detail to yourself, or you'll dilute your own legend.'

Another group of soldiers approached the galley and Steiner almost collapsed against the mast with relief. Walking among the soldiers with her head held high was Kristofine. She looked utterly defiant – if she had cried during the night she resolutely refused to shed her tears now. She had never looked more beautiful. Kristofine nodded curtly to the sergeant as she was brought aboard.

'Good morning,' she said, as if she were a passenger and not a prisoner.

The sergeant nodded to her. 'And good morning to you. We'll make a small cabin available to you while we travel, but Steiner stays on deck. He's too dangerous to remain out of sight.' Kristofine stepped forward and gave Steiner a long, lingering kiss before the soldiers took her away. Steiner watched until she disappeared from view.

'You'll keep her safe?'

'As if she were my own daughter,' replied the sergeant.

'Other soldiers might . . .' Steiner couldn't finish the sentence.

'Yes,' agreed the sergeant. 'Other soldiers might. But the captain runs a tight ship and my men and I are better than dogs, so she'll be safe, Vartiainen. You have my word on that.'

'Where are we going?' Steiner didn't expect an answer but the sergeant seemed unusually affable given Steiner's crimes. The sergeant looked out to sea and to the north.

'You'll find out in good time.'

CHAPTER THIRTY-FIVE

Kimi

Kimi woke to the dim light of a brazier. She coughed and tried to cover her nose but her hands were bound together.

'What's that smell,' she croaked, her throat dry and sore. She was in a cavern wider than Romola's ship, the ceiling unseen in the darkness. Water ran freely down the walls and collected in a stream at the centre, burbling as it coursed over pebbles and rusting plates of armour. There was no wood in the rusted iron brazier, nor was it coal. Kimi huddled closer to the ruddy light. The burning peat gave off a malodorous smoke that made her head ache. There were other braziers around the cavern, all shedding a sombre light. It was then she remembered being clubbed unconscious as Marozvolk was pulled down by the gholes. She shuffled forward on her knees and inspected her bonds more closely.

'Frejna's teeth,' she whispered. The slender rope was made from hair. Human hair if she had to guess. She opened her mouth to call out for her friends just as a chill breeze swept into the cavern. Kimi stared with widening eyes, mute with shock, as an immense serpent entered the cavern from a narrow tunnel. It was vastly different in every way to the

stunted juvenile dragons she'd fed on Vladibogdan. The
creature was the colour of sour milk at first glance, but as
Kimi looked harder she realised there were motes of sickly
green shining in its iridescent scales. The serpent half-slithered,
half-crawled on four wiry legs that grasped at the walls as
much as they grasped at the floor. Most disturbingly of all,
the serpent moved silently despite its great size. 'Veles,' Kimi
whispered to herself in disbelief. For a moment it was hard
to think, breath would not come and every muscle froze. The
creature turned, coiling about itself like a rancid ribbon in
the wind. Scars the colour of pitch and dried blood ran down
its back. The serpent paused at each of the braziers, stirring
them up with a single claw, causing them to glow more
brightly. Kimi feigned sleep as the dragon came near, yet she
could feel an overpowering presence beside her. Kimi opened
an eye just enough to see and almost flinched as the dragon's
maw hovered over her. It sniffed at her, snuffling down the
scent of her. She clamped her eyes shut and prayed to Frøya
out of desperation. Veles gave a barely audible growl, so deep
and low that she felt it more than heard it. May Frejna's eye
not find you, she thought. The sound of screaming filled the
cavern and for a moment she feared she had surrendered to
her terror. Veles had moved off across the cavern when she
dared to open her eye again. A dozen gholes dragged three
men into the chamber. Each was attired in black with a heavy
travel cloak. Each wore a sheath on his belt but their weapons
had been confiscated or lost in the fight. Kimi looked around
the cavern with growing dread. Where was Marozvolk? Was
Tief here somewhere?

The gholes dragged the first of the men forward and he
screamed out in Solska. 'No, please, no!'

Veles swung his great wedge-shaped head down so his snout
was pointing at the man's chest. The man's eyes widened in
fear and Kimi could tell he was shaking, even from the other

side of the cavern. She slid away from the brazier, hoping the shadows might make her less noticeable.

Veles lifted one great foot from the ground and scored the man's forehead with a single claw. A bead of blood shone in the ruddy light and Veles snorted. Something like smoke emerged from his nostrils and the cavern became heavy with the stench of sulphur.

'Please, just let me go,' said the man. 'I'll forget I ever saw you, I'll tell them I never came here.'

Veles remained perfectly still, or so it must have seemed to man in front of him. Kimi watched the dragon's tail snake around, a sliver of metal glittering at the tip. The man barely flinched as the tip of Veles' tail whipped around behind him, piercing his flesh with a deft touch.

'Please. Anything but this!'

Kimi watched in horrified fascination as the man's hair turned snow white in the space of a few breaths. No sound escaped the man's mouth as he began to stoop, his skin wrinkling and shrivelling as he grew gaunt. A moment later the man slumped on the floor, his youth devoured. Veles pulled the blade from the man's back with the tip of his tail, which curled gracefully around behind him. Kimi struggled at her bonds as a terrible panic suffocated her.

So, you are awake, my Yamali jewel. Kimi froze as if she had been struck. The words had appeared in her mind without the need for sound to bring them to her ears. She had witnessed this before with Silverdust. Slowly, she forced herself to her knees, then her feet, shaking so hard she was sure she would fall. She stood up and took a deep breath.

'You can speak?'

Of course I can speak. You don't live as long as I do without mastering a number of languages. I am an expert in every tongue that is spoken in Vinterkveld, and a few that history has forgotten. I do not merely speak. I converse.

The serpent slunk across the cavern but maintained a respectful distance from her. She eyed the tip of the dragon's tail and the dagger that had been secured there with a breathless dread. His face was long and contained every shade of parchment and polished bone, with a rabble of jutting teeth, some broken, others blackened, most sharp as daggers and just as long. Kimi stepped around the blunt tip of his jaw until she could see one eye, at least a hand's span wide. The orb was ringed with a diseased red, while the centre bore a cloudy rheum that made the iris indistinct.

You've been very busy since arriving in my kingdom. Veles snorted another plume of sulphurous smoke. *Many of my children are missing, and many that remain have lost hands and arms.* The dragon made a peculiar noise that was neither growl or purr and Kimi wondered if the creature might be laughing.

'Oh no,' said Kimi, her eyes drawn to the corpse at the far side of the cavern. Slowly at first, the dead man rolled onto his side, then pushed himself up onto hands and knees with tremulous effort. The head turned first one way and then the other, as if trying to remember where he was.

Of course, I've had to refresh my ranks. And new recruits are so hard to find these days.

'Oh no,' whispered Kimi, too appalled to think of anything else to say. Veles turned to the other men.

These three are Okhrana, not merely soldiers or hired thugs. Imagine the Emperor sending his most prized Okhrana to Izhoria after all these years! There must be something here he really wants. Veles turned his blind gaze back to Kimi and snorted another stinking plume. *Or someone.*

'Don't kill them.' Kimi surprised herself even as the words fell from her lips. She forced herself to her feet and looked Veles in the eye. 'Don't make them into gholes. Please.' Killing Okhrana was bad enough, but seeing them changed so horrifically was more than she could bear. Veles made the strange sound that was neither growling or purring again.

I have read their minds and they seem convinced they are tracking the bearer of an artefact. One of the Emperor's most treasured, most powerful, most ghastly artefacts. Imagine such a thing. Just imagine such a fantastic bauble fetching up in dreary Izhoria. Perhaps you know something about this, my Yamal jewel? Or should I say, my Yamali thief?

'I'm not a thief. And I didn't choose to come to Izhoria. I merely want to get to Khlystburg.'

You have the Ashen Torment and you will give it to me or the lives of these men will be forfeit. Though only the stars know why you'd want to save the lives of your persecutors. Of course, humans never did make much sense to me. So squeamish.

The gholes became restless and the men in their grasp stared at their comrade with undisguised horror. Veles cast a look across the cavern and the gholes forced the men to their knees.

Can you not see that I'm doing you a favour by killing these men, my Yamali thief?

'I'm not a thief.'

I can make these Okhrana go away. The serpent drew himself up so he towered over Kimi. *And all I want is one little artefact in return.*

'I don't have it,' said Kimi. 'I wore it on a chain around my neck and it was lost in the fight.' She felt the something heavy brush against her thoughts, not a physical sensation, but something unsettling. Panic set in as Kimi realised the serpent was attempting to read her mind.

It seems you are a closed book, my Yamali thief. Veles reached forward with a claw larger than Taiga's sickle. The tip of the blackened bone touched Kimi lightly on her throat, then traced a line down to her breastbone.

Of course, this is most unfortunate. To lose such an artefact is unthinkable. Unconscionable even! And I am denied the simple pleasure of reading your mind to see if you speak falsely. You leave me no choice but to kill them.

'Wait! No! I lost it during the fight!' Kimi's heart raced and a deep disgust rose within her.

Veles withdrew from her, moving in an explosion of curling coils and sinuous movement. He arrived by the cavern entrance just as more gholes arrived. Kimi's heart nearly stopped in her chest as she laid eyes on Marozvolk. She was being dragged by four gholes and Kimi prayed that the woman was unconscious rather than dead. A grim-faced Tief entered the room on his own two feet, though his hands were bound.

'Please don't hurt them,' shouted Kimi. 'I lost the Ashen Torment in the swamp. I would give it to you right now if I had it.'

Veles reared upright, sat back on his haunches, then slipped two claws of one vast foot around Marozvolk, catching her under her arms. He lifted her closer, as if inspecting a favourite doll. Marozvolk's head lolled to one side but she did not wake.

Perhaps this one is more important to you than the Emperor's Okhrana? Perhaps she too is a Yamali thief? Veles held her closer to his muzzle and sniffed again. *I smell the arcane on this one.* He turned his rheum-blinded eyes back to Kimi. *Are you certain you do not want to tell me where the Ashen Torment is?*

Kimi thought of the shattered artefact hanging from its chain at the circle of stones; she thought of Taiga, sleeping and vulnerable.

'I lost it. I lost the Ashen Torment in the fighting and . . .'

Veles set down Marozvolk's limp body and scored the forehead of the nearest Okhrana. His tail whipped around a second later, and the man aged in the space of a few heartbeats.

'No, please! It's broken, shattered into pieces,' shouted Kimi. 'All that remains is a shard. Nothing more.'

I have met ones such as you before. Spirited and stubborn. Surely it is of no great concern to you whether my trinkets be broken or whole.

Kimi looked around the cavern and the single tunnel leading out. She saw Tief, bloodied and bound, eyes wide, and worse yet Marozvolk, who had still to wake.

'If I tell you where it is will you give me your word that all of my friends can leave Izhoria unharmed?'

You want me to give you my word? How quaint. Let me consider it for a moment. Veles turned and dispatched the last of the Okhrana with a languid grace, no doubt carrying out an unholy tradition that had been repeated hundreds of times. The man died without a sound, his mind fled. His body aged and withered, only to stand with effort moments later, another ghole for Veles to command.

I have considered it. Veles loomed over Tief and extended a single claw just above his forehead.

'Don't hurt him!' shouted Kimi, though it was anger not fear that drew the words out of her. She didn't care for the callous way the dragon gamed with her, nor the helplessness of her situation.

I give you my word that your friends will die next unless you tell me precisely where the Ashen Torment is.

'It's at the stone circle! I left it at the stone circle.' Tief gazed at Kimi with a look of dread and disbelief in his eyes. She had damned Taiga to almost certain death, and worse yet the dragon would likely make a ghole of her.

What stone circle?

'We made our camp there. It's where your gholes found us. Where they captured Marozvolk and I.'

Veles drew close to her and stared from one diseased eye. Kimi had no way of knowing if he was entirely blind; certainly the serpent's lack of vision hadn't slowed him down. He gave another snort so loud that Kimi shrank back behind the brazier, feeling foolish and small.

*We will see if the Ashen Torment has been destroyed as you say
it has, and what mood takes me upon my return. Perhaps I will
release you and your friends after all. It is good to try new things.
Can you possibly imagine how incredibly tedious it is to live in a
swamp for over a hundred years?*

Kimi stood up again, confused by the dragon's ramblings. His
mood seemed to weave and coil as much as his body, and his
anger flowed and ebbed so quickly she could barely follow it.

'I imagine it's lonely more than anything else.'

*Dragons are not social creatures, little thief. Though I confess, I
find these conversations a pleasant diversion.*

Veles snorted a plume of sulphurous smoke and turned
away, gesturing to his followers with a black talon. A handful
of gholes marched Tief across the cavern, while another mob
dragged Marozvolk and deposited her at Kimi's feet. Veles
watched all of this as he moved slowly across the cavern,
slinking and prowling in a way that unnerved Kimi.

*The stone circle, you say. How curious. I have no recollection of
such a place.* Suddenly he was a flurry of looping coils and
whiplash motion, disappearing from the cavern, his tail clat-
tering against the tunnel mouth as he left. The gholes turned
as one and raced after their master, leaving the cavern in
silence.

CHAPTER THIRTY-SIX

Kjellrunn

Kjellrunn emerged from Sundra's bedroom the following evening, taking small steps, one hand pressed to her side and the throbbing pain that resided there. Sundra spoke at the altar in a low and calm voice. Trine stood just behind her, attired in the dark garb of Frejna's priesthood. Every so often Sundra would pause to let Maxim translate a sentence or two. A small congregation of roughly thirty townspeople had gathered on the low benches. Some listened attentively, while a few stifled tears for the recently departed and others sat with their heads bowed in contemplation.

'She got what she wanted,' whispered Mistress Kamalov, emerging from the shadows. 'It is a real temple now.'

Kjellrunn eyed Trine and felt a pang of annoyance. 'That should be me up there. Sundra asked me to be her initiate.'

Mistress Kamalov gestured to the stairs behind her and soon they were back in Kjellrunn's room where they could speak without fear of interrupting Sundra's service.

'Perhaps you should be by the altar,' said the renegade Vigilant. 'Or perhaps it is better you study with Sundra *and* with me.' She perched on the edge of the table and inspected the room. Kjellrunn felt faintly embarrassed her former master had not seen the simple chamber, though in truth there was little to see. At one point, not so long ago, she had shared the kitchen of a woodcutter's chalet with the woman. Every afternoon they had trained together, but now Trine had usurped her in Mistress Kamalov's estimation, and Sundra's too it seemed.

'It seems you dislike Trine as much as she dislikes you,' added Mistress Kamalov.

'I don't dislike her . . .' said Kjellrunn before being silenced by a stern look from her former master.

'Kjellrunn. I see with my own eyes how you two girls circle each other. Like cats, yes?' She hunched her shoulders in imitation of a cat with its hackles up and mimed claws with her bony fingers.

'I'm not a cat,' said Kjellrunn, her mind drifting to the very same creature she'd imagined in the doorway the previous day. Mistress Kamalov crossed her arms and frowned.

'Horseshit.'

'I dislike her because she's unbearably rude.' Kjellrunn sat down on her bed. She took a deep breath as the pain flared in her side before subsiding. 'Did you send her to spy on me?'

Mistress Kamalov chuckled with a distinctly unhealthy rasping sound.

'Is that what you think? I sent a spy?'

'I don't know what to think,' confessed Kjellrunn. 'So much has happened since we came here and I've struggled to make sense of any of it. All I know is that Trine always seems to be close by with a sour look on her face. She seemed desperate to be your new apprentice—'

'More horseshit,' said Mistress Kamalov. 'All the novices are mine now. Who else will teach them? You think I know anything about the secrets of House Plamya? House Zemlya? Of course not. All I can do is stop these children being a danger to themselves. Trine is not my only apprentice. They all are.'

'She's never had a kind word for me.' The more Kjellrunn thought about it the more she realised she barely knew the girl. 'And now she's the new initiate of Frejna. That was my position.'

'Sundra needed an assistant and Trine is the only girl the same age as you. Sundra could not ask the boys to do such a thing. They fidget too much.'

'So why does Trine hate me so much?'

Mistress Kamalov looked away and smiled. 'When I was on Vladibogdan there was another woman, a girl, who also studied at Academy Vozdukha. Natalya Sokolov. She came from a good family in the Vend Province and had all the airs and graces you might expect, along with all the pomp and arrogance.' Mistress Kamalov rolled her eyes, a curious gesture that belonged to a much younger woman. 'Whatever I did Natalya had to do it better. She had to be more skilled with the arcane, earlier to rise and later to bed, more thorough in her studies. There was no end to the ways in which Natalya Sokolov set herself up against me.'

'How did you beat her?'

'Beat her? There was no need to beat her. She graduated from the academy and was posted to the Novgoruske Province. I heard she hunted down three gangs of bandits and was famous within the Synod for a time. She used her powers so freely that she died of a strange wasting sickness. It is common to people who draw on the arcane power of the air.'

'That's awful.' Kjellrunn grimaced.

'But not as awful as Natalya was. She will not be missed. My point is, some people convince themselves you are their enemy, or that they must best you in some way. Some people need opposition in order to feel alive, yes?'

'So . . . you're saying Trine is in competition with me?'

'It would seem so.'

'And there's no great conspiracy or reason to hate me?'

'The conspiracy is simple! She is an angry young woman with a stick up her backside. She is much like you in this way. Perhaps this is why she dislikes you so much. You remind her of herself, except you are fair whereas she is dark, in hair and temperament.'

Kjellrunn laughed wearily, then winced and pressed a hand to the crossbow wound. 'I do *not* have a stick up my backside.'

'Of course. And birds have been known to fly north for winter.' Kjellrunn couldn't help herself from grinning. She had missed the wizened old *kozel*. 'I cannot believe you thought I would send a spy.' Mistress Kamalov shook her head. 'As if I have time to worry about you with a temple full of children running around and barely any money to feed them. Idiot.'

'Fine. I'm an idiot.' Kjellrunn stared at the renegade Vigilant, suddenly serious. 'But now it's time you told me what's going on with my powers and my anger. I need to learn why I can't go near the shore without . . .' She waved one hand, searching for the word. 'Whatever it is that happens.'

'Very well,' said Mistress Kamalov. 'You have made it clear that you do not take these powers lightly. That is to be commended.'

'So you're willing to teach me again?'

'If you are willing to be taught,' said Mistress Kamalov.

Kjellrunn nodded. 'I'm willing. I want to learn how to control this. I want to stop being scared of this.'

'Good.' Mistress Kamalov smiled. 'We have wasted a lot of time, yes?'

The very next morning brought an abrupt change of routine. The temple steps and sombre readings of Sundra's black book had been exchanged for a gentle walk to the shore.

'How is your wound?' asked Mistress Kamalov as they walked the nearly empty early-morning streets of Dos Khor.

'It hurts less than I was expecting,' replied Kjellrunn, pressing tentative fingertips to where the crossbow bolt had split her open.

'Students with access to the powers of earth often heal at a faster rate. Those with the powers of water *and* earth faster still.'

'Why is that?'

'An old Vigilant I knew used to say people are made of water and minerals.' The old woman cocked her head as if she half-believed it. 'Or perhaps you are simply more tough than you look.'

The sea was choppy that day and an endless procession of waves advanced towards them. White crests flourished here and there across the Shimmer Sea. The waters crashed against the shore with a rousing susurrus while the sky was overcast with streaks of pale blue breaking up the endless grey. Kjellrunn almost felt at home.

'What do we do now?' she asked as they trudged through the dunes and past the stone hand.

'We sit.'

'That's what Kolas asked me to do.' Kjellrunn half-winced, half-grimaced. 'It never goes well.'

'Perhaps.' Mistress Kamalov stared at the sea and pouted. 'But I am not Kolas. Sit.'

Kjellrunn did as she was told and listened to the sea meet the shoreline as she had done so many times before.

'Tell me now,' said Mistress Kamalov, in a voice barely louder than the tide. 'What do you feel?'

'The usual dread. I want to run away. I feel . . . irritated?'

'Irritation is the first step towards anger,' said Mistress Kamalov. 'These feelings, they come from inside you or from the sea?'

'I'm not sure.' Kjellrunn took an uneasy breath. 'There's a feeling that comes from the sea, but there's also something in me.'

Kjellrunn started as the old woman took her hand. 'Breathe, Kjellrunn. Close your eyes. This is not easy but I am here with you. Think of our conversation in the temple that night you fell asleep by the altar.'

They sat for a long time and finally Kjellrunn felt a shift. It was easier to sit here with Mistress Kamalov's guidance; she could feel the woman next to her even as the presence in the sea grew steadily stronger.

'The feelings are mine,' said Kjellrunn. 'The dread is for Steiner and my father. Dread that I may never see them again. The anger is for the Empire and all the suffering it's caused us. The anxiety . . .' She struggled for the words, took a breath. 'The anxiety is that I don't know how to change things.'

'And the presence in the Shimmer Sea?'

'It knows me. I can't tell you how I know that. Whatever is out there knows me, it hears me, it feels what I feel.'

'Yes.' Mistress Kamalov squeezed her hand and Kjellrunn opened her eyes. The old woman was smiling at her. 'This was my sense too.'

'Do you know what it is?'

'Those who study with Academy Vozdukha are able to summon birds as you have seen many times now. Also strange winds and storms, as you saw in the street the day you were wounded. Academy Plamya can conjure fire and smoke, sometimes from their own bodies, but also from thin air. Voda can move water and Zemlya practitioners have no way of summoning anything.'

'I don't understand,' said Kjellrunn. 'Where does that leave me?'

'Every now and again a student has a foot in two worlds. A Vigilant with a mastery of fire and earth could summon a dragon, given enough time.'

'And me?'

'You, Kjellrunn, have a mastery of earth and water far beyond your years. You can summon something far rarer than even the mighty dragon.'

Kjellrunn rose to her feet and stared out to sea, feeling the immensity of something far larger and older than herself, something that held a deep knowing.

'I'm not sure I'm ready for that,' she said quietly.

'I am not sure you have a choice, Kjellrunn.' Mistress Kamalov stood up and pulled her shawl about her. 'You need to learn control, or your fears of hurting other people may be realised all too soon.'

'What happens now?'

'You are wounded, yes? Now we go back and you eat something, perhaps have a nap.'

Kjellrunn nodded. 'But we'll come back later?'

'No, we will train near the temple. The sea is too much of a distraction for you, and that is the last thing we need.'

Mistress Kamalov made her way back up the beach towards Dos Khor, head bowed against the wind. Kjellrunn snatched one last look at the Shimmer Sea, searching for some clue of what waited beneath the waves.

'You know me,' she whispered to the sea, and the words brought some measure of relief. 'You know me. I don't have to be afraid of you any more.'

CHAPTER THIRTY-SEVEN

Silverdust

The mood around the Imperial Palace was frantic as Silverdust made his way outside. Not even a fine drizzle could dampen the spirits of the soldiers, messengers, Envoys and nobles who gossiped and speculated. Everywhere, the same name was uttered with a reverence usually reserved for the Emperor.

Steiner Vartiainen.

Silverdust lingered on the steps of a side entrance. He stood in the shadow of a vast column that supported the roof, sheltering from the weather. The palace stables were close at hand and messengers arrived and departed on horseback every few minutes. A torrent of information swept by, an irresistible stream of it. Silverdust caught glimpses and flashes of thoughts and feelings, heard fragments of conversations. A messenger lurched from the doorway with a small bottle of wine. Dark circles beneath his eyes hinted that he had ridden through the night. The messenger took a moment to pull up his hood, before heading towards the stables on another errand. Silverdust stepped before the man, blocking his way.

What has happened?

'I don't have time for the likes of you,' sneered the messenger.

You will make time for the likes of me. I am an Exarch and I asked you a direct question.

'The messengers don't answer to the Synod. Never have. You can stuff your request up your arse. I bear a message from the Emperor himse—' The messenger, all of seventeen summers perhaps, and weighing no more than a soaking wet tabard, found himself pinned to the wall by his throat.

'Gkk! Get off of me, you halfhead. I am—'

This will not take long.

'Get off me. Gah! I can't breathe!' And just as abruptly the messenger was let down. His legs buckled as he slid down the wall and slithered to the ground. The messenger glowered at the Exarch from his seat on the floor.

Thank you. I have everything I need. Silverdust bent down until he was face to face with the messenger. *You have been very useful, Andrej. Glory to the Emperor.*

'What did you just do to me? Wait . . .'

The Exarch drifted away, pondering on what he'd gleaned from the messenger's mind.

'How do you know my name?' called the messenger, but Silverdust paid him no heed. Steiner had been true to his word, creating a string of uprisings across the continent. Silverdust had learned everything the messenger knew about the disturbances in Virag, Trystbyre, and Vostochnyye Lisy in the space of a heartbeat. The knowledge came with a darker truth: Exarch Zima hunted Steiner and Marek was in Imperial hands. Even righteous anger and a sledgehammer could get you only so far, it seemed.

Silverdust thought upon all of this as he wended his way from the Imperial Gardens. Something felt amiss and for a long time he struggled with what it might be.

Streig.

The soldier was nowhere to be seen. Silverdust felt the old loneliness return, the gentle stifling of enforced solitude. It is good that he got out now, thought Silverdust. Someone should survive. Bad enough he had lost his own life all that time ago, but if he could save just one soldier, well, that would be a glimmer of hope in the onrushing darkness.

The Voronin District was just as wretched in the drizzle as it had been in the mist. Silverdust gave thanks for waxed robes and pulled the hood into place more securely. It would not do for a cinderwraith to be caught in such weather. The rain could achieve in seconds what seven Okhrana had failed to do. The patrons of the inn grumbled at the Exarch's passing, eyeing him warily. Silverdust was faintly surprised that the place was open, given the events of the previous night.

In time the rain ceased its lazy descent from the steel grey sky and Silverdust resumed his place on the inn's roof. All night he waited on the roof of the inn, keeping watch and reflecting on what had happened.

It was morning when Streig appeared, walking beside a lieutenant in the street below. The citizens of the Voronin District cleared the way with fearful looks on their faces. They had barely had the chance to recover from the earlier violence. Rumours were circulating furiously regarding the many corpses it produced. More soldiers followed behind, not merely the ten men they had travelled with from Vladibogdan, but a full troop of thirty men marching in lockstep.

'Hoy there!' shouted Streig from the square below. The city folk shrank away from the sudden appearance of so many armoured men. 'I'm coming up with the lieutenant,' shouted Streig. 'Just to talk, nothing more.' He held up empty hands. The thirty soldiers spread out across the square, a handful of men blocking off each exit.

'Exarch.' Streig bowed. He had his helm tucked under one arm and carried a letter in one hand. The lieutenant removed his helm, revealing a veteran with a shaven head and a deeply lined face. There was a hard look about him, but Silverdust could sense his fear. The lieutenant had no wish to suffer the same fate as the Okhrana the night before.

What does the letter say?

'We are to depart for the docks immediately and set out for Arkiv Island,' said the lieutenant. 'We believe Steiner Vartiainen is in hiding there.'

I was led to believe I am on trial for the downfall of Vladibogdan and for fraternising with the Vartiainen boy.

'Permission to speak freely, Exarch?' said the lieutenant. Silverdust nodded.

'The Emperor is well aware that Envoy de Vries likes to foment competition among members of the Holy Synod to earn her favour.'

Not unlike the Emperor himself.

The lieutenant walked to the edge of the roof, using one hand to steady himself on the parapet.

'The Emperor is also aware that the Envoy is trying to divest the responsibility of what happened onto someone else.' The lieutenant stared down to the square below. Silverdust could tell the man was thinking about the dead Okhrana and how long it took to fall from such a height.

You were saying, lieutenant?

'What? Yes. The Emperor is keen not to lose any more Vigilants, given the circumstances. The fate of Vladibogdan fell to Ordinary Shirinov. You can prove your loyalty to the Emperor by following the orders in the letter.' Silverdust didn't need to read the letter to know what game the Emperor had set out for him.

I am to capture Steiner Vartiainen.

'No, Exarch. That task is for Father Orlov and Envoy de Vries. You are tasked with hunting the former Matriarch-Commissar.'

I am expected to best Felgenhauer? Her powers are considerable.

'It's all in the letter, Exarch. We must head for the docks at once. Time is of the essence.'

And if I refuse?

'Then I walk away and leave you here,' said the lieutenant in a calm voice, ignoring the fact an Exarch of the Holy Synod had suggested treason. 'The Emperor is giving you a choice, Exarch,' added the lieutenant softly. 'That's not something that happens often, especially in the Imperial Court.' There was something in the lieutenant's tone that gave Silverdust pause.

You refer to the Sokolov boy? Silverdust took a moment and reached out with arcane senses, working softly so as not to disturb the veteran. *You are from the Vend Province, are you not?*

'I am, Exarch. I served the Sokolov family for a long time. Now if you'll please come with us. We can speak more once we've boarded the ship.'

CHAPTER THIRTY-EIGHT

Steiner

'You're really going to leave me tied to this mast all the way to . . .' Steiner frowned. 'Where are we going?' He'd spent the night drowsing against the mast or shivering in the deep chill of the small hours. A soldier had approached in the night and draped an extra cloak over his shoulders. His hands were coldest and he'd bunched them into fists in an effort to retain any heat. The dawn failed to bring much-needed warmth.

'Now you mention it,' said the sergeant, 'it doesn't seem like the most civilised of methods.' He'd taken off his helm to reveal a long face; he lacked the usual pale complexion so common to Solmindre men, and his hair was a rich brown. He chomped an apple as he walked in an unhurried circle around Steiner, looking out over the Ashen Gulf.

'Have you got Spriggani blood in you?' said Steiner. 'I have friends that look just—' The sergeant stepped in close.

'Keep your voice down.' He looked over his shoulder. 'Any other soldier would kill you just for thinking such a thing.'

'Do your men know?'

'Of course they know. It's not my men that concern me, it's the sailors. If you want to get off this ship alive you'll keep your mouth shut.' The sergeant threw the half-eaten apple over the side of the ship and put his helm back on.

'I'm sorry,' whispered Steiner. 'At least tell me where we're going?'

'Arkiv,' said the sergeant. 'We're going to Arkiv.'

Steiner was released from the mast a few hours later. A small cabin without a window was made free to him. The door had three locks and was barred from the outside. The only light crept around the gaps in the timbers of the ship. This was where he spent the rest of the journey, worrying about the fates of Marek, Kjellrunn, and Kristofine in the gloom.

'Not long now,' said a voice outside the door. 'You can come up on deck if you give your word not to start any trouble.'

'You have my word,' croaked Steiner. He hadn't spoken in days and his throat was dry. The locks clicked and the sound of scraping wood could be heard as the bar was lifted. The door creaked open and the sergeant waited outside, his helm under one arm and a gruff look on his face.

'Any trouble and the girl goes to Khlystburg,' said the sergeant, loud enough that the people on deck most likely heard him. 'And trust me, you don't want that.'

'No need for threats,' said Steiner. 'You have my word.'

'And no more talk of Spriggani blood either,' said the sergeant under his breath. He led the way to the main deck where Kristofine waited. She held Steiner close when it was clear no one would stop them. Steiner bowed his head and squeezed his eyes shut against her hair. For the first time in days he felt a fleeting moment of relief.

'I'm sorry,' he mumbled. 'I nearly got us all killed.'

'He's your father,' she said, and hugged him closer. 'Stands to reason you'd try anything.' She looked him over and wrinkled her nose. 'You look half dead. And you smell like it too.'

'I feel half dead,' replied Steiner. 'I just haven't decided which half yet. And you?'

'I'm fine,' she said softly. 'I didn't get far in that rowing boat. Once the cart overturned I surrendered.'

'There it is,' said the sergeant, 'Arkiv Island. Jewel of the entire continent.'

Steiner stared in disbelief. Never had he seen such architecture. Every street was lined with buildings of stone, not a wooden home among them. There was no sign of the thatched roofs or simple cottages of Nordvlast here. The city possessed a vastness that demanded attention, a grandeur of scale. The roads were not the winding lanes of Virag or the narrow alleys of Vostochnyye Lisy. Broad thoroughfares ran through the city in straight lines, wide enough for three carts side by side.

'That's not a row of houses in the same style, is it?' Steiner said, nodding towards a four-storey building not far from the docks. It had been painted white, and the window frames and doors were all black-varnished wood. Sunlight reflected from window panes finer, straighter and clearer than Steiner had ever seen. 'That's the same building stretching all the way along that street.'

The sergeant nodded. 'It's the naval college. It's like that on four sides, and the courtyard in the centre can hold two hundred men on parade.'

The ship drew closer to the island and Steiner stared in awe at the docks. Four Imperial ships waited for fresh crew, cargo and orders. Their masts formed a loose forest against the early-morning skies.

'The fleet is based here?' asked Kristofine.

'For a long time now,' said the sergeant. 'The Emperor wants them to relocate to Khlystburg, but there are significant bureaucratic hurdles slowing the process down.'

Steiner couldn't decide if the sergeant sounded happy about this or not. 'Surely the Emperor's word is law?' he asked.

'Law isn't necessarily reality,' said the sergeant, then pointed to another part of the city. 'That's where we're headed, the Great Library of Arkiv. It holds the largest collection of books and arcane artefacts in the world.'

'Why are we being brought here?' said Kristofine.

'Maybe they want to know about the boots?' said Steiner. The sergeant gave a low chuckle.

'You ever wonder why you're so fortunate with that hammer?'

'I'm strong, and the sledgehammer . . .' He stopped for a moment.

'How much training have you had?' said the sergeant. 'Fighting, I mean.'

'None,' admitted Steiner. 'But I think I'm a natural.'

'I don't doubt it,' said the sergeant. 'But that's not the whole truth of it.'

The ship put in at Arkiv docks as close as it dared to. The waters were full with all manner of fisherman's boats. Commercial ships set sail for Slavon, Vend or Novgoruske Provinces. Steiner and Kristofine were taken to shore in a small boat with no less than six soldiers.

'Almost there,' said the sergeant, though Steiner wasn't sure who the words were meant for. He stared east towards the horizon, where the choppy swell of the Ashen Gulf stretched out, seemingly forever. A desolate feeling stole over him, like a deep cold and driving rain.

'That way lies the Midtenjord Steppe,' said Kristofine.

'And Khlystburg?' he asked. She nodded with a sombre look.

'Shackles,' said the sergeant. The pair acquiesced and Steiner wondered how many more days they'd remain alive. There would be no escape this time, he was sure of it. The sergeant guided them onto the pier and the soldiers bundled them onto a simple cart. They were both given an extra cloak.

Steiner closed his eyes and shivered next to Kristofine, who whispered soft words of encouragement. Before long the cart had arrived at the Great Library. The building was clad in white marble and stood some five storeys tall. Every window was flanked by wooden shutters painted in eggshell blue.

'Are you sure this is a library?' said Steiner. 'It looks more like a palace.'

'Knowledge is more important than royalty here,' said the sergeant.

'This place makes the rest of the world seem like a series of hovels by comparison,' said Kristofine. Steiner nodded, too tired to speak. The front of the Great Library featured seven columns, all hewn from black rock, perhaps sixty feet tall.

'What are those?' asked Kristofine as they mounted the steps.

'Each column represents one of the seven virtues,' replied the sergeant. 'I can never remember them, probably on account of not having any myself.'

The main doors loomed a dozen feet high, decorated with golden figures of men and women all reading, scribing or debating.

'We're not going that way,' said the sergeant, steering them away from the crowds that queued to gain entrance. They were taken to a smaller door at the far side of the Great Library, spirited through dim grey corridors, turning left and right and seemingly back on themselves. Down dusty stairs they went, through half-remembered locked doors, all the while weighed down by silence and the shackles around their wrists. Up more stairs and back outside, blinking in the daylight after the darkness of underground. They were in a courtyard the length and width of a galleon, and thick square towers stood on the far side, all joined by a stout wall. A few dozen people milled around wearing robes of various hues and clutching books; many were smoking pipes. They all stared with arrogance or curiosity on their pale faces.

'We shouldn't have come this way,' said one of the soldiers. 'We're bound to be seen.'

'Do you know a better way to get up there?' replied the sergeant, nodding towards one of the towers. 'Come on.'

'What's wrong?' said Kristofine, seeing Steiner's expression darken.

'Towers. Khigir nearly burned me alive the last time I was in a tower.'

'But you *escaped* that tower,' she replied quietly.

'Yes, with help.' Steiner sighed. 'I don't think any of my friends are coming, this time.'

The ground floor of the tower held nothing but broken furniture and thick dust. They mounted spiralling steps until they were short of breath and their thighs were heavy. A heavy wooden door awaited them and two soldiers stood guard, bearing two-handed axes.

The sergeant removed his helm and spoke quietly. A guard opened the door with a thick iron key and gestured that they could enter. Sitting behind a desk was a Vigilant with a mask fashioned after an open book. There were no features to the mask, save for the two eye holes. The mask bore an inscription, but Steiner couldn't decipher the words. The Vigilant rose from the desk, fingers steepled, and said nothing.

The sergeant removed their shackles and slung them on a nearby table, the sound shocking in the quiet. Steiner had been expecting a room full of shelves laden with tomes, but instead five chairs had been spread in a loose semicircle around the fireplace. A bed had been jammed into one corner, the sheets rumpled. Scraps of parchment were scattered across the floor and what looked like a trio of bird cages stood near the window, all covered in thick black velvet.

'I did the best I could,' said the sergeant to the Vigilant. 'But there's a good chance they know he's here. I don't know how much time we have.'

The Vigilant nodded and unfastened the book-shaped mask. Steiner's eyes widened in shock. A Vigilant never removed their mask, not in front of anyone, even other Vigilants. The woman that looked at Steiner was in her forties, with strong features and a dimpled chin. Her chestnut-brown hair was caught in a ponytail at the nape of her neck.

'You don't recognise me,' she said, and a small smile appeared on her lips. 'Why would you? You've never seen my face before.'

'Felgenhauer?' Steiner stared, a rush of feelings leaving him breathless. The Vigilant nodded and smiled.

'How do you know it's her if you've never seen her face?' asked Kristofine quietly.

'I recognise her voice,' said Steiner, grinning. He paused a moment, then looked at the Vigilant. She was tall enough to be the Matriarch-Commissar he'd met on Vladibogdan. 'How did we first meet?' he asked.

'You had just been brought to Vladibogdan. You struck Shirinov with your hammer while defending the boy Maxim. Where is Maxim?'

'Anyone could know that,' said Kristofine. 'Anyone from the island, anyway.'

'You have a point,' conceded the Vigilant. 'I admire your caution. At times like these it pays to be wary of new faces.' Felgenhauer, if it was her, stepped forward and inspected Kristofine as if she were a soldier on the parade ground. 'And who might you be, and where do you hail from?'

'Cinderfell of course,' replied Kristofine. 'Everyone had to leave after Steiner slew Shirinov on the beach. Besides, I was better off with Steiner.' The Vigilant and the sergeant shared a look and the sergeant gave an almost imperceptible nod of his head.

'She's with me,' said Steiner. 'And I wouldn't be here without her. You can trust her.'

The Vigilant nodded. 'Ask another question, Steiner.'

'While I was on the island Felgenhauer tried to teach me something,' said Steiner. 'What was it?'

The Vigilant smiled at the memory. 'I tried to teach you to read, Steiner. It's me, I promise you.'

Steiner stepped towards her, his whole body trembling from tiredness and fear and cold. She held out her arms and he fell into them with tears of relief in his eyes.

'They got Marek, they got my father,' was all he could say.

'I know,' she replied. 'But now I have you, and I'm never letting go.'

A hot bath was waiting in the room below, along with clean clothes. Steiner and Kristofine were left alone to wash and rest. A pot of tea and two mugs had been left beside the bath and Kristofine sipped while Steiner bathed. Neither of them said anything for long minutes.

'And you're sure it's her?' said Kristofine finally.

Steiner nodded and slowly stood up from the bath, every joint aching.

'I always forget quite how covered in scars you are,' said Kristofine, eyeing his wiry frame. He held out his arms and stared at the back of his hands.

'Bats,' he replied, 'and any number of small cuts from various fights.' His expression hardened. 'I earned all of these the hard way, and I suspect I'll earn some more before we're done.'

Kristofine took her turn in the bath after fresh water had been brought to them. Steiner dressed and drank tea. He slumped on the bed and stared at the daylight shining through the window, savouring the moment of peace. It was easy to forget they were in the heart of the Solmindre Empire, tasked with killing the Emperor and trying to find Marek.

'Do you ever wonder what it would have been like to run my father's tavern in Nordvlast with me?' said Kristofine.

'Is that the life we might have had?'

Kristofine shrugged, sending ripples across the bath water. 'I suppose. If not for the Empire.'

'And we'd grow fat and happy together?' Steiner smiled. 'That sounds like some kind of bliss.'

They slept for a short time.

A knock on the door roused them some time later and soon they were upstairs in Felgenhauer's chamber again.

'Please, sit.' The Vigilant gestured to the chairs. She stood near a window, her eye always straying to the courtyard below, ever watchful.

'So you're with my nephew,' said Felgenhauer to Kristofine, and for a moment Steiner heard the authoritative tones of the Matriarch-Commissar he remembered from Vladibogdan.

'I am,' replied Kristofine. 'Steiner and I were . . . friends before he was taken.'

'And now you're something more than friends?' A playful smile quirked the corner of Felgenhauer's mouth.

'You could say that.' Kristofine looked away.

'Marek always had a good eye when it came to women,' replied Felgenhauer. 'It seems you take after your father.' Steiner grinned and Kristofine blushed.

'We were told you were running a mercenary company in the Slavon Province,' said Steiner. 'Where we told wrong?'

Felgenhauer smiled. 'A pretty misdirection, or bait. It was a good way of luring out those who would try and track me down.'

'Like us,' said Steiner.

'And a handful of Okhrana,' said Felgenhauer, as if this were a minor inconvenience. 'I've been pretending to be this miserable wretch for some time now' – she indicated the open book mask on the desk – 'and running a few dozen spies from here. I don't have much influence, but whispers reach me eventually.'

'You knew I was coming?' said Steiner.

'I heard Tikhoveter was killed halfway through sending his message,' replied Felgenhauer. 'And then you disappeared for weeks. No word of you anywhere after the street battle in Virag.'

'We travelled east,' said Steiner, 'and were captured by bandits. Kristofine won them over.'

'And that's how you took out the garrison in the mountain pass.' Felgenhauer shook her head. 'Virag, Trystbyre and Vostochnyye Lisy are now on the lips of every Vigilant in the Empire, and in the hearts of every person who would see it fall.'

'So people know about us?' asked Kristofine. 'They know people are fighting back?'

'Very much so,' said Felgenhauer. 'They're calling you the Lovers. Your fame has reached every town in every province and the Emperor is seething.'

'That's all well and good,' said Steiner. 'But I need to rescue my father.'

'We eat first,' replied Felgenhauer. 'Then I'll take you to meet someone in the Great Library.'

'We don't have time,' said Steiner. 'I need to find Marek.'

'You'll want to make time for this,' said Felgenhauer.

'So who is it then?' said Steiner.

'All things in time.' Felgenhauer glanced out of the window. 'They may have useful information about the Emperor, but they refuse to speak to me. Only a Vartiainen will do.'

CHAPTER THIRTY-NINE

Taiga

Taiga woke alone in the stone circle, aware of the dim firelight beside her and the ghostly moon far above. The clouds hung in the night as sheets of gossamer and her breath steamed on the chilly air. The night sky, so black and forbidding these last few weeks, was alive with translucent ribbons of amethyst and jade. Flat stones rose from the ground all around, like the blunt teeth of some vast creature.

'Tief?' Her voice did not sound like her own. It returned to her a moment later, a distorted echo. 'Kimi?' No one replied. She lifted her head, feeling weak from the poison and too scared to look at the wound in her side. She took a moment to warm her hands on the dwindling camp fire, but felt no heat. Panic began to rise in her chest and she stared at her hands, trying to make sense of the forbidding midnight hour.

'What's happening?' Taiga wondered if she was dreaming, or delirious with poison. The lights in the sky continued their sinuous dance, amethyst and jade light weaving about one another.

'Tief? Anyone?' Her voice came back to her a moment later, sounding flat and dull. A grey cat, barely more than a kitten, appeared by her face and headbutted her shoulder before purring loudly.

'Mmmrr?'

'Hello, little one. Where did you come from?' Another grey cat appeared alongside the first. It sniffed Taiga briefly before losing interest and grooming the other cat aggressively.

'Hello, Taiga Tiefdenker.' A face appeared in the darkness, and Taiga realised there was a gap in the stones. The woman who stepped into the light was neither Spriggani nor Yamali but something of both, with dark lovely skin and large features. Ivy leaves had been woven into her flowing brown hair and her pale green gown shimmered softly in the moonlight. A silver sickle and a dagger hung from her belt, a halo of soft light shining from the blades.

'I see you've met Lelse and Diplo.' The woman indicated the two cats. One had curled up beside Taiga and snored gently, while the other gnawed on the remains of a rabbit carcass by the fire.

'Those are good names for cats,' replied Taiga. 'Good names.' A pang of unease coursed through her. 'How is it you know my name? Have we met before?'

'Hello, Taiga Tiefdenker,' said a second, older voice before the woman in green could reply. A second woman appeared beside the first, differing from her companion in every way. Her hair was the stark white of an old woman, her gown shimmering jet. The polished skull of a small bird had been sewn onto her vestments over the heart. Two crows alighted on the stones and stared down at the camp fire. They gave muted squawks before taking wing again, leaving as abruptly as they had arrived.

'I am dreaming,' said Taiga. Without knowing why, she wanted to shed tears, feeling a deep and terrible grief. She remained beside the camp fire, not trusting herself to stand, not trusting her body after the ghole's poison.

'You are not dreaming,' said the woman in green with a gentle smile.

'We have come to take you away from all of this suffering,' said the woman in black. 'For you have suffered so very greatly, Taiga Tiefdenker.'

'It is time for you to take your rest,' added the woman in green. She knelt down beside Taiga and one of the grey cats hopped onto her thighs, insisting on being stroked.

'Who are you?' asked Taiga. 'Where are my friends? Where is my brother?' She feared she would not enjoy the answer to the last question.

'Your brother will be joining us shortly,' said the woman in black. A dark expression flitted across her face before she turned away.

'That's a lie,' said the woman in green, stroking her cat. 'As well you know.'

'Tell me who you are,' said Taiga, afraid for herself and Tief in equal measure.

'All of these long years and you don't recognise me?' said the woman in green. 'Do you not recognise Frøya?'

'Oh no.' Taiga pressed a hand to her mouth. 'Oh no.' If the goddess had come for her she must surely be dead.

'I heard my name called from these very stones and so I came to you.' The woman in green looked around and smiled ruefully. 'I had forgotten this shrine existed.'

'I am not dead,' whispered Taiga to herself. She stared at the woman in green with a pique that sharpened to anger. The sheer audacity of claiming to be a goddess was preposterous. Gently at first, she sat upright, surprised when she felt no pain. Her dress was whole, the torn fabric smooth and clean and fine.

'What happened to my . . .?'

'And I am Frejna,' said the woman in black. 'We have come for you, Taiga Tiefdenker. We have watched your loyalty all these long years and now it is time to go.'

'Do you take me for a fool?' Taiga stood up though she felt

faint, fuelled by her irritation. 'Where is my brother? Where are my friends?'

'Blood was shed within the standing stones,' said the woman in black, pointing at rabbit carcasses. 'Sacrifice. This by itself was enough to ensure my attendance, but now your life has come to an end and it is my duty to escort you to what lies beyond.'

'That wasn't a sacrifice.' Taiga pointed at the cooking pot. 'Anyone with eyes can see that my friends made rabbit stew.'

'And someone has cleaned and cared for the shrine,' said the woman in green. She gestured to the base of the stones. Taiga squinted into the darkness, seeing the firelight catch on the engraved symbols.

'I don't know anything about shrines,' said Taiga. One of the cats was rubbing itself affectionately against the backs of her ankles.

'I know this is hard for you, Taiga Tiefdenker,' said the woman in green. 'But your body can not withstand the poison. You will not survive this night. Come with us now, my priestess.'

Taiga drew a panicked breath. Her hands were suddenly ice cold and the moon above far too bright. The lights in the sky continued to dance, so reminiscent of the lights of her homeland further north.

'No! I will not leave my brother in the swamps of Izhoria.' Taiga turned to Frejna. 'No! Pass me by and leave me be. It is not my time and I will not go.'

'If I leave you here,' said Frejna, her expression stern, 'you will exist as a lost soul and nothing more. You will be a phantom haunting the land for no good reason.'

'Good reason?' said Taiga. 'I have a reason to live! We are journeying to Khlystburg to kill the Emperor. Surely you want vengeance on the Emperor for what he has done to your followers?'

Frejna looked away and stood near the gap in the stones, and for a terrible moment Taiga thought the goddess might step out of the circle.

'Don't go! Please.'

'So you believe I am who I say I am,' said Frejna without turning. Taiga looked down at her feet, saw how much her hands were shaking, how her breath raced fast and shallow in her chest.

'Fine. It is as you say it is. You are Frøya and these are your cats, Diplo and Lelse, just like the stories of my youth. And you are Frejna, and somewhere out there are your crows, Se and Venter.'

The death goddess nodded but said nothing, looking out into the night. The crows returned, settling on the standing stones with a great commotion of wings and squawks.

'He comes,' said Frejna, pulling a long knife free of her sleeve. The silver blade was engraved with a dozen words in a dozen languages and every one of them meant death.

'You mean Tief?'

'Hush now,' said Frøya softly. She held up a finger to her lips as if scolding a small child. Taiga was about to protest when the serpent reared up in the darkness. Its skin was the colour of spoilt milk and almost glowed in the moonlight. It moved across the swamps with a half-slithering, half-walking motion, its great head casting about this way and that.

'We have to go,' breathed Taiga. Frøya shook her head and held a finger to her lips once more. She moved close to Taiga and whispered in her ear.

'It cannot see us here. It cannot see us within these stones.'

Taiga watched with dread as the serpent slunk into the night, escorted by packs of gholes, running through the long grasses and cold waters. 'These creatures are an abomination to me,' said Frejna once the creatures were a good distance away.

'Veles,' said Taiga. 'He has my brother, doesn't he?'

Frejna concealed her silver knife in her sleeve and shook her head. 'I am sorry for your brother, truly I am. My powers outside of this circle are not what they once were. To fight Veles would be foolhardy.'

Taiga looked to Frøya. 'Please, send me back. There is so much to be done. Tief needs me. My friends need me.'

'No one needs anyone,' said Frejna, sounding as bitter as the deep chill in the air. 'There is no friendship in the world now, no loyalty, no love. It is as if people do not live at all. Soon the Empire will rule over everything. An entire continent of fear and suspicion, loathing and greed. It will be as if men barely lived. What matters death if there is no life, Taiga Tiefdenker?'

'But we're trying to change that,' said Taiga. 'We're fighting back, trying to find a way to stop the Empire.'

'I have collected the souls of so many of my people,' said Frejna with a deep sigh. 'So many souls executed by the Empire. It is better that we end too, once and for all.'

Taiga crossed the stone circle to where a chain glittered in the moonlight. The artefact hung from one of the standing stones. Taiga picked it up, holding the last fragment of the Ashen Torment before the goddess of winter, wisdom and death.

'Do you know what this is?'

'Of course I know,' scolded Frejna. 'It is an affront to everything I stand for. It is an affront to the natural order of things.'

'Not any more,' said Taiga. 'It's been destroyed. A young man from Nordvlast turned down all the power of the Ashen Torment. He set free all the souls bound to it out of his sense of friendship and love and loyalty.'

Frejna held up one hand and waved off Taiga's words, shaking her head. 'This world grows cold, there is nothing here for gods any more. Nothing.'

'Is there no way I can change your mind?' asked Taiga.

'Our time is done,' said Frejna. 'The years of our followers come to an end, just as I and my sister must come to an end.'

Frøya rose to her feet. The cats slunk out of the stone circle, disappearing into the night.

'Please, Taiga Tiefdenker, come with us. You of all people should not be left to such a lonely vigil. I would hate to think of you alone here.'

'I will not. I will stay here for my brother.' Taiga was shaking still, but shaking with anger now. The death goddess turned to her with a dark expression, holding up a forbidding finger and opening her mouth to speak.

'No, you listen to me!' shouted Taiga. 'We never lost faith in you two. Never! When the Emperor rounded up the men and executed them in the woods we prayed to you. When others were sent to Novaya Zemlya we called out for your blessings. Even when my family was sent to Vladibogdan for years on end, through toil and hunger we stayed faithful.' She was almost nose to nose with the sombre goddess, her hands clenched into fists. Now, at the very point of death, she felt more alive than she had ever been.

'You will not abandon us now! It's time you made good on every prayer we ever made. It's time you rewarded our devotion.'

Frejna shook her head and stepped out of the circle. One moment she was there and then Taiga could see only the endless miles of the Izhorian swamps.

'Fuck.'

Frøya began to laugh and took Taiga's hand in her own.

'She's not going to forget that in a hurry,' said the goddess, and continued laughing.

'Why are you laughing?' Taiga stared through the gap in the stones at the endless mists of Izhoria in shock. 'She just left me here to haunt the swamps as a shade for all eternity.'

'No one has ever spoken to Frejna like that and it's just about the funniest thing I've ever seen.' Frøya continued to laugh a moment longer before she composed herself. 'You spoke the words that I couldn't bring myself to utter. If only I were as brave as you, my priestess.'

'What happens now?' said Taiga, almost too afraid to ask. 'What happens to me?' Frøya knelt down next to the sleeping body of a pale and frail-looking Spriggani woman who slept by the camp fire. Somehow Taiga hadn't seen her until now.

'Who is that?'

'This poor unfortunate is you,' replied Frøya. 'Or your body at least.'

'Frøya save me,' whispered Taiga on instinct.

'I fully intend to,' replied the goddess with an impish smile. She fussed at her belt a moment and removed a pouch there. 'A pinch of this,' she said happily. 'A kiss of that.' She pressed her lips to the palm of the other hand. 'Ready?'

Taiga nodded and realised she was holding her breath. Then she realised she couldn't very well hold her breath if she were no longer in her body.

'Being dead is very strange.'

'I wouldn't know,' said Frøya, though she sounded distracted. The goddess pressed her hand to the wound in Taiga's body and whispered a long chain of breathy and sibilant syllables. Her hand glowed so brightly Taiga had to close her eyes.

A bright and powerful sun rode high in the sky, rousing Taiga from sleep. She blinked awake with a start and looked around.

'Frøya?' She suddenly felt very foolish. 'Tief? Kimi?'

No replies, just the dead stares from three rabbit carcasses. Taiga pressed her fingers to where the ghole had slashed her open, but the skin was smooth and unbroken.

'She did it! She did it.' Taiga grinned at the sunlit sky and shouted as hard as she dared. 'I'm alive!' She stumbled around the camp fire, delirious with joy, brushing her fingers over the stones and whispering her thanks to each one. 'I'm alive!' Finally she reached the Ashen Torment, hanging from its chain. Gone was the grey fragment of shattered stone. In its place was a jade green dragon, a perfect copy of the original sculpting.

'What?'

Kimi Enkhtuya

Taiga nearly dropped the artefact. She looked around, leaning through the gap in the stones to see if anyone hid beyond her sight.

Kimi Enkhtuya

Taiga picked up artefact and studied it anew.

'It's you, isn't it? You're telling me who you belong to.

Kimi Enkhtuya

Taiga gathered her things and packed as best she could. Her sickle and dagger were not the dull and slightly bent blades she remembered. Both reflected the sunlight from their perfect silver surfaces, both were heavier and larger than she remembered.

'May Frejna's eye not find me,' said Taiga to the blades, 'and may Frøya keep me close.'

Taiga stepped out of the circle just as a lone ghole loped past, splashing noisily in the swamp. It turned its cowled head in her direction and hissed, flexing its claws.

Kimi Enkhtuya said the artefact.

'We'll find her,' said Taiga, hefting the silver blades. The ghole ran at her, arms reaching, black talons glinting in the sunlight. 'Nothing can stop me now.'

CHAPTER FORTY

Kjellrunn

Kjellrunn's afternoons were now spent in an old watchtower just a few minutes' walk from the temple. Mistress Kamalov had chosen the building, venturing up the curving stairs to the highest room. She had opened the creaking shutters on the first day and they had enjoyed the view over Dos Khor together.

'I've asked Trine and some of the older novices to look after the younger ones,' said Mistress Kamalov. 'It's important we remain undisturbed.'

Kjellrunn's time was spent meditating, developing her arcane senses or lifting shattered pieces of masonry. For the first time since Kjellrunn had arrived in Dos Khor she felt truly at peace. She could think clearly, slept deeply, ate well, and looked forward to each day a little more than the one before. The quiet of the tower was a balm to the anger and frustrations of the recent months and a refuge from the comings and goings of the temple.

But the peace was not to last.

Feet slapped on the stone steps below the practice room. Kjellrunn opened her eyes and looked to her teacher. No one had interrupted them before and Kjellrunn experienced a pang of alarm.

'Calm yourself,' said Mistress Kamalov after a moment of reaching out with her own powerful senses. 'It is only Maxim.' A frantic knock on the chamber door followed. The boy almost tumbled into the room, breathing hard.

'Not the slavers again, surely?' muttered Mistress Kamalov, rising to her feet with a grunt.

'Romola is back. The *Watcher's Wait* has been sighted to the north-east.' Maxim looked to Kjellrunn, worry etched into his brow. 'She's not alone. Two ships are following.'

'Imperial?' asked Kjellrunn.

'Hard to say for sure at this distance,' said Maxim. 'But Sundra says we should assume the worst.'

'That sounds like Sundra,' admitted Kjellrunn. 'Come on!'

They hurried to the beach to find the high priestess of Frejna and the rest of the novices clustered around the base of the sculpture. An uncomfortable buzz of fear and irritation lingered on the humid air. The same scene was being played out further down the coast, where a smattering of the local people had gathered at the docks. Kjellrunn frowned, eyes straining for some clue of what was to come. Romola's dark red frigate raced ahead, sails billowing in the wind, crashing through the waves.

'She's coming in awful fast,' said Maxim, almost wincing.

'I don't think she intends to drop anchor and disembark nicely,' replied Kjellrunn. A bright lance of fire erupted from one of the ships behind the *Watcher's Wait* and sped forward. A moment later a dull crumping sound carried over the water as the arcane fire smashed into the mainsail of Romola's ship. The novices on the beach released a collective sigh of dismay.

'It seems they have at least one Vigilant aboard,' said Mistress Kamalov. Her shoulders sagged.

'Why is Romola leading them here?' asked Kjellrunn. No one answered, they could only watch in horrified fascination as more bolts of arcane fire streaked across the sky towards the *Watcher's Wait*. The mizzenmast caught fire, trailing smoke as the frigate cut through the waters of the Shimmer Sea, coming ever nearer to the shore.

'What will we do?' asked Maxim.

'We'll fucking burn all of them,' growled Trine.

Sundra shot her a dark look. 'You are an initiate of Frejna,' said the older woman. 'Try to remember that.'

The *Watcher's Wait* was close now. Kjellrunn could see the crew running this way and that on the deck, attempting to quench the hungry flames.

'We have to go,' said Mistress Kamalov. 'There could be as many as sixty soldiers on those two ships and half a dozen Vigilants. We won't stand a chance.'

Kjellrunn fixed her gaze on the Imperial ships and curled her lip. She was tired of running and tired of hiding. She was tired of fearing the Empire, but most of all she was tired of fearing herself.

'Children,' said Sundra in a loud but calm voice. 'We're going to have to leave the temple and head north to—'

'No.' Kjellrunn's eyes remained fixed on the Imperial ships. 'We stay.'

'Have you lost your mind?' replied Sundra.

'The people in those ships think they are chasing down pirates,' said Kjellrunn. 'They have no idea we're here. That gives us the advantage of surprise.'

'What are you going to do?' Trine sneered at Kjellrunn. 'Meditate at them? I'm sure that will help.'

'Why don't you go back to the temple, initiate,' replied Kjellrunn. 'I have no use for you.'

'Kjellrunn,' said Mistress Kamalov softly, 'this is madness. Even with your considerable—'

'The next nearest town is Nadira,' said Kjellrunn. 'And that's days away. We'll starve before we reach it. We have to stay and fight.'

'I'm not staying here with you,' shouted Trine. 'You tried running away just last week.' Kjellrunn felt the patience drain out her. The familiar heat of anger kindled. 'You don't have a clue,' continued Trine, louder now, playing to the audience of novices around her. Kjellrunn clenched her jaw and her fists. 'You and your brother are just witless fools from Nordvlast.' Trine was close now, jabbing a finger into Kjellrunn's chest. 'We all know you're too scared to use your powers . . .' Her voice trailed to nothing as Kjellrunn floated into the air a few feet. Kjellrunn's entire body tensed and the great hand sculpture behind her snapped clean in two with a deafening crunch. Trine's eyes widened and the other novices scattered. The fingers of the stone hand, some ten feet long, floated in the air for a moment, then flipped forward in a long arc. Everyone watched in open-mouthed disbelief as the stone smashed into the prow of the nearest Imperial ship. The bowsprit snapped clean off and the sculpture tumbled over the deck, mashing a handful of crew to pulp. Kjellrunn looked down at Trine with an icy calm. The sand the girl stood on was very wet, along with her britches.

'You were saying something about being scared?' said Kjellrunn in a deathly quiet voice. Trine broke into a flat run, heading towards the temple.

'Kjellrunn!' Mistress Kamalov looked pale.

'I need you to summon a headwind, Mistress Kamalov. But not until Romola's ship makes the shore. Get the novices to help you.' Kjellrunn floated a few feet higher. 'Let's keep those Imperial dogs at sea for as long as we can.' More and more lances of arcane fire shot towards Romola's red frigate. Smoke billowed from the masts as the sails came apart, fluttering down as ashes and lengths of blackened canvas.

'Winds! Now!' shouted Kjellrunn. The *Watcher's Wait* ploughed into the shallow depths of the beach. Men and women began leaping into the water before it had stopped moving. One or two pirates had caught fire, their screams carrying over the restless waves. Kjellrunn gazed at the Imperial ships and thought of the day Steiner had been taken from Cinderfell. She thought of leaving their home, and being parted from her family, but most of all she thought of the moment the Okhrana had killed Verner.

'What is that?' said Sundra, pointing out to sea. A terrible shadow moved under the water and a vast fin emerged from the waves, long, blunt and grey.

'It's come to help,' said Kjellrunn.

Mistress Kamalov and six novices, including Maxim, had gone to the water's edge, arms held aloft, faces set in fierce concentration. A keening gale rushed overhead, shrieking as it raced over the rooftops of Dos Khor. The Imperial ships tried to stow their sails but the crewmen were caught off guard by the unnatural wind. The galleons slowed and Kjellrunn allowed herself a triumphant smile. The Vigilants responded with arcane fire, but the fiery bolts were slowed by the headwind. The novices scattered as the lances of fire impacted on the beach. Great showers of sand were thrown in all directions and the novices flipped the sign of the four powers at the ships. A pair of boys cast their own arcane fire back towards the ships but the bolts missed their mark and splashed into the sea.

'Kjellrunn!' shouted Mistress Kamalov over the wind. 'This isn't working. We're simply buying time. We will be dead the moment they come ashore.'

Kjellrunn gritted her teeth, every muscle tense with all the rage and grief of the last few months.

'Time is all I need.'

The dark shadow under the water convulsed and a leviathan rose up from the Shimmer Sea. Its body was larger than Imperial galleon in front of it, shining grey in the fierce sunlight. Water sloughed from great vents in its sides and blunt fins could be seen in the foaming tide. The leviathan had no face as such, no eyes with which to regard the world; the only feature was the cavernous maw that yawned open. There were no teeth, only an inescapable darkness in that vast opening.

'Frejna save us,' said Sundra as she dropped to her knees in reverence. The leviathan slammed down on the galleon. The ship's stern was lost from view as the colossal mouth swallowed the Imperial vessel. Kjellrunn could hear the crew screaming as if she were aboard. Bright flourishes of arcane fire were launched from the prow of the ship, impacting against the immense creature's head. Kjellrunn felt pinpricks of heat at her brow, which only served to fuel her anger. She gritted her teeth and the leviathan closed its vast mouth, then sank below the waves once more, taking half the ship with it. The screams of dying men sounded in the distance as the vessel sank, slipping beneath the waves with terrible speed.

'Kjellrunn,' whispered Sundra. 'The water!' They watched in horror as the leviathan's passing sent up a great wave, an inrushing storm tide.

'Away from the shore!' shouted Mistress Kamalov, shepherding her novices back up the beach. The arcane wind dwindled and a wordless panic gripped the novices. Romola's crew were now swimming and stumbling to get out of the sea even as the leviathan's wave rose behind them. The second Imperial ship let down its stowed sails and the Vigilants aboard turned their attention to the leviathan. They cast great arcs of fire at the creature, but the colossus remained beneath the waters where the fire could not harm it.

'Get away from the shore,' bellowed Kjellrunn. The first of Romola's pirates pulled themselves from the sea, half-mad with fear as a curving wall of water rose higher and higher behind them. Three more bolts of arcane fire rose from the Imperial ship, heading towards the shore.

'Sidewind!' shouted Maxim, throwing his arms into the air and frowning hard. Mistress Kamalov and the other novices followed his lead. Kjellrunn watched with growing dread as the lances of fire sped towards them in graceful arcs. Maxim gave a wordless shout, desperation writ large across his young face. Mistress Kamalov fell to her knees but her arms remained aloft, forcing the wind to do her bidding with every ounce of her being. The yellow streaks of arcane fire curved away, impacting on the beach a few dozen feet further along. More pirates emerged from the sea, glancing over their shoulders at the great wave that followed.

'We must shelter in the town,' said Sundra as she hid behind the remnant of the sculpture. 'We cannot win this battle on open ground, Kjellrunn!'

The leviathan's wave broke upon the shore, bringing a tangle of bedraggled pirates with it. Novices were knocked off their feet, and Mistress Kamalov was lost from view as the surge swallowed her completely. Rylska the pirate all but collided with Maxim as the water dragged her inland. There was a startled moment of recognition before Maxim clung to the tall woman's back. She headed up the beach with loping strides, breathing hard, her red hair shining wetly. The Imperial ship had come about, beaching itself so the starboard side looked over the beach.

'Birds!' bellowed Kjellrunn. The Vozdukha novices responded, reaching out with arcane senses to summon gulls, crows, and hawks. Mistress Kamalov emerged from the swirling water and gasped for air, then pulled off her headscarf.

'Gods damn you,' she muttered, before rejoining the Vozdukha novices. A handful of Zemlya novices had remained further up the beach, searching for larger rocks. They lifted the stones with their powers and pelted the deck of the ship. Kjellrunn watched with grim satisfaction as the Vigilants and sailors on board stumbled and ducked to avoid the rain of stones.

'We can do this,' said Kjellrunn. She floated down to stand beside Sundra. 'We *have* to do this.'

The soldiers had disembarked in two boats and headed towards the shore, working their oars hard. The first of them jumped over the side of the boat and the water reached his waist. Moments later there were thirty black-armoured men in the water, clutching shields and maces, roaring battle cries.

'To me!' shouted Kjellrunn. She had scaled the broken sculpture and stood on its summit. Pirates and novices alike formed around the shattered hand and drew blades and marshalled their powers. Of Romola there was no sign and Kjellrunn's heart sank for a fleeting moment before her attention turned to more arcane fire arcing through the sky towards them.

'Break left!' yelled Kjellrunn as she leapt from the stone. As one the rabble of pirates and novices sprinted away from the sculpture and moments later lances of fire smashed down, sending clouds of sand billowing across the beach and blackening the shattered hand.

The soldiers were free of the Shimmer Sea now, storming up the beach towards them. Kjellrunn hesitated and looked for Mistress Kamalov. The press of bodies parted a moment to reveal the charred and burned corpses of those who had not evaded the Vigilant's fire just moments before. Mistress Kamalov knelt on the blackened sand, her face a mask of misery. Her eyes rolled back in her head and she slumped forward. She was the deep black of charcoal from her neck to the backs of her legs.

'No!' Kjellrunn forced her way through the crowd as the soldiers clashed with the outnumbered pirates. 'No.' Kjellrunn knelt beside Mistress Kamalov, almost too afraid to touch the old woman. Her eyes opened and a single tear dripped to the scorched sand.

'Gods, I hate the Empire,' said the old Vigilant.

Kjellrunn stared at the old woman's back, the crisp flesh and singed hair. 'Are you just going to kneel there and let them kill your teacher without consequence?' Mistress Kamalov closed her eyes and sighed for the last time. Kjellrunn rose to her feet, lifting a handful of stones with the arcane as she did so. A moment later an Imperial soldier was pelted in the side of the head, knocking him off guard. The pirate fighting him forced the tip of his blade inside the soldier's shield and rammed the sword through a gap at the shoulder. The soldier screamed and went down.

Sundra stalked the sands like an avenging shade. Clad all in black, the Priestess turned one soldier after another to stone with her dread gaze, but she had become separated from the novices and pirates. Kjellrunn ran to protect the priestess and tripped. The air was knocked from her lungs and she stared at her feet. A dead novice lay in the sand, face bloodied and skull broken. The handiwork of a soldier's mace. Her name was Surya. Kjellrunn was floating in the air again, so angry she could barely speak or think. The Vigilants on the ship were preparing to come ashore in one of the small boats.

'Consequence,' whispered Kjellrunn through gritted teeth. No one saw the leviathan emerge from the Shimmer Sea; it rose over the beached ship like a terrible cloud, blocking out all light. The sailors cried out in horror as the colossal creature slammed down, snapping masts, shattering the hull, crushing all in its shadow. The ship split in two and all fighting on the beach ceased as people turned to stare at the shocking spectacle. The Vigilants tumbled into the water, followed by spears of the broken mast and torn canvas. The leviathan released a forlorn wail and Kjellrunn shuddered with agony, as if she had suffered a thousand splinters.

A great roar went up from the pirates and the novices joined in, a wordless shout of joy and triumph. The soldiers hesitated but there was nowhere to go and no one to support them.

'Consequences,' whispered Kjellrunn before her vision dimmed and the ground rose up to meet her.

CHAPTER FORTY-ONE

Silverdust

They stood at the back of the Imperial galleon on the port side. Father Orlov had taken up a similar position on the starboard side and together the two Vigilants summoned arcane winds to fill the sails of the ship, sending it speeding across the choppy waters of the Ashen Gulf. The sky was banded with the colours of evening. Vivid orange simmered into pale grey, the grey fading into blue and becoming ever darker. The sun busied itself, appearing to sink into the waves.

'I wasn't sure if you'd come with us,' said Streig.

Vigilants pretend to be priests but we take orders just as readily as soldiers. It is ingrained in us.

'You didn't come with us just because you're an obedient little soldier,' said Streig, catching sight of himself in the mirrored surface of Silverdust's mask. The reflection was decidedly warped, stretched thin and unclear, much like his obedience.

What choice did I have? I could not leave Khlystburg without drawing attention. Such a move would provoke questions. The Emperor would not grant me a further audience after our performance at court.

'It was a performance all right,' said Streig, sounding more like a Virolanti farmer than he intended.

I asked you to absent yourself. I asked you to get clear, to get to safety.

'And I would have, but I wanted to see if you succeeded. I wanted to see if you received the audience you wanted so badly.'

Things did proceed as I had hoped.

'But he knew you,' said Streig, stepping closer and dropping his voice, even as the arcane gale shrieked over their heads. 'He knew your name. Serebryanyy Pyli. I saw it in his eyes. He knew you and he was afraid.'

We are all afraid of the past in some way. Silverdust had no wish to divulge to his friend why the Emperor had reacted so.

'I think I deserve some answers. I've stuck by you this far.'

That is true, and do not think your loyalty has gone unnoticed, but there are some secrets that are too dark, too old, too much a part of me, so that I can hardly bare to think let alone speak of them.

Streig looked over his shoulder. Envoy de Vries slunk past, glowering at the pair of them as she went. Silverdust could tell she was mulling over any number of possibilities, and that she had been rebuked by the Emperor for the deaths of his Okhrana. The Envoy disappeared through a door and Father Orlov continued with the task at hand. Silverdust reached out to Streig with his arcane senses. The soldier knew full well his questions regarding the Emperor would remain unanswered and tried another angle.

'Are you not worried that Orlov and de Vries will try and kill you once we reach Arkiv? She's already moved against you once.'

It has been difficult for me to know who to trust for a long time now, even on Vladibogdan. This is not so different. All I ask is that if you can save yourself you do so. You should not even be on this ship. Better you desert and head back to Virolanti as I suggested. I do not want your death on my conscience, Streig.

'I have no intention of dying,' said the young soldier, and

for a moment Silverdust wished that bravado alone might sustain Streig in the time ahead.

Dimitri Sokolov had no intention of dying either.

Streig turned to watch Khlystburg retreat into the distance behind them. 'We hunt traitors and Vigilants even as we speak of treason ourselves. For the first time I can admit to myself that I'm not sure what side I'm on any more.'

There are no sides any more. Only survival.

'There are still sides,' said Streig. 'There are those against the Empire and those that stand for it.'

True enough, but what does the Empire stand for, and is it worth saving?

'There'll be chaos without the Empire,' said Streig.

Chaos is ever present, and never more so than now. Steiner wishes to create an uprising because it appeals to his heroism and sense of justice. I rebel as an act of atonement. De Vries too acts against the Empire in her own way, hoping one day she will sit on the throne.

The arcane winds continued to howl and Silverdust and Father Orlov reached into the sky to draw on more power. The ship's captain clung to the wheel with a grizzled determination, no stranger to the Holy Synod and its eldritch ways.

'Act of atonement?' Streig frowned in confusion. 'Atonement for what?'

Silverdust cursed himself for the slip, but he'd revealed something of himself and Streig was too clever to fall for misdirection and deserved better than lies. *Do you remember I told you it was the Spriggani who originally offered to teach the Emperor about the arcane?*

'But then they declined.'

Some of them declined, certainly. But not all of them.

'Serebryanyy Pyli,' said Streig. 'You taught him how to use the arcane back in the Age of Fire.' He shook his head with the impossibility of it. 'But that would make you nearly a hundred years old.'

Silverdust gestured to the blank mirror of his face. *This has not always been my mask. Such longevity provokes questions.*

'Unless you're the Emperor.'

So it would seem.

Streig stood quietly for a time, watching the arcane winds fill the sails above him. 'Over a hundred years?'

I have been a cinderwraith for forty years. It was not my intention to die on Vladibogdan but . . .

A look of anger clouded Streig's face. 'Was it the Okhrana? Did the Emperor send them?'

Silverdust wanted to laugh, touched by the righteous anger of his companion. *I had long since covered my tracks, but using the arcane does spiteful things to the human body and old age found me wanting. I died in my sleep one night and woke in the forges beneath Vladibogdan. Suddenly I knew first-hand what the Emperor was doing to the failed novices and realised that everything I had done to empower him had been the gravest of mistakes.*

'Atonement. I can see why you'd feel responsible. But what of the Matriarch-Commissar? Surely you're not going to kill her. You and she want the same thing.'

In truth, I do not know what the Matriarch-Commissar wants outside of protection for her family. Her motives are known only to her. Arkiv may well be a place of many misunderstandings and mistakes, but mostly it will be a place of death.

'You mean to hunt her?'

Such success would almost certainly grant me an audience with the Emperor, and I could finally undo the mistake that has lingered across these long decades.

'I never thought you'd go against Felgenhauer,' said Streig. 'She's famous. She's infamous. Her powers are—'

Considerable. Yes. Silverdust turned to Streig and grasped him lightly by the shoulder. *Do not put yourself at risk unnecessarily, Streig. I would be greatly aggrieved if anything happened to you.*

'Whatever happens, you and I are getting through this.' The young soldier had the audacity to grin as spoke. 'Mark my words.'

Silverdust wanted to believe him, but common sense and foresight told him otherwise. There would be much death on Arkiv island.

CHAPTER FORTY-TWO

Steiner

'Do we really have to wear these?' said Steiner as they stepped into the courtyard. The purple robes nearly reached the ground and the cowl wouldn't sit straight on his shoulders, though he was glad for the warmth it provided.

'Be sure to pull the hood up,' said Felgenhauer, who wore the open book mask once more. 'There are eyes everywhere.' She handed Steiner a hemp sack and he knew the contents immediately, a reassuring weight. 'Just in case,' she added quietly. Her presence calmed him despite the strangeness of their situation.

'Where are we going?' asked Kristofine. She tied the belt around her own robes and pulled up her hood. Somehow she made it look effortless, whereas Steiner felt he was drowning in fabric.

'The Central Library,' replied Felgenhauer. 'It's the oldest part, containing tomes forbidden to the Empire's citizens.'

'But not to its Vigilants,' said Steiner.

'Even the academics and Imperial historians aren't allowed to set foot where we're going,' said Felgenhauer. 'We'll need to stay alert when we reach the top floor.'

They headed across the courtyard without the soldiers and

entered the Great Library through wooden double doors stained blue and finished with varnish.

'Not exactly the old school house in Cinderfell, is it?' said Steiner. Kristofine smirked. Felgenhauer led them through a series of interconnected rooms all lined with mahogany shelves. The smell of dust and parchment hung heavy on the air and a faint susurrus of whispering could be heard at each junction. Much of the place was lush with shadow, and searchers in the stacks held aloft glass lanterns against the endless dark. The library dwellers nodded reverently to the Vigilant and watched her pass with reverence. Staircases took them higher, until they reached the fourth floor. One room led to another, and every so often the maze of shelves gave way to a clearing. Every space was the same, filled with four desks and four chairs. It was quieter here and Steiner wondered if they were completely alone in the dim shelf-lined avenues.

'How do you know where you're going?' he whispered. Felgenhauer pointed to small brass signs attached to the shelves, but Steiner couldn't read them. 'Directions?'

Felgenhauer nodded.

'This is my idea of Hel,' muttered Steiner. 'All these books and I can't even read the signs.' They emerged in yet another room but this one had a black iron staircase that swept upwards in a graceful curve.

'This is where I leave you,' said Felgenhauer. She gestured to the staircase. 'I'll wait here.'

'What?' asked Steiner. 'Who are we meeting?'

'They asked me not to say,' replied Felgenhauer. She leaned closer. 'But be deferential, or the meeting could be painfully short.'

Steiner reached out for Kristofine's hand and they took the stairs upwards. The top of the building had a cupola with tall windows and yet more bookshelves. Glass cases that stood tall as grandfather clocks contained weapons or armour, to Steiner's surprise.

'What happens now?' whispered Kristofine. Steiner shrugged even as he caught sight of an older man in white robes. He was tall, broad-shouldered and youthful-looking despite the dark hair shot through with white. The man held a stack of five books and was slotting them back into place on the shelves with a look of careful consideration.

'Hoy there,' said Steiner in Nordvlast, and immediately regretted not greeting the man in Solska.

'Hoy there,' replied the man with a wry smile. His beard was also shot through with white, and his dark eyes were filled with amusement. 'Not often I hear that tongue between these four walls. Perhaps you're in the wrong country?'

'I'm Steiner, this is Kristofine. We were sent for, but we don't know by whom or why.'

'Uncertainty always makes people anxious,' replied the man, slotting a book back into the gap on the shelf in front of him. 'But I always rather liked it. Makes things more exciting, I think.' The man turned away from them and went about his task.

'Great,' said Steiner under his breath. 'I love cryptic arscholes.'

'Do you know who we're supposed to meet?' asked Kristofine, following the man across the room.

'Oh yes.' The man nodded slowly, smiled again, and turned back to his books. 'Barely anyone ventures up here. I have the place to myself.'

'And will you tell us who we're supposed to meet?' said Kristofine, a note of impatience creeping into her words.

'You're here to see me.' The man stood a little taller, clearly impressed with himself. Steiner disliked him intensely. 'I'm Ving.' He turned to Steiner. 'I like her. Spirited. If you get bored you can leave her here.'

Kristofine frowned and opened her mouth to speak but Steiner squeezed her hand. 'Deferential, remember?' he whispered.

Ving chuckled and looked Kristofine over.

'I don't see myself getting bored anytime soon,' said Steiner, standing in front of Kristofine. 'What sort of name is Ving?'

'An abbreviated one. And you're the latest in the line of Vartiainen men.' Ving looked him over. 'Did you forget to eat this week?'

'Times have been hard,' admitted Steiner.

'They say your grandfather, or is it your great-grandfather?' Ving shook his head. 'They say he was seven feet tall with shoulders like an ox, which is fabrication, of course. Still, he was bigger than you, if memory serves.'

'You didn't know my great-grandfather,' said Steiner with a scowl.

'Deferential, remember?' Kristofine whispered.

'I did,' replied Ving, 'just as I know you're carrying his sledgehammer in your sack. It's not polite to turn up to a simple conversation with a weapon like that. Especially given my history with it, but you're not to know about that sorry tale.'

'Are you always this obscure with your visitors?' said Steiner.

'We're done with deferential then?' said Kristofine. Ving chuckled and shelved the last of the books.

'I suppose Felgenhauer told you to bow and scrape to me.' Ving chuckled again. 'A nice touch. I like her, she's very thoughtful for a human. I understand she's your aunt?'

Steiner nodded. 'What do you mean, "for a human"?'

Ving gestured to a pair of leather couches and bade them sit. A low table lay between the couches and a decanter of wine stood on a silver tray with some glasses.

'Best thing you people ever did,' said Ving, as he poured

the wine. 'And the only thing that makes my imprisonment tolerable.'

'This doesn't look like any prison I've ever seen,' said Steiner, looking at the neatly ordered bookshelves. 'And I've been to Vladibogdan.'

'I heard you all but destroyed Vladibogdan,' said Ving, sitting back on the couch and sipping his wine. 'And the Ashen Torment along with it. I imagine that seized the Emperor's attention.'

'I imagine the Emperor is feeling uncertain about a few things,' said Steiner. Something about the arrogant librarian made him want to boast, put the man in his place.

'Just think on it,' said Ving. 'You lead an uprising on an island barely anyone knows about, you fly a dragon across the Sommerende Ocean and kill a Vigilant, then you destroy one of the most powerful arcane artefacts in all of Vinterkveld. Not content with freeing all the dragons beneath the island, you go on to stage three acts of open violence against the Empire in Virag, Trystbyre and Vostochnyye Lisy.'

'Credit where it's due. Virag was down to my sister and some friends.'

'These are uncertain times, Steiner,' continued Ving as if he hadn't heard. 'And you are the source of the Emperor's uncertainty. He hates you. I, on the other hand, am invigorated by uncertainty. It is the food and drink that so rarely reaches this place.'

'I suppose when you lay it out like that,' said Steiner.

'You couldn't have known Steiner's great-grandfather,' said Kristofine. 'That would make you close to ninety years old. No one lives to such an age. And besides, you don't look much older than fifty.'

Ving chuckled in a deep baritone. The sound gave way to laughter, and eventually glimmers of tears could be seen at the corners of his eyes. He laughed until he was breathless and took a while to compose himself.

'You're right,' said Kristofine quietly. 'He really is an arsehole.'

'Are you going to explain what's so funny?' said Steiner.

'Steiner,' said Ving, suddenly serious. He sat forward on the couch and put his glass down on the table. 'The dragons you saw were young, am I right?'

'It was awful.' Steiner nodded as he remembered. 'They didn't last longer than perhaps thirty years, but they were huge—'

'No, they were not. The dragons you saw were adolescents at best,' said Ving. 'Dragons mature more slowly than men. It takes around a hundred years before one can truly call one's self an adult.'

'So the dragons I saw were just kids?'

Ving chuckled again. 'I like you, Steiner. I don't get many like you up here. In fact I don't get anyone like you up here.' Ving sipped his wine. 'So these "kids", as you call them, don't have the full benefit of their powers. Dragons aren't just big lizards, no matter what the Emperor used to tell the common folk; dragons were masters of the arcane.'

'I know about the arcane,' said Steiner.

'But you don't know as much as the dragons do,' said Ving a smile halfway between smug and condescending. Steiner wanted to punch it. 'They're not limited to the four elements like you humans are. Dragons knew the deeper mysteries, the power over life and death. The power of transformation.'

Steiner stood up slowly and backed away until he was standing behind the couch. Kristofine followed, her eyes darting from Steiner to Ving and back again.

'Frøya save me.'

'Steiner, what's going on?' whispered Kristofine.

'Ah,' said Ving. 'And here I was thinking I'd have to spell it out to you, or give you a demonstration. I hate doing that, I usually rip my robes in the process.'

'You're not just Ving,' said Steiner.

'I did say it was an abbreviation.'

'You're Bittervinge, father of dragons.'

Ving sighed happily, sipped his wine, and sat back on the couch with a crooked smile. 'And you managed to remember my title. Impressive.'

Kristofine frowned. 'Did you hit your head during the voyage over here? He's just an old man that's spent too much time on his own with too many books.'

'There's always one,' said Ving. 'Look, it's just not practical to be a dragon when you're imprisoned. You take up too much space, your appetite is commensurate with your size, and it's difficult to read books when you have claws instead of hands. I'm not going to lie to you, I miss flying every day I'm in here, but it's the wise choice. And besides, I need to maintain the Emperor's fiction that he killed me, or rather your great-grandfather killed me.

'My great-grandfather?'

'And with that sledgehammer no less,' said Ving. 'He was named Steiner too.'

'This is ridiculous,' said Kristofine, crossing her arms. 'I've heard some drunken horseshit in my time but this is something else.'

'If what you're saying is true,' said Steiner, 'then you know the Emperor better than anyone alive.'

Ving nodded. 'Of course I do.'

'You were defeated by him, enslaved by him—'

'Get to the point, Steiner.' All trace of amusement slipped from Ving's face. 'I have no wish to dwell on past defeats.'

'So you've been here ever since thinking how you'd kill him if the chance presented itself. You've been here for over seventy years thinking about it.'

Ving began to smile again. 'You're not as foolish as you look.'

'So I'm told,' said Steiner, taking his seat on the couch once more. 'I need you to tell me what I need to know to kill the Emperor.' The sledgehammer lay in the hemp sack, resting across his knees. Ving's gaze lingered on the hidden weapon and shook his head.

'It's near-impossible to kill the Emperor now. Even your brutish hammer won't smite the life from that twisted husk.'

'Why not? The hammer seems to do well enough against everyone else.'

'The hammer was made to strike true,' agreed Ving. 'And more than that, it's cast from the same material as the staircase you've just climbed.'

'Black iron?'

'Dragons can endure most things.' Ving looked as if he might spit. 'But black iron is not one of them.'

'So how do I kill the Emperor?' said Steiner. 'Tell me how to do this thing.'

'Only two blades in all of Vinterkveld can kill the Emperor,' said Ving. 'I know this because I made them myself in the late stages of the war. One the Emperor kept for himself and the other was stolen from me by a sibling.'

'A sibling?' said Kristofine.

'He was born from the same clutch of eggs.' Ving gestured vaguely. 'My title may be "the father of dragons" but that's simply because I rose to prominence, my fame going before me.'

'Who was this light-fingered sibling of yours?' asked Steiner.

'His name is Veles. He took one of the Ashen Blades and replaced it with a fake. I discovered the switch but Veles had hidden the original. I ripped the wings from his back and still he refused to tell me where it was. In the end he escaped to Izhoria and surrounded himself with an army of dead souls. If I ever get free of this place . . .' Ving looked away towards the windows with a terrible frown. Light streamed in and caught motes of dust as they floated lazily on the air.

'So I have to break in to the Emperor's palace, find the Ashen Blade, and kill him with it?' said Steiner.

'Or hunt down Veles in the swamps of Izhoria, fight your way past his legion of undead, kill a dragon, and claim his blade for yourself, yes.'

Steiner pressed a hand to his forehead and released a long, despondent sigh. 'Frøya save me.'

'Did you think assassinating the Emperor would be a simple matter?' asked Ving, pouring more wine for himself.

'We were under no illusions,' breathed Kristofine, 'but this is beyond anything we could have imagined.'

'And yet it will happen,' said Ving. 'I feel it. A change is coming to Vinterkveld, and perhaps you will be the agent of that change, and perhaps there is another.'

'What do you mean? Is someone else trying to kill the Emperor?' said Steiner.

'I only know what the bones tell me when I cast them,' said Ving.

'And what do they say?' pressed Kristofine.

'They say a warrior queen rises in the south. They say she has endured unimaginable hardship. They say she is coming north, but to what end I cannot tell.'

'What else?' asked Steiner.

'A power comes from the sea, something that has slept many long decades.'

'And my father?' asked Steiner as he stood up.

'The bones say nothing for him,' replied Ving. 'He is unimportant in the times ahead.'

Steiner took the sledgehammer out of the sack and stood up.

'He's not unimportant to me.'

'Destiny cares not for sentimentality, Steiner. Your father's future has little bearing on the ultimate outcome. He has played his part.'

Steiner lay the metal head on the man's shoulder. 'My father's future has every bearing on me. I'll kill this entire continent to get him back if I have to.'

Ving looked at the sledgehammer and grew pale. He glowered at Steiner and brushed the weapon aside.

'Such bravado. Still, it has always been the way of the Vartiainen men.'

'Let's go,' said Kristofine softly. 'He's been useful in his own way.' She took Steiner by the hand and they headed towards the staircase.

'Steiner,' said Ving, rising from the couch. 'If you do kill the Emperor, if you do take throne, don't make the mistakes I made and don't make the mistakes of the Emperor.'

'That was never my intention. I simply want the Empire to stop taking children from the Scorched Republics. I want them to stop splitting up families. Destroying families.'

'Nature abhors a vacuum, Steiner. You will be drawn to the throne, and your mistakes will be recorded for all of history.'

'What mistakes?'

'Power is intoxicating. It is cruel and unfeeling. The desire to be in control, to be admired, to be untouchable. All of these things will take you away from your truest self.'

'Steiner has something that you and the Emperor never had,' said Kristofine, lingering at the top of the black iron stairs.

'And what is that, my spirited child?' said Ving, his patronising smile fixed on his handsome face once more.

'He has me,' she said with a smile of her own. 'I'll keep him honest.'

'She's right,' said Steiner. 'I couldn't have done any of this without her.' He took a moment to look at his proud and brilliant woman as she faced down Bittervinge. 'She'll keep me honest if I find myself in charge of things, but I have bigger problems to worry about right now.'

'That you do,' said Ving. 'Problems like finding your way
into the labyrinth beneath the Imperial Palace. Go now.' He
waved them off with a shooing gesture. 'Go to your problems
and don't get caught by the Emperor's men. Even now they
are coming to kill you.'

CHAPTER FORTY-THREE

Kimi

'We assumed the worst when you didn't return,' said Kimi. She twisted her wrists against the hair rope that bound her. The silence was broken by the sound of water dripping down the sides of the cavern. The wind would faintly shriek down the tunnel adding to the misery of the place. Tief sat by the brazier of stinking peat, head bowed in exhaustion or shame. Kimi suspected he was feeling a touch of both. Or perhaps the feelings were her own. She hadn't wanted to tell Veles where to find the remnant of the Ashen Torment, but the dragon had left her with an impossible choice.

'Veles will kill Taiga when he finds the camp,' said Tief. His words were grave, his tone flinty. 'Or his gholes will.' Tears were running down his cheeks. 'Why did you tell him where to go, Kimi? Why did you tell him where Taiga is?' Kimi had no answer and checked on Marozvolk as a distraction. The renegade Vigilant was still unconscious. Kimi bent over to listen and was rewarded with the faintest sound of breathing.

'Kimi.' Tief didn't shout, but his voice was an angry hiss that startled her all the same. 'My sister is going to be killed because you told Veles where our camp is.'

'He was going to turn you into a ghole.'

Tief looked away and grunted in frustration. 'My sister . . .'

'Is that what you wanted? To be turned into one of those things?'

'If it means keeping Taiga alive, then yes.' Tief glowered at her and struggled with his bonds.

'Our best bet is that Veles brings Taiga back here,' said Kimi. 'Maybe he will let us go after all.'

'Our best bet?' Tief shook his head. 'Wishful thinking is one thing but this is foolishness.'

'Be grateful you're alive at all,' said Kimi. They settled into a sullen silence and Kimi slunk around the cavern looking for anything that might help them escape. The water continued trickling down the walls and a spiteful chill filled the cavern.

'Frejna's teeth,' she muttered, looking into the water.

'What is it?' Tief was on his feet and edged towards her, picking his way across the uneven ground.

'A corpse, more of a skeleton really.'

'Perhaps he doesn't turn everyone into a ghole,' said Tief, kneeling down to get a better look at the body. 'Some he eats.'

Kimi searched the stream at the centre of the cavern, her boots sloshing in the icy water.

'There's plate armour here.' She grinned. 'And a knife.'

'What use is a knife going to be against a dragon, halfhead?'

'We don't have to kill the dragon, we just need to free ourselves.' She retrieved the blade from the water, and began sawing through Tief's bonds.

'Human hair,' he said, grimacing. 'I've seen a few things but this . . .'

'Hold still,' chided Kimi. 'I don't want to cut you.'

The dagger was fairly blunt and it took far longer than either of them wanted, but soon they were free. They spent breathless moments searching the detritus of the stream, stumbling over old bones, finding curios but nothing much of use.

'Our gear is over there,' said Tief, pointing at the mouth of the tunnel. 'I saw it when I was brought in.' No sooner had he said the words than Veles appeared like a vengeful spirit, twisting this way and that as his coils propelled him forward. Kimi's heart leapt as the dragon descended upon her, one clawed foot seizing her around the throat and shoulders. Veles lifted her off the ground so quickly the air was squeezed from her lungs, then slammed her into the cavern wall. She was high enough that any fall would surely break her.

It was not there! The Ashen Torment was not where you said it would be. There is no camp. You lied to me!

Kimi stared in wide-eyed dread at the dragon, too stunned to speak. Veles craned his sinuous neck forward and sniffed, then stared upon her anew with a seemingly blind eye.

I may not be able to read your mind but your Spriggani friend is quite a different matter. Tief stared up at the serpent and glanced at Kimi in alarm.

The dragon cocked its head for a moment and regarded the Spriggani.

'Get out of my head, you old snake,' shouted Tief, pressing his palms to his eyes. He bent over double and moaned.

Veles licked his lips and returned to face Kimi. *You are no mere Yamali thief. How extraordinary! Royalty! Royalty, here, visiting me at my seat of power.*

The dragon lowered her to the floor of the cavern with a father's care, then lowered his head and closed his diseased eyes.

'Is . . .' Tief stared with disbelief. 'Is he bowing to you?'

Kimi nodded slowly. 'What will happen to us now?'

Why, you must stay, of course! My hospitality has been sorely lacking and for that I give you my most sincere apologies. Had I known of your lineage sooner our relationship would have begun quite differently, I assure you! The dragon straightened up and looked around the cavern in the manner of someone who has just received unexpected guests. *I will find you food and we will talk of our great nations and what it is to rule! Come now! Come! Warm yourself by the brazier while I make the necessary preparations for my royal guest.*

Tief and Kimi picked their way across the room and knelt down by Marozvolk.

'Is he . . .' Tief touched two fingers to his temple and looked at the wingless dragon.

'Imagine living in a swamp for over a hundred years with only gholes for company,' replied Kimi. 'I think that's enough to send anyone out of their mind.'

'Or any*thing*,' said Tief, watching the pale serpent issue orders to the gholes. Marozvolk stirred and mumbled a sound.

'Hoy there!' said Tief with a smile, dashing over to her. 'She's waking up.' He took Marozvolk's hand in his own and leaned forward. 'How are you feeling?'

'Well, I was held underwater by four undead monsters until I lost consciousness.' Marozvolk coughed for a time and pressed a hand to her forehead. 'But I've had worse hangovers to tell the truth.' Tief gave a long low chuckle and Kimi let herself be caught up in the sound, allowing herself a smile.

'So we're friends now, are we?' said Marozvolk, eyeing Tief with a wary expression.

'Friends,' said Tief. 'You fought to keep Taiga safe?'

'I did.'

'Then we're friends. And I'm a damned fool for ever doubting you.'

'Where are we?' asked Marozvolk, looking up at the roof of the cavern.

'We've been captured by Veles himself,' said Tief. 'My sister is still out there, somewhere in the swamps, fighting for her life, and he has close to thirty gholes coming and going.'

'We seem to be royal guests, rather than prisoners,' added Kimi.

'Oh. That's good,' said Marozvolk sleepily. 'Less chance of being eaten.'

Veles slept at the mouth of the tunnel, his huge body an ample impediment to even the idea of escape. The gholes surrounded him, sitting against the cavern walls, cowled heads bowed in the imitation of sleep.

'They'd only track us down if we did manage to leave,' said Tief. 'We've no chance of reaching Taiga, even if we could find her.'

'She may have survived the poison,' replied Kimi, but in truth she thought it would be kinder to pass away in the shadows of the standing stones. At least Veles wouldn't raise her as one of his gholes that way.

They'd found a dry, flat space in the cavern and a clutch of gholes had brought more peat, but it was too damp to burn. Marozvolk slept soundly while Kimi and Tief watched the slumbering creatures with disgust and fascination. They huddled together for warmth and Kimi was acutely aware she hadn't bathed in weeks.

'I don't understand how he missed the standing stones,' said Kimi, her thoughts lingering on Taiga.

'Not exactly an abundance of landmarks in Izhoria,' said Tief. 'And a circle of upright stones nearly the height of a man is difficult to miss.'

'Perhaps the mist . . .?' Kimi shrugged. 'And those eyes of his. I'm not sure how clearly he sees.'

'He sees you clearly enough, your highness.' Tief smirked. 'I think he likes you. Me, not so much.'

The pale serpent had presented gifts soon after discovering Kimi was royalty. Every last thing had belonged to the people he'd killed; all spotted with rust, waterlogged or broken.

'He gave you a blanket, didn't he?' said Kimi.

'A dead man's blanket.' Tief wrinkled his nose. 'Enough to make your skin crawl. Still, it was good to eat the Okhrana's food. Frøya knows they won't be needing it.'

Kimi watched the dead Okhrana, now gholes, sitting obediently by their master. They were barely distinguishable from their unholy kin. She thought one of them had gone missing, but it was hard to tell in the mass of bodies.

'I don't want that to happen to me, Tief. I don't want that for any of us.'

'I'm not sure there's much we can do to prevent it, besides being eaten.' Tief clutched his stomach, grimacing as it rumbled. Kimi couldn't miss the sound.

'Hungry?'

'Ravenous. We used up the last of the Okhrana's food last night, or morning, or whatever time it was.'

'I think they sleep during the day,' said Kimi, indicating the gholes. Time was meaningless in the cavern. The only constant was the sound of dripping water and the bitter chill. Veles shook his great wedge-shaped head and the gholes stirred, jumping up and hopping about like a flock of carrion birds.

You are not the only ones who are hungry.

Kimi looked at Tief in surprise. The serpent was able to project his words a considerable distance. She worried how much of their conversation the serpent had heard.

'This can't be good,' whispered Tief. 'It's not as if Izhoria is teeming with animals. I'm likely to be the main course.'

'It will be fine,' said Kimi, though in truth Veles' unpredictable nature brought a terror all of its own. The pale serpent stirred and slunk across the cavern. The gholes banded into groups of threes and fours and departed.

I have been sending my children out into the kingdom to look for both food and these standing stones you speak of, your highness.

Three nights now I have sent my children. Veles reared up and Kimi shrank back on instinct. *They have found nothing.*

'The swamps are treacherous and confusing,' said Kimi, standing up in an effort to feel less small. 'I wouldn't know how to get back to our camp.'

This is my kingdom, Your Highness. These are my lands, there are no mysteries for me here. Nothing! For over one hundred years I have roamed the mist and not once have I seen these standing stones you speak of.

'I promise to you by my royal blood that I speak the truth,' said Kimi. She fought down a fierce tremor of fear as the conversation soured.

The Ashen Torment here in Izhoria after all of these years. My brother's greatest work. Veles' tail swished behind him. *Of course, even the Ashen Blades pale by comparison.*

'I've not heard of those,' said Kimi, keen to keep the serpent talking lest he decide on another form of entertainment. Veles curled around, coiling, until the tip of his tail hovered in the air just an arm's length from Kimi's face. A dagger had been strapped into place at the tip, though the blade was dull and unremarkable in the gloom of the cavern.

And yet you have seen it in action. By the power of this blade do I keep myself young. It drinks the life of others so that I may remain in this world. The Ashen Blade is a prize beyond measure, though it can never give me the wings that Bittervinge so cruelly ripped from my back.

'How awful,' said Kimi, struggling to think of something more sincere to say. 'Perhaps you could tell me more about your life before you came to Izhoria?'

The dragon's tail whipped away, taking the Ashen Blade from Kimi's sight. Veles lowered his head until his snout was just feet from her face. He sniffed and for a moment Kimi was sure he would consume her in a single brutal bite.

Your friend is thinking of escaping, your highness. It consumes his every waking minute. Perhaps you too are thinking it is time to take your leave.

'I am,' she replied. It seemed pointless to lie. 'I seek to kill the Emperor.'

Veles retreated a dozen feet and clawed at the stones for a moment.

A worthy ambition. Why have you set yourself such an impossible task?

'He kept me prisoner for five years. He'll send his armies south to Yamal when he learns I escaped the island of Vladibogdan.'

I too sought the Emperor's end. Even now he kills my children. These last three nights I have lost many gholes. It grieves me that they lie in the swamps, rotting and festering.

'I think they're already rotting and festering,' muttered Tief. Veles hissed and turned his sightless gaze on the man. Tief shrank behind Kimi.

'Sorry,' he whispered.

'You think the Empire is in Izhoria?' asked Kimi. 'Killing your . . . children?'

Who else would do such a thing? Who else would hunt my gholes?

'Perhaps the armies are already on their way south,' said Kimi.

Or perhaps they come looking for you, Your Highness. I think that it is time to withdraw my hospitality.

'Let's not be hasty,' said Tief, holding out his hands to placate the vast serpent. 'We don't know for sure that it's Imperial soldiers killing your gholes.'

Even so, you cannot give me what I want. I seek the Ashen Torment and you have not led me to it.

Veles slunk about the cavern, like a cat stalking prey. His tail moved with a mind of its own and Kimi's eyes were fixed on the dull blade that would drain the life from her.

'We could look for the standing stones with you,' she said, desperate and afraid.

The standing stones that I have not once seen in over one hundred years. I think not, Your Highness.

'Tief, what do we do?'

'I was about to ask you the same question,' he replied, taking her hand as they backed up against the rough, stony wall. Three gholes chose that moment to race into the cavern and Veles whipped his head towards the source of the interruption. One of the gholes was missing an arm and another had been scored open, cut from sternum to gut. Such a strike would have meant death for any other creature. A dim light appeared on the far side of the cavern, emanating from the tunnel mouth, growing steadily brighter. A figure stood silhouetted there.

'Taiga?' Tief sounded as though he could barely bring himself to say her name.

'I am the high priestess of Frøya,' said Taiga calmly to the pale serpent. 'All of your works are an affront the natural order of this world, and you will surrender to me or die, you gutless coward.'

Veles coiled back at such a rebuke, then hissed in fury. The serpent sprang towards Taiga, racing across the cavern with jaws stretched open.

CHAPTER FORTY-FOUR

Kjellrunn

Kjellrunn awoke in her own bed. Sunlight marked the deep brown floorboards in long slashes of gold from where it crept in through the blinds. Her body lay heavy and unresponsive under the thin sheet and flashes of the previous day came back to her in a jumble of shocking images. The leviathan of course, with its eyeless visage and vast maw, but also what had seemed like a constant rain of fiery lances, falling all around them. Kjellrunn made a sound, part gasp and part moan.

'I figured you'd be asleep for at least another three days, right.'

Kjellrunn lifted herself onto her elbows. Romola was sitting on a chair at the foot of the bed with a book in one hand and a half-eaten apple in the other. She was wearing cream-coloured robes, clothes more common to Dos Khor, rather than her usual flamboyant attire. For a moment Kjellrunn thought she saw a grey cat sitting beneath the pirate's chair, but decided it was a trick of the light when she looked again.

'You're alive,' breathed Kjellrunn.

'I washed up on the shore just after you passed out. Good thing I did or Sundra might not be in the land of the living any more. She was a touch outnumbered.'

'How many people did we lose?' Kjellrunn blinked and for a brief moment she was back on the beach, kneeling beside Mistress Kamalov, the stench of burned flesh overpowering.

'A few of the novices died on the beach. About a third of my crew never made it ashore.' The pirate grimaced, then shook her head. 'But that's a whole lot better than I was expecting, right. I'd have lost everyone if we'd tried to fight them at sea.'

Kjellrunn sat up and swung her legs out of bed, then pressed a hand to her mouth to hold back her sobs. 'Mistress Kamalov.'

'There was nothing anyone could have done.' Romola sighed. 'She was a force of nature, but they had so many Vigilants aboard their ships. Powerful Vigilants.'

'So much fire,' said Kjellrunn, remembering the bombardment.

'So much fire,' agreed Romola. 'We managed to save the hull of the *Wait*, but the masts are all for shit and we'll have to salvage the sails from the Imperial galleons. Looks like you're going to have a lot of guests for the next few weeks.'

'Why did you lead them here?' said Kjellrunn, her expression hardening, loss shifting to something darker. 'This was supposed to be our hiding place from the Empire. We were supposed to keep the novices safe here. I was supposed to be safe here.'

'You're right to be angry,' said Romola softly. 'But I was desperate and we had a run of bad luck. We were taking on water as we passed Dragon Tear Island heading south. That's when they spotted us, and that's why I headed here. I'm sorry.'

Voices echoed up the stairs from the temple below as Kjellrunn struggled to accept Romola's apology. She pushed herself off the bed and opened the window shutters. Two crows perched on the roof of the building across the street. They called out noisily and fussed at their tail feathers. Kjellrunn nodded to them as if meeting old acquaintances. The sound of people at their chores drifted up to her. There would be a lot to organise with so many dead.

'You hungry?' Romola stood up and flashed an awkward smile. 'I don't know too much about summoning sea monsters, but I'm guessing you might have an appetite.'

'I'm not sure I can walk far,' said Kjellrunn. 'I feel like I'm dreaming. My legs are . . . numb?'

'I guessed that too,' said Romola, offering her hand.

'And I'm seeing things.' Kjellrunn shivered. 'Are there two crows on the roof across the street?'

Romola nodded. 'Nothing wrong with your eyes. Unless I'm seeing things too.'

'And a grey cat? It was here just a moment ago when I woke up.'

Romola shrugged. 'Come on. Time for you to meet your petitioners.'

'What are petitioners?'

'Worshippers of Frejna, come to pay their respects to the goddess and her prophet. They've been outside since about midday.'

'What prophet?'

'You, of course.' Romola smiled. 'They're calling you the Stormtide Prophet. The wounded girl who summoned a leviathan to protect the town from the Empire.'

'I'm not wounded.'

'You were shot by a crossbow just days before. Remember? Maybe you hit your head in all the fighting.'

Kjellrunn pressed her fingers to her side. The crossbow wound was all but healed. She'd leapt towards the slaver to prevent him shooting Mistress Kamalov but now her teacher was dead.

'I can't meet anyone right now,' said Kjellrunn, misery a cruel weight on her every breath. 'It's all I can do to speak. So much has happened. Mistress Kamalov . . .'

'Mistress Kamalov would be proud of what you did and everything you've achieved. You'll feel different after some tea. Proper Shanisrond tea, mind. None of that Yamali filth.' Romola pulled Kjellrunn to her feet and wrapped a firm arm around her shoulders.

'Kjellrunn. I'm sorry for leading them here, but you and Sundra and Mistress Kamalov were my best hope for getting my crew to safety. Thank you.'

Kjellrunn nodded, seeing the sense of it. 'I'm having tea then,' she said with a weary smile.

'I'll help you down the stairs,' replied Romola.

'The Stormtide Prophet,' whispered Kjellrunn, trying out the words that came to shape the coming months.

CHAPTER FORTY-FIVE

Steiner

Steiner and Kristofine looked for Felgenhauer in the library but there was no sign of the Vigilant. A shaft of light shone from above, following them down the spiral stairs and into the dusty gloaming of the stacks.

'Where did she go?' whispered Kristofine. Neither of them strayed from the black iron staircase for fear of getting lost amid the dark maze of shelves.

'I'm more curious *why* she left,' said Steiner, 'and why she left us without a lantern.' A jingling sound could be heard in the darkness, muffled by countless tomes slumbering on their shelves.

'Ving did say that even now men are coming to kill us,' said Kristofine, straining to hear the sound.

'I thought you said you didn't believe him?' replied Steiner quietly.

'It was the only thing he said I did believe. I've heard some tall stories in my time but . . .' Kristofine looked over her shoulder to the source of the noise. The sound of metal on metal drew closer and Steiner feared it was a prelude to soldiers wearing mail and plate.

'Get behind me,' he said, lifting the sledgehammer and

rolling his shoulders. A soldier holding a lantern rounded the corner of the shelves ahead of them. He held out an empty hand to show he meant no harm.

'Easy.' Slowly he reached for his helm and removed it, revealing the face of the sergeant who had brought them to Arkiv.

'Where's Felgenhauer?' said Steiner.

'A message arrived that needed her attention,' replied the sergeant. 'Follow me.'

'I should know your name if we're to be on the same side,' said Steiner.

'Tomasz.' The sergeant gave a curt nod, as if meeting them for the first time. 'How did you like our guest?'

'He's an insane old fool,' said Kristofine with a scowl. 'Tried to convince us he's a dragon. How ridiculous.'

Tomasz said nothing and they followed him through the library. They had to hurry in order to keep up with the sergeant's stride.

'Let's say he is what he says he is,' said Steiner after they'd descended a flight of stairs. 'Why doesn't he simply walk away?'

'Black iron,' replied Tomasz with a grim smile. 'They can't stand being near black iron. It makes them sick and dizzy at a range of a few feet. Over a long enough period they lose consciousness entirely.'

'The staircase to the cupola?' said Steiner.

'And the window frames,' added Tomasz, 'and the top of the dome. I imagine there's a fair amount in that hammer too.'

Kristofine stared at the sledgehammer. 'But I thought it was enchanted?'

'It is,' replied Tomasz. 'Enchanted to strike true and find its mark, with black iron to smite the sense out of any dragon you cross paths with. It was that weapon that won the war over seventy years ago.'

Steiner, who had always borne the hammer with reverence, now looked at the weapon as if it were a new-found relative.

'Frøya save me,' he whispered. 'Ving was telling truth about the hammer, and the staircase.'

'That may be, but I still don't believe he's a dragon.' Kristofine frowned. 'Tomasz, have you ever seen him in his . . .' She struggled for the word. 'Other form.'

The sergeant shook his head. 'Truthfully no, but soldiers older than me remember him up there when they were just raw recruits, and they say the veterans before them spoke of Ving too. Whatever he is, he's been in that part of the library for decades.'

'Only the Emperor could hide a dragon in plain sight,' muttered Steiner. Tomasz led them past a clutch of students and the academics stared at the soldier with sullen expressions.

'Why do they look so upset?' asked Kristofine.

'Soldiers only enter the library to arrest people caught in the forbidden sections, and all the students want to read the forbidden texts. Most likely they assume I've just arrested you.'

'This place is stranger than anywhere else I've been,' said Steiner.

'Anywhere?' said Tomasz, his tone incredulous.

'Almost anywhere,' said Steiner, remembering the horde of cinderwraiths in the forges beneath Vladibogdan. They hurried down another flight of stairs where yet more rooms of books waited.

Felgenhauer was waiting in the courtyard when Tomasz finally led them outside. The Vigilant was flanked by her cadre and a handful of porters hefting crates. Many of Arkiv's academics strolled the edges of the courtyard in conversation with their colleagues. All took note of the soldiers in their midst. 'That was a total waste of time,' said Kristofine before anyone could say anything. 'He didn't tell us anything useful.'

'That's not true,' replied Steiner. 'Ving told us the Emperor is near invulnerable to everything except a weapon called the Ashen Blade.'

Felgenhauer nodded. 'We can't worry about that now. We have to leave. I've had word from one of my spies at the Imperial Court. Orlov and Silverdust are en route to Arkiv.'

Steiner smiled widely at the familiar name. 'Silverdust! Shouldn't we wait for him to arrive?'

Felgenhauer shook her head. 'The Emperor himself has charged an Envoy and the two Vigilants to hunt us down—'

'What? Silverdust would never . . .' Steiner lowered his voice, keeping a watchful eye for the academics in the courtyard. 'Silverdust wants the Emperor dead as much as we do.'

'We can waste time speculating about Silverdust's motivation once we're off the island,' replied Felgenhauer. 'Come on.'

It took some time to drag and carry the soldiers' possessions to a waiting cart. Kristofine slipped an arm around Steiner's waist, sensing his hurt.

'Silverdust,' she said simply.

'I trusted him. Frejna's teeth, I trusted him. He knows all of it, the whole story. He knows about Kjellrunn and my Spriggani friends and Kimi.'

'I'm sorry, Steiner.' She let him go and addressed Felgenhauer. 'Can I get my sword back? I don't fancy being unarmed if we get caught.'

'I'm not sure how useful it will be against two Vigilants and an Envoy,' replied Felgenhauer, handing Kristofine her weapon.

'More useful than not having it, I imagine.'

Finally they were ready to depart. The soldiers followed behind the cart and kept a brisk pace despite the weight of their armour. Steiner stared in wonder at the buildings and the wide cobbled thoroughfares.

'How did I miss all of this the first time?' he said.

'I think you were suffering from exhaustion,' replied Kristofine. 'You slept most of the journey from the docks to the library.'

'She's right,' said Felgenhauer. 'You looked like a ghole when you arrived.' The cart continued on its way, bumping and jolting along the roads. People stood aside at the sight of the Vigilant and the many soldiers following behind.

'I don't understand why Silverdust is working against us,' said Steiner, feeling another pang of betrayal. 'After everything that happened on Vladibogdan.'

'The Emperor can be *very* persuasive,' said Felgenhauer. 'It's why I went rogue before I reached Khlystburg. Besides, Silverdust has always been a mystery. Even on Vladibogdan I never had the full measure of him.'

'But you know he's a cinderwraith?' said Steiner.

Felgenhauer went very still. 'What?'

'That's why he's so old, immortal, or undead.'

Felgenhauer breathed out slowly. 'All this time and I couldn't see what was right in front of me.' She pondered on what Steiner had said as the cart creaked and bounced through the city. 'But the other cinderwraiths passed on when you destroyed the Ashen Torment. Why didn't Silverdust go with them?'

'I'm not sure any more,' said Steiner. 'I thought I could trust him.'

'Perhaps you could, for a while,' said Felgenhauer.

'But not any more,' said Kristofine as the cart arrived at the docks. Steiner jumped down and stared out to sea.

'When did the message arrive?' he asked.

'While you were in the Great Library,' said Felgenhauer. She followed his gaze out to sea.

'And when did your contact say the ship left the Imperial Court?'

'She didn't give me a precise time,' admitted Felgenhauer. 'She simply said she had heard a rumour of the Emperor's command.' Steiner, Kristofine and Felgenhauer all looked at a small speck of darkness on the horizon, far out to sea in the Ashen Gulf.

'There's no way they could have arrived here already,' said Kristofine. 'Khlystburg is miles away.'

'But with a good wind the journey could be made in a fraction of the time,' said Steiner. 'And Silverdust studied at Vozdukha Academy.'

'You mean like Mistress Kamalov?' Kristofine stared out to sea. 'Oh, no.'

Felgenhauer swore in Solska and slammed a fist against the side of the cart. A few of the soldiers ceased unloading and watched the oncoming ship.

'Why are we waiting?' said Kristofine. 'The sooner we board a ship the sooner we can leave.'

'Silverdust also has a mastery over fire,' said Felgenhauer, 'and his mastery over the sight is greater still.'

'No one ever detected witchsign at such distances,' said Steiner.

'He will,' replied Felgenhauer. 'And then they will give chase and burn any ship we board while we're helpless at sea. We have to stay on the island.'

The ship was closer now. Steiner could see the sails billowing at their fullest, yet no breeze troubled the docks at Arkiv.

'We stay and hide, and hope to sneak away later,' said Felgenhauer. 'Or we fight and hope the gods smile on us.'

'We don't know that that ship is from Khlystburg,' said Kristofine. 'We should go while we have the chance.' By now the soldiers had realised that something was amiss. They stood nearby, chatting and gesturing at the oncoming ship. Tomasz approached Felgenhauer.

'It has Khlystburg markings. I fear the worst. We should head back to the city. It's the best way to remain safe.'

'But I have to find my father,' said Steiner.

'No,' replied Felgenhauer. 'Right now we need to stay alive. That's all.'

Steiner shook his head, a disappointment settling on his chest. 'Damn you, Silverdust,' he said from gritted teeth. 'I'll kill him myself when we find him.'

'Come on,' urged Tomasz from the cart. 'Let's not attract any more attention than we already have.'

Steiner was not so impressed with the Great Library as they returned.

'This is madness,' he said, scowling. 'How are ten soldiers and a Vigilant going to survive all the resources of the Empire?'

'Silverdust is a graduate of Academy Plamya,' replied Felgehauer, 'but he wouldn't dare use fire in the Great Library. He'd need a pardon from the Emperor himself for damaging the books.' They headed into the darkness and several students flinched at the sight of so many soldiers marching side by side.

'We stick together,' said Felgenhauer. 'There are basements and catacombs here that people barely remember.'

They wound their way into the Great Library and Tomasz gestured that they stop in a clearing between the many shelves.

'We get some rest and stay quiet,' said the sergeant. 'They may pass us by.' Soldiers were posted as lookouts elsewhere in the endless avenues of bookshelves. A deep sound reverberated through the stacks, as much felt as heard. The soldiers roused themselves and Felgenhauer paused to listen. The sound came again, a peal of bells rung in unison.

'They've sounded the alarm,' said Felgenhauer, rubbing her forehead wearily. 'I had hoped they would hunt us quietly.'

'The whole island will have heard that,' said Steiner. 'Nowhere is safe to us now.'

'We move,' said Tomasz. He nodded to his soldiers and they paired off, taking moments to tie bandages around each other's arms.

'What's that for?' said Kristofine.

'So they can tell friend from foe in the next few hours,' replied Steiner. 'One soldier looks much like another in armour.'

Tomasz gestured to a nearby doorway. 'Through here, we'll go deeper.'

Kristofine and Steiner headed off but a shadow moved in the gloomy doorway. Kristofine gasped and stumbled backwards as a soldier lunged out, mace raised and black cloak swirling behind him. Steiner stepped forward, dropped to one knee and swung in one motion. The sledgehammer took the Imperial soldier across the shin and Kristofine dived sideways just in time to avoid the armoured man collapsing on top of her.

'Careful!' she chided.

'Not much room to manoeuvre,' said Steiner, rising to meet the next soldier who emerged from the doorway.

'I've found them!' shouted the loyal soldier. A backswing from the sledgehammer smashed into the books and the Imperial soldier took advantage of Steiner's hesitation.

'These shelves are pissing me off.'

Other Imperial soldiers rushed towards Felgenhauer's cadre and sounds of combat rang out in the library behind them. The soldier attacked Steiner but the mace embedded itself in the shelf near Steiner's face. Kristofine swung her blade and caused a din as the pauldron took the worst of the strike, yet the soldier's head snapped to one side on instinct. Steiner slammed the butt of the sledgehammer handle against the soldier's faceplate, knocking him off balance. Kristofine raised her sword and cleft the man's hand from his wrist. The man folded in on himself, cradling the maimed limb, making strangled noises of shock.

There was a dull thump from behind as an entire shelf was knocked sideways and a holler of alarm as one of Felgenhauer's followers was lost beneath it. More Imperial soldiers emerged from the gloom.

'Felgenhauer!' shouted Steiner. 'We're outnumbered!' The way behind them was blocked with the wreckage of the vast bookshelf. The sounds of men dying filled the air and no help came.

'Strike for the face,' Steiner told Kristofine, 'one, two, three.' They dived forward as one, Kristofine's blade a shimmer of steel in the lantern-lit gloom. The soldier instinctively raised his mace to block her strike, and that's when Steiner jabbed the black iron head of the sledgehammer at the man's faceplate.

'What are you doing?' shouted Kristofine.

The soldier's head snapped back and Steiner jabbed down twice, connecting with one knee and then the other. Space opened between the two fighters and Steiner gritted his teeth and unleashed an underhand strike that took the soldier under the chin, felling him instantly

'Difficult to swing side to side in here,' he replied, eyeing the next two soldiers. A great commotion sounded behind them and the Imperial soldiers paused. Steiner dared a glance over his shoulder to see Felgenhauer lifting the bookshelves with the arcane, gesturing the the wood and books to levitate. Tomasz emerged from his place of entrapment and swore in Solska.

'Steiner, Kristofine! Get down!' barked Felgenhauer. Kristofine grabbed Steiner's arm and pulled him sideways and down as the wrecked shelves and dozens of heavy tomes sped forward as if fired by a catapult. The Imperial soldiers fell back as an avalanche of literature hit them. When Steiner dared to look up he saw the doorway was now thoroughly blocked with the wreckage of the bookshelves.

'We go a different way,' said Tomasz, grabbing Kristofine by the arm and pulling her up. Steiner looked around to see the bodies of fallen men, though it was difficult to tell which casualties belonged to which side. Three of the corpses were not corpses at all but statues from where Felgenhauer had petrified them with her arcane gaze.

'Run,' said the Vigilant, pointing along a main avenue between the shelves. 'Back to Ving if you have to.'

'Would he help us?' asked Steiner.

'You'd have to get him out of the tower first,' said Felgenhauer, 'and I trust him less than I trust Silverdust.'

Steiner nodded and headed towards the centre of the library, the sounds of fighting fierce and deafening behind him.

'We can't leave her now,' he said, gesturing back to where Felgenhauer was using the arcane to punch, smash, petrify and maim any enemy soldiers who came close.

'I think she can hold her own,' said Kristofine, watching the carnage with growing horror. 'Come on.' They fled into the darkness with only Kristofine's lantern to light their way, turning left and right until nothing made sense.

'We're lost,' she complained.

'Over there!' said Steiner, pointing to where the curve of the black iron spiral staircase could be seen. A figure waited, silhouetted by a shaft of pale light from the floor above.

'That can't be Ving,' said Steiner. 'He couldn't tolerate standing on the iron stairs.' They drew closer and the lantern light revealed a Vigilant's garb, the mask a handsome face with nine stars down one side.

'I am Father Orlov,' said the Vigilant calmly. He stood on the bottom step with his fingers laced. 'Your actions killed many of my colleagues on Vladibogdan. You will surrender to me now.'

'Steiner,' said Kristofine, her eyes darting from side to side. Imperial soldiers emerged from behind the shelves nearby.

'Felgenhauer,' said Steiner under his breath. 'Where are you?'

CHAPTER FORTY-SIX

Kimi

'Taiga!' The word had barely left Tief's lips before Veles plunged into the tunnel where his sister had appeared just moments before.

'What the Hel is she doing?' said Marozvolk. There was no way Frøya's priestess could survive the charging serpent.

'Wait!' Kimi laid a hand on Tief's shoulder as they watched Veles disappear from view, scuttling up the tunnel in a fury of claws and tail. Three gholes had arrived just moments before Taiga had appeared, almost knocked aside by their draconic master. One of the wretched creatures was missing an arm, but the nearest of the gholes turned to Kimi and hissed, flexing black talons. In life the man had been tall and heavyset, and the ghole was his dark mirror.

'I think we're in trouble,' said Marozvolk, moving behind the nearest brazier.

'But I'm a guest,' said Kimi. 'I'm Veles' guest. Surely they won't—'

'I don't think they care.' Marozvolk took a breath and whispered gently. Nothing happened and her eyes widened in shock. The gholes hissed louder and the largest of them took a step closer.

'I'm not changing!' said Marozvolk. 'My skin. The arcane. It's not working!'

Kimi led her friends to the flat ledge at the side of the cavern, pausing to pull the old dagger from where she'd concealed it in her boot. No sooner had she drawn the blunt blade than two of the gholes sprinted towards them. Kimi settled into a low stance, knife held out before her, heart pounding in fear. The larger ghole gave a terrible roar that pierced the frantic silence. Kimi watched in confusion as the second creature attacked its kin from behind, catching the larger ghole around the throat with a sickle. A silver dagger was held high, gleaming with a light all of its own.

'What in Frøya's name?' said Tief.

The second ghole stabbed the larger one with the dagger, over and over until the creature fell to its knees, then pulled hard on the sickle. The larger ghole's cowled head came free, smacking against the cavern floor. A gout of black ichor burst from the severed neck and the air was filled with an unholy stench. The second ghole turned the sickle on itself, cutting through the cowl and hacking off the robes to reveal a familiar face.

'Taiga?' said Tief.

'I can't believe that worked,' she said, kicking off the mouldering fabric. 'They really are quite stupid.' The remaining ghole fled from the cavern, still clutching its severed arm. Tief ran forward and embraced his sister.

'What? I don't understand . . . How?' Kimi and Marozvolk stared in wonder before Kimi had the sense to ask.

'Who was that in the tunnel mouth?'

'Oh.' Taiga smiled. 'That was an illusion. I haven't done one of those for a long time.' She chuckled.

'But you're just an initiate of Frøya,' said Tief, eyes wide.

'Yes, when we were first taken to Vladibogdan I was just an initiate. Things change, big brother. Now come on. Veles

will be back before you know it.' They ran, with questions
burning on their lips, barely believing their fate could change
so quickly. Taiga led the way, a nimbus of light glowing from
the silver sickle and dagger she carried.

'This way!' Taiga led them into the tunnel, then turned left
into a smaller cavern, not much more than a dead end in the
rock. All manner of gear had been stacked up against
the walls, much of it wrapped in oilcloth.

'What's this?' asked Marozvolk.

'Weapons,' said Kimi with a smile as she unwrapped the
first oilcloth. 'Lots of weapons. Veles is quite the collector.'

'I can't believe you're alive,' said Tief, holding his sister by
the shoulders. Tears shone at the corners of his eyes.

'No time for that now. Find a weapon or something useful
and let's be gone.' Taiga narrowed her eyes. 'There's something
not right about those braziers. That smell . . .'

'There'll be no outrunning him,' said Kimi. 'We need the
best weapons we can lay our hands on.'

'We can't possibly fight a creature that size,' said Tief. 'Have
you lost your mind?'

'We don't have a choice,' replied Kimi, lifting a two-handed,
double-edged sword from the pile. It was as fine craftsmanship as she had ever seen.

'Pah! Are you going to be able to wield that thing?'

'I was head blacksmith in the harshest forge in Vinterkveld,'
replied Kimi. She twirled the great blade backwards, making
a figure of eight in the air. 'I think I can handle it.'

'I know a place we can hide,' said Taiga, 'above this very
cavern, but we'll need to be quick.'

No sooner had they emerged into daylight than Taiga was
pointing to the top of the hill. Rain sheeted down, falling
diagonally, a fierce wind chasing it across the swamps.

'We go up,' she said gleefully, then sprinted ahead. Kimi

and Marozvolk exchanged a puzzled look and dutifully followed.

'This must be the only hill in all of Izhoria,' wheezed Tief as they climbed the steep slope. The mail armour he'd found in the dragon's stash was slowing him. Kimi had insisted he wear it along with the crossbow slung over his shoulder. Marozvolk had chanced across a padded leather coat that reached her knees and a sturdy circular shield hung from her left arm.

'Is that the sword I bought you in Virag?' said Kimi.

Marozvolk nodded. 'It's not every day a Yamali princess buys me a sword. I wasn't going to leave without it.'

Kimi had also found a mail shirt, though she wondered how much good it would do against Veles' teeth. Another collection of standing stones awaited them at the top of the hill, just like the shrine they had camped in before.

'Wait,' said Kimi. 'Taiga, you need to tell us what's going on. How are you still alive? Do you have a plan?'

'At first I didn't really believe it was happening and then I realised I was going to die.' The priestess smiled so broadly that Kimi wondered if her brush with death had left her unhinged. 'Then I lost my temper a little bit but it worked out fine in the end.'

'Taiga.' Tief stared at his sister, concern etched into his lined face. 'You're not making any sense. Who gave you those silver weapons?'

'Frøya did! They're Frøya's very own, or they were before she gave them to me.' Taiga reached into the neckline of her dress and plucked at the chain that lay hidden there. 'I almost forgot.' A moment later she had removed the artefact from around her neck and held it out to Kimi in both hands with reverence. The chain was familiar, the bronze links were delicate yet dark with age and bore a faint green patina, but the finely-crafted stone dragon had been replaced with something else, something that glittered green in the dismal light.

'What is this?' said Kimi, eying the jade dragon. 'Where is the Ashen Torment?'

'This *is* the Ashen Torment,' said Taiga. 'It's been calling for you ever since I woke up.'

'I don't understand.' Kimi couldn't bring herself to take the artefact, horrified that it had somehow been made whole again.

'Perhaps I'm not explaining myself very well.' Taiga sighed. 'I met the goddess. She took the poison out of my body and gave me her very own sickle and dagger. She must have made this for you while I was sleeping.'

'Frejna's teeth,' muttered Marozvolk. 'She's completely lost her mind.'

'Yes! Frejna was there too.' Taiga stroked her silver weapons. Kimi wondered what the ghole's poison did to a person's mind. Taiga held out the necklace. 'Will you take this from me? It's very insistent that you do.'

Kimi obeyed the priestess of Frøya and held the jade dragon up higher so it caught the sombre daylight.

'But I haven't worshipped Frøya for years,' said Kimi, 'not since I was sent to Vladibogdan. I'm sorry, Taiga, but I don't believe in her.'

'Perhaps it's time to rediscover your faith in the old ways.' Taiga looked over her shoulder. 'And quickly.' Kimi looked down the hillside to where five gholes were scrambling up the grassy slope. They ripped clods of earth from the ground as their claws sought purchase. Kimi slipped the chain over her head and tucked the artefact inside her shirt.

Kimi Enkhtuya

'What the Hel? It speaks!' Kimi jerked backwards, trying to get away from the artefact hanging around her neck.

'I did warn you,' said Taiga, drawing her dagger and sickle.

'What a pair we are, the high priestess fighting alongside the champion of Frøya, facing down the undead hordes in the misty swamps of Izhoria!'

'She's completely lost it,' muttered Tief, shaking his head.

'Be grateful she's still alive,' replied Marozvolk.

The gholes were close now and Kimi let out a great war shout as Taiga raised her silver blades and uttered an invocation to her goddess. The gholes paused, as if staggered by the words alone. Kimi stepped in and swung the great sword, snarling with fury. A moment later and a ghole's head tumbled down the hillside, the corpse followed, arms and legs flailing as it went. Marozvolk mashed her shield into the cowled face of another ghole, knocking the creature off its feet, while Tief stamped a solid kick into the chest of the next of them, sending it back down the slope.

'Frejna's teeth, I hate these things!'

Kimi dodged backwards to avoid the raking claws of the next attacker. She stepped to one side and spun the blade, removing the ghole's fingers in a single swipe. The ghole collapsed forwards on the grassy slope and Kimi brought the full weight of her weapon down, snapping its neck.

Marozvolk was fending off her own attacker with the shield she had stolen, jabbing her sword tip at the creature's cowled face, but the ghole ducked backwards. Tief dashed in and dropped to one knee, slicing the ghole across the hamstring.

'Now finish it!' he shouted. Marozvolk kicked the ghole over, then took her shield in both hands and straddled the creature's chest, bludgeoning its skull with the metal rim. The ghole's head came apart with a series of wet smacking sounds. Taiga had dispatched the last of the foul creatures by the time Marozvolk has regained her feet. Spattered in black ichor, Marozvolk looked at her comrades, wild-eyed and trembling.

'Are you hurt?' asked Kimi.

'I can't change to my stone form,' said Marozvolk with

panic in her eyes. 'I can't change.' Her breath came fast and shallow. They watched the lone ghole run back down the slope, loping across the swamps with a fevered haste.

'They'll be back with more,' said Taiga. 'Let's head to the shrine. We can hide there.'

'What are you talking about?' said Tief.

'Don't worry, big brother. I'll look after you. I'm the high priestess of Frøya, blessed with the honour of carrying her holy symbols.'

Tief raised his eyebrows and sighed. 'You're serious about this, aren't you? You really believe Frøya saved your life.'

Taiga nodded. 'We can hide at the shrine, just as I did the night the goddess came.'

'You've made a believer out of me,' said Kimi. 'Let's get moving and hope Frøya is listening. We need all the help we can get.'

The rain was still falling when they reached the shrine and all were wet to the skin, teeth chattering.

'Maybe we'll drown before Veles arrives,' said Tief. 'I think I'd prefer that.'

'Tief,' said Kimi with a chiding frown, 'that kind of talk isn't helping.' Taiga slipped through the gap in the standing stones and looked around. The shrine looked older than the last and one of the stones had slipped out of alignment with the rest. Taiga raised her eyebrows at Marozvolk.

'So, what did you do?' asked Taiga.

Marozvolk shrugged. 'What do you mean?'

'How did you re-consecrate the shrine when I was poisoned?'

Marozvolk looked at Kimi, who returned her blank expression with one of her own. 'Consecrated?'

'We made rabbit stew,' said Marozvolk, 'and Kimi was muttering about murdering Frøya if anything happened to you.'

Taiga grimaced. 'No. That doesn't sound right at all.'

'Wait, I cleaned out those engravings,' said Kimi, pointing to the base of each stone. 'They were furred with moss. Perhaps that helped?'

'The symbols are very sacred to her,' said Tief, nodding. 'At least that's what Sundra always said.'

All four of them knelt before the stones, picking the verdant green moss from every groove and swirl with the tips of their knives and daggers.

'And then I polished it a bit with my cloak.' Kimi demonstrated. 'Like this.' The others followed suit and then stood up to admire their work.

'So now what do we do?' said Tief, cleaning his blade.

'I don't know.' Taiga's shoulders sagged. 'She didn't tell me.'

A great thundering roar of frustration sounded from outside the stone circle, carrying across the swamp like a rumble of thunder.

'He must have returned to the cavern,' said Marozvolk quietly.

'Now we're for it,' growled Tief, wiping rainwater out of his eyes.

'Wait,' said Taiga softly. 'Frejna said something about blood. The shedding of blood, symbolic of a sacrifice.'

'Don't look at me,' said Tief. 'I'm not dying just to consecrate a shrine.'

'You don't have to die,' said Taiga.

'Then what?' said Tief.

Kimi rolled up a sleeve and drew her knife. 'I think maybe this.' She cut her forearm and winced, then smeared her blood on the tallest of the stones. Taiga dropped to her knees and began praying. Tief, Kimi and Marozvolk waited, barely daring to breathe until finally Taiga fell silent and stood up.

'Did it work?' said Tief, shivering in the rain.

'I've no idea,' said Taiga. She drew her holy weapons. 'But the shrine is consecrated again. I have done my part.'

'I thought you had a plan!' shouted Tief. The rain slackened and grey clouds shifted, colossal and vast as they were. Taiga busied herself bandaging Kimi. Marozvolk slipped through the gap in the stones and Kimi followed her a moment later. They stood together in the sheeting rain looking for a sign of the gholes, or worse still, Veles himself.

Marozvolk sighed and shook her head. 'Between her religious ecstasy and his constant bickering we may as well cut our own throats now.'

Kimi Enkhtuya, said the artefact in Kimi's mind. It sounded like a wind chime in a gentle breeze, though it did little to calm her. Kimi touched her fingers to the jade engraving, so like the Ashen Torment and yet not.

'Tell me what you do,' she muttered to the artefact. 'We need a miracle. Just tell me what you do.'

But the jade dragon remained silent.

'At least the rain has stopped,' said Marozvolk as the first of the gholes crested the side of the hill.

'Come inside the circle,' said Taiga quietly. 'Quickly!

'What use will that do?' said Marozvolk.

'Before, when the goddess came, she told me that circle is beyond the sight of Veles and his kin. They can't see it.'

Kimi and Marozvolk entered the standing stone circle but the gholes were still running towards them.

'It's not working,' said Tief, eyeing the unholy creatures with growing panic. Taiga stared at the standing stone that had come loose, leaning at an angle from the others.

'Perhaps it's damaged somehow,' said Taiga. 'I'm sorry.'

'We fight,' said Kimi. 'No more bickering, and no more religious nonsense. We fight and we fight hard. Understand me?' For once Tief was speechless. He dropped to one knee and readied the crossbow.

'Frøya's champion should not say such things.' Taiga shook her head. 'The goddess is not nonsense.'

'Tell that that to him,' said Marozvolk as Veles emerged over the lip of the hill, some forty feet away.

'We stand together,' said Kimi, 'and try to cut the bastard's tail off. The dagger will kill you just as easily as his claws.'

The gholes were approaching at a flat run and Veles scrambled behind them, his pale body coiling and surging furiously across the wet grass.

'May Frejna's eye not find me,' said Kimi as she stepped out of the stone circle, hefting the sword over her shoulder.

CHAPTER FORTY-SEVEN

Silverdust

Silverdust stalked through the Great Library of Arkiv like a vengeful shade and Streig followed close behind. The aura of argent light played about his feet, illuminating the pressing darkness that surrounded them and gilding the many bookshelves in a silver glow.

'I can hear fighting,' said Streig. Silverdust nodded.

As do I. The Exarch reached out with arcane senses, past rooms of tomes and countless shelves of books. He felt the panic and snarling hatred of minds locked in combat.

'What are we waiting for?' pressed Streig.

I am not waiting. I have no wish to rush to my death or for you to rush to yours. I am trying to find someone.

'Felgenhauer? You're really going to hunt her down?'

Come now, quickly.

Silverdust set off and Streig struggled to keep up, weighed down as he was by the heavy armour, mace and shield. They pushed past a heavy door and emerged in another shelf-lined room where a black iron staircase coiled up into the ceiling. Father Orlov stood on the lowest step facing another side of the room, with one hand raised. Somehow Orlov hadn't noticed their approach, too intent on something else. Soldiers flanked either side of the staircase, weapons held low. Many had slung their shields across their backs.

'You will surrender to me now,' said Father Orlov. Silverdust knew this was no simple boast and drew closer until he could see Steiner and a young woman who appeared transfixed by Father Orlov's enchantment.

'You should be surrendering to me,' replied Steiner. He looked more scarred and weathered than Silverdust remembered but there was no doubt that this was the thorn in the Emperor's side; the sledgehammer was proof enough of that.

'I think not,' replied Father Orlov, reaching out with an open palm. The air shimmered as the arcane domination took hold and both Steiner and his companion's expression became blank, their gazes unfocused. Silverdust had seen the enchantments of Academy Voda before, but it was a rare thing to witness such power.

'You will drop the weapon,' commanded the Vigilant. Steiner complied and the sledgehammer slipped from his fingers and hit the floor. The relief of the soldiers was almost palpable; no one wanted to fight the dragon rider, it seemed.

'Now draw your knife and kill the girl, we have no need for her.' The girl flinched at this, shaking off the enchantment and stumbling away. Steiner tried to speak as his hand reached for the knife at his hip.

'K-Kristofine . . .' was all he managed. The woman slipped and fell against a bookshelf, then turned to Steiner with an expression of horror. The soldiers at the base of the stairs stirred uneasily, shocked at what they were about to witness.

Protect her. Silverdust pointed at the girl and Streig rushed forward, mashing his shield into the face of one of the soldiers.

Orlov! Silverdust lifted his reflective mask, revealing the cinderwraith beneath, his scream a vast exhalation of fire. Father Orlov dashed forward, preternaturally fast, and fled into the maze of bookshelves. Silverdust turned his fiery breath on the soldiers, igniting two of them in a heartbeat. They began to scream as they roasted inside their armour.

Steiner blinked in shock as if jerked awake. 'What happened to me?' He snatched up his sledgehammer.

An enchantment to ensure your obedience.

Silverdust surged through the library after his prey and Father Orlov snatched a glance over his shoulder just as Silverdust reached him.

'A cinderwraith?' he snarled in disgust.

So it would seem.

Silverdust grasped the Vigilant's face and suffused the mask with heat and Father Orlov began screaming as the metal burned his face. For a moment the Vigilant slumped against the bookshelves, then seized a heavy tome and smashed the Exarch in the head.

'Off of me!' mumbled Orlov through burned lips. Silverdust stumbled sideways before composing himself. A javelin of arcane flame appeared in his hand as three soldiers emerged from the darkness, staring in confusion from one Vigilant to another, unsure whom to attack. Silverdust hurled a streak of flame at the nearest of them but the fire passed through the soldier and impacted upon some shelves a dozen feet behind. The illusion flickered and the soldiers faded. Father Orlov had fled in the confusion and Silverdust reached out for the Vigilant's presence but found nothing. Orlov had shielded his mind.

Damn you, Orlov. Damn your ambition and damn your slavish devotion to the Emperor.

Silverdust spent long minutes retracing his way back to the centre of the room. The black iron staircase was easy to locate but Steiner and his companion were nowhere to be found.

Where are you, Streig?

A flurry of movement erupted from a junction of shelves nearby. Father Orlov approached at a run, a slender blade grasped in his fist. Silverdust summoned a javelin of fire, but the Vigilant responded with a blast of cold air from an outstretched hand. The arcane fire in Silverdust's hand flickered and failed as Father Orlov pulled back his arm to thrust forward. The blade glittered too brightly and Silverdust felt a rare pang of fear.

'Get away from him!' Steiner bounded out from the darkness, sledgehammer swinging, cursing loudly in Nordspråk. The metal head smashed into Father Orlov's chest and he sank to one knee, wheezing pitifully.

You should have fled when you had the chance, Orlov. Silverdust stood over the Vigilant. His hands began to smoke and then burst into flames once more.

'The Emperor charged me with killing the Vartiainen boy.' Orlov raised his head, revealing the burned and scalded mask. 'And I will see it through to the bitter end.'

A great gale caused doors to slam all through the many chambers of the Great Library. Fires danced manically as the wind whipped past and smaller flames were extinguished. Soldiers were buffeted as the wind howled and Silverdust was smashed into the shelves as the wind reached them. Steiner dropped to his knees and shielded his face with one arm as books were wrenched from the shelves in a furious tornado.

Silverdust fired off arcane bolts of fire, yellow flame streaking through the darkness, but none found their mark. The fire guttered out in the high wind before it could reach Father Orlov. Soon the shelves at the base of the black iron staircase were aflame, books smouldered and smoke was swept up in the tornado.

'You will surrender to me,' wheezed Father Orlov, climbing to his feet with one arm wrapped around his broken ribs. The winds dipped and Silverdust felt a strong compulsion to do as the man said. 'You will surrender to me!' said the Vigilant with more conviction. Silverdust found it difficult to move, difficult to think. Something was wrong but he was powerless to resist. Orlov came closer and the Exarch felt something snag against the fabric of his vestments. He looked down through the fog of confusion to see a slim dagger protruding from his chest. The arcane tornado that had shrieked through the library with such ferocity was now silent. Silverdust raised his hand to remove the dagger, fearful for what would happen when he did.

How?

'It's no Ashen Blade,' admitted Father Orlov, struggling to breathe. 'It's barely an echo of that blade.'

But enchanted all the same.

'It belonged to Dimitri Sokolov.' Orlov paused to draw down another wheezing breath. 'The Emperor gave it to me should you turn traitor.' He was about to say more when a sledge-hammer flashed through the darkness, but Steiner's strike went high and slammed into the black iron staircase above Father Orlov's head. 'Leave us now!' bellowed the Vigilant, and Steiner dutifully turned away. Silverdust felt the enchantment break as Orlov's attention turned to Steiner.

'Time to finish this,' said Father Orlov. He pulled the knife from Silverdust's chest and held it before the Exarch's throat.

I agree. The Exarch punched upwards with both fists, turning them into bright blades of fire, roaring with all the hatred and disgust of his long life. The fiery blades pierced Father Orlov's chest, emerging from the man's back in searing yellow. Silverdust stood up, arms raised high with Orlov screaming in agony above him. The Exarch wrenched his arms apart and the burned corpse fell to the floor in two pieces. Dimitri Sokolov's enchanted blade clattered in the darkness.

Streig? I need you.

Silverdust slumped to his knees, largely on instinct. It had been a long time since he'd had legs to betray him. Strange what the human mind was capable of, even when denied the body.

'Silverdust!' cried Steiner, dropping to his knees and holding the Exarch's hand.

Steiner. It is good to see you again. Your fame goes before you.

'What was that?' Steiner eyed the still-burning corpse of Father Orlov.

Father Orlov. It seems he trained at both Academy Vozdukha and Academy Voda. He used an enchantment on you. And on me.

'Can you stand?' Steiner picked up the dagger; it was polished to a bright gleam and looked brand new. 'What happened?'

Father Orlov wounded me.

'But cinderwraiths can't be hurt by simple blades.'

Silverdust knew he had worked out the truth of it, but Steiner clung to the denial all the same.

This is not a mundane blade, Steiner. The Emperor gave it to Orlov specifically to kill me.

'But how did the Emperor know you're a cinderwraith?'

It seems I said too much at the Imperial Court. The Emperor must have guessed my secret.

'Oh no,' said a woman's voice in the darkness. Steiner's companion approached with Streig close behind. She was a pretty, tear-stained girl and Silverdust could feel waves of concern emanating from her.

And who is this?

'I'm Kristofine.' She knelt down beside Steiner. 'Thank you for saving us. When the Vigilant spoke I was powerless, I couldn't . . .' She held one hand to her mouth, the words too frightening to say, even with Orlov dead.

You have done well, Streig.

The soldier nodded but said nothing. Flames continued to flicker and dance on the books and shelves until Silverdust extinguished them with a thought and a gesture. The black iron staircase gave a groan and crashed down among the shelves, sending up a great cloud of ash and burned pages.

'I didn't think I hit it that hard,' said Steiner. He coughed and looked embarrassed. Sounds of fighting were close at hand and Kristofine took the shining blade from Steiner.

'I swear to Frejna,' said Streig, 'I will murder everyone who comes this way.'

'Let's hope it doesn't come to that,' said Kristofine. 'We have to move. Silverdust, can you stand?'

I fear Father Orlov's parting gift may be permanent. He touched fingers to the tear in his vestments where the blade had pierced his chest. There was no pain, for the Exarch's body had long since passed, but a feeling of terrible dread suffused him. A tendril of soot-dark smoke emerged from the wound and trailed into the air before dissipating.

'No, dammit, no!' Steiner seized the Exarch by his shoulders and held him close.

I do not have long left, Steiner. It is of paramount importance that you leave the island. Go now. Please. You promised Kimi to lead an uprising. Fulfil that promise.

'We can't just leave him here,' said Kristofine. 'Come on, Silverface! Get on your feet.' For a moment the Exarch wanted to correct her, then thought better of it. Silverdust found himself pulled upright and carried through the library. Streig put an arm around his shoulders.

'I'm not leaving you here,' said the young soldier, his mouth a flat line, jaw clenched.

My friend . . . Silverdust lost his train of thought as another wisp of soot escaped from the wound in his chest.

'Fall back to the centre!' The voice was unmistakably Felgenhauer, loud enough to carry from somewhere else in the library. She marched out of the darkness, and though she wore no mask Silverdust knew who stood before him.

The former Matriarch-Commissar looked at the Exarch, saw his vestments battered and burned, saw the cinderwraith beneath and the way he pressed a hand to his chest.

You are speechless for once, Felgenhauer.

'You have a lot of questions to answer, Exarch, but now isn't the time.'

A handful of soldiers emerged from the gloom, battered yet resolute.

'Things are bad.' Silverdust recognised the man from Vladibogdan, a sergeant called Tomasz. 'Many have fallen and a few more are lost among the stacks.'

Another soldier stumbled around the corner of a bookshelf and the others turned against him, hefting their axes. It was the lieutenant from Khlystburg.

He is with me. Silverdust reached out for the man. *What is your name, lieutenant?*

'I'm Reka.' He paused a moment to look over the faces of the wanted rebels. 'I guess I know which side I'm on. What happens now?'

'We head to the docks,' said Steiner. 'It's the only way off the island.'

'And how will we get down from the fourth floor?' said Streig. 'This place is crawling with soldiers, and the Envoy is here somewhere.'

'Leave her to me,' said Felgenhauer. 'Come on.'

'Wait!' said Steiner, looking upwards. 'What's happening?' The plaster flaked off the ceiling above them, then fell away in great chunks. It sounded as if the building were shaking itself apart. The circular gap where the spiral staircase had met the floor above began to split and crack. Something dark was trying to force its way through.

'Look out,' shouted Felgenhauer. She sent up a great wall of force that shielded them from a rain of smashed timber, shattered plaster and falling books. It took several moments for everyone to recover. All eyes turned to the ragged hole in the ceiling in the shocked silence that followed.

'Frøya save us,' whispered Kristofine.

'Look at the size of him,' whispered Steiner.

I did tell you I was a dragon. Bittervinge's words appeared in their minds like golden chimes. He had resorted to telepathy, for his mouth could no longer produce human sounds. His great snout dipped into the room from the floor above, followed by his wedge-shaped head and long sinuous neck. The father of dragons was covered in black scales that gleamed like polished obsidian, while his horns and claws were purest ivory. Black lips peeled back from pale teeth, each as long as Steiner's thigh. Sitting on Bittervinge's neck, holding onto his horns to support herself, was Envoy de Vries. She smiled triumphantly.

'The Emperor said I could use all means at my disposal to destroy you, Steiner. And seeing as I am so outnumbered' – she patted the dragon's head affectionately – 'I made a deal.'

Silverdust looked into the Envoy's eyes and despaired.

CHAPTER FORTY-EIGHT

Steiner

Steiner watched in horror as the father of dragons descended from the upper floor of the library, bursting through the ceiling above. Dust and books rained down as Bittervinge landed on huge claws. His long black tail snaked down, following in heavy coils. The floor buckled and groaned under the colossal weight and the building shuddered once more.

'Look out!' shouted Steiner. Too late, Bittervinge disappeared from view, falling to the floor below as the timbers surrendered under the dragon's bulk. Steiner turned to run, almost blind with dust, but the floor dropped out from under him. His hand lashed out as he fell and he received a handful of splinters for his troubles, but he clung to the ruined timbers despite the pain.

'Help!' Steiner called out as the dragon sprawled among the ruin of bookshelves and countless tomes. Bittervinge had opened up a hole in the library some thirty feet across through two floors. The Envoy had clung on to the dragon's horns and glared at Steiner, hanging from the floor above by a single hand.

'I don't know how much longer I can hold on!' Kristofine's face appeared above as Bittervinge collected himself below, his great jaws snapping beneath Steiner's dangling feet.

'Steiner the Unbroken?' shouted the Envoy above the din, almost hysterical with laughter. She held on to the dragon's vast horns, sitting behind the base of his long head. 'I was expecting more.'

Kristofine grabbed Steiner by the arm and hauled him up. There was a frenzied moment as he dragged himself over the lip of broken wood and Bittervinge's head rose higher.

And now I will avenge myself upon the Vartiainen bloodline.

'Not today, halfhead.' Steiner swung hard as Bittervinge lunged for the kill. The sledgehammer caught the dragon in the teeth as the jaws closed down. Steiner's arms jolted so hard he almost dropped the weapon, and Bittervinge's head snapped to one side. The Envoy shrieked as she slipped from her seat behind the ivory horns and fell, slamming into a black-scaled shoulder before plummeting to the book-strewn floor below.

'We can't win against that,' said Kristofine in a shocked and reverent whisper. 'We need to flee to the docks.'

'We won't stand a chance if we fight him in the open,' replied Steiner from between gritted teeth.

Bittervinge swung his head back towards them, a fierce growl in his throat so loud Steiner could feel it in his chest. Teeth raked through the air and Steiner dropped to one knee to avoid the savage bite. Kristofine, just a few feet behind him, found herself lifted off the ground. She clung to the side of the dragon's snout and slammed Sokolov's dagger into Bittervinge's scaled face. The dragon roared in pain before he reared upright, then shook her off.

'Kristofine!' Steiner watched as the woman he loved slipped from the dragon's muzzle and fell to the floor below. He reached out to her and to his shock her descent slowed.

'What's happening?'

Felgenhauer appeared beside him, one arm extended towards Kristofine, using the power of Academy Zemlya.

'Keep the dragon busy.' Felgenhauer narrowed her eyes. 'I have a score to settle with the Envoy.' She jumped off the shattered floor to the storey below, slowing her fall with the arcane.

'Why do I have to fight the dragon?' muttered Steiner as Bittervinge fixed his gaze on Sergeant Tomasz and Lieutenant Reka on the far side of the hole in the floor. Silverdust and Streig appeared by Steiner's side.

Come. We must help them. They will not stand a chance.

The Envoy had recovered from her fall, but was limping badly, trying to escape from Kristofine, who picked her way across the debris of the library with her sword in her hand.

'This isn't part of the deal,' shouted Envoy de Vries, staring up at the dragon.

Did you really think I would help you usurp the Emperor? asked Bittervinge, projecting the words to all present. *I wished only to be free, Envoy.*

'We made a deal!' shrieked Envoy de Vries, hobbling away from Kristofine.

Dragons do not make deals. We take what we want.

Felgenhauer landed in the jumble of books and shelves just as Bittervinge swung his tail. Kristofine dived to the ground but Felgenhauer took the force of the blow. The Matriarch-Commissar was lifted from the ground and slammed into a bookshelf twenty feet away. She slumped down unmoving among the countless tomes.

'Steiner!' shouted Lieutenant Reka. 'If you're going to do something, do it now!' The lieutenant had fetched up a length of broken timber and was using it as an unwieldy pike to keep the dragon from devouring him whole. Sergeant Tomasz swung his mace as the dragon's head came close, but Bittervinge was unconcerned by such weapons. The dragon raised one claw and a low droning sound filled the air. Steiner knew dragons were magical creatures, but had never seen

one use the arcane as a Vigilant did. Reka released the improvised pike and watched in dismay as the timber snapped in
two above his head. The pieces sped across the library to land
in the darkness, leaving Reka unarmed. Bittervinge pressed
home the attack and raised his other claw to rend Sergeant
Tomasz apart, and Steiner leapt forward. Tomasz fell back as
the sledgehammer slammed the claws aside and the dragon
hissed with fury.

You will not survive, Vartiainen.

Silverdust conjured a javelin of fire and hurled it into the
dragon's eye, causing Bittervinge to stumble sideways, almost
crushing Envoy de Vries on the floor below.

'This isn't part of the deal,' she screamed, dodging out of
the way as best she could on her wounded leg. Kristofine
had collected herself, and ran forward, but the Envoy drew
a blade of her own and dropped into a low crouch.

'I'll not die to a lowly peasant!'

Kristofine thrust forward with her sword and the Envoy
parried it, smashing her elbow into Kristofine's face. Steiner
was so intent on the fight below that he almost failed to
notice Bittervinge had rallied. The wedge-shaped head darted
forward, twisting sideways in a blur of teeth and black scales.
Streig shoved Steiner out of danger and was swept into the
air, his cloak snagged in the dragon's teeth. Bittervinge bit
down and Streig scrambled higher onto the dragon's face to
avoid being eaten. The soldier gripped hold of Sokolov's blade
where it protruded from the dragon's muzzle and pulled
himself up. Bittervinge roared and the library was filled with
the sound of his pain.

Streig must not fall! Silverdust swiped left and right, both of
his hands bright blades of fire that scored deep grooves in the
dragon's black scales. Bittervinge reared up and Streig disappeared from view, hurled through the hole in the ceiling to
the floor above.

'Frejna's teeth!' Steiner stared in shock. Streig wasn't the only one in trouble.

'Throne save me,' sneered the Envoy as she parried another of Kristofine's hasty strikes. 'You even fight like a peasant!' Wounded as she was, the Envoy sidestepped and blocked all of Kristofine's strikes, smirking between exchanges of blows. In a fit of frustration, Kristofine drew back and thrust down with her sword, point first into Bittervinge's tail. A sinuous ripple passed through the dragon's body and its head whipped around to the source of the pain.

You dare wound me!

Kristofine ran towards the Envoy at a flat sprint as Bittervinge's head thrust towards her in maddened fury. Kristofine dived to the side at the last moment and it was the Envoy, not Kristofine, that disappeared into the vast maw.

'This isn't part of the deal,' screamed Envoy de Vries before the dragon flicked its head back and bit down. The snapping of bones silenced everyone.

Steiner.

Silverdust appeared by his side, one hand pressed to the wound in his chest. Smoke continued to escape from the Exarch's body.

'We have to get you out of here,' said Steiner.

We will not survive this unless we defeat the dragon here. You know this, Steiner. Live up to your bloodline.

'But it's all bullshit,' said Steiner. 'My great-grandfather didn't kill Bittervinge, so what chance is there for me?' The dragon extended his great wings as best he could, causing more ruin in the devastated library.

It is true. The dragon's words sounded in their minds in a sing-song golden sound that was at odds with Bittervinge's terrifying appearance. *Your great-grandfather did not kill me, that much is obvious, but he laid me low all the same so that the Emperor could capture me and contain me.* Bittervinge became still, staring down at them as his torso heaved with laboured breaths.

Then the Emperor betrayed your great-grandfather and told everyone it was he that had struck the vital blow. His bodyguard was celebrated as a hero, but the Emperor became legend, all from a single lie, perfectly told.

'We all want the same thing,' said Steiner, staring up at the black-scaled dragon. 'We all want the Emperor dead. You could fight with us!'

Bittervinge didn't move, his torso continuing to huff with each great breath. The smell of blood was on the air and Steiner tried not to think about Envoy de Vries.

It is true. I do wish for the Emperor's death. I have wished for the Emperor's death for a very long time. Seven decades of dreaming, wishing my tormentor finally gets what he is owed.

'So join us!' shouted Steiner.

There is however one thing I want more. The dragon lowered its head.

Steiner took an uncertain step back. 'And what's that?'

The end of the people who helped defeat me. The end of the Vartiainen line and the destruction of that hammer.

Bittervinge lunged forward, fanged maw suddenly wide. Steiner swung the sledgehammer and felt the dragon's angular cheekbone shatter under the force of the blow. Silverdust punched forward with one hand, a blade of arcane fire burning bright. Steiner fell sideways as his strike took him off balance, watching in horror as the Exarch disappeared into the dragon's mouth.

'Silverdust!'

Bittervinge's vast head continued to thrust forward across the shattered floor of the library like the prow of some deadly ship, throwing up a wave of books and broken shelves.

'No!' Streig stood at the edge of the shattered floor above and stared in disbelief as Silverdust was swallowed.

The end of the Vartiainen line is nigh!

Steiner ran forward and leapt, throwing himself onto the dragon's muzzle, grasping hold of the dagger hilt that protruded from Bittervinge's face. The sledgehammer rose and slammed down into the burned eye. The dragon flinched and convulsed under the black iron sledgehammer. Below, Kristofine plunged her sword through the black scales, causing another ripple of pain to course through the dragon's body.

Far above, Streig had wrested an ancient great sword from a shattered display cabinet. He leapt from the floor above, black cloak billowing behind him.

'Silverdust!' The great sword tore into the dragon's wing and sliced through the leathery membrane, opening a long wound. Bittervinge flicked his head to one side, dislodging Steiner, who sailed through the air to land on a pile of books with a grunt. The dragon flapped his wings as best he could in the confines of the library and Streig crashed to the floor below, the great sword spinning from his grasp.

'Steiner!' screamed Kristofine, as she stood before the terrible creature with her simple weapon held out before her with a trembling hand. 'Steiner, I need you!'

The dragon lowered its head, craning its neck, the foot-long teeth and powerful jaws drawing closer to Kristofine with every heartbeat. Steiner started sprinting towards the dragon, slipping on debris, fearing he wouldn't make it in time.

'Steiner!' Kristofine's voice broke as the panic took hold of her. The dragon's jaws spread wide and it lunged forward. Kristofine was lost from view as the horned head closed down on her.

The dragon jerked as if shaken, then hesitated.

Felgenhauer rose from the wreckage of the library like a vengeful shade, her robes torn and dusty, her expression murderous. She held up one forbidding hand, her eyes the dark grey of granite. Bittervinge trembled and shook, but could not close his jaws on Kristofine, who cowered beneath him. Veins of grey spread across the black scales as the arcane did its work. Teeth fossilised in seconds under the Matriarch-Commissar's petrifying gaze. The dragon slashed at Felgenhauer with a claw but the Vigilant threw up a ward of force to block the rending talons. Bittervinge's tail followed moments after, lashing out, breaking Felgenhauer's concentration as it slammed against the ward. The Matriarch-Commissar stumbled backwards under the onslaught but did not fall.

'Damn you!' seethed Felgenhauer from between clenched teeth. Kristofine chose that moment to thrust upwards with her blade, the point piercing the soft underside of Bittervinge's throat. Kristofine's sword stuck between the black scales of the dragon's neck as it turned away, leaving her unarmed. Bittervinge stared at Kristofine and drew back a taloned claw for the killing blow as Steiner ran several feet and leapt from the shattered floor, the sledgehammer's swing carrying him forward.

'Bittervinge!'

The dragon swung his wounded head around as Steiner smashed into him, knocking teeth loose, sending cracks through the petrified face. Steiner slammed into the wall of teeth, nearly falling to the ground before grabbing a jutting fang.

I have you now, Vartiainen.

The dragon flicked his head up and Steiner spun loose, tumbling through the air. For a moment he stared down into the dragon's petrified and bleeding maw. The sledgehammer slipped free of his grasp and time slowed.

'Steiner!' Kristofine screamed from far below. He was dimly aware that Felgenhauer was running forward and Streig had become trapped under one of the dragon's claws. The sword they had bought for Kristofine in Virag protruded from the dragon's throat. All the trials and challenges of the last few months flickered past, pointless and fleeting. Bittervinge extended one claw and held Steiner in the air, suspending him with the power of the arcane. A deep and malevolent chuckle filled the library.

At last, Vartiainen. You will die.

Steiner stared down in shock and blinked. Silver light was emanating from Bittervinge's chest. The dragon shuddered and coughed, then writhed to one side. The silver light grew brighter, streaming out of the dragon's throat, glowing faintly from between every scale.

It burns!

Steiner plummeted to the ground, saved from injury by Felgenhauer, who slowed his descent with a gesture. Kristofine ran to him and they fell into each other's arms.

What trickery is this? Bittervinge stumbled away from them, colliding with the remnants of the shattered floor above. The silver light became more intense and black scales flaked off, revealing scorched and smouldering flesh beneath. Bittervinge clawed at his chest in agony, writhing and convulsing.

'What's happening?' whispered Kristofine.

'Silverdust,' said Steiner. 'It has to be Silverdust.'

'We should go,' said Felgenhauer. A wave of heat washed over them and the books closest to Bittervinge sparkled into flame.

'I think you're right,' replied Steiner. 'We fall back.'

The dragon was a walking torment of terrible burning. Scales slipped and fell and the vast creature stumbled, drunk on pain, roaring louder than anything Steiner had ever heard.

'Where's Strieg?' shouted Steiner above the din.

'There's no time,' replied Felgenhauer.

A ripple passed through Bittervinge's body, and Steiner was sure it must be the convulsion that heralded the creature's death. The dragon's jaws parted and a great gout of flame annihilated a section of the library in a heartbeat. Bittervinge's fiery breath was a great streak of near-white heat with tongues of orange reaching towards the ceiling. For a brief moment the fire glowed silver and Steiner was certain the dragon had purged himself of the cinderwraith Exarch. Bittervinge hunched down on the floor, then sprang upwards, bursting through the ceiling of the library itself.

'Frøya save me,' whispered Steiner. 'He got free.' The shattered ceiling began to sag and collapse under the heat of the fire and Kristofine tugged at Steiner's hand. Felgenhauer led the way, as they fled from the ruins of the greatest library in Vinterkveld.

'Silverdust,' was the only word Steiner could say when they finally emerged outside. The library succumbed to the grievous damage, the walls and dome collapsed inwards and exhaled dust and ash. Bittervinge's prison was no more.

CHAPTER FORTY-NINE

Kimi

The rage that infested Veles was tangible, Kimi could almost taste it, like coppery blood in her mouth. Her fingers were suddenly numb and her guts had turned to stone. The gholes who ran ahead of their master were infected by his rage, hissing with fury as they raced ever closer. Suddenly a ghole in the centre of the oncoming horde flinched backwards. The creature stumbled a moment, then collapsed to its knees.

'That's one,' said Tief, reloading the crossbow as fast as he could. Kimi ran forward and swung the two-handed sword in a bright arc of shining steel. Two gholes dropped to the ground to avoid it while another lost its head entirely. Kimi felt a jolt of pain race across her shoulders as the blade bit deep. She gripped the hilt more tightly in response.

'Two!'

Taiga held up the holy weapons of her goddess and shouted loud and clear above the chaos. The five gholes nearest to the priestess hesitated as if confused and another fell as if struck. Taiga wasted no time and raked at the closest with her sickle, then slammed the dagger into the creature's cowl. The ghole went down without a sound.

'Three!'

Marozvolk had already severed the arm of one ghole by the time Kimi glanced at her. She batted aside rending claws with her shield and stabbed the creature in the guts.

'Hit it in the head!' shouted Tief.

'I know what I'm doing!' bellowed Marozvolk, ripping the blade free of the ghole's stomach. Entrails spilled out and the ghole stumbled backwards, then tripped on its own guts. Marozvolk threw her sword up a short way and caught it in a reverse grip, then slammed the point down into the creature's head. 'Four!'

Black-clad bodies surged around them like an angry sea threatening to drag them under at any moment. Kimi swung wildly with the blade, hoping to stay clear of the poisonous claws if nothing else. A crossbow bolt whistled past her shoulder, finding its mark and taking down another ghole.

'Mind where you're pointing that thing!' she shouted over her shoulder.

'Five,' shouted Tief as he ran back towards the standing stones to reload. The hateful gholes were close on his heels and Marozvolk stepped in front of him, slamming the rim of her shield into one creature's face before slashing through the knee of another.

'Reload faster,' she shouted.

Taiga stood beside Kimi and slashed left and right with her shorter blades as Kimi used her longer sword like a spear to jab viciously.

'We're split up,' complained Taiga as a ghole's claws raked her vestments, narrowly missing the flesh beneath.

'Kneel!' shouted Kimi. The priestess obeyed without a word and Kimi flipped the blade over her shoulder and spread her feet wide. She whipped her arms about her head so the two-handed sword cleaved a wide circle. The gholes, who had crowded them so completely just moments before, collapsed backwards. Taiga sprang up and finished one of their unholy number, shouting triumphantly.

'Six! At least!'

Kimi surged forward, decapitating another ghole as it reeled from her attack. The sun emerged from behind a cloud, bathing everyone in majestic light, and the gholes hunched lower; a few screeched in irritation and stumbled away from the melee.

'And seven!' shouted Taiga.

'Wait,' said Kimi, struggling for breath. 'Where is Veles?' She looked over her shoulder just as the vast serpent reared up from behind the standing stones. Marozvolk was still defending Tief from the gholes, unaware of the pale and sinuous danger behind her. Veles darted forward, his wedge-shaped head split wide to reveal blackened and cracked teeth.

'No!' shouted Kimi, but the serpent moved with alarming speed. Marozvolk turned and began to dive sideways just as Veles struck. He seized her about the waist with his cruel jaws and snatched her up into the air. Kimi was powerless to prevent the serpent mounting the standing stones. The sword slipped from the renegade Vigilant's hands and Veles tossed her in the air, catching Marozvolk so her legs were in his mouth. Blood stained the jaws of the pale serpent but Marozvolk let out a furious cry. She began to punch the serpent even as it bit into her. Kimi ran forward as Marozvolk punched with fists of stone, knocking out ancient teeth and cursing at the top of her lungs.

'You will not take me!' shouted Marozvolk through blood-spattered lips. Kimi sprinted around the standing stones, bringing her sword down on Veles' tail with every sinew of her body. The two-handed sword ripped through the tip of the dragon's tail and the creature jolted. Kimi gripped the sword by the crosspiece and slammed the blade through the bleeding stub of Veles' tail, pinning the creature to the ground, or so she thought.

Such was Veles' fury that the stone circle came apart. Marozvolk was flung aside, landing at Kimi's feet as the dragon ripped its tail free of the ground. The serpent slammed her with its sinuous body and for a moment nothing made sense. The ground slipped free and the sky tumbled deliriously beneath her. She fell into wet grass and felt a sharp pain in her shoulder.

Everything became dark.

You will give the Ashen Torment to me.

Veles was waiting when Kimi's eyes fluttered open. There was no part of her that didn't hurt. She was lying on the ground a dozen feet away from Marozvolk, but the renegade Vigilant wasn't moving.

'No,' whispered Kimi, but the truth was plain to see in the renegade Vigilant's unblinking eyes; they stared unseeing at the grey skies, the spark of life extinguished. Marozvolk was gone. 'No.'

The gholes had formed a circle and two of their number stood behind Taiga and Tief. Both had been captured during the fighting and both had been forced to their knees. The gholes held poisoned claws against Tief and Taiga's throats, waiting for the command from Veles. Kimi pulled herself to her feet, almost sobbing with pain and despair, trembling with agony.

The Ashen Torment can never be stolen or taken by force. Veles slithered around the outside of the ruined stone circle, keen to keep the gholes between himself and the woman who had wounded him. *Bittervinge made sure a key part of the enchantment meant the artefact had to be given freely.*

Kimi nodded slowly, the pain in her shoulder so intense it made her head swim. She reached for the chain around her neck with her good arm, pulling the jade dragon from beneath her shirt.

'Frøya,' she whispered. 'Your high priestess is in grave danger, Veles himself has desecrated your shrine, and I stand here half-dead, supposedly your champion.'

Who are you speaking to? Veles reared up, daring to thrust his head into the circle of gholes.

'I'm speaking with my goddess,' said Kimi. The wind dropped and all was still on the hillside. Kimi lifted her good arm, and the jade dragon dangled on the bronze chain, reflecting the sunlight. The pain in her shoulder abated and the sun shone with renewed brightness. Kimi's gaze fell on Marozvolk's ruined form and a host of feelings swirled within her.

Give it to me! Veles writhed with impatience.

Kimi gritted her teeth and closed her eyes. The word that escaped her lips was of no language she had ever spoken, louder than any sound she had ever made, filled with all of her loss and anger and despair. The jade dragon flashed brightly and the circle of gholes exploded into fine dust, leaving only blackened rags to mark their passing.

What is this? You said you carried the Ashen Torment! Veles coiled about himself, hissing in confusion and fury. Kimi stooped to retrieve her sword, expecting to be driven to her knees with the pain of her wounds. She reached forward and saw that her arm was surrounded in a nimbus of light, the same light that played about Taiga's silver weapons.

This is unthinkable!

Kimi looked into Veles' face and breathed deeply, feeling the now-familiar weight of the two-handed sword. Veles flexed his cruel claws.

You are thieves from Yamal. Thieves and liars! You are no better than any other lost soul who stumbles into this province! Worthless!

Kimi watched the serpent tense, ready for when Veles lunged up and forward with bleeding jaws wide open.

You are nothing!

Kimi felt no fear as she stepped aside, graceful and swift, feeling half-drunk or dreamlike. Veles smashed his long face into the ground where Kimi had stood barely a heartbeat before and the earth shook beneath her feet. Kimi hefted the two-handed sword and thrust forward before the serpent could recover himself, burying the blade to the hilt in his vast diseased eye. She felt the metal scrape on bone and pushed harder, putting her weight behind the pommel, twisting the blade as she leaned forward. Veles clawed at the ground and then became rigid. He twitched once before a terrible exhalation escaped his scaly lips.

'I am a Yamal princess,' said Kimi. 'And you just killed my friend.' She twisted the blade and ripped it free from the dragon's skull.

They buried Marozvolk at the site of Frøya's shrine the following day. The rain did not trouble them and the ever-present mists of Izhoria failed to return. The sun rose that morning and bathed the land in a gentle temperate light. They had used the standing stones to create a sarcophagus of sorts, though it had taken the whole day to lift them.

'This is as good as it's going to get,' said Tief, wiping away a tear. Taiga knelt beside Marozvolk's resting place and prayed to Frøya. Kimi surrendered to her grief and a series of violent sobs wracked her body. All day she had held the feeling inside so she might finish the sarcophagus. Tief held her close until the tears passed.

'She spoke of moderates within the Empire,' said Kimi. 'And I mocked her for it. She regretted not coming to find me sooner while I was trapped on Vladibogdan, said she was trying to work out who she was.'

Tief nodded. 'She was a hero for the sagas, is who she was.'

Kimi dashed away tears with the back of her hand. 'She

didn't want to go to Yamal at all, but she came anyway. She came for me.'

'She was so young,' said Tief. 'But what a woman. As dangerous as Frejna herself, armed or not.' They watched the sun set over Izhoria as Taiga finished her blessings over the sarcophagus. Now the mist had cleared, the sunlight reflected from the many stretches of water in golden yellows and warm oranges. For a moment it seemed as if the whole country were aflame. They ate in silence though Kimi could scarcely bring herself to think of food, much less consume it.

'I let her down,' said Kimi when the meal was done.

'No,' said Taiga softly. 'She came with us to kill the Emperor. We all knew the risks. We have to see it through now to honour her.'

'Honour?' Kimi snorted a derisive laugh. 'There's not much honour left in Vinterkveld.'

'No, there isn't,' admitted Tief. 'But she died defending me, even though I doubted her. And she died fighting for you, even though you had your differences. I say we follow her example.'

'I let her down,' repeated Kimi.

'It was Veles' awful braziers that killed her,' said Taiga as the sun finally slunk beneath the gilded horizon. 'The smoke they gave off, you see? The smoke affected her ability to draw on the arcane.'

'So why were you not affected?' said Kimi.

'Vigilants draw the arcane from dragons, while priestesses draw power from their goddesses.'

Kimi stood up, stalked over to the corpse of the dragon, then gave it a hefty kick in the face. A moment later she was crying again, her anger fled.

'Feel better?' said Tief. He prodded the dragon's head with his boot.

'Not really.'

'Would it help if we raided his horde again? You might find some armour, or money.'

Kimi shrugged. 'It might.' She put an arm around him. 'I'm going to miss her,' she said, glancing over her shoulder at Marozvolk's grave.

'I know,' he said. 'I'm going to miss her too, believe it or not.'

CHAPTER FIFTY

Steiner

They prepared to leave the island of Arkiv on a schooner the next day. A change of clothes and a square meal had cured some of their problems, but Steiner, Kristofine and Felgenhauer had slept poorly during their night at a dockside inn. A dire plume of grey smoke hung over the ruins of the library in the centre of the city, as the fire continued to rage, devouring the many books within. People on the docks talked openly of the dragon seen escaping from the scene of devastation. Few knew the real story of what had occurred the day before, but rumours were already growing, being embroidered and passed on.

Steiner waited by the boarding ramp to the ship and kept a keen eye on the street, wary for trouble.

'This feels too much like Virag for my taste,' said Kristofine.

'You're not wrong there,' admitted Steiner. The sledge-hammer was concealed in a sack though his hand grasped the handle all the same.

'How much longer?' said the schooner's captain. He was a heavyset man in his fifties. The lobe of his ear was missing, along with one of his eye teeth, and his hair was long and lank, a greasy black.

'As long as you can spare,' replied Felgenhauer, appearing

on the boarding ramp and joining them on the dock. 'It took a lot of courage to do what they did.' She wore a blue robe like the academics, and a cream scarf over her head. The captain nodded and attended to his men.

'Streig?' said Steiner.

'I don't think so.' Felgenhauer shook her head. 'He was down when I saw him, mostly likely trampled to death when Bittervinge started to burn.'

'Lieutenant Reka?'

'Hard to tell. Maybe he escaped. It was very chaotic at the end. I wonder if Tomasz or any of my men made it out.'

'It doesn't seem right that we should survive and they . . .' Kristofine pursed her lips and became very still.

'Why don't you go to the cabin and get some sleep?' said Steiner softly. 'We're all shattered.' Kristofine nodded and headed up the boarding ramp.

'How is she doing?' asked Felgenhauer when Kristofine had disappeared below decks.

'I'm not sure. I'm not really sure how I'm doing, if I care to be honest. I can't believe Silverdust was there, and before I knew it he was gone.'

'He killed Orlov?'

Steiner nodded. The terrible power of Orlov's enchantment came back to him and he shuddered at the memory.

'He cut the bastard clean in two. Huge fiery blades sprang from his hands. I've never seen anything like that before. He saved my life.'

'And for that I will always be grateful,' said Felgenhauer.

'It strikes me we're wanted now,' said Steiner.

'Wanted?' Felgenhauer raised her eyebrows. 'That's some understatement. Besides, we've both been wanted for months.'

'My point is . . .' He dropped his voice. 'I can't call you Felgenhauer in the open. You have a first name, don't you?'

'You can call me Nika.'

'Hoy there, Aunt Nika.' Steiner gave an impish smile and Felgenhauer rolled her eyes.

'Don't ever call me that again, I feel like I aged an entire decade in a heartbeat.' They stood together, nephew and aunt, watching the business of the docks play out, ruminating on what had gone before, overhearing snatches of gossip as the sailors went about their tasks.

'We should go,' said Felgenhauer. 'The captain's already taking a huge risk just being seen with us. I can't ask him to wait any longer.' She made to board the ship. Steiner pointed down the street. Two mules pulled a cart led by a woman wearing purple academic robes. 'Do you know her?'

Felgenhauer looked over her shoulder and a slow smile crept across her face.

'Drakina. She's one of my contacts on the island.'

As the woman approached it was clear there were men riding on the cart. Many were bandaged and all were attired in burned academic's robes. Drakina was a blonde woman in her twenties, pale and serious in equal measure.

'I found a few waifs and strays.'

The men who climbed down from the cart were heavyset, and had no more studied books than Steiner had. Tomasz nodded to Steiner and they clasped forearms.

'It's good to see you again,' said Steiner.

'I saw you fight,' replied the sergeant. 'If I didn't know better I'd say you were unhinged.'

'You wouldn't be the first,' replied Steiner with a grin.

'Or the last. And thank Frøya for that.' The sergeant headed up the boarding ramp.

'How bad was the fire?' said Felgenhauer.

'It still burns even now,' said Drakina. 'Thankfully it didn't spread to the city, but . . .' She shook her head. 'All gone. All of it. And to think, there was a dragon living in our midst this whole time.'

'Any survivors? A young soldier called Streig perhaps?' asked Steiner, watching the men climb down from the cart as fast as their wounds would allow them.

Drakina shook her head. 'No one by that name. These men only survived because they had the good sense to flee when the dragon appeared.'

'He didn't make it,' said Steiner. 'Not Silverdust or Streig.'

'Or Lieutenant Reka,' added Felgenhauer. 'And half a dozen of my men. All gone to their rest.'

'There's something you should know before you leave,' said Drakina. 'I've heard whispers on the wind. Something shocking has happened.'

'You mean more shocking than Bittervinge trying to kill me and everyone I know?' said Steiner.

'Almost.' Drakina stepped closer and dropped her voice. 'They say two Imperial galleons were destroyed in the south. A Vigilant aboard managed to send a message, but it doesn't make much sense. They say a sea creature rose up and attacked them near a small town called Dos Khor. Something about a young girl with vast powers summoning a leviathan.'

'Kjellrunn.' Steiner was suddenly very light-headed. 'Frejna's teeth, that's my sister.'

'We don't know that, Steiner,' replied Felgenhauer.

'They're calling her the Stormtide Prophet,' said Drakina. 'Everyone in Khlystburg is waiting for the Emperor to give the order to invade Shanisrond.'

Steiner hefted the sledgehammer. 'Maybe we should get to Khlystburg and stop him from giving that order.'

'Drakina,' said Felgenhauer. 'I may never see you again. Make sure people know what really happened here. Make sure they know why we rebelled, why we fought. Make sure they know why we're fighting still.' Drakina nodded.

'I can wait no longer,' said the schooner's captain.

'I'm ready,' said Steiner. 'Let's find my father.'

CHAPTER FIFTY-ONE

Kimi

They spent another night on the hilltop. Kimi had no desire to shelter in the cavern where she had been prisoner. A weary calmness settled over the three of them as they grieved and healed. Dawn came in a procession of gentle golds and somehow Taiga still had something worth eating in her bags. This alone felt like a miracle.

Kimi Enkhtuya. The artefact whispered her name cheerfully and Kimi allowed herself a smile as she pressed the jade dragon to her chest.

Izhoria remained free of the mist that had haunted them over long weeks of their journey and the way north was clear.

'Frejna save me,' muttered Tief. He was looking west from under the blade of his hand, squinting into the distance.

'What is it?' asked Kimi.

Tief extended an arm to where three dots floated in the sky.

'Surely it can't be . . .' Taiga trailed off, a look of disbelief on her weary face.

'We can't outrun them,' said Tief. The three dots were closer now, their outlines revealing wings and sinuous tails.

'And we can't fight them,' added Taiga. 'Not three of them.'

Kimi walked over to where Veles' head lay on the hillside. She took a moment to climb up on his neck, then rested her two-handed sword point downward on his brow, striking what she hoped was an intimidating pose.

'What are you doing?' asked Tief.

'I'm a Yamal princess and a dragon slayer,' said Kimi. 'Even if no one lives to tell this tale, this is the way I'll meet my end.'

The dragons swept in low and graceful over the swamps and banked around the hilltop before doubling back. One by one they landed, their wings sending ripples through the grass. Kimi recognised the nearest of them, the eggshell blue underside and scales that contained all the colours of autumn. It was the dragon she had conversed with from the prow of the *Watcher's Wait*. She felt a stirring of hope. The dragons huffed and flapped their wings before settling down; one was azure while the other was a granite grey. Tief and Taiga edged closer to Kimi, who stared at the dragons with a look of patient resolve.

You killed Veles.

Kimi started in surprise. The last time she had seen the juvenile dragons they had been limited to thoughts and feelings, and that communication was only possible due to Sundra's help.

'You can speak now,' said Kimi.

We have had many weeks to grow and master ourselves. We grow still, and there is much left to learn. You may call me Namarii.

'Veles took us prisoner and killed one of my friends,' said Kimi. 'We had a reckoning.'

Namarii prowled closer; eyes the colour of amber surveyed the corpse and the dragon snorted a plume of smoke.

I know nothing of this dragon. He was not present with us when we were trapped beneath Vladibogdan. Namarii turned his gaze to the north-west, as if he might see the wretched island from half a world away. *And this Veles did not come to free us. Just as well you put an end to him. Besides, he has no wings. Pitiful.*

'You don't want revenge for your slain kin?' said Kimi, almost too afraid to ask the question.

In truth, you are more kin to us than Veles ever was. You fed us in the darkness, treated our sores, wiped down our wings. Your words helped free us.

'How did you know to find us here?' asked Taiga, clutching her hands together.

Veles cried out as he died, he cried out with the arcane. Those who can hear such things cannot have missed his dying words. Every dragon and human who can whisper on the wind will know of his passing.

'Shit,' said Tief. 'Every last Imperial soldier will be coming this way, coming to find us.'

Perhaps. Namarii shook his wings and settled down on the hilltop, crossing his claws like a cat. *The Emperor has other problems. A young girl in the south channels powers far in excess of mine, and Bittervinge himself has escaped the Great Library, though I confess I do not know where this library is.*

Kimi took a moment to ponder on all this. She stepped down from Veles' carcass and laid her sword down. Tief looked at her with concern plain to see in his eyes.

'What will you do now?' said Kimi.

Many of my kin seek only to survive, grateful to be alive after so long in the darkness beneath Vladibogdan, but survival is not enough for us. We three seek vengeance on the Emperor. We do not desire dominion over man as the older dragons did, simply to see justice done. You feel the same the way. Namarii blinked the huge amber eyes. *I can almost taste your need for it.*

'Well,' said Tief with a broad smile. 'If we're all heading in the same direction perhaps you could give us a ride north—'

'Tief!' Kimi glared at him.

'Why should Steiner be the only one to ride a dragon?' countered Tief.

It will be as you say. Namarii looked around the hilltop *But first we eat and then we rest.*

'What will you eat?' asked Kimi. Nothing lived Izhoria, nothing edible. Namarii eyed Veles' corpse and snorted a plume of smoke.

'I can't imagine he'll taste too good,' said Tief, making a sickened face.

We have eaten worse.

They left later that day, and Kimi's head was full of plans even as her heart grieved for Marozvolk. One by one they took to the air on their vast mounts, awed at the prospect of gaining such powerful allies. Kimi felt the raw power of the dragon beneath her as she was borne aloft.

'Nothing can stop me now,' whispered Kimi as the wind whipped past and Namarii's wings sped her towards Khlystburg and the Emperor.

Acknowledgements

While a novel may only have one name on the front it's fair to say the manuscript passes through many hands before it reaches the reader. I'd like to thank the following people for helping to usher *Stormtide* into the world:

Firstly Natasha Bardon for taking a chance on the series (and on me).

Vicky Leech has been a powerhouse of enthusiasm, insight and a joy to work with.

As much as I love words I also love pictures, so thanks to Nicolette Caven for the map and Micaela Alcaino for my book covers.

My agent Julie Crisp has kept things ticking along nicely and I'm very grateful to her.

Jen Williams and Andrew Reid have always been on hand for moral support and a fine selection of GIFs.

Huge gratitude to Robin Hobb for not only reading Witchsign, but also reviewing it and offering a cover quote. It's not unlike receiving an A* on a particularly long piece of coursework from a favourite teacher.

I'd like to mention Matt Rowan, not because he helped

with the book per se, but because he's a fine friend, cat-sitter and roller of odd-shaped dice.

Lastly I'd like to thank my wife for sleeping in late, so I can write uninterrupted in the mornings.